Ice
Angel

Ice Angel

CHARLOTTE HAPTIE

*Hodder
Children's
Books*

A division of Hachette Children's Books

A Catalogue record for this book is available from the British Library

ISBN 978 0 340 89418 7

Typeset in Berkeley by Avon DataSet Ltd,
Bidford on Avon, Warwickshire

Printed and bound in Great Britain by
CPI Bookmarque, Croydon

The paper and board used in this paperback by Hodder Children's Books
are natural recyclable products made from wood grown in
sustainable forests. The manufacturing processes conform to the
environmental regulations of the country of origin.

Hodder Children's Books
A division of Hachette Children's Books
338 Euston Road, London NW1 3BH
An Hachette UK Company
www.hachette.co.uk

for
Fionnuala and Jason
Tess, Cormac and Róisín

Chapter 1

Zachary Jump climbed down into the cool, still air of the water cave. For as long as he could remember he had made sure that his father heard the news first, whatever it might be.

And this was the best news of all.

He breathed deeply. Trying to calm down. Failing. Then he blurted out:

'We're going to do it, Dad. Me and Clovis. We're going to take the Ice Angel van out on the road again and sell ices, just like you did.

'I've finished with school. I'm no good at studying. Clovis is leaving as well. You know he's two years ahead of the other kids his age on account of his brains. He's passed all his exams. He's going to be apprenticed to Meakin's the Map Makers.'

He paused. The only sounds were the spring bubbling into the pool between the rocks – quietly occupied, like something alive – and his own breathing. Slower now.

He couldn't remember his father Balthazar's face. That

didn't matter. He closed his eyes.

'It'll be just like when you were here,' he whispered. 'Clovis can fix the van. He's great with engines. Just like you were. Are. And I can drive. Sort of. We've got the Recipe Book. I can make the ices and stuff. Cooking's the only thing I can do . . .'

Zack shivered and hunched himself into Balthazar's ancient coat. It was much too broad in the shoulders.

The ice cave lay beyond the water cave, deeper in the mountain. Snow was stored back there, packed into blocks. Clean, spotless snow waiting to be made into ice cream and sweet fruit ices: untouched for twelve years.

'Except climbing. And balancing . . .' he grinned. 'Things goats do. Anyway, we were going to start in the spring. I mean, we still are. With the van. And then today I found her. The Ice Angel herself. Hidden. Did you hide her?'

Somewhere outside he could hear his mother calling him.

'That's where she belongs. That's why the van is called the Ice Angel, isn't it? It must be. And you're going to be proud. I'm sure you are.'

He could hear his mother more clearly now. Not far away: probably on the short path down from the house above the caves.

Still, for another full minute, he didn't open his eyes. The air no longer seemed cold against his face. The palm of his hand was pressed against the rock but the dampness and the chill had been replaced by warmth.

He felt, as always, that something was close enough to touch. Almost. Something familiar from long ago.

Then he opened his eyes and stood up; the breath of the cave swirled up around him again, restless and cold; he nodded to himself and set off with quick, springy strides, back out into the winter sunshine.

Chapter 2

The house and the caves were far below on the mountainside. Zack and his mother had been climbing for over an hour. Zack ahead as always. Almost dancing on the path and the rocks.

His mother Mariette following, cautious and grim-faced. She stopped to catch her breath and looked behind her. The steep plunge of the great mountain fell away into space. She had a dizzy glimpse of the lights of Rockscar City where it clawed up from the harbour. The sea beyond, fading into the coming dark.

She turned back to face her son on the treacherous path.

'Are we nearly there?' she asked, sharply. Her heart was racing, as urgent and scared as her voice.

Zack peered down at her and drew his tattered sleeve across his face. His nose and eyes were streaming from the cold.

'What's the matter, Mum?'

She didn't reply. She had guessed what he had found: she knew exactly where it was hidden.

He pulled aside some branches and scrambled up on to a narrower, overgrown path.

'There are wolves up here,' called Mariette, struggling after him. 'And bears. And . . .'

'Mountain lions,' he called back. 'Who knows, maybe big hairy trolls . . .'

'Don't even speak about the trolls . . .' Mariette muttered. 'Just because you've never seen one . . .'

He had heard her.

'Well you've never seen one either,' he retorted. 'Or have you, Mum?'

No reply. The wind whispered and spat.

'Here,' he called, a moment later, still somewhere ahead.

'Here,' she whispered to herself. Remembering so horribly clearly this steep climb. In the dark. Alone. Struggling with a burden that was breaking her heart.

She caught up with him now, her breath rasping, and he was gesturing with his long skinny hands, the way he always did when he was excited: his coat torn, his eyes gleaming—

'I found her when I was looking for another way to get up to the glacier.' He was talking quickly now. 'She's just the most beautiful, beautiful, not thing, you can't say thing . . .'

Mariette pulled her knitted coat more tightly around her. The air seemed filled with the taste of ice. She grabbed Zack's arm as if one of them might fall.

The bushes had grown, of course. But she recognized the

mouth of the little cave. She had managed to block it with rocks on that dreadful night. There, in that cleft, she had wedged her lantern. The sled she had dragged so far up the path had broken, finally, here.

She had not left the pieces on the path. They might have given away the hiding place. She had dragged them home and burnt them, one at a time, on the fire.

Those rocks, the ones she had used to block the cave, had been only as big as she could roll with all her strength. Last summer Zack would still not have been strong enough. Now, it seemed, he was.

She watched as he crouched down and crawled into the cave. She followed him, marvelling and grieving at the power which must have drawn him here. Her son, finding the inheritance she had laboured so terribly to hide.

'So, what do you think?' whispered Zack.

And a moment later they were side by side, crushed together, and there was the treasure Zack had brought her to see.

It was a wooden statue, just over a metre tall, shot through here and there with shards of blue-green aqua-crystal. A young woman, perhaps a girl, with a serene and lovely face. She stood with her hands clasped on her chest. Her curved wings arched up behind her shoulders and framed her with the shape of a heart.

Zack frowned to try and hide his pride: waiting for his mother to speak.

Mariette said nothing.

Then she suddenly struggled backwards and stood up again in the harsh, cold air. She took a few steps away and staggered; saw herself, in her imagination, spinning down, down and tiny, to the roof of the forest below. A useless mother who had failed to protect her sons.

'How long do you think she's been here?' called Zack.

'Since you were two years and three days old,' she said. 'And Clovis was six weeks. Twelve years ago.'

An instant later and he was in front of her, facing her.

'When Dad disappeared?'

She just stared at him.

'But how do you know?'

'I put her here,' she said simply.

Zack rocked back on his heels.

'You knew she was here? You put her here?'

'I was trying to protect you. And Clovis. All of us, Zack.'

She waited. Another pause.

'She's Dad's, isn't she? She went on the front of the van and the van was called after her. And you hid her here? After he disappeared?'

As always when he, or Clovis, spoke of their father, Mariette felt her face become locked and stern. Even now.

'Yes.'

'I bet you'd have hidden the van in here as well, if you could.' He gave her a shaky grin. She had kept the shed near the house locked, she'd even planted bushes in front of the doors; but it had not stayed hidden from Zack and Clovis for long. They had forced the rusting lock when Zack was seven.

She didn't smile back.

There was a sound from somewhere up the mountain. Very faint. The howl of wolves.

'Let's go down now, Zack,' she said, speaking briskly as she might have done when he was small: trying to sound as if nothing important had happened and everything could go on as before. 'Clovis will be home before us. He'll wonder where we are.'

But Zack was still thinking. When he had found the angel and rushed home to fetch Mariette he had realized that his mother might be sad, or puzzled; but he had secretly hoped that she might actually be pleased. Instead, and not for the first time, she had shocked him with another fragment of the horrible puzzle about his father.

Balthazar Jump had worked as a mechanic in Rockscar City; but that was just in the day. By night he was an outlaw. He had inherited the secret Jump family spring, sweet water from the glacier that leeched into the caves under his house. At night he went down into the city selling delicious ices and giving away bottles of water to those who needed them.

It had been, and still was, illegal to sell water, or ices, without a special licence. And only the immensely powerful Scarspring Water Company had a licence.

Nevertheless, Balthazar, in the long tradition of his family, had continued to sell his ices illegally for many years. Then, one night, he had disappeared.

However much Zack and Clovis discovered, the story was never complete. Even now, even though his mother looked so strange and scared and sort of smudged, clutching her coat around her, shuddering, he knew that she was also, skilfully, shutting him out. She had more to tell. She always gave them the smallest piece she could. 'Crumbs for the starving,' Clovis had once said. 'Just enough to keep us alive.'

'Well, we're alive all right,' whispered Zack and added immediately and loudly, 'wait. I'm bringing her down.'

'Zack!'

'She belongs with us.'

Mariette wanted to drag Zack out of the cave, bundle him down the path . . .

'The angel has belonged to the Jumps for generations. She's very, very precious and ancient, Zack. Your father used to say that she was like the spirit of the water. He used to say that she protected him . . . The Scarsprings would love to get their hands on her!'

'They won't get their hands on her,' said Zack, already crawling back into the cave.

'Zack! No! Please, please DON'T!'

No reply. And he was too big, of course, for her to drag or bundle him anywhere ever, ever again. Here he came, out of the cave, carrying the angel. He had taken off his coat and wrapped it around her. His pale hands and face were already tinged blue with the cold.

'Don't want to damage her,' he said over his shoulder.

'But if the Scarsprings find her . . .' Mariette realized that her voice had risen to a scream. She was wringing her hands. 'All these years I've made sure you were safe. I've hidden the past away. I've tried to give you and Clovis a chance for a normal life. But if they found HER in *our house* . . .'

'They won't find our house,' said Zack, very determined now. 'They haven't found it in hundreds of years. And anyway, she won't be in the house, she'll be on the front of the ice van, where she belongs—'

Mariette gasped as if he had punched her.

He was talking too fast to stop: 'Anshelm Scarspring and his steward Golightly have had it all their way in Rockscar for too long, Mum. Just because Scarspring managed to get himself elected Mayor. Just because the Scarsprings own all the springs and wells. Fresh water is like gold in the city. You've said it yourself. He can charge what he likes and he does. He doesn't care—'

'But Zack—'

'You said Dad was the only one who ever stood up to them. Storing ice in our caves. Going about in his van at night, selling ices, giving away bottles of water. Just like the Jumps have always done, right under the noses

10

of the Scarsprings—'

'Listen, Zack, listen please . . .' Mariette's voice was shaking.

'Well. we're going to stand up to them now, just like he did. Clovis has got it all worked out. We're going to get the van going again, Mum. Clovis can do it. And we're going to start making beautiful flavoured ices and taking water to people who can't afford it. Just like Dad did.'

'But Zachary, listen.' She was fighting tears, she didn't want him to see how afraid she was. 'But Zachary, they are dangerous. Steward Golightly is dangerous. He is a dangerous ruthless man. Once he gets an idea he is like a man *possessed*. He means to control the whole, the whole Scarspring *empire* one day. They have always wanted our spring, they just could never find it. And there are other reasons, very important reasons, why you must never go near him. Never.'

'Are you saying they made Dad disappear?'

Mariette didn't speak. Nor, for a moment, did she move.

Zack turned and made his way slowly down the path. Very, very soon, it was hard for her to pick him out among the rocks and the scrubby trees, dim in the icy twilight. She knew when he stopped, though. She knew, without seeing, that he was staring back, looking for her, waiting for her. Then he shouted:

'I don't want to be apprenticed, Mum, I couldn't stand it. You know I couldn't . . . And you don't want me to go off to sea, do you?'

She said nothing. Her father had been a sailor: she didn't trust the sea.

'Do you?'

She heard the crunch of his boots on the path as he came back towards her, empty-handed. He had put the angel down.

'Don't try and trick me by making this a choice between the Ice Angel and the sea. There are plenty of other ways you could make a living.'

'But I've got to do this,' he said, softly. 'Clovis feels the same. We're doing it for Dad. It's our . . .' he struggled for the word, '. . . birthright. It's what we've got to do.'

Chapter 3

Far below, fog was filling the winding, climbing streets of Rockscar City. It was a dense November fog, part sluggish freezing sea mist, part brown chimney smoke, part darkness. Wagons, lorries, buses and large, lumbering, blunt-nosed automobiles pushed through it, their lights glowing, their windscreen wipers thudding slowly to and fro. They splashed through the puddles, drenching the scooter-riders, sending freezing spray on to the pavements and the hurrying, hunched pedestrians.

Each one had a guardian of some kind bolted or lashed to the front, facing the road ahead just like the figureheads on sailing ships which face the pitiless sea. There were animals, birds, dragons and monsters, stately women and warriors. Some were beautifully carved and painted: others made from scrap metal crudely welded together. The guardians on the wine-red cars of the Scarspring family were always silver mountain lions.

These guardians were to protect against danger; against the wild animals of the wilderness who might come hunting in the city, bears, wolves and mountain lions; and against something else.

The songs and legends and fireside stories of trolls in Rockscar were as old as the history of the people themselves. There were some who still spoke of trolls in hushed voices. And everyone, even the most educated and scornful, even those who laughed together at the very mention of trolls . . . everyone had a guardian when they took to the road.

Rockscar was a port city, facing the harsh sea. But the people feared the wilderness more, and the wilderness lay behind the city, and reached down on each side of it, surrounding it. If the trolls had existed, this was their stronghold. The legend was that they were an ancient and terrible race, who had lived on the mountains since the beginning of time. They hated the doings and the buildings of men and came down into the city by night, unseen, causing accidents and disasters. In truth, everyone still barred their doors: especially when the wind blew down from the wilderness, bringing the smell of the green wild woods, the great forests and the vast, unknown darkness.

All the guardians had a certain power, because the people believed in them and felt reassured. But none were as beautiful, or as truly powerful, as the angel that was hidden in the cave in the mountains; and then found and claimed by Zachary Jump, her rightful companion.

Chapter 4

It had been a long and busy winter. Zack and Clovis worked on the Ice Angel van in the shed below the house beside the entrance to the caves. Clovis was a patient person of science and invention. Zack marched about, standing in paint pots, knocking things over: desperate for everything to be finished so that he could try and drive the van out on to the Wolf Road. (The small matter of learning to drive had still to be accomplished. He planned to learn as he drove.)

The van was made from silvery metal. She had a chunky elegance, all long lines and smooth curves, with the big bonnet of a truck and a tall chrome radiator on the front. And she was tough: built for outwitting the police and the Scarsprings, sneaking round back streets and coming home up the rocky Wolf Road in the black and secret dark.

They found hidden places where rust was eating at her joints and her reinforced panels and they cleaned it all away. They scrubbed and waxed and polished her over many hours. Clovis took her engine to pieces and put it back together twice. Zack went to run-down garages on the outskirts of the city where they didn't ask to see your papers, and bought new brake cables and headlamps. The wheels were more of a problem, until Mariette showed them where Balthazar had hidden four new ones in the water cave.

'He certainly planned ahead,' said Clovis, as they struggled to roll the last one up and out through the cave entrance.

Zack grunted. He had wrenched his shoulder and the wheel had just gone over his foot. He had a grim suspicion that Clovis was stronger than him, despite being younger, shorter and rounder.

'Nothing to it,' he gasped. He stopped, to breathe a bit more.

'I mean, you know, if he was going to disappear, why would he get the new wheels and put them away and everything?' persisted Clovis, who wasn't even out of breath. Zack comforted himself with the thought that he, Zack, could run further without getting tired.

'I think it's all more evidence for the theory that he didn't intend to disappear at all,' added Clovis. 'What's wrong with your shoulder?'

'Old hunting injury,' said Zack. 'Wrestled with a bear. He could have got the wheels and then decided he had to disappear afterwards. Simple.'

Neither of the brothers ever used the words 'ran away'. Nor did they say out loud, 'murdered'. Always, always they

16

cradled their father's dreadful absence in gentler words. Disappeared. Missing.

'I found a dial that might be some sort of music thing, last night,' said Clovis, starting to push the tyre by himself. 'I didn't actually play it though. Thought you might like to be there. And Mum.'

'Let's do it now,' said Zack. 'I mean, I'd love to go on with shifting all these wheels and stuff, but you must be tired . . . it's getting dark . . .'

'Was it Mum's old teddy bear you wrestled with?' asked Clovis, as they climbed the short path to the house, stepping off it here and there, to avoid triggering the alarms. 'You should always approach them from downwind, you know, so they can't get your scent.'

Chapter 5

Only the Wolf Road came this far up the mountain, and that was pitted and treacherous. No one used it: except the wolves. No one hunted here. The fear of wild beasts and trolls was too strong in the city.

The house was locked into a crevice in the rock, behind dense trees, and it fitted cunningly back into the mountain; each floor a different shape and smaller than the last. It was built like a ship, protected by bolted plates of metal, and it had been the stronghold and the hiding place of the Jump family for over six generations.

Now Zack and Clovis Jump marched in through the front door, still chatting earnestly about wrestling bears.

Mariette earned a living by knitting clothes to her own designs. Balthazar had built her a knitting machine the size of a grand piano. It stood here in the living room. She was standing behind it, intense with concentration, wearing the large ear protectors Clovis had made for her. The knitting machine knitted very loudly.

When Balthazar had been running the Ice Angel

and risking arrest, a complex alarm and security system had protected them from discovery should any uninvited visitors, like the police, discover their house. No police, or anyone else, had ever found the house: then or since. At Mariette's insistence this system was still primed and working and was still tested on the first Friday of every month. This house alarm was the only sound that could penetrate the ear protectors.

'Listen to this, Mum!' yelled Clovis. 'There's a dial in the van that says "voice".'

She pointed at the knitting machine and then at her watch.

'She can't hear you,' said Zack. 'She just needs to finish something.'

They went back down to the Ice Angel, parked outside the shed. The angel was fixed in her place in front of the radiator, gazing calmly ahead. Clovis climbed up into the cab and slid along the seat and Zack followed him.

'Maybe it's just a wireless,' suggested Zack. The dashboard had been cleaned and polished and extra dials, buttons and levers extended along it right to the passenger door. These were the new controls added by Clovis: most of which Zack still hadn't been allowed to touch yet.

'Absolutely not the wireless,' said Clovis. 'That's the wireless, there.' He pointed to a row of red and gold knobs. They were each labelled with one of the five broadcasting houses based in the city, including the illegally-run Barnacle Radio.

'Well, I'm not going to be able to reach half of all these controls and things when I'm driving,' said Zack. 'What does this one do?' It was a lever that appeared to have been made out of a bath tap.

'DON'T!' cried Clovis. 'That's the Emergency Defensive Ice Dispenser. It's not ready yet!'

'The what?'

'Did you want to show me something, Clovis?' Mariette had come down. She was standing, hugging her arms around her, with the ear protectors tucked into her belt.

'What do you mean, defensive?'

Zack stopped speaking. Clovis had turned the elegant dial marked 'voice' and a girl's voice suddenly sang out into the still air.

'TURN IT OFF!' screamed Mariette.

Neither of the boys moved. The girl was singing very beautifully in a language they had never heard before.

'TURN IT OFF! TURN IT OFF!' Mariette scrambled in through the passenger door, pushed and climbed over Zack, gave a yell of frustration at the sight of the dashboard and began grabbing and slapping at the controls.

'WHAT HAVE YOU DONE, CLOVIS! I CAN'T FIND ANYTHING!'

The windscreen wipers swept across the windscreen, the horn sounded, powerful headlamps lit up the trunks of the nearest trees, the doors automatically locked themselves, and, finally, Clovis and Mariette together wrestled the dial marked 'voice' to the off position.

The voice faded and fell silent.

'Do you realize how far that travels?' demanded Mariette.

Clovis unlocked the driver's door and struggled out and down to the ground. He was giving this question his usual thought and attention.

'On a clear night,' he began, 'when there's no wind, because wind would, of course, affect it, for example an easterly, down to the city, although we are shielded by the mountain, might carry the sound, although not very far, whereas a southwesterly, off the sea—'

'BE QUIET!' yelled Mariette, jumping down beside him.

Zack slid across the long tattered seat and lowered himself after her. He caught his brother's eye and saw his own bewilderment neatly reflected.

'I didn't want you to, to restore this thing in the first place. We were all right. We were managing. But you are your father's sons. I knew I couldn't stop you. Not now.' She seemed smaller and more tightly packed than ever. Her eyes were bright. 'Not now Clovis is going to start his apprenticeship. I can't keep you as babies. And then you do something so STUPID. What will you be like driving this thing around if you put us in danger even before you go down the mountain? That singing can be heard for miles . . . You must promise me that you never,

ever turn that dial again, Ever.'

She was starting to cry. Zack tried to put his arm around her and she sidestepped him.

'It is a long way down to the city from here,' said Clovis, slowly. 'We never hear anything from there. Not even on a still night. We don't hear the bells, and they're very loud . . .'

'We hear the ships though, don't we, in the fog?' snapped Mariette.

'Mum,' said Zack, lowering his voice as if he were trying to calm a frightened animal, 'You're not saying that girl singing was as loud as a ship's foghorn, it's nothing like the same.'

'The foghorn sounds a note at a very low pitch, which travels much further than a high one,' said Clovis earnestly.

'You don't understand what you're dealing with,' said Mariette. 'And I want all of us to go inside NOW.'

She herded them up the path to the house. Then she slammed and bolted the door. The tension closing around them like a fist.

'I really don't think there's anything to worry about—' began Clovis.

Mariette silenced him with a flash of her eyes.

Zack peered through the half-closed shutters on the small window by the door.

'Everything seems to be all right,' he said, hopefully.

'Promise me you won't use that voice thing ever again, Zack,' she said. 'Someone might hear it.'

'But that's the whole point—'

'Never, never let her sing, Zack. Never. It's very ancient. You never know who's listening.'

'How can it be ancient?' said Clovis. 'It's a gramophone record or something. I don't know where, exactly, in fact, I can't see *how*, but it must be inside the van somewhere—'

'Shut up, Clovis,' said Mariette, still fixing her gaze on Zack.

'I promise,' said Zack.

Chapter 6

The family sat in front of the fire, sipping cocoa and eating crumpets. The oil lamps threw shadows on to the varnished wooden walls. It was windy on the mountain outside: a southwest wind bringing a faint smell of the sea.

Zack was consulting a large book of handwritten recipes. It was bound in thick cardboard and bent with age. Some of the writing was his father's, some the sloping copperplate hand of his great-grandfather. A few recipes, almost too faint to see, had been recorded by ancestors now faraway in time.

'*Take one sprigge of freshe pepperminte leaves,*' he announced, '*and the pulp of one large mango. Do adde two tablespoonfuls of the juice of the fruit of the lemone and* . . . can't read that . . . *of sugar. Mango Gran-it-a. Sweet chopped ice in a tubbe.* Sounds great. You have to keep sort of chopping it up as it freezes. Do you think we could do that, Mum? There's loads of little tubs in the attic.'

Both Zack and Clovis looked at Mariette, who was mending a shirt and using tiny, angry stitches. She had

24

hardly spoken since they had come indoors.

'You will need more than just Mango Granita,' she said abruptly, without looking up. 'The night workers in the newspaper offices, the journalists and the typesetters they always went for the sorbets, they're cheaper because they're easier to make. And they liked iced black coffee with the best brown sugar and bottles of iced fruit drinks.

'The granitas were for the richer customers, special orders for parties and dinners. And the people at the broadcasting houses, they were very particular. The nurses at the hospital were always fond of anything with chocolate, from what I remember.

'Then there's the syrups. Balthazar always had raspberry, strawberry, blackcurrant, chocolate, honey, mint . . . I made all of it, by the way. Everything. I haven't got the time to do it now. You'll have to do it yourselves.'

Clovis and Zack watched her. She had never told them quite as much about their father's business before. She bent over her sewing, her dark red hair shot through with silver, glittering in the firelight.

'But very little ice cream, made with you know, milk and cream,' said Zack. This was to prompt her to continue: he and Clovis knew the answer.

'Only the best ice cream,' she said, quietly. 'The milk came from one certain farm where your father believed the animals were treated kindly. He was a man of very high principles.'

There was a great crack from the wood in the fireplace. A spark arced up into the air and landed on the hearthrug. Clovis stamped on it. The wind sang in the chimney: a particularly eerie sound, like whispering voices. The chimney led through pipes that divided and redivided, dispersing the smoke in different parts of the forest above. Giving nothing away.

'There's supposed to be a storm coming,' said Mariette.

She stood up and closed the inside wooden shutters on the one window. The room was filled with warmth and shadows and the sound from the fire.

Zack opened the book at another page and found a sheet of paper, folded in half. He unfolded it.

'What?' demanded Clovis, who had seen his face.

'It's his,' said Zack. 'It's his list.'

'List of customers?' said Mariette, in a neutral voice, without looking up.

Chapter 7

Later, as she usually did at eight in the evening, Mariette leant over and turned on the massive wireless set. There was a buzz of interference, she adjusted the tuning dial and a man's voice announced the beginning of the news in smooth and sonorous tones.

'Good evening from all of us at Excelsior Broadcasting. Here are the headlines tonight,' he said. 'Mayor Anselm Scarspring has asked for calm after a third explosion in the district of Storm Hill caused damage to a number of buildings. He confirmed that the Scarspring Water Company, of which he is Managing Director, are currently looking for new sources of water in the area. They are also prospecting for water on the edge of the wilderness beyond Storm Hill. The Mayor informed this programme that although explorations so close to the wilderness are hazardous they are necessary because a dry summer next year could lead to water shortages.

'The Scarspring family announced today that they would be donating the money to build the new community centre in Storm Hill. They have now given more money to charities and city improvement projects than any other family since records began. The Mayor himself has been nominated for an Excellent Citizen award. The award is given for exemplary conduct in personal and business life and was first given to the founder of the Child of Flowers Charity Hospital.

'In a separate incident police have informed us here at Excelsior Broadcasting that the dredging of part of the Cat's Tail, an open sewer, in Pedder's Town, is a matter of routine maintenance only, after a sluice became blocked. The public are asked to stay away from the area to avoid traffic congestion.'

Zack snorted.

'The weather department has issued a storm warning this evening. The midnight freight train to the mainland has been cancelled.'

'Put Barnacle on, Mum,' said Clovis. 'This is rubbish.'

Now there was the hiss and crackle of more interference, and a woman's voice, warm and husky and confiding; as if the speaker were sitting next to them here in the living room.

'... Excellent Citizen award because he is the most extremely squeaky clean mayor anyone can remember. Well, goodness me, listeners. Does Anshelm Scarspring have no private life? And are all his business dealings so straightforward? Is he really so wonderful? Let us know your views, listeners. Better still, let us know your evidence. All communications will be kept strictly confidential.

'We have received information that the body of a man has been found in the Cat's Tail, the notorious stinking and steaming sewer which runs through Pedder's Town. As you know, good people, the Cat's Tail is nasty, nasty, deep and nasty and is flanked by high walls for its entire length to stop just this sort of tragedy from occurring.

'A very shy little bird has told us that the unfortunate gentleman who has been fished out of it this evening may well be Mr Jeremiah Pimm, a perfectly harmless greengrocer with a gambling habit. Did he jump off that high wall or was he pushed, ladies and gentlemen? Neighbours tell us that he had been visited recently by your friend and mine, Steward Golightly. Was the good steward asking for money? Rumour has it that he lends money to people like Pimm who have big gambling debts. The trouble is, he charges a very high rate of interest. Coincidence? Here in the Big Barnacle nothing is ever quite what it seems . . .'

There was a surge of interference, and the woman's voice became more distant. Zack and Clovis were both scowling with concentration, trying to hear.

'It's the wind bending the aerial. Turn it off,' said Mariette abruptly, without looking up from her sewing. The aerial was hidden in a tree and vulnerable to storms.

'Now!' she added, when neither of them moved.

'This is Momma Truth, bringing you news and

views from Barnacle Broadcasting, the voice of the outlaw truth here in the Big Barnacle, otherwise known as Rockscar City. I'll keep talking, people, as long as you keep listening . . .'

Zack shrugged, shook his head and turned the volume down. Mariette always wanted the Barnacles turned off before the end. And he and Clovis always wanted to hear more.

'Put the serial on,' said Mariette. 'I'd like a bit of humour.'

'It's not supposed to be funny,' said Zack.

'That makes it funnier.'

'Our evening serial here on Excelsior Broadcasting,' boomed the wireless suddenly, in a very clear and cheerful voice. 'The adventures of Dinah Dibbs, private detective. Last night Dinah returned home to visit her parents. Her father, Captain Jake Dibbs, has just come home from the sea . . .'

'Oh good grief,' said Clovis. He opened his book on the history of the development of the Wind Shadow scooter: the most expensive, powerful and elegant scooter on the market. His bookmark was a strip of very old dried banana.

There was a burst of music. 'Sponsored by the Scarspring Water Company,' added the announcer brightly.

Mrs Dibbs: 'Oh, Dinah, how lovely to see you, would you like a cup of tea?'

Dinah: 'Not straight away, Mum, I've just called in at the new juice and coffee bar the Scarsprings have opened on Shepherd's Lane, so I'm not really thirsty.'

'ONE,' chanted Zack and Mariette in unison.

Mrs Dibbs: 'Your father is outside checking on his pigeons, he'll be really pleased to see you. How is that new case you're working on? The one about the diamond tiara that dissolved in the rain?'

Dinah: 'I've traced the stranger who was seen carrying a small briefcase in a suspicious manner. He owns the Cinema Misterioso on Shady Avenue. He has a motive. The cinema roof was damaged in the storms last month and I suspect he doesn't have enough money to pay for the repairs.'

Mrs Dibbs: 'Well you know, I was just saying to your father, the Scarspring Water Company do offer financial help to businesses in that sort of situation. For a share of future profits they will make very reasonable loans.'

'TWO,' intoned Zack and Mariette.

Sounds of a door opening and closing.

Captain Dibbs: 'So, how's my favourite detective?'

Sounds of a hug.

Dinah: 'It's great to see you, Dad. The duchess's tiara was stolen by the owner of the Cinema Misterioso while she was asleep during a very clever film. The thief replaced it with a fake before she woke up. But the fake stones dissolved in the rain when she was queuing at the hot dog stand afterwards. Fortunately the real tiara was insured with the Scarspring Insurance Company.

'THREE!'

Mrs Dibbs: *'What will they think of next? I think I'll just put the kettle on.'*
Sounds of a tap running and a kettle filling with water.
Sounds of the kettle coming to the boil. It starts to whistle.
Mrs Dibbs: *'There's nothing like a nice cup of tea.'*
Sounds of the kettle being put back on the hob, a cup of tea being made.

Chapter 8

Zack and Mariette stared at each other. Clovis looked up from his book.

In Mr and Mrs Dibbs' cosy kitchen the impossibly fast-boiling kettle had stopped whistling. However a very similar, high-pitched note was still screaming in the Jump family living room.

This was the house alarm. It sounded exactly as it always did when they tested it on the first Friday of every month, which they had done for as long as Zack could remember. Except today was Thursday, and they were not testing anything.

Mariette turned off the wireless. Outside the wind slammed into the mountain as if the sea itself were coming to their door.

The alarm was attached to a number of sensor plates buried just under the leaf mould on the forest floor around the front of the house and on the path down to the caves and the shed. Very occasionally it was triggered by a bear. The wolves and mountain lions did not come so close.

Everyone waited. If it were a bear, which, of course, it must be because it always was, then a second lower-pitched tone would tell them so. This was thanks to a mechanism which took into account the approximate weight of the creature that had stood on the sensor plates and, crucially, the number of feet, or paws, involved.

Clovis lifted his mug towards his lips and then lowered it again without taking a sip. For the first time ever the second sensor had not been activated.

Silence.

Mariette's face went white. Her blue eyes were wide with fright.

Then suddenly a clamour of creaks and whirring sounds came from inside the walls and under the floorboards. Zack jumped to his feet. Clovis spilt his drink. The room seemed to be starting to move.

'Stay still!' hissed Mariette.

Both boys froze. Something was happening just above the fireplace. The picture of Zack and Clovis, aged four and three, had swung out, flipped over and locked smartly back into place. They all stared at the back: now facing into the room. It was an old and faded newspaper picture of Carmine Scarspring, grandfather of Anshelm, receiving the Order of Merit for Public Service from a harassed-looking civic official. Underneath it said, 'Another Proud Moment for Rockscar City'.

'Beautiful,' whispered Clovis. 'We are *such* loyal citizens.'

All around them bookshelves were ducking out of sight, taking with them their libraries of Balthazar's potentially troublesome books on the maintenance of vans, freezers and ice houses. Other shelves rose up in their place, or folded down out of the walls. They were already loaded with very dusty, but harmless books about gardening, stamp collecting and knitting; some of which appeared to be glued into position.

There was a thud from the kitchen. This was the sound of the locked safe containing their real birth certificates and other family papers: it was sinking into the floor. The whole house above them was muttering and juddering with life as cupboards, boxes and shelves in every room moved and concealed themselves.

Mariette snatched the Recipe Book out of Zack's hands, climbed on to the back of the sofa, balanced, wobbled, and jabbed her finger at a knot-hole on the varnished wooden ceiling. An entire panel slid sideways, revealing a secret compartment. Swaying and cursing, Mariette reached up and pushed the book inside.

'There might be a whole posse of them,' said Mariette, rapidly. 'Someone must have heard that ridiculous singing. They certainly work fast—'

'It's not possible, Mum—' began Clovis.

'Be quiet, Clovis! It could be Golightly himself. You didn't think of that, did you?'

'But we're miles and miles from the city, Mum!' insisted

Clovis. 'And no one knows we're here. And no one's *seen* the Ice Angel for years. I don't see how anyone could find us. I don't see why anyone should be looking. Not even Steward Golightly. We're not a threat to him—'

'That singing *travels* for miles and miles, Clovis,' said Mariette, evenly. 'The Jumps and their spring and their Ice Angel van was and will always be a threat to the Scarsprings. And Golightly is our enemy.'

Zack's heart pounded. He could feel the sweat on his palms and his forehead. He had been about to say that maybe it was hunters: people from the city who had strayed far out of their way and up into the wilderness. But she had driven his own thoughts clean out of his mind.

Zack and Clovis moved closer together.

Mariette was at the shuttered window, straining to hear through the sound of the storm. There was a vibration like a small earthquake. They all felt it through their feet.

'That'll be the boulder rolling across the mouth of the caves.' She straightened her clothes and patted her hair: her eyes fixed on the door.

'The wonder of hydraulics,' whispered Clovis, his voice shaking.

'What about the Ice Angel?' cried Zack.

'Locked in the shed,' said Clovis.

There was a noise behind them.

'SSH!' hissed Zack.

They both looked at him.

He pointed at the reassuring door with its big iron bolts and reinforced timber crossbars. Built to resist a battering ram, probably.

There it was again. A thud. A knock. Spaced out. Bang . . . bang . . . bang.

Mariette took a deep breath.

'You open it, Zack, then keep behind it. You too, Clovis, that way you'll both be out of sight. If they've found the van I'll say it was abandoned on the Wolf Road and I've been restoring it. I'll say I thought it was a hot dog van, all right? I didn't know it had anything to do with water. I don't know anything about water. I make sweaters.' She looked from one boy to the other.

'If it is a troll, or more than one troll, I will shoot it. Or them.'

'WHAT?'

They backed away from her as she strode across to the sofa. The sofa which had been there all their lives. She knelt beside it, reached underneath, pulled a catch and the cushioned seat rose up.

And inside, clean and ready for use. A hunting rifle.

'A gun,' whispered Zack. 'You've got a gun.'

'You can't mean it, Mum,' breathed Clovis.

'Shut up, Clovis,' said Mariette, softly. 'Zack, open the door.'

She crossed the room.

Zack and Clovis crept after her. Then Clovis went

and stood by the wall.

Another bang on the door. It seemed to be coming from low down.

'They're kicking it,' groaned Zack.

Slowly, shaking, he slid back the first bolt. Then the second. He squared his shoulders and turned the key in the lock. He heard the click as Mariette cocked the rifle.

With the magical speed of thought, Zack imagined Scarsprings, imagined a troll, whatever that would look like, imagined the blast from the rifle . . . screams and blood . . .

He opened the door. He forgot to keep behind it. The wind roared through the trees and smacked in his face.

There was no one there.

'Keep back,' hissed Mariette. She stepped up to the threshold and confronted the darkness, her hair and shawl streaming.

'What's that?' whispered Zack, bending down.

'Keep BACK!' said Mariette. 'Stay in the house!' She was starting to close the door again, pushing against the storm.

'There!' said Zack. 'There. Don't shut the door. Look!'

He jammed his foot in the doorway.

'Zack!'

Zack crouched down. He held out his hand into the swirling, booming night.

'Come here,' he whispered. 'Come here. We won't hurt you.'

A small dog stepped out of the dark: he was tattered and scarred and wiry. 'I don't believe it,' whispered Mariette. 'I don't believe it.' And she stared at the dog, and backed a few steps away, as if she were seeing a ghost.

Chapter 9

For a moment nobody moved. Zack, still crouched on the floor, Clovis' eyes round with terror, Mariette still holding the rifle. The dog peered from one face to another and then turned and stared determinedly at the doorway himself.

'Let's close it, Mum,' whispered Clovis. 'I don't think there's anyone there.'

She didn't speak.

Between them, Zack and Clovis swung the heavy door shut.

Mariette lowered the gun. She was moving in a leaden way now, as if all her muscles had suddenly become stiff.

'Cup of tea?' said Zack, trying to grin. 'Special Scarspring blend?'

Mariette looked at him and his grin froze and died. Very slowly, she walked to the fireplace and leant the rifle against the side of the chimneybreast.

'Is the safety catch on?' asked Clovis.

'Don't try and be clever,' she whispered. 'You don't know anything about guns.'

She went into the kitchen. Zack glimpsed her face as she turned to close the door. A stranger. A mask. He looked at Clovis.

'I wasn't trying to be clever,' said Clovis.

'I know.'

They both looked at the rifle. They did not touch it. Or even walk over to it. They just looked at it.

'The barrel is all carved,' said Clovis.

'Chased, isn't it?' said Zack, quietly. 'Don't they call that chased? When metal is all decorated like that?'

'Yeah, chased,' said Clovis. 'And that stuff. Mother-of-pearl. It looks, sort of . . .'

'Expensive,' said Zack. 'And it's got initials on, here. Do you think that's the person who made it?'

There was a loud yawn and the two brothers turned round very fast. In the dread strangeness of the moment they had forgotten they had a dog in their living room.

He was sitting up, looking at them: his fur, neither very short, nor very long, was curly and dripping. His whiskers sparkled with droplets of water. His ears were very large and unevenly shaped and stood up like sails.

'He must have got lost in the dark and the rain and everything,' said Zack, squatting down and holding out his hand. 'We won't hurt you.'

The dog put its head on one side.

'It's him hurting us that worries me,' said Clovis. 'Look at those teeth.'

41

The dog did seem to have rather impressive teeth: somewhat yellow.

'He could have been wandering for days,' said Zack. 'He's sort of battered looking, isn't he, look at his ears, and his tail.'

'He's not thin,' said Clovis, thoughtfully.

The kitchen door opened and they both spun round again, two soldiers on guard.

Mariette. Some warmth had returned to her face. Not much, though.

'The first bell went off, and then the second one didn't,' she said. 'Something crossed those sensor plates on two legs. Something that must still be out there now.'

The dog suddenly scrabbled noisily to his feet: he had big feet and long claws. With the gaze of each of them upon him, and skidding slightly on the polished floor, he stood up on his hind legs and began to totter across the room.

The Jump family stepped out of his way in various directions.

The dog reached the hearthrug, still balancing. Then he stopped, swayed and fell over heavily and sideways. He lay down and put his chin on his front paws.

'Are we saying that he was walking about in the forest on his hind legs?' breathed Mariette, finally.

'I think *he's* saying that,' said Clovis.

They all stared at the dog. He stared back. He did have an unusually knowing expression.

'And how did he knock on the door?' added Clovis.

'Maybe with his nose,' said Zack. 'Maybe he's escaped from a circus or something. There was a circus in Pedder's Hill Park in the summer. He could have been wandering about for weeks. Let's give him something to eat.'

A pause followed. They could hear the trees outside moaning and straining in the relentless wind. Now a great handful of hail hit the outside shutter of the window like stones, making Mariette flinch.

'The alarms haven't gone off again,' added Zack. 'There can't be anyone else out there.'

'He could have a listening device installed inside him,' said Clovis.

'Are you mad? You are so obsessed with science and stuff! What sort of listening device? A microphone? Who would have installed it? Installed where, exactly?'

'It's just weird, that's all,' said Clovis.

'Are you suggesting we put him back out of the door in this weather? If a lion or a wolf doesn't get him he'll die of exposure anyway.'

'We'll keep him tonight,' said Mariette. 'Then we'll think about it tomorrow. Get him something from the kitchen, Zack.'

She lifted out a stone from the side of the fireplace and began pulling back levers to reset the alarm and rearrange the house. The room creaked into life again. Bookshelves dived out of sight and were replaced; the panel in the ceiling opened; the boys' portrait swung back into position.

'Did Dad ever have a dog, Mum?' asked Zack, over his shoulder, on the way to the kitchen.

Mariette didn't reply.

'Or a gun?' whispered Clovis, following him. 'I thought he was supposed to be a man of peace.'

The kitchen was small and warm and smelt of baking. Zack felt something relax in his chest: his muscles were like fists unclenching. For a moment he thought he was going to cry.

'Maybe we should ask Dinah Dibbs,' he said quickly. 'Except, of course, she's not real. And worse still, she's sponsored by the Scarsprings, which goes against her.'

He'd wanted a dog for years. He started pulling things out of cupboards – biscuits, tins of stewed fruit – a paper bag split open and dried peas showered over the floor. Clovis started trying to scoop them up with his hands.

'Sometimes I think Dad's not real,' he said. 'He's like someone in a story. And we can't get into the story to find him.'

'We'll find him,' said Zack.

There was a hubbub of voices from the living room: Mariette had put the wireless on again.

'Once I get out and about in the van, meeting his old customers, getting to know people. We'll hear stuff. Information. We'll find him for sure.'

'So, do you think she would have used the, er, firearm?'

'It certainly looked like that to me.'

The brothers began crawling about on the tiled floor collecting the peas, while the dog stood unnoticed at the kitchen door, watching them.

Chapter 10

Later, without anyone objecting, the dog followed Zack up the various stairs, including the narrow spiral ones that led up through the trapdoor into his tiny room.

The room was a crooked shape, with a small round window looking out over the tops of the trees. The storm had blown the sky almost clear and the moon rode on the last, high, threadbare clouds.

Zack watched as the dog turned round and round on the end of the bed, finally faced the window, and curled up. Did all dogs have such big feet? Did they all fold their ears down like that? Weren't dogs' ears either up or down, folded or unfolded?

'Zack? Zack, are you asleep?'

Zack jumped. Even though it was only Clovis' voice, muffled by the trapdoor.

'Possibly,' called Zack. 'But you've completely cured me. Come in. It's not bolted.'

He looked back at the dog again: yes, those ears really were folded over those eyes.

The door creaked open and Clovis' head, and then his shoulders, rose into view. He was carrying a candle. The light threw shadows across his face and made a halo out of his curly hair.

The dog's ears sprang up like sails.

'Found something,' said Clovis in a mumble.

'What? Aren't you coming up?'

'You come down. It's in the attic.'

It was necessary to go down from Zack's room, along a narrow sloping passage, through Clovis' larger room, full of maps and things to do with maps, and up an ancient ladder.

'Where's Mum?' whispered Zack.

'Still up. Doing a new knitting pattern or something.'

'So what's the big mystery?' They were on the rickety ladder. Zack was talking to his brother's ankles.

'Something must have gone wrong after the alarm went off. I came up here to fetch some parchment. A sort of chest thing has come out of the wall. It must have got stuck. It hasn't gone back in. I've never seen it before.'

They hauled themselves into the attic. As Zack followed Clovis, and climbed up on to the dusty floor, the dog appeared behind him, his expression thoughtful, his front paws clinging on to the top rung of the ladder.

'Have you seen that?' exclaimed Zack. 'And I didn't even think dogs could climb ladders. Must be the unexpectedly large feet.'

'That whole dog is unexpected,' said Clovis dryly.

The dog scrambled up through the hatch and licked a cobweb off his nose.

'Anyway,' continued Clovis, sounding suddenly miserable, 'there it is. It's there. I think it's a map chest. I saw loads of them at Meakin's when I went for my interview.'

The attic was small with a pitched roof and yet another hatch, this one leading to the series of ladders up to the lookout platform in the trees. The mountain was very steep here, the attic fitted into the very top of the deep triangular cleft where the Jumps had built their house. One tiny window, black against the night.

Zack looked around, blinking. There were the familiar piles of boxes and the sacks of wool, the train set and the pirate ship and the jungle fort made of painted wood and canvas. There also, were the reinforcements for Clovis' ever-increasing army of map-related equipment, otherwise stored in his bedroom: rolls of parchment and paper, bottles of ink, measuring tapes and a half-painted globe.

And there, sprung out of a place on the wall which had always looked like rock, and was, in fact, the side of the mountain, brushed over with whitewash . . . there was the chest. It was long, narrow and carved and it was bound along the edges and over the corners with what he presumed must be brass.

The lid was partway open. The inside, a mouth of darkness.

'So, what's in there?' whispered Zack.

'A picture and stuff,' said Clovis, softly. 'I think it's something to do with Dad.'

'Really, a picture? A picture of him?'

Neither of them had ever seen a photograph of their father.

'No. I think he must have painted it. Remember Mum said he fancied his chances as an artist at one time? She wasn't very polite about it.'

'Should we take it downstairs?' said Zack. He felt as if he were in some sort of danger. 'I mean, this is good, isn't it? A picture by Dad. She'll want to see it, won't she? And I mean, I want to see it . . .'

'I think she's seen it already,' said Clovis, slowly. 'I think she knows it's here and she can come and see it whenever she likes.'

'What?'

'Think about it, Zack. We've never seen this chest before, right? We both come up here from time to time. It's not exactly small. We couldn't have just not noticed it. Right?'

'Right,' said Zack.

'So, this chest must have been hidden in the wall all our lives, just about. Perhaps a connection has got loose somewhere. Don't you see? Normally this is out of sight all the time. Then tonight, either when the alarm went off or when everything was rearranging itself back to normal, this must have come *out* of the wall. Something went wrong.'

Zack frowned. 'But if it's always hidden in the wall how would Mum know it's there? How would she have ever seen it?'

'My guess is she knows. She knew about the rifle inside the sofa. She knows about everything. We're the ones who are always getting surprises.'

'So you think she just hasn't told us?'

'Yes,' said Clovis. 'It would hardly be the first time.'

They stood together without moving.

'So I came to get you,' added Clovis.

'Right,' said Zack.

He took three steps across the room to the chest and knelt down. He could see a roll of canvas inside and some other things wrapped in material. Newspaper at the bottom. He reached in very cautiously, as if the chest were full of rage and might slam down on his arm.

'That's the picture,' said Clovis. 'I didn't unroll it. I just sort of looked down the middle.'

While the dog sat down, watching intently, Zack and Clovis spread the picture out on the floor and held it flat with jars of ink.

There was a long silence.

'What exactly do you think it's about?' whispered Clovis.

There was a title printed neatly by hand along the bottom: 'The Garden of the Trolls'.

For a moment Zack thought that he had never seen anything like it. Then he was washed over with a memory, covering him like a wave and then receding, leaving him shaking inside. A room. Could it have been this room? And a smell of something. And a man. Was he smiling? Or was he crying? And these colours, these many shades of blue and green and the flowers and trees and animals, filling the canvas . . .

'I remember something about painting,' he said. 'I remember him.'

The light from Clovis' candle flickered and went out. The wick had burnt down into the pool of wax and drowned. Much fumbling as he took a new one from his pocket and lit it: the match flaring in the window, reflected like a golden eye.

'Tell me anything, anything about what he was like, anything you can remember.'

Zack knew that Clovis was desperate: but there was almost nothing to give him.

'He was upset,' he whispered, at last. 'And I was scared. I think maybe they were arguing. I'm not sure.'

'Oh God I hate being younger!' cried Clovis suddenly. 'I hate not being able to remember anything! You can remember him. You said before you can remember the smell of him, when he picked you up . . . and you don't look much like me, or Mum, so you must *look* like him, too . . .'

Zack was so amazed that he knocked over one of the jars holding the picture flat on the floor. It rolled loudly across the attic. The dog trotted after it.

'But you *are* like him, Clovis, you're terribly like him. You like maps, didn't Mum once say he liked maps? Plus you're great with engines and scooters, taking them to pieces and fixing them, just like he did. If I take something to pieces it just stays in pieces.'

Clovis shook his head and looked away from him, back down at the picture of the flowers and trees.

'Perhaps there really is a place like this. Perhaps it's somewhere in the wilderness and he found it.'

'There's nowhere in the wilderness where this sort of stuff would grow,' said Zack.

Clovis sighed and pulled out the bundle of material. The first thing he found was a cylinder which looked to be carved out of bone, with a silver stopper on one end. He handed it to Zack.

Zack gently loosened the stopper. His heart was racing. He tipped the tube and a piece of parchment fell out. This was a very different sort of picture. Very old. At first it looked like something from a fairytale: there was a blue-green sea monster and a grey dragon. And yet there was also something familiar about it . . .

'Squeeze your eyes a bit,' said Clovis, suddenly.

'Squeeze them?'

'Yes, make it blurry.' Clovis was squinting at the parchment as if he were looking into the sun.

Zack half closed his eyes. The sea monster, the grey dragon, the fierce-looking giant . . . all lost their vivid detail: they became shapes.

They became a map.

'It's a map!' said Zack. 'The monster is the sea. The dragon is Rockscar City. The whole thing looks like a kid drew it to me. The giant is, the giant is—'

'He's the wilderness and the mountains. It's all taken up by the giant. The giant is the wilderness. And look who's here—'

Zack looked. He didn't need to screw up his eyes anymore. There she was, surely it was her, the angel from the front of the van: small and beautiful.

'She's right over the giant's heart,' he said.

'And here, what do you make of this?'

There was a small circle in the top left-hand corner of the map, roughly drawn, containing a picture of a man, or at least, a person, and a blurry animal, perhaps a dog.

'It's like a signature,' said Clovis.

'You know what I think,' said Zack. 'You know what I think. This isn't a giant. This is a troll. And this is his territory, the wilderness and the mountains.'

'A troll,' whispered Clovis. 'You mean sort of representing the wilderness, like the dragon is representing the city? You mean the troll is the wilderness? Not real, obviously . . .'

'I don't know. Mum seemed to think trolls were pretty real tonight.'

They stared at the map. The dragon appeared to be made of stone and metal. It was breathing a blast of flame, scorching the ground black around it. The troll, if it was a troll, was an enormous man with massive legs and arms, six fingers on each hand, short forked antlers, beard reaching his feet . . .

'He's got wolves in his beard,' said Zack.

'And that could be a mountain lion,' said Clovis. 'And a bear, look . . .'

'Let's look at the newspaper,' said Zack. He felt as if they were stealing. He moved quickly, picking dusty newspaper cuttings out of the bottom of the chest and handing them to Clovis. The dog sniffed each one in turn: then he stuck his head in the chest and sniffed every inch of that too.

'These are really old,' said Clovis, abandoning the map. 'Listen to this, *Archibald Scarspring Esquire, owner of the Scarspring Water Company, today pleaded guilty to a charge of disorderly and threatening conduct—*

'Archibald!' exclaimed Zack. 'Which one is he? I've never heard of him.'

'Well you wouldn't have done,' said Clovis, still scanning the piece of newspaper. 'Look at the date. This happened over ninety years ago . . . *following an altercation which took place in the Anchor Ale House in the area adjacent to the docks known as SugarTown between Mr Scarspring and a seafaring gentleman, Captain . . .*

'I can't read that bit, it's all worn, where the paper was folded, anyway . . . . . . *witnesses confirmed that the Captain had asserted to the company gathered in the tap room of the*

Anchor that there are no such things as trolls. He had referred to the belief in such creatures as an antique superstition, meriting as much serious consideration as the legendary notion of the existence of mermaids.

He also remarked that anyone espousing such a belief was likely to be simple-minded, ill-educated or mad. Mr Scarspring took exception to these comments and an unseemly exchange followed, involving language unsuitable for inclusion in this paper.

Both men had partaken freely of beer and spirits. There was an exchange of blows ended only by the intervention of the landlord.

Mr Scarspring, who is well-known for his quick temper and his intemperate habits, apologized to the court. However he insisted that trolls not only exist but that he himself had encountered one in the mountains when he was a young man. He said he could not describe its appearance, as it had no recognizable form or shape.

Outside the court he was asked by a journalist from this newspaper for his response to the respectful suggestion that he suffers from the sickness of mind known as the Curse of the Scarsprings. This condition has been noted in several members of this illustrious family over the generations. The sufferer sees things which are not there, known as hallucinations. He or she then becomes obsessed with the task of persuading others that what they have seen is real.

Mr Scarspring was re-arrested a few moments later for assaulting the journalist in question . . .'

Clovis turned the paper over. 'That's all.'

'Oo-er,' said Zack, grinning. 'The Curse of the Scarsprings.'

They looked at the other faded newspaper fragments. They all referred to trolls. In one case, thirty years before Zack was born, trolls were blamed for damage to the foundations of a new road being laid across the east side of the mountain on land otherwise described as wilderness. This road had never been finished after the earth removed during the day was repeatedly put back during the night. Attempts to recruit men to stand guard had failed and the enterprise had been abandoned completely after heavy machinery and equipment were thrown into the sea, again during the night, by person or persons unknown.

'No more cuttings?' asked Zack, after they had both read everything they could find.

Clovis shook his head.

Zack unwrapped the rest of the bundle of material: closely attended by the dog.

A fob watch slid on to the floor. Then there was a flash of gold and something else fell too. Something that could roll, and did roll; tracing a curve on the dusty boards; stopping close to Zack's feet.

Neither of them spoke.

In silence they each picked up an item and turned it over in their hands.

Zack had the watch. It looked very old. The silver case had tarnished to black and was dented and scratched. The back was engraved with a flowing letter J. 'This is a bit personal,' he said softly.

'Not as personal as this,' said Clovis, his voice shaking. A battered gold ring glinted in his palm. There were four tiny blue pearls set in a row along it, and a space where a fifth must have been lost. It was a broad ring, made for a big hand.

They didn't look at each other.

'He's dead for sure,' whispered Clovis.

'No,' said Zack quickly. 'He was always in danger. Something may have happened and he might have left to protect us. He might have had to take a new identity and it might have been safer not to wear such a, you know, such a distinctive ring that people might recognize—'

There was a sound from somewhere below them: the dog stood up, his ears swivelling.

'Zack?' called Mariette. 'Clovis? Where are you? What are you doing?'

Footsteps.

'We're OK, Mum,' yelled Zack. 'We're just, we're just . . .'

Clovis was frantically rolling up the picture. Zack snatched up the parchment map and slid it back into the tube. He almost dropped the stopper. He glimpsed another piece of paper right at the bottom of the chest. Only small. Yellow and old and folded up. No time to look at it now. He grabbed the newspaper cuttings and bundled up the fob watch.

57

A moment later they were both throwing all their weight on the lid of the chest. It began to close very slowly. Almost at the last second it suddenly slammed shut, there was a crunching sound and a grinding of cogs somewhere in the wall and it slid backwards. A fake piece of wall, stone set on a wooden panel, rumbled into place in front of it.

'Are you in the attic? Whatever are you doing there at this time of night? I thought you were both in bed!'

There was no doubt about it: she was right below them now. The ladder began to rattle. She was coming up. Clovis, his eyes enormous, pointed to the floor: it was the ring. Zack grabbed it and shoved it into the pocket of his dressing gown.

'We're just going up to the lookout, Mum,' he called. This was horrible.

'What do you want to go to the lookout for? It's dark. You won't be able to see anything. What do you want to see anyway?' Head and shoulders through the trapdoor. Her face shadowed in the candlelight.

'It is a full moon, Mother,' said Clovis, in a stilted, formal voice. 'There's no harm in checking the road, after what happened tonight.'

She stared at him as if she were about to say something. Then she nodded slowly and started back down the ladder. A swift, furtive glance at the place where the chest had disappeared so tidily back into the wall.

Chapter 11

The storm had passed. However, even in the stillness left behind, the lookout tree creaked and sang to itself. It was a wilderness cedar. The tallest and broadest of the trees that grew in the wilderness.

A series of small platforms led almost to the top, linked by pieces of ladder and tarred rope so that climbers could steady themselves. Everything was slippery, wet and cold. As Zack climbed, in the moonlight, reaching one platform, then the next, the trunk of the great tree grew narrower and the branches offered less and less protection. Worse still, the other smaller trees nearby reached as far as they could and then one by one were gone; until the drop gaped wherever he looked.

He was near the highest platform of all now. He stopped for a moment, leaning against the peeling bark of the trunk, very alone between the earth and sky. He could feel the ring in his pocket. He closed his fingers around it. Then he drew it out and looked at it closely: it felt smooth and worn with age.

Zack slipped it on to his finger. Not his ring finger, it was too big for that. He put it on his middle finger. Even then, it was a little loose. He felt it slide against his skin. Someone had worn it for a long time, he was certain. Maybe that person had never taken it off. Maybe, in the end, someone else had taken it, carefully, from a hand that was already cold. Or maybe they had pulled it, indifferent, perfunctory . . . . and shoved it in an envelope labelled 'personal effects return to relatives' . . .

The tree pitched in a stray gust of wind and he hugged the trunk. 'He's dead, for sure,' Clovis had said.

Zack climbed on, weary and aching, until at last he reached the final platform and the cold air engulfed him. He looked out, beyond the foot of the mountain and the distant, twinkling city far below, and saw the silver glimmer of the sea.

At the same moment something brushed against his leg and he stifled a scream: it was the dog.

'You are one heck of a climber,' he said, daring to stroke the top of the dog's head. He thought of the places where he had stepped from one branch to another, his free arm clamped as far as it would reach around the tree trunk, his eyes almost shut against his fear.

'You are one heck of a climber,' he said again.

The dog yawned. For a moment Zack thought that he had raised his eyebrows. Except surely dogs didn't have eyebrows: and didn't raise them either.

Clovis had told Mariette that Zack was going to look at the Wolf Road.

No harm in actually doing it, although, surely, if anyone had been there, they would be far away by now. He took the oilskin bag that held the binoculars out of its hiding place, strapped to the tree. Then he scanned the black roof of the forest, the crouching mountain to the left and the still, sparkling sea.

He focussed on the place where the Wolf Road emerged into view from the trees, a long way below. It curved to the right, like a grey shadow on the paler grey of the rocks and scrub on either side. Impossible to tell from this distance, in the moonlight, how hard it would be to drive the Ice Angel down there.

Then he saw dark shapes, wolves, a hunting party, spread out and fast-moving, and he heard their voices raised, only once; before they were gone again and part of the night. An owl sailed past him.

Now he saw something else on the Wolf Road. Something that made his heart lurch with fright.

And the mysterious dog at his side whined softly.

Chapter 12

Clovis had not been asleep. He was sitting up in bed propped on pillows, chewing anxiously at a piece of bread and honey. The room was full of books and maps. There were all kinds of maps on the walls, including a scale map of the Jump family bathrooms: all drawn by Clovis. He had been making maps since the first day he could hold a pen.

'Is Mum still up?' asked Zack. 'Where is she?'

'In her ro . . . om,' mumbled Clovis, through the mouthful. 'Are you sure it wasn't fireflies?'

'Oh yeah, fireflies going at twenty miles an hour.'

'Could have been blown by the wind. You can get local twisters, all so . . .orts of things—'

'IT was NOT fireflies and IT was NOT being blown by the wind. It was a tail light. A little red light, following the road, smooth, sailing along.'

'That road is full of potholes and all sorts and after this rain it would be like a stream, the water runs right down it, that's what makes the potholes and the cracks—'

'But I saw it, Clovis.'

'I'm just saying,' Clovis had finished his bread, he was brushing crumbs off the blankets, 'how could a bicycle or a scooter or whatever go smoothly. You keep saying that it was going smoothly and I'm saying how could that happen on that road surface in those conditions . . .'

'I don't KNOW how,' cried Zack.

'It would be bump, bump, bump.'

'But I DID see it.'

'I know you did.'

They both fell silent. The dog had gone to sleep on the end of Clovis' bed. He started to snore. Zack produced a hairy piece of chocolate from his pocket and ate it.

'Someone was on the road,' he said, eventually. 'There's never been anyone on the road before.'

'I know,' said Clovis.

Even though they were both exhausted they sat there a little while longer. Zack ate a large piece of bread. Then he drew the ring from his finger and Clovis fetched a magnifying glass.

They looked at it together, running it between their fingers, feeling the weight, touching it and holding it as if it could connect them straight to its owner.

'I think it's very old,' said Clovis. 'Maybe a family heirloom, you know, passed down. These are blue pearls, aren't they? They're very rare, aren't they? And one is missing. Looks like it came out a long time ago.'

'You try it on,' whispered Zack.

But Clovis just held it, still looking at it under the magnifying glass. 'These are hallmarks. Special little marks inside that tell you who the jeweller was, or when it was made, or something . . . you should wear this.'

'What?'

'You're the driver. You wear it. When you go out in the van. All the time. Just don't let Mum see.'

'Why not you? You could wear it when you start at Meakin's. Or we can take it in turns.'

'You wear it, Zack,' said Clovis, his eyes rimmed with tiredness. 'You know it's his. You wear it. She scared the heck out of me tonight. I didn't know this whole Ice Angel thing was going to be so dangerous.'

'But when you think about it we're just two people, with one little van,' exclaimed Zack. 'And the Scarsprings own everything else. I mean I know we've always kept out of their way, I know they were our enemies in the old days—'

'For many generations,' interrupted Clovis.

'Yes, for many generations, but nowadays they are so powerful, why should they bother with us?'

'So what do you think happened to Dad? And why do your think our mother, the nice woman who knits, actually has a rifle hidden in her sofa and knows how to use it? She is not only extremely scared of the Scarsprings, especially Golightly, she is also terrified of trolls.'

'Are you saying we now believe trolls actually exist?'

'Well Mum certainly seems to, something she's never

exactly emphasized before. She is prepared to shoot one dead on our doorstep. Bang.'

Zack thought of Mariette pointing the rifle into the night.

'What I mean is,' said Clovis, 'she has some reason or reasons to take everything very seriously and it must be to do with Dad. He didn't run off and he didn't get sick and die. I think that she believes that either it was something to do with the Scarsprings *or* a troll killed him one night. On troll territory, just like it says on that map: on the Wolf Road.'

Zack couldn't speak.

'It's a logical conclusion,' persisted Clovis. ' That's why she's been in such a state about you and the van and selling ices again. And hasn't she's always stopped us going down to the Wolf Road? Telling us all about the wolves and the lions and the bears. Have you ever heard of anyone being attacked in broad daylight by wolves? And the mountain lions stay higher up, don't they? And the bears are vegetarians.'

Zack discovered that he was clutching the ring in his fist. He uncurled his fingers and stared down at it, not seeing anything . . .

'You wear that thing,' Clovis whispered. 'It feels . . .' He hesitated. 'At the risk of sounding unscientific, it feels good. There's something good about it.'

And so it was decided.

Chapter 13

They had called the dog Moe. He was sitting on the long seat in the cab of the Ice Angel, next to the passenger door, wearing a safety harness especially designed for him. Clovis was in the middle: Zack behind the wheel. (It was a ship's wheel.) Zack and Clovis were wearing harnesses too. All they had to do was sit down and the harness shot out from several directions and locked itself over their chests. It was a new invention, which Clovis had been working on most of the night.

'Fine,' said Zack. 'Really good. Except I do need to be able to move my arms to drive.'

They had struggled with the harnesses for a while. In the end, Clovis had detached the self-locking mechanism.

Now they were ready.

Mariette had gone down into the city by the usual route, through the water cave, the ice cave, then the tunnels and caverns which led to their secret entrance near the outskirts of Storm Hill. Also the hiding place of the Jump family scooters.

By now she would be putting on her pink pearl-finish helmet, her black rain cloak and her pink gauntlets and steering her Favolosa Mark C scooter out of the final tunnel. Then she would lock the iron gate behind her and push the Favolosa down the overgrown path through the trees to the place where it met the road along Storm Hill Ridge: on the very edge of Rockscar City.

When she left, Clovis had been reading books on map making. Zack had been struggling with a chocolate and chilli sorbet. He had had so many disasters trying to make the ices that he had started inventing his own recipes.

But now they were here, in the cab of the Ice Angel. The engine was coughing and choking. Clovis was holding up a library book called *The Art of Driving the Automobile and Van*.

'It's a maiden voyage, like a ship,' said Zack, surveying the now extremely complicated dashboard. 'Right. The plan is we do not under any circumstances get out of the van, right? It's very solid. We'll be quite safe as long as we don't get out—'

'You're over-revving,' yelled Clovis.

'I'm what?'

'Get your foot off that pedal!'

The Ice Angel leapt forward like a greyhound—

'Not that pedal!' bawled Clovis.

They shot out of the shed, past the entrance to the caves, drove over some tools and equipment and thundered down the short slope to the potholed and pitted track. Birds shouted in panic. A mountain goat jumped out of sight. Moe, his ears back, his hackles up, made a sound somewhere between a snarl and a scream—

'Brake!' yelled Clovis.

They were gaining speed.

'I AM braking!'

'That's not the brake, *that's* the brake – steer! Steer!'

They just missed a boulder. They ploughed through a small lake of floodwater. They reached the place where the track joined the Wolf Road. Soon there would be hairpin bends, dreadful drops and ravines . . .

Clovis heaved on the handbrake. It jammed.

Zack, his face cartoon-terrified, his lips moving without making proper words, started punching wildly at the buttons next to the steering wheel—

'What are you doing! Stop!'

'Trying to . . . HORN . . .'

There was a bear on the road ahead of them.

The Ice Angel thudded and bounded towards it—

Zack clenched his hands even tighter on the wheel—

Moe was thumping at anything he could reach with his paw—

'Emergency stop!' cried Clovis—

Zack pressed the red button with the picture of the skull and crossbones on it, the van lurched to a tremendously impressive halt, the safety harnesses worked very well, the bear ambled thoughtfully into the forest, the horn finally sounded and—

'What the . . . what the . . . what . . .' spluttered Zack.

'Internal sprinklers,' said Clovis. 'In case of fire on impact.'

'But there wasn't an impact!'

'At least the air bed didn't go off.'

At that moment the air bed did go off, filling the cab with rapidly expanding floral camping mattress.

Clovis had designed this particular safety feature so that the mattress would not reach where Moe sat, right over by the passenger door, because he was too small and it would be dangerous. While Zack and Clovis fought with the mattress Moe took the opportunity to bite at the clasp on his harness, free himself and jump out of the window.

It was sunny and warm on the Wolf Road.

It was still raining in the van: voices were raised in there.

'Don't press that!'

'I'm just trying to turn . . . this . . . thing-g . . . off . . .'

'Just let me get at the—'

'Aah!'

The Ice Angel, being a van designed for the transportation and sale of ices, had various doors. Among them, one at the back where the ramp could be lowered to allow the driver to emerge with his refrigerated cart.

This door had just flung itself open. The ramp descended

with a crash. Zack fell out of the cab and charged round the back to see what was happening: a scooter rolled smartly down the ramp, reached the bottom and fell over sideways.

Clovis arrived shortly afterwards: he had just managed to turn off the sprinklers. Zack was jumping up and down, dripping wet and gesticulating . . .

'We are here,' he exclaimed. 'Somewhere on the Wolf Road, a famous dangerous place,' he looked around, trees, rocks, more trees and they all seemed to be watching him, 'and you've, you've tipped this, this scooter . . .'

'Emergency escape vehicle,' said Clovis, calmly.

'You've tipped this, this emergency escape vehicle—'

'Well, help me pick it up then,' interrupted Clovis.

Between them they heaved the scooter upright. It was black and silver, an early Bellisima, beautifully banded with gleaming chrome.

'What's that down there?' asked Zack. 'Is that bit broken?'

No, you idiot, that's the kick-start. This is really old. It's a Series 2. They didn't bring in the starter switch on the handlebars until Series 4.'

'Is this the one that was in the back of the shed?'

Clovis nodded. He had taken his handkerchief out of his pocket and was wringing it out. He started wiping mud off the running board, where the scooter had hit the ground. For a moment they both forgot where they were and the fact that they were very wet.

'I've cleaned it up a lot,' said Clovis. 'It needed a new headlamp and some other stuff. And some of the chrome had to be rubbed down. Rust.'

'Do you think it was his?'

Clovis shrugged.

Zack was starting to shiver. 'I'm freezing.'

'Me too.'

Zack looked around again at the enormous pine trees, hemming them in on both sides of the road. The mountain, and other mountains beyond, loomed savage and glittering with snow. Even the blue spring sky seemed harsh.

Now that the sprinkler was off the Ice Angel was silent, except for one or two muffled clicks and creaks as the engine cooled.

It was beautiful and frightening and very, very quiet on the Wolf Road.

'Let's get out of here,' said Zack, softly.

They rolled the scooter back into the van, lifted the ramp and locked it in place.

'Look at that,' whispered Clovis. "Where the ramp was, and over there, look . . .'

A single tyre track ran straight across the road. It was clearest near the back of the van where the mud was soft. Then it scoured a patch of shingle, disappeared over some stones and reappeared in softer ground again: just before it was gone, heading into the forest.

Moe had been chewing the cover of the *Art of Driving*

book. He stood up and trotted over. Zack and Clovis stared at the track. Moe sniffed it.

'You think someone came out of there?' Zack pointed to the forest on one side of the road. 'And went in there?' He pointed to where the track disappeared again. 'On a scooter?'

They crept towards the edge of the road. There had once been a gully there, it looked to be the remains of a drainage ditch, clogged with mud and debris. Then, of course, the forest reared up, huge and ancient. Dense, green darkness. The floor a mass of moss and the rotting carcasses of trees long dead: scattered rocks, half hidden, like buried bones. A great platform of white fungus jutted out of a stump.

Zack's heart was pounding.

'Anything could happen here,' he whispered.

'I know,' said Clovis.

They both ran back to the cab. Moe, left behind, stood for a moment staring into the forest, at the place where the tyre track seemed so improbably to plunge between the pines. Then he followed them and jumped into his seat.

Behind the wheel Zack gasped and pointed wordlessly through the mud-splattered windscreen. A mountain lion had come out of the trees and was walking along the road ahead of them.

'I thought you said they never came this far down the mountain,' he whispered.

'Looks like I was wrong,' said Clovis, not moving.

Moe made a small sound: meaning unclear.

'Do up Moe's harness,' said Zack. 'Let's get out of here.'

Zack had read in the *Art of Driving* book about how to do something called a three-point turn. Clovis hissed instructions, holding up the book and guessing at the bits with teeth-marks. Moe whined softly. They did a thirty-point turn and set off slowly for home.

Absolute silence after that: until they were chugging in through the doors of the shed.

'So,' said Clovis, 'that went well.'

Chapter 14

'It can't have been a scooter,' said Zack, later. 'Do you think it could have been a wheelbarrow?'

'Even if it was a wheelbarrow,' said Clovis, 'there still had to be someone pushing it. Who? Why? And anyway, no footprints.'

They were sitting by the fire drinking cocoa after a great drama of activity trying to get their clothes dry before Mariette came home. Two pairs of steaming socks dangled from the mantelpiece. Zack had accidentally set fire to his jumper. Clovis, always more cautious, had only singed his coat.

'I think it was a hunter. The one who rides about in the dark and has a tail light,' said Zack.

This seemed the only explanation of the tyre tracks on the road and they fell silent for a moment. The thought of a hunter so near the house was frightening.

'Perhaps it was a bear on a unicycle and it had escaped from the same circus as Moe the Mystery Dog,' said Clovis.

'Or a troll,' said Zack. 'Cycling home after a long day in the garden. A troll on a unicycle.'

'Wouldn't its feet be too big for the pedals?'

'Definitely.'

Mariette had opened the front door.

They stopped talking.

She stared at them for a moment. She was still wearing her black rain cloak. The pink pearl-finish helmet hung from her arm by the chinstrap; the gauntlets were sticking out of the top of her shopping bag.

'Next time you two take the van out and get it all splashed with mud,' she said, 'please clean it afterwards. Your father always did.'

Zack started coughing. Clovis slapped him on the back.

'And also, now you are so very big and important and going out and about without any idea what's what, I'd like you not to make jokes about trolls. No jokes about them at all.'

'Why not?' said Clovis, his voice very cool. 'Is there something we should know?'

Mariette didn't blink. She looked from one son to the other. Her voice, when she finally spoke, was cold and steady. The voice of the woman who had pointed the rifle, just where a person's heart would be.

'I can't stop you from driving your father's van,' she said. 'I can't stop you going down into the city and selling the ices. This is Rockscar. People grow up fast. Just make sure that you keep away from the Scarsprings and Golightly. And never get out of the van on the Wolf Road.'

'Are trolls real?' Zack blurted out. 'Did a troll kill our father?'

He would rather have cornered the mountain lion.

'Balthazar Jump was a dreamer of dreams,' she whispered, at last. '*His* father was sensible. *He* closed up this house and brought up his children down in Storm Hill. Balthazar lived down there until he was seventeen. You didn't know that, did you? But his grandad never forgot the house and the Ice Angel van and Balthazar listened to him, and he decided to come back up here and follow the crazy family tradition after all.

'He was a dreamer who thought all manner of things might be possible. Including trolls. His grandfather had spoken to him about them when he was a boy. He would much rather talk about trolls, and other fancies, and about his precious Ice Angel van, and his good works taking our healing spring water to the needy. He would much rather talk about all those things than the practical matters of life. I had to deal with those. All of them.

'He thought that the figure of the angel was wonderful, just like you do. He thought she had the power to save him from danger out there in the wilderness on the Wolf Road . . .'

There was a silence. Zack and Clovis both stared at their mother.

'But it was all rubbish,' she said. 'He was gone . . .' Her voice broke. Her eyes were filling with tears. Not the sort of tears she would allow her sons to wipe away for her: tears of bitterness and rage.

'He was *gone*. And there *she* was, still so prim and proper and calm and beautiful, still sitting on the front of the van . . .'

'You mean you found—' began Zack.

But Mariette turned away from him and slammed the kitchen door behind her.

'Why don't you just stop asking her things?' said Clovis, almost in tears himself. 'It's not worth it. It's like being beaten up.'

Chapter 15

Zack had rushed around shopping in the fruit markets, collecting supplies of milk and cream, cutting ice in the cave and, of course, preparing the ices. The kitchen was unrecognizable, busy with stainless steel utensils, bowls and chopping boards and baskets of fruit. Huge pans on the stove; overpowering smells of hot sugar and berries; jugs of cream; chillis hanging from the ceiling. Blocks of dark chocolate as big as bricks. Mistakes and crises and spillages all over the place.

Now it was the night before Clovis started his apprenticeship at Meakin's the Map Makers. Clovis was sitting in the living room packing and re-packing his bag. Pencils, measuring rules, a bottle of indelible ink, pens with various types of nib, two apples and a piece of chocolate in gold paper.

'You're not going to live there,' said Zack. 'You'll be home tomorrow evening, just like school.' He had the Recipe Book open on his knee.

'I will be home,' said Clovis. 'And I will have my tea and

sit here and listen to the radio and all the normal things. But I will have embarked on the great adventure of map making. I will never be quite the same again.'

Zack groaned.

'It's a miracle that you've got this apprenticeship,' said Mariette. 'Just don't mess it up. Don't go arguing with Mr Meakin like you do with me.'

'I will not argue with him,' said Clovis, solemnly. 'I just wish he was going to pay me a bit more, that's all.'

'Don't concern yourself with that,' said Mariette. She was bending over her sewing. Zack realized that she was hiding her face.

'Shut up,' he whispered. He tried to kick Clovis, but couldn't quite reach.

'I'd just like to be able to bring home more money,' said Clovis, demonstrating the capacity for persistence so much admired by the teachers at Storm Hill School.

'I'm sorry if you feel we don't have enough, Clovis,' snapped Mariette. 'There is only me and I've done the best I can.'

'I was only saying—' began Clovis.

'I've been looking at the list of places that Dad visited. I've been trying to work out a route,' said Zack, quickly.

Mariette bit through her sewing thread with her neat, sharp teeth.

'Excelsior Broadcasting House,' said Zack. 'Studios nine and ten. Late night performances. I'm planning to take

Crushed Vanilla with Ginger Crystals, Coffee and Bitter Chocolate with Frozen Crystallized Orange Lumps, I invented those today when I was trying to make something else. Mango Granita, Burnt Sugar and Toffee Fingers, that's because, you know, the sugar got burnt, Lemon Sorbet . . . with bits in . . . I think we can do all those . . . But it says featherplum here, next to Excelsior Broadcasting House, is that a sort of ice cream that they really liked, or something?'

'Featherplum was the name of the director at Excelsior Broadcasting,' said Mariette. 'Edgar Featherplum.'

'Really, that's his name? Great, I didn't see how feathers could make very nice ice cream.'

'He *was* the director,' said Mariette quietly. 'It's a while ago, remember.'

'The Child of Flowers Charity Hospital. I've got something really brilliant for the nurses. Cherry and Cream Vanilla Bombes and Chocolate Sparkles with Pecan Frosting.'

Clovis spluttered with laughter.

'Or it might be Twinkling Chocolate Sauce,' added Zack, undaunted. 'Depending on whether I can get the chocolate to set. And then there's the Midnight Café, Lemon Shark Street. But that's all been crossed out.'

He could see out of the corner of his eye that Mariette had put down her sewing and was watching him.

'And it says here, Candlemas, Totter Hill Pump, as many crates of our water as possible. Collect empty bottles. Try to get people to queue to avoid young, old and infirm being knocked over . . . no charge.'

'Excellent,' said Clovis. 'I was wondering how we'd find out safe places to, you know, sell stuff.'

But Mariette's voice was spiked with ridicule. 'So, you two are just going to march in the doors of Excelsior Broadcasting and announce that you've got illegal ices for sale?'

'There are various possible strategies—' began Clovis.

'One, it is twelve years since your father last took the Ice Angel into the city. I think there is just a small chance that different people might be working at Excelsior Broadcasting by now. Two, your father had passwords which he exchanged, for example with the security guard at Excelsior and at the Child of Flowers Charity Hospital, so even if the same people are there, you won't get anywhere because you don't know what to say.'

Moe grunted and rolled over on his back: he was lying on the hearthrug.

Zack looked at him, feigning calm.

'You're just a couple of know-it-alls. Know-it-alls who don't know anything,' said Mariette. 'You'll be arrested on your first night out.' And she sounded triumphant: or at least Zack thought she did.

Clovis started to speak, slowly, but he didn't have time to say anything much—

Zack was on his feet and shouting before he'd even decided to stand up.

'Stop making fun of me as if I'm some stupid little kid! I'm his son! You have to tell me *everything* I need to know!'

Mariette remained perfectly still, her fists clenched. For a moment it seemed as if she were going to say something, perhaps something very important. Then she leapt to her feet and ran out of the room and they heard her running on, up the stairs; then running again, away up into the house.

Zack picked up a log, held it over his head and threw it at the fire with all his strength. Another, burning log bounced out on to the hearth and the rug and the wooden floor, sparks, smoke, flames—

Clovis was scrabbling about, stamping, kicking things, yelling, Moe was on the high window sill—

'Help me, you idiot!' shouted Clovis, pushing the flaring log with the poker. The log fell apart in the middle, its red glowing heart spreading and flickering: Clovis pulled the rug out from under it, kicking the burning pieces back over the hearth stone. He slammed the rug down, stamped on it.

Mariette came back into the room. She stepped over scattered chunks of smouldering wood as if they were always there. She was holding a piece of lined paper: yellowed with age. Zack recognized it. He had seen it at the bottom of the chest hidden in the attic wall.

'These are the passwords, Zachary,' she said. 'He always kept a list, just in case. The Midnight Café was crossed out for a very good reason. Stay away from it.'

Chapter 16

It was early next morning and Zack, Clovis and Moe were walking quietly through the caves. They had already passed the spring and the ice store, and now they were climbing the stone staircase which led deeper into the mountain. Pale shafts of sunlight slanted down from somewhere very far above them. The steps were narrow, worn and slippery.

There was, of course, no banister. They climbed in silence and they guided themselves step by step with their left hands against the cold rock. Moe was behind them: Zack could hear his claws scratch against the stone.

The floor of the next cave was almost flat. They always followed the same path, passing the rock that looked like a tree and the rock that looked like a woman holding a child. The roof was high, too high to see properly. Bats flickered across the beam of the lantern like black ash.

Then down and down through a twisting tunnel, towards the sound of running water. The walls glistened where the light touched them. They walked more slowly because the way was uneven. Moe sauntered on ahead, scrabbling over low rocks. The air was damp and cold.

'Nearly there,' remarked Clovis wearily.

They had been walking for three-quarters of an hour. Now they unlocked an iron gate, locked it carefully behind them and followed a smooth passageway that curved back to the south.

Another gate: Zack put out the lantern.

At last they came to the small cave where their scooters were waiting. Zack's blue and silver Bellisima Series 5 and Clovis' much-modified white and gold Favolosa Mark B. Mariette's pink Favolosa Mark C was here, too, neatly covered by a piece of tarpaulin.

Much wrestling with wet weather gear, helmets and gloves. More gates to lock and unlock and a long section of tunnel. Finally, the concealed wooden doors, faced with sheets of stone, which hid the Jump family's private way home.

They had only a small way to go before they reached Storm Hill Ridge, the quiet stretch of road that looped up through the common land and then plunged steeply back down into Storm Hill. As always, the boys pushed the scooters very carefully out of the low-growing trees.

Zack and Moe were escorting Clovis to Meakin's to provide moral support.

They set off on the gleaming rain-washed road. Zack following Clovis. Moe, also wearing a helmet, sitting behind Zack. A bright, fresh morning. The road curving upwards briefly, like a smile.

'I feel sick,' Clovis explained, half an hour later. 'I'm having a nervous reaction to a new situation.'

They were standing on Parchment Street outside Meakin's the Map Makers in the district known as the Flower Market.

'You look terrible,' agreed Zack. 'Do you think they ever get lightning flies here?'

Lightning flies were small, extremely fast-moving and deadly poisonous. One bite could kill a person. Everyone on the island knew that you must lie down and cover your face if they attacked you. They particularly liked faces.

'Oh, thanks *very* much,' said Clovis. 'They are, of course, extremely rare. They come from somewhere very hot in crates of tropical fruit and are therefore mainly seen down by the harbour. They're only active for a few days in the middle of summer. And it has to be a very hot summer. And neither of us have ever seen one.'

'They're too fast to see,' said Zack, cheerfully. 'Everybody knows that. You just see a blur and then it's all over.'

'Shut up.'

The street was narrow and cobbled and crowded and the shops were a mixture of wood and brick, with many overhanging bay windows and pointed gables. Meakin's had a gold-painted sign with a picture of a globe. The shop next door was a perfumier: they had a picture of a perfume bottle.

There were other map makers further down the hill. The city of Rockscar was famous for the making of sea charts and maps of all kinds. However, as Clovis had already explained several times to Zack, none of these were as famous or as long established as Meakin's.

'S'cuse me, gents,' said a boy, much the same age as Zack, bustling down the pavement pushing a handcart. 'Some of us have got work to do.'

The cart was packed with bunches of flowers in metal buckets.

'Had a row with your girlfriend?' enquired Zack. 'Pretty bad, was it?'

But the boy had seen Clovis' scooter: his manner changed.

'Is that the Mark B?' he enquired, reverently. 'Where did you get those brackets for the mirrors?'

'I made them myself,' said Clovis. 'Two extra mirrors on each side.'

The boy whistled through his teeth. Immediately Moe jumped down from the seat of Zack's scooter and looked urgently around.

'Dog with a helmet, responds well to whistle,' remarked the boy. 'Excellent mirrors. And the third lamp?'

'Took it off a Mark C,' said Clovis. 'Takes a bigger bulb. Had to modify the electrics a bit.'

'Bet she moves.'

'She does.'

'And the flames were painted on by a professional?'

'No, we did them ourselves.'

'Beautiful.'

'We wanted some shark's teeth or something too but there wasn't enough room—'

'Good uphill? How big is the engine?'

'Excuse me, excuse me, you're blocking the pavement,' gabbled a man with a black, padlocked briefcase. He had a dog with him too: a magnificent, terrible wolf-like dog on a rope. Big enough to ride, with a spiked collar and massive jaws.

This dog had just arrived at the place on the pavement where Moe was standing.

'Mind your little animal,' said the man, talking faster and faster. 'This is the new guard dog from the shop where I work. I've got jewellery in here,' he patted anxiously at the briefcase. 'I'm a courier. I'm having a terrible morning. He's part wolf, you know. He's already bitten someone in Parchment Street. The boss insisted I bring him. He's got a nasty temper.'

Zack spun round. Moe was still standing in the other dog's path, still wearing his scooter helmet: something which surely affected his credibility in this sort of encounter.

The guard dog drew back his lips. He was white-furred and ice-eyed. A part of the mountains. Altogether in the wrong place.

He expanded to an even greater size. He snarled a deep, long and terrible snarl. He strained forward. He was crazy with the grief of wild creatures in the hands of men. He was going to eat Moe personally.

'Steady, Cruncher,' muttered the courier, his face shiny with sweat.

Cruncher lunged at Moe and was only held back by the courier throwing all his weight on the other end of the rope.

Before there was time for anyone else to think, Moe calmly and very swiftly raised a paw and flicked at the chinstrap of the helmet with one of his unexpectedly long claws. A claw considerably longer than Zack had thought it was earlier that morning.

The helmet fell off.

Moe's face and his big ears were revealed. He did not growl or snarl or raise his hackles at Cruncher. But he did tilt his head back, and craned his neck, so that he could look Cruncher in the eyes.

Cruncher stopped everything he was doing. Then he made a tiny sound: almost a whimper. His shoulders dropped, he sank down. He lay on the pavement. The courier, still clinging to the rope, toppled backwards into the gutter.

Cruncher placed his head on his paws and looked up at Moe. He wagged his tail very slowly, sweeping the cobbles.

'Dominance thing,' whispered Clovis. 'He's telling Moe that he knows Moe is the boss.'

'And why exactly would Moe be the boss, here?' muttered Zack.

'No idea,' said Clovis. 'But he is unexpected.'

Together, they helped the distressed courier to his feet.

Moe bent down and sniffed Cruncher nose to nose. Then he jumped on to the seat of Clovis' Favolosa and stared up the street as if none of this had anything to do with him and Cruncher, now very calm, stood up again.

'He's never done that before,' breathed the courier, brushing at his clothes. 'How did you get him to do that, then?'

'I didn't do anything—' began Zack.

The door of the map maker's opened behind him.

'Move on, everyone,' yelled the boy with the flower cart. 'Nothing to see.' He added quietly to Clovis. 'This your place of work? Excellent dog. I'll call in some time. Like to ask your opinion about a noise my Bellisima is making.'

'Ah, I thought it must be you,' said someone in the sort of voice that is gentle and hard to ignore. Mr Meakin himself stepped out over the threshold of his shop. He was a dark-skinned man with white hair, a red satin waistcoat, enormous glasses and a pencil stuck behind his ear.

'Clovis Greenwood,' he said, pleasantly. 'Welcome to Meakin's.'

All through school, and for as long as they could remember, Zack and Clovis Jump had been obliged to conceal their real name.

Chapter 17

The long evening shadows of the trees reached across the Wolf Road.

Zack, Clovis and Moe stared fixedly ahead. Zack was clutching the steering wheel, hunched forward, eyes narrowed in determination. Clovis and Moe also had their eyes partly shut but this was because they were scared. Moe was growling softly.

Mariette's goodbye had chilled them to the bone.

The Ice Angel juddered and bounced over the gullies and potholes. Moe yelped. Zack slowed down. There had been one late frost since he and Clovis had completed their spectacular trial run, and then some days of cold sunshine. They reached the Wolf Road: it was hard, gleaming here and there with crystals of ice.

No one speaking. Black spikes of the pines against a sky of pink and peach and pearl. One star.

Past the place where they had stopped before. Dim shapes of deer disappearing between the trees. Clovis cleared his throat and Moe and Zack both jumped.

Further still. How long had they been going now? Half an hour? Probably more.

Suddenly the world seemed to be flung open on the left side of the road. A steep rocky slope to the tops of trees far below. Waterfalls.

'Easy does it,' said Clovis, through clenched teeth.

Zack began to steer round a long steep corner. The Wolf Road was creeping back on itself like a snake. Zack was biting the inside of his mouth: his knuckles ached as he gripped the wheel. A dense cluster of trees again. It seemed darker now. Another bend as the road clung to the mountain. The van only at the speed of a man walking. A horrendous sound as Zack hauled on the controls.

'You're *in* the lowest gear, you can't get any *lower*. Concentrate on the *brake*. Keep *braking* . . .' hissed Clovis.

The road evened out: for a short distance, it was almost flat.

Then a dreadful drop plunged away from them on the left-hand side. No trees this time. Barren. As if the mountain had been wounded. A giddy tumble of strewn rocks.

A deep chasm filled with the twilight.

Zack's heart was pounding: he tried to unclench his hands on the wheel. With difficulty, because everything about driving was difficult, he stopped the van. Intending to rest for a moment. They were next to a giant wilderness cedar, standing alone, on the very edge of the ravine. Moe suddenly started to howl.

'SSH!' hissed Zack, pointlessly.

Clovis had both hands over his ears: his face screwed up. Moe's head was thrown back. The howl went on and on.

It ended, at last, on a fading, falling note that seemed to come from some ancient place in time. Moe opened his eyes and looked away, through the window, into the ravine.

Silence. Clovis, very slowly, removed his hands from his ears.

In a flurry of inexperience and curses Zack started the van again. They bumped forwards. Clovis leaned across and switched on the headlamps. The road began another descent and another long curve into more towering trees.

A wolf ran across in front of them. Then another. Zack threw his weight on to the brake pedal.

'I don't believe this,' he whispered.

The wolves stood still. Their bodies dark and hard to discern. Their eyes like bright gold coins.

Clovis dimmed the lights. Now the wolves were revealed, big, scarred and powerful. They were joined by a third. All stood and stared at the Ice Angel van.

'Well,' whispered Clovis, 'it is their road.'

Zack nodded.

'We just stay in the van,' added Clovis.

Zack nodded again. Were all wolves this big?

'What do you reckon they're actually, you know, doing?'

The wolves started to walk closer. They came right

up to where the angel stood on the front of the radiator. They walked past her to the side of the van where Moe was sitting.

One of them, the largest and most battle-scarred, loomed up on his hind legs, put his front feet on the door and brought his face to the window. Both Zack and Clovis made tiny sounds of terror and dismay.

The wolf was black, grey around the muzzle, with a scar running down from one ear, lost in the shaggy fur of his neck. His eyes were light blue. He was separated from Moe only by the thickness of one piece of glass. Glass which he could surely shatter with a single blow. He stared at Moe and Moe turned and stared back, sitting very straight, his harness, of course, still crossed across his chest.

A moment passed. The wolf dropped down again on to the road.

The boys watched in silence. All three wolves walked a little way ahead and then turned towards the mountain and disappeared into the black trees.

Clovis swallowed loudly. 'They seem to have gone,' he remarked, his voice a little higher than normal.

'Yes,' said Zack.

'And your plan is to drive along this road on a regular basis. Most nights in fact?'

'Yes,' said Zack, fiddling with controls. The windscreen wipers suddenly shuddered across the windscreen; a jet of foamy water sprayed up from the bonnet.

'Does the windscreen need washing?'

'Possibly not,' said Zack. 'I thought that was the switch for the heater. Ah, here we are—'

The radio blasted into the cab, alive with crackles and buzzing—

'. . . and it's not long now until the next election, listeners, when we will all have a chance to vote for Mayor Scarspring again, or *not*,' whispered Momma Truth. 'Here at Barnacle Radio we like to ask the questions that other people don't. Is Anshelm Scarspring really the big-hearted public benefactor we all know and love?

'Why does he never seem to move a muscle without seeking the advice of Steward Golightly, an *unelected* person who is *nothing* to do with the City Hall but is a big player in the Scarspring money-making machine. Nobody seems to quite trust our handsome friend Golightly, do they? He has been accused of blackmail, threatening behaviour and all sorts of other nasty little crimes over the years, but he always gets off one way or another. Strange.

'Well, all I can say is, I wish I had someone to do all my dirty work for me. Saint Anshelm is a very lucky man. On the other hand, they do say Golightly practically *owns* the police. Perhaps he owns Saint Anshelm too. Who's the real boss, I wonder . . . That's all we've got time for right now. Have a nice evening out there in the Big Barnacle.'

Zack turned the radio off. He looked at the squadron of

levers and buttons and decided to forget the heater this time.

'If the Mayor's office ever found out who Barnacle Radio are, he'd close them down for sure,' said Clovis.

'They're like us,' said Zack. 'They offer outlaw news and we're going to offer outlaw ice cream.'

The road curved out of the forest for the last time. They came round below a jagged wall of rock and the salt smell of the sea washed into the cab.

The mighty city climbed towards them. Gaudy with lights and possibilities. Zack stopped the van and they sat in silence. Months of thinking and hard work had propelled them to this moment. He grinned at Clovis.

'Kings of the Mountain,' he said. They knocked their fists together.

'Kings of the Mountain,' said Clovis, grinning back.

Then Zack started the engine and for the first time in over twelve years the Ice Angel crept down into the city of Rockscar. Sleek as an otter into a sparkling pool. It was eight o'clock and the high tide bell was tolling.

* * *

After Balthazar had disappeared, Mariette Jump could not leave the house without her babies because there was no one to look after them. So, in the first weeks after he was gone, she slung them on her chest and her back, wrapped in blankets. She could not bear to stay indoors. They slept, lulled by her lonely heartbeat and the swing of her stride as she wandered the tracks made by wolves and bears and lions and deer, the rifle pointing ahead, ready to fire. Searching for some sign, some clue. Sometimes, on those early desperate nights, even calling his name.

Tonight, again, she could not stand to stay at home. As Clovis and Zack set off down towards Rockscar, she had run swiftly through the maze of paths. She had reached the place where they had stopped by the deep ravine. She had seen the tyre tracks of the Ice Angel and she knew that they had gone safely on their way.

She had not followed them any further.

The wolves did not frighten Mariette, although she saw their prints now, by the red light of her lantern. It was something else which froze her in this place, on the edge of the barren ravine. In the end, she had always come here: on those dread nights of searching.

And now a memory, more real than the present, spread suddenly before her eyes. The first night: the first search. The first time he had not come home.

Mariette saw the Ice Angel slanted and tilting across the narrow, stony road. The driver's door hanging open; the headlamps still on. The angel herself, serene on the front. And the light of that winter dawn, uncaring and cold, showing scattered objects – a shoe, a rifle, something glinting – and blood, dark, terrible blood, already drying on the ground.

She had crept forward. This was the ravine which Balthazar called 'the Garden of the Trolls'.

Suddenly, incomprehensibly, she had felt the air surge up and swirl around her. And then, as she had started to scream and to run towards the stricken van, stepping on things, stepping on blood, she had been engulfed by the smell of lowland summer flowers, here, in the bitter cold, where there was nothing but rock and pine.

Jasmine, roses, lily-of-the-valley.

How could this be?

And for Mariette, afterwards and always, those sweet, gentle scents were like the whisper of death.

Chapter 18

Zack, Clovis, Moe and the Ice Angel were in SugarTown. And they were there because they had got lost.

Even at this early time in the evening SugarTown was simmering. This was the harbour district. Whenever the tide was high, day and night, pilots guided ships through a maze of reefs and wrecks and shallow deadly water into the deep safety of Rockscar harbour. And, day and night, sailors from far countries filled the bars and the hotpot curry houses and the shindig rooms and music halls of SugarTown, spending their foreign money and drinking and gambling their way through their few days on shore.

Then they would go, back to their ships and their long voyages. Except for those who had been arrested or murdered. Many old scores were settled in SugarTown, where almost everyone was far from home.

It was not a good place for two boys, a fairly small dog and a beautiful, silvery ice cream van with an angel on the front.

'It was fine until we came to that junction, and the road was closed, and I said right and you went left,' Clovis was saying. Teeth gritted like a milling machine.

'You *said* left . . .'

Zack wound down the window to try and read a sign and was slapped in the face by the combined smells of the sea, rotting fish and stale Canary Beer.

'I said *right*. And I strongly suggest that you close that window. I *am* the map expert here. Plus it is always you who gets left and right muddled up.'

'Well, map expert, get us out of here, before someone decides to push us into the harbour.'

'There's another left turn in about half a mile . . .'

'Half a mile?'

'Don't turn before that, we'll be in—'

Zack stopped to let a group of men amble drunkenly across the road in front of them. The pavements were already crowded, although the night had only recently begun.

They were outside the swinging wooden doors of a place called 'Mollie's Shindig Rooms'. Shindig rooms were rented by the night and used to hold parties involving bootleg alcohol, music, dancing and fighting.

There was a thump on the side of the van and a woman pushed her face up against the window next to Moe. Or was she a man? Zack looked round and this person smiled a scarlet-lipped, gold-toothed grin and beckoned to him. He took his foot off the brake and the Ice Angel stalled.

'Great,' muttered Clovis.

Now there was shouting. Despite the early hour, it seemed that there was already trouble in Mollie's establishment.

Just as Zack was trying to start the engine for the third time, several figures came hurtling out through the doors, arms and legs flailing, hats flying, all of them lunging and staggering into the road. Perhaps it was a fight, but it was not a very serious one. And they all forgot it when they saw the Ice Angel.

Within moments the cab was surrounded. Voices were shouting in a language Zack and Clovis had never heard before. Someone was trying to get the driver's door open. A man hauled himself up on to the bonnet, brandished his tobacco-stained fist at Zack's face through the windscreen, splayed his square fingers, grinning horribly, and then curled them back, stroking his palm—

'He wants money,' groaned Clovis.

The man was now drawing his finger across his own loose-skinned, sun-blasted throat.

'Or he's going to kill us.'

Zack struggled with the ignition key. It had become slippery with sweat.

Then Moe snarled: an extraordinary, deep and savage sound. Much louder than either of them had ever heard him snarl before. Out of the corner of his eye, Zack thought he saw him grow bigger, much bigger, until his head was jammed against the inside of the windscreen, jaws open, teeth huge, eyes burning—

The engine jumped into life. Outside the man on the bonnet screamed, his face only inches away from the blood-curdling, gold-eyed monster on the other side of the glass. He flung himself sideways. Everyone, all around the van, was trying to get away.

'Now!' yelled Clovis.

They inched forward, the engine rumbling softly, and then hurtled ahead, tyres screeching, and swung around the next corner; up a steep hill; past late night shops and bars and barrows selling fried fish; up out of SugarTown, on and on, as if the Devil himself was snapping behind them.

Finally they were in darker, quieter streets. Zack slowed the van almost to walking speed, still staring straight ahead.

They stopped completely across the mouth of an alley leading back down towards the harbour. The beam from the lighthouse dazzled briefly in the shapeless dark. Slowly, Zack allowed himself to turn and look beside him.

'I know,' whispered Clovis, hoarsely.

There was Moe, in his harness, sitting next to the passenger door. A scruffy, medium-sized dog, shaggy fur, large ears.

'Did he get, did he get . . . bigger?'

'It did look like it,' said Clovis. 'Just for a moment.'

'But how . . . ?

'I don't know.'

Moe raised a paw and licked it daintily.

'Seems normal now.'

'Yes.' Clovis swallowed. More of a gulp. 'Normal now. Optical illusion thing. Just seemed bigger because he was, you know, snarling. Good thing he did, too. Momma Truth says there's gangs down there, smugglers and stuff, always having shoot-outs with the police. In fact, police don't go down there much, she says . . .'

'We're still lost,' said Zack, eventually.

'Better than dead,' said Clovis.

More silence. Then Clovis scrabbled down in the foot well and retrieved the map.

'We're in Lemon Shark Street,' said Zack, peering at a sign bolted to the nearest building. 'Sounds familiar. Is it familiar?'

Clovis frowned at the map. 'We can get from here to Excelsior Broadcasting House fairly easily. Excelsior Broadcasting is in Excelsior, obviously. This is MockBeggar. Better keep the doors locked. Go straight ahead. We need to turn left, but not yet.'

Zack drove on along the street: after the noise of SugarTown, MockBeggar was eerie and furtive.

'It's like we're being watched.'

On past shops locked for the night with wooden shutters across the windows. A cat darted along the pavement. Here and there the grimy, orange glow of an upstairs light. And some basements, down below iron railings, also lit.

'Workshops,' said Clovis, in a low voice.

He wound down the window a very small amount. They smelt the distant sea and the closer smell of grease and cooking. Sewing machines hummed and clattered somewhere. The mumble of a radio.

'Sweatshops, more like,' said Zack.

MockBeggar was known as a place where it was easy to get a job without the right identity papers, so long as you didn't mind working for almost nothing, and sharing a room with the fleas and rats.

'Maybe they'd like a present of some bottled water,' said Clovis.

But Zack didn't hear him. He stopped the van. He was staring down a narrow passageway, barely lit, cluttered with bins.

'I knew I'd heard of Lemon Shark Street,' he said, breaking into a grin. 'Look at that.'

There was a lamp on the wall about halfway along the dark of the passageway. A door underneath. A blue neon sign was flickering on and off: just one word, 'Midnight'.

'I bet it's the Midnight Café, the place from the list, the one that was crossed out.'

'Crossed out for a reason,' said Clovis.

They both stared. Then Zack wound down his own window. There was the faint sound of music playing.

'Nice tune,' said Zack. 'Maybe they'd like some ice

cream to go with it.'

'It was crossed out,' said Clovis. 'Mum said—'

'Twelve years ago, probably more,' interrupted Zack. 'The reason might be really out of date. Perhaps they just didn't pay their bill. Might be under new management.'

The door under the lamp creaked open and a man came out in a billow of sound. He disappeared further up the passageway. The door closed.

'Saxophone,' said Zack.

'I think we should go.' Clovis rustled the map. 'We turn left soon. We're not that far from Excelsior Avenue, it's half past nine already. We need to get going.'

But Zack had turned off the engine. He took off his harness. Briefly checked in the periscope.

'I'm just going to have a look.'

'*No*, don't, we've only just escaped from one situation, I don't like the look of this whole place, let's just *go*—'

Zack was already opening his door. Clovis, always practical, stopped trying to persuade him and unbuckled Moe's harness instead. 'Moe's coming with you,' he said. 'I'll stay with the van. *Don't be long.*'

Zack and Moe stepped off Lemon Shark Street and were engulfed by shadows.

Chapter 19

Zack made his way towards the lamp and the neon sign, past dustbins and stacks of crates and filthy, barred windows. The passageway ran between two brick buildings: at the far end he could see the glow of a street light. A long way off.

Moe sniffed the air: keeping close.

A hubbub of voices coming from somewhere, and again, the blossoming sound of the saxophone.

They reached the door.

Zack didn't intend to go in: at least, not yet. He had thought that perhaps there would be a window, or a poster board, or some other clues about the café and what went on there.

Nothing. Just this sombre wooden door, unusually tall. At the top, way above Zack's head, there was a coloured glass fanlight. Warm, red glass, lit from inside.

Balthazar had come here: he must have stood here, at this door.

Zack glanced back at the van. He could just make out

Clovis' silhouette in the window: radiating concern.

Moe whimpered softly.

Without allowing himself to think anymore, Zack picked up a wooden crate, dragged it as quietly as possible over to the door and stood it on end. Then he climbed dangerously on top of it.

Straining, on the tips of his toes, he pressed his face to the fanlight. Saw a world washed in shades of dull, smoky red. A narrow foyer, a desk, a sign saying 'coats and umbrellas'. And a man sitting on a stool reading a newspaper. Possibly the largest man Zack had ever seen. Wearing a suit, hat pushed to the back of his head. Fingerless gloves on his huge hands.

Zack's breath had steamed the glass. He raised his arm, almost losing his balance, and wiped it with his sleeve.

A woman came out from a curtained doorway to the left of the desk. In contrast to the man with the newspaper, she looked tiny. Her hair was piled high and decorated with some sort of net, her dress looked velvety, her heels were like stilts.

She and the man talked for a few moments while Zack watched them, spellbound, his heart racing. Here were two people who might actually have known his father. Who might even know something about what had happened to him.

The scene disappeared into mist again.

Zack tried to wipe the glass as he had done before, leant a little too far one way and the crate lurched and then skidded and fell over with a crash, leaving him hanging on briefly to the top of the door frame. Before he, too, fell.

The door flew open. Light blazed into the passageway, revealing Zack on the ground and Moe, hackles raised, beside him.

The big man stared, then leant down all in one very fast, violent moment and picked Zack up by the front of his coat. He held him in one shovel-sized hand and Zack's feet dangled and kicked like the gallows.

Moe growled. A very deep, dangerous sound.

'What have we got here?' asked the man, breathing into Zack's face. His own face made of meaty slabs, eyes small, bloodshot and mean.

Zack sucked in a mouthful of air and it rasped in his throat. He twisted, trying to swing his fist at the man's chest. Heard himself making a choking noise.

'Balthazar Jump,' he gasped. 'Ice Angel. I'm his son.'

The big man blinked, narrowed his eyes, broke into an unfriendly grin as if at a joke. Then allowed it to slide off his face.

'Where did you hear that name, boy? Where did you hear that name?'

Mo growled again.

'Put . . . me . . . down . . .'

'Stop squirming and spitting, you bone-faced runt. Tell me how someone like you knows the name of a hero like Balthazar Jump. You don't look fit to be speaking that name!

You look like you should be swanning around Merchant Hill in a silk suit with all the other toffs—'

'Let him go, Mittens!' shouted the woman. 'Look, he's got Balthazar's dog! Let him go, now!'

Zack saw the man swivel his head, peering towards the sound of the growling which was growing louder and more threatening by the second.

'Trolls take us,' muttered the man. He dropped Zack on the ground and Zack stayed there, swallowing air. He barely noticed that Moe stood over him, facing the big man, hackles up, teeth bared. His mind was screaming with a single thought: *One punch from this brute and I'll be dead.*

He heard the slam of a metal door. The Ice Angel. And then Clovis was running towards him. Clovis was helping him to his feet. And something strange and extraordinary was happening.

The big man and the tiny woman seemed under a spell: they were staring at Clovis.

'Did somebody just say something about being the son of Balthazar Jump?' said the big man to Clovis.

'I didn't say anything,' said Clovis, evenly. 'I just came to try and stop you killing my brother.'

He stared up into the big man's face and added, 'Or die with him.'

'You can stop flexing your small muscles,' said the big man. 'No one's going to do any killing.'

'You could have fooled me . . .' began Zack, and started coughing.

'Did he say he was Balthazar's son?' The big man indicated Zack with a jerk of his thumb, still talking to Clovis.

Clovis nodded.

'And you? It's you we're looking at.'

'I'm his son too,' said Clovis.

'We can see that, darling,' said the woman, softly. 'You've a strong look of your mother around the eyes, and her colouring, of course, the dark red hair, but you're very like Balthazar, too. Bless his soul.'

'We're both his sons,' insisted Clovis.

'Of course you are,' she added. 'I'm afraid my husband is forgetting things and being very rude. I can see the resemblance between you two boys, of course I can. It's obvious you're brothers—'

'No it isn't,' interrupted the man.

She frowned at him, then looked back at Clovis, speaking slowly. 'You'll have to forgive us. It's been a very long time. And your brother, well, he looks like, he looks more like . . .' She trailed off, darting a glance at the man. 'Mittens, I think you owe this young gentleman an apology.'

The big man stared at her: then he stared at Zack. Then he looked at Moe, who looked straight back at him.

'I'm sorry,' he said gruffly, holding out his hand to Zack. 'I must ask you to forgive me. A lot of time has passed, as Tiny said. Now I think about it, it all makes sense. My name's Mittens. And this is my wife, Tiny. She's the boss around here.'

'I'm Zack,' said Zack. Clovis nudged him. He took the proffered hand and shook it reluctantly. Felt his own hand crushed in a grip of iron and wool.

'May the trolls take me,' said Mittens, 'if I ever again misjudge a member of Balthazar Jump's household. Whoever they may be.'

'And this is my brother Clovis,' said Zack. More handshaking.

'And your beautiful dog, I wouldn't like to argue with him,' exclaimed Tiny, now crouching next to Moe and scratching the top of his head. 'He hardly looks a day older.'

Zack and Clovis exchanged puzzled glances.

'Do come in,' said Tiny.

Zack realized that the foyer had filled with people. The music had stopped. In fact, one of the several people crowding in front of the desk was holding a saxophone. Another big man, although not as a monumental as Mittens, this time wearing a green hat.

Everyone shuffled and rearranged themselves. All of them were staring.

'We'll go in the lounge,' said Tiny. 'Someone ask Nanette to bring two hot chocolates for our guests.'

And she led the way through the curtained door and Zack, Clovis and Moe followed, entering a long low room, with dark walls and thick dark carpet. Pools of amber light revealed small tables, each with a cloth and a flower in a cup. There were booths along the walls with upholstered seats, a small dance floor and an even smaller stage.

The man with the green hat started playing something soft and sad on the saxophone. Another man joined him on the double bass; then Tiny stepped on to the little stage too and began to sing in a crackly, intimate voice. Two couples stood up and started to circle the floor.

Meanwhile the members of the Jump household were escorted to a table by Mittens and given red mugs overflowing with chocolate and cream. Moe, under the table, had a saucer of gravy. Zack sipped the hot chocolate. Licked cream off his lips.

Mittens stood awkwardly beside them.

'So, how *is* your mother?' he said suddenly.

Clovis started coughing.

'Fine,' said Zack.

'I suppose she told you what happened. I'm not proud of myself. Not proud at all. I was angry. Angry for her sake. Always wanted to protect her. But I shouldn't have . . .' He stopped speaking.

Tiny had finished her song. She was staring at him from the stage. Frowning some kind of warning.

'I shouldn't have,' repeated Mittens. 'Not that he couldn't look after himself. Little vermin.'

'Shouldn't have what?' said Zack.

'Mariette never did quite forgive me. I don't blame her. Very pleased you've come now though.' Mittens addressed most of this incomprehensible speech to Clovis. Then turned to Zack, fumbling his words. 'And you. Very pleased to meet both of you. Very pleased you're both here . . .'

'You've said enough, Mittens,' said Tiny, her voice like a rasp.

'Did she never tell you?' Mittens looked from Clovis to Zack and back again.

'Tell us what?' said Clovis.

'Mittens,' said Tiny. 'I don't think we need to worry the boys about history just now, do you? If they don't know what you mean, I'm sure we don't want to go raking things up that happened before they were born.'

Mittens nodded slowly. Put his hand to his face and rubbed his eyes. Still wearing the fingerless gloves.

'Sorry,' he muttered. 'I thought she must have sent them.'

Zack looked at Clovis.

'Nobody's sent us,' said Clovis.

'But we're here to sell ices,' said Zack. 'Just like our dad did.'

'Of course you are,' said Tiny. 'Excuse me.'

There were more customers arriving. Tiny bobbed back and forth greeting people, returning, patting Clovis on the shoulder. Offering more chocolate. While Mittens, no longer wanting to talk, it seemed, took his leave very politely and went back through the curtained doorway: presumably to the desk in the foyer.

'What do you make of that?' whispered Zack.

Clovis shook his head.

'What do you think he was talking about?'

'No idea,' whispered Clovis.

The wall next to Zack was covered in black-and-white photographs of Rockscar celebrities. Actors that he recognized from films. Musicians. Then he blinked in shock. There was a picture of Anshelm Scarspring, looking much younger, with Tiny sitting on his knee, holding up a glass, drinking a toast or something, smiling . . .

He nudged Clovis and jerked his head. Watched Clovis' eyes grow round.

At that moment Tiny herself came and sat down with them again.

'May I?' she asked, taking a marshmallow from the untouched island floating on Zack's chocolate.

'Is that Mr Scarspring?' asked Zack.

She peered up at the photograph: then she looked at Zack.

'Yes, dear, I believe it is. Some years ago. All sorts of customers come to the Midnight Café. Rich and poor. It's always been that way. We don't ask any questions and neither do they. We've had the Chief of Police sitting where you're sitting now. And we've had one of those smuggling families from SugarTown, what were they called? They had their own table for quite a while.'

She took another marshmallow. Zack had the impression she was choosing her words carefully. 'You won't meet him here, dear, if that's what you're wondering,' she said, not looking at him, dipping the marshmallow in the cream. 'He used to come here a long time ago. But he doesn't now.'

More customers were arriving. The door to the kitchens swung open. Zack glimpsed a man in a chef's hat, a fog of steam.

'If you're going to be buying from us, and getting people like the Scarsprings in here,' said Clovis. 'We have to think about security. Our understanding with you will be that you do not tell anyone where you are getting your supplies. We don't have a licence to sell ices or water. We could be arrested.'

Zack looked at him in amazement: Clovis the businessman.

'I do understand that,' said Tiny, smiling slightly. 'You are outlaws, just like the people who sell us untaxed spirits and cigars. Except with water, it has always been more serious. I told you, we don't ask questions. And it is really a very long time since Anshelm Scarspring was here, or his friend, Mr Golightly. Over fourteen years, Mittens saw to that.'

'We have all the things our dad used to have,' persisted Clovis. 'Water ices, granitas, ice cream, sauces, cones and bottled spring water.'

Tiny grinned. 'Do you still have the Raspberry and

Blackcurrant Swirl? It should go with my clothes.' She was wearing a dark red velvet dress. 'What do you think, Mr Zachary?'

Zack tried to smile.

'The Ice Angel is outside,' added Clovis, speaking with increasing speed. 'Zack's older than me. He's done most of the work. It was his idea. He's got it all organized. He's absolutely brilliant at making original and interesting ices and *he* found the angel to go back on the front of the van.'

'The Ice Angel van is here now? Outside right this minute?' exclaimed Tiny, clapping her little girl hands. A diamond ring flashed like a firework against her brown skin. 'I must go down and see it! We must all go down! This is a great night for Rockscar . . .' She put her hand on Zack's arm and he flinched. 'And it's lovely to see Balthazar's dog again. Even though he is so scary.'

She looked fondly down at Moe and he wagged his tail. 'He hardly looks a day older.'

While Clovis accepted a top-up out of the steaming chocolate pot, Zack enquired as to the whereabouts of the toilets.

On his way there he had to go through the crimson bar, with its dainty chandeliers, and then up a narrow staircase. The staircase was lined with more photographs, all in black and white or sepia, many embellished with scrawled signatures. Returning a few minutes later he stopped midway down the stairs as if he had walked into a wall. There, among the smiling, carefree faces, he saw one he recognized.

Mariette.

She looked wild and young. She was holding a microphone, surely the same large microphone that Tiny had been using half an hour before.

Zack thought he could make out the man with the hat and the saxophone, looking slimmer and slightly out of focus in the background.

But it wasn't the background that interested him just then. It was the man standing next to Mariette, his face close to hers, smiling, apparently singing into the microphone with her. For a tiny, magical slither of a second Zack thought that perhaps this was Balthazar. The first photograph of Balthazar he had ever seen. But it wasn't Balthazar and he knew it at once.

It was the man Barnacle Radio said did the dirty work for Mayor Anshelm Scarspring. His friend and steward, looking younger, almost fresh-faced, with his hand on Mariette's arm: their shoulders touching. Stefan Golightly.

Chapter 20

Half an hour later Zack, Clovis and Moe were back in the dark on Lemon Shark Street, where it was beginning to rain. They unloaded several frosted boxes and a crate of bottled water.

Tiny had paid them more than they'd hoped for the ices. She also told them about how things stood these days at the hospital and the Excelsior Broadcasting House and who to ask for and how. If anyone seemed unconvinced they were to mention Tiny herself.

Zack had intended to ask her, and anyone else who had known Balthazar, if they knew what had happened to him. Even if they had no idea, which is what he expected, he had planned to ask them to talk about him, anything.

But he kept quiet.

At last they all climbed back into the van and set off.

He felt as if his whole body was made of wires, and they were pulling tighter and tighter. One touch, one word and he might snap into a million screaming pieces.

Rain was rattling on the roof: the windscreen wipers

swished and thudded to and fro, to and fro. No one spoke.

They were toiling up through streets of shops and boarding houses. They passed a group of men digging in the road. Scarspring employees, fixing a drain. Every drain, every gutter and every pipe in the city belonged to the Scarsprings, and bore their crest. Every house had a copper and brass water meter the size of a trunk bolted to the wall. It was impossible to turn on a tap anywhere without closing your hand over the embossed head of the mountain lion and the tiny insistent writing around it, 'we possess'.

They were on the outskirts of Excelsior. The road was desperately steep: Zack tried to take the Ice Angel down a gear.

'Once again, you're in the lowest gear you've got,' muttered Clovis, looking straight ahead.

Zack dragged on the gearstick. A dreadful crunching and grinding from the engine, the van shuddered to a halt, seemed about to go backwards, then struggled forwards again with a groan.

'Weird, wasn't it, what she said . . .' he shouted above the noise.

'Must be rubbish, of course you look like Dad, you must do.'

'Not that! Not that!' The engine was suddenly quieter but Zack was still yelling. '*Of course* that's rubbish. Not that. I mean what that woman Tiny said about Moe. About Moe being Dad's dog. He can't be. Where's he been all this time? I mean, Dad didn't have a dog—'

'Next right,' said Clovis.

'I mean, Mum would have mentioned it.' Zack shivered, although the cab was warm.

'Do you want to bet?' said Clovis.

'I saw a picture of her, by the way, when I went up to the toilet.' Zack paused, perhaps because he was concentrating on looking for the turning. The rain blew in a mist across the road in front of them. 'She was with someone.'

'Yeah, Golightly,' said Clovis, staring straight ahead. 'I saw it too.'

'You saw it?'

'You're not the only person who's ever needed a toilet. It was when you and Tiny were cooing over the sherbet twists. *Right*, turn *right* here.'

They turned right, mounting the pavement briefly and just missing a telephone box. This was Excelsior Avenue, parallel to the harbour but high above it: almost flat, lined with trees.

'STOP!' screamed Clovis.

Someone was crouching right on the corner in the middle of the road. All in black. A shadow on the cobbles.

The Ice Angel lurched dramatically to a standstill, rocking from side to side. Zack peered into the rain and the dark and the gleaming puddles. Then, his heart thundering, he flung open the door and jumped out.

This was it. He'd killed someone.

For sure.

Clovis and Moe came charging round from the other side.

The hunched figure was still hunched. Right in front of the bumper of the van, and the calm, gazing angel.

'Oh no, no, no,' gabbled Zack.

Clovis was down beside the person already. Moe, meanwhile, was looking up the empty avenue, his nose twitching.

'I'm all right,' said a clear, quiet voice. And the person stood up. His hood fell away from his face as he moved. A boy, about Zack's age: a thin, pale brown face and dark hair.

'I expect you're wondering if you drove into me,' he said. 'I can assure you there is no damage. You stopped just in time.'

'Why didn't you move?' enquired Clovis, sternly.

'I'm sorry,' said the boy. 'I was distracted. I found this on the road, just here, it belongs to my cat Fisher. I've lost her, you see. I'm out looking for her. I've been looking for her every night.'

'Well, you won't find her if you get run over,' said Clovis.

'I'm sorry,' said the boy again.

'If you get run over you'll be dead,' persisted Clovis, who was much shaken.

121

'The man says he's sorry, Clovis,' muttered Zack, frowning at his brother.

'What I'm saying is logical, if you sit around in the middle of the road, especially near a corner, in the dark, in the rain, with this sort of visibility—'

'Shut up, Clovis,' said Zack. 'What is a cat fisher, anyway?'

'No, my cat is *called* Fisher,' said the boy. 'Oh, what a beautiful guardian.' He was looking, of course, at the angel. 'That is the most beautiful guardian I've ever seen.'

Zack looked at the thoughtful face of the angel, gilded by the streetlights.

'Yes,' he said. Awkwardly.

No one spoke for a moment.

'And you've got a very good guard dog,' added the boy pleasantly. 'Very unusual-looking too.'

Both Zack and Clovis looked round at Moe who was still in the middle of the avenue. He had moved a short distance away to a place where he could see beyond the van, back the way they had come, as well as ahead. He was standing like a soldier at attention, his hackles slightly raised, and as they watched he slowly and repeatedly turned his head, looking one way, then the other, sniffing the air, ears swivelling. He certainly looked as if he were on guard.

'I expect you love him with all your hearts, just like I love Fisher,' said the boy.

Zack and Clovis exchanged glances. Clearly this boy had never been to Storm Hill School, where such language would have put him in physical danger.

'I don't understand why Fisher's collar should be here,' added the boy. 'We don't live anywhere near here. I have to face the fact that she has been taken deliberately. But I have not received a ransom note.' He was running the collar through his long fingers.

Something sparkled on it. A gemstone? On a cat's collar?

'I have put signs in shops offering a reward,' said the boy.

Moe gave a low bark. Almost a growl. Everyone looked to see why. A long, dark car was sliding to a halt under the trees some way off, where the avenue began to curve itself out of sight. An expensive engine purred into silence. The driver's door opened and a uniformed man stepped out. It was hard to tell at this distance but Zack was almost sure that the guardian on the front of the car was a mountain lion.

Scarsprings.

Clovis leapt back into the van and turned off the engine and the lights. The Ice Angel seemed to recede into its own darkness under the trees.

The uniformed man opened one of the back doors of the car. Someone climbed out. A woman? No, a man in an opera cloak.

'They've parked outside Excelsior Broadcasting House,' whispered Clovis.

Zack nodded: watching.

Both men stood for a moment outside the grand doors. Then the doors opened, and they disappeared inside.

Zack shivered. If they had not almost run over this extremely strange person out looking for his cat, he and Clovis would have been in that foyer right now. They might even have got the refrigerated ice cart out of the van. What on earth would Scarsprings be doing at Excelsior Broadcasting in the middle of the night?

He turned to the others. Only Clovis was there.

'He went,' said Clovis. 'The moment he saw the man get out of the car. Swift and silent as a bloody assassin. Off down that alley.' He was pointing into the shadows between buildings on the other side of the road.

'Probably wanted across the city for demanding money with menaces,' said Zack.

'He whispered something under his breath.'

'I thought you said he was silent.'

'I think he mentioned the name Golightly. And I think we should go *now*, by the way.'

Zack whistled softly.

There was a dreadful scratching and scrabbling behind them. Then a thud. Moe had jumped in through the driver's window, fortunately half open, and was already sitting in his seat, whining and muttering.

'I agree with the Unexpected Dog,' said Clovis. 'Definitely a good idea.'

But Zack stayed a moment longer with the rain dripping down from his hair and into his eyes. He stared at the powerful car, crouched like a cat under the trees.

He whispered, 'I'm just going to have a closer look,' and he started walking, slowly, keeping to the side of the road, ignoring Clovis who was saying something sensible.

A milk lorry rumbled past, then one of the Rockscar taxis, white with a green light on the roof. Zack glimpsed a woman's face at the window. He was very near to the Scarspring car, still on the other side of the road. The rain had stopped and the long bonnet and the silver mountain lion sparkled with drops of water. The windows were very dark. Special glass, probably.

There might be someone else sitting in there right now, waiting for Steward Golightly to come out. Anselm himself might be in that car. If so, Zack had never been so close to him before.

Without knowing exactly what he was going to do, Zack came out from the protecting shadow of the trees, walking into the road and towards the car.

He didn't get far.

First of all he thought he felt something brush against his shoulder, then a black shape swerved in front of him, indistinct, not quite formed, and he stumbled backwards as if someone had pushed him. He definitely felt hot breath on his face.

He took another step backwards, holding his hands up to protect himself. From what? Something big and dark, backing him on to the pavement. He thudded into a tree trunk. He couldn't move at all.

Within seconds the doors of Excelsior Broadcasting opened. Steward Golightly came out with his opera cloak swirling and the man in uniform followed. Golightly seemed well-pleased with life. He said something to the chauffeur, who laughed. They stood for a moment in the newly-washed spring night, talking in low voices, sharing a joke. Then the chauffeur opened the doors and they got back into their car.

Still Zack didn't move.

The car moved off, as quiet as a car could possibly be, away down the avenue.

Zack felt the breath on his face again, saw something blurred and bulky, felt its energy as it went past.

He stayed exactly where he was.

Clouds had parted above the trees: there were stars.

'Are you all right?'

Clovis. Looking scared.

'I'm fine,' said Zack, surprised to hear his own voice.

'Well, you don't look it. What happened? I thought you were going to, to try and *speak* to that Golightly bloke, then you just sort of disappeared.'

126

'I was here,' said Zack.

'Did he see you?'

'I don't think so.'

'You look a bit weird. Are you coming back to the van?'

Zack nodded.

'Only Moe ran off. I thought he was following you. And then I couldn't see him. And then I followed him, and, oh, there he is . . .'

Moe sauntered towards them from somewhere further up the road, tail wagging.

'Did you see anything?' asked Zack, as they climbed back into the van.

'Golightly, you mean? Small, springy individual? Like the photo taken with our very own mother in an offbeat joint in MockBeggar, that we were never supposed to visit?'

Zack frowned into the dark. He hadn't meant Golightly. He remembered the darkness pressing him back out of sight under the tree. It seemed too difficult to explain.

'Yeah,' he said softly. 'Him.'

Chapter 21

There were crystals of coffee on crooked barley twist sticks, little pots of dark chocolate and raspberry sauce, crunchy Mango Granitas, frosted Pineapple Icicles, Lemon Sorbets with ginger crumble . . .

'People, people,' sang out Mr Featherplum. 'This is a live performance. We start in ten minutes. Your co-operation would, as always, be appreciated . . .'

The cast of *Dinah Dibbs, Girl Detective* weren't paying their director much attention. They were gathered around the silvery ice cart, handing over money, mmming and aahing and oohing and talking with their mouths full. Zack, wearing a white hat, was dispensing things as quickly as he could. He accidentally squirted his foot with vanilla and chocolate sauce. He dropped a splodge on to the well-worn carpet.

Mr Featherplum bounced and fretted. His eyes looked red, he kept sneezing and checking his watch and the large clock on the wall.

'Remember, people, we have three new characters today

and still only four microphones, generosity please, I hate to see pushing and shoving and remember I have an *allergy . . .*'

The studio had smelt of perfume, stale sweat and wet raincoats when Zack arrived. Now it was delicious with the sweet smell of sauces.

Nobody looked as Zack thought they should. He had always imagined that Dinah Dibbs was a rather small earnest-looking person, not dissimilar to the art teacher he had liked at Storm Hill School. However, the woman who played Dinah was big and much older. She had a cheerful, hearty face and swept about grandly in a long dark blue dress. When she spoke, it was disconcerting. She was having a Chocolate and Maple Honeycomb.

'I remember this,' she said to everyone. 'You've got to try it. I never thought I'd eat anything so yummy again.' And there was Dinah's girlish voice, light and tripping as the voice of the art teacher who had once whispered to Zack that he might well have talent if he could just apply himself.

Captain Dibbs was hopelessly slim, elegant and beardless. All wrong. But then, when he spoke, his voice was deep and deliberate and sounded just like the good, extremely boring Captain, after all.

'Excellent, excellent,' he said, easily drowning out the chatter around him. 'The water here in Rockscar has such an appalling taste, even the best recipe can never quite cover it up, I gather it's because it filters down through various flavours of mountain. I can't help wondering if these delicious ices actually come from a different source—'

'Be quiet, Frederick,' said the unrealistically young and pretty woman whom Zack had been told played the comforting, tea-making, Scarspring-advertising Mrs Dibbs. 'We don't ask.'

'Well I'm an inlander and maybe it's different for me but I would have thought that we all agree that the Scarspring ices are frankly inedible,' said Frederick, who seemed to have more opinions of his own than the Captain and no inhibitions about expressing them. 'They're all the colours of the rainbow, bright pink, lime green, goodness knows what they've got in them, but they all taste of Rockscar water, a flavour I will not miss when my contract with this delightful show finally runs out—'

'Don't say another word, darling,' hissed the Dinah Dibbs woman, amid similar advice and anxious glances from everyone else standing nearby. Zack stared fixedly down into the Raspberry Sorbet. Was it supposed to be lumpy like that?

'The Scarsprings have done so much for Rockscar,' said Mrs Dibbs, loudly.

'And we are so grateful that they sponsor this show,' added someone else.

Frederick the inlander seemed, finally, to get the message. 'Wonderful people,' he said. 'I've always said so.'

'I'm sure we've all enjoyed our refreshments,' puffed Mr Featherplum, fiddling with the four microphones. 'And I do hope we've all had a chance to look at our scripts. I've made a couple of minor changes, of small ... atchoo! Small changes and ... atchoo!' He produced a huge white handkerchief from his pocket, dabbed sweat off his face and neck and then blew his nose loudly.

'Do forgive me, terrible allergy, five minutes to go, people, remember when the Maharajah bursts into the room and demands his jewels back I want proper screams from the ladies ... a little too slow to react in rehearsal, but, of course, that's why we have rehearsals, even for such remarkable talents as yourselves ...'

'Excuse me,' whispered a voice behind Zack. He turned, a chocolate-lined cornet in one hand and a scoop of Orange Sorbet in the other. Someone was standing in the doorway.

'Ah!' Mr Featherplum weaved and bustled up beside him.

'Excellent, Miss Frankie, scripts everybody. Hand them round, my dear. Three minutes to go, scripts for next week, hand them round ...'

'Hello,' said the girl in the doorway to Zack. 'I've heard about you.' She was neat and small with short, dark curly hair, light brown skin and grey eyes. Zack took all this in at once, as if she were under a spotlight.

'You'll spill that,' she giggled.

He just managed to catch the Orange Sorbet in the

cornet. It was for one of the new characters, the man who was playing the Maharajah: a short man with freckles and long red hair.

'Thanks,' he said. 'I'm an absolute bundle of nerves. I've only got two lines tonight and I keep getting them wrong. I *demand* the *return* of my property, I demand the return of *my* property . . .'

'Two and a half minutes,' cried Mr Featherplum. 'At your microphones please, I'm afraid you really must leave now Mr, er, Mr, er . . . much as we have all enjoyed your, er, er . . .atchoo! Your *ices*. Remember what we discussed in rehearsals, for tonight's episode we want tension, we are looking for tension, the mood is tense, become the mood people, become the mood . . .'

The girl with the scripts grinned at Zack and pushed her way into the throng, handing out the bundles of typewritten sheets, exchanging greetings. How old was she, for goodness sake? And what did she mean, she'd heard of him? How?

He went to put his scoop back in the gleaming stainless steel bucket.

At that moment, he heard a very tiny voice coming out of the cart.

'And silence,' announced Mr Featherplum, who had just been making another speech about the mood for tonight.

Everyone bustled around the microphones. The sound effects woman was standing behind a table that was laden with coconuts, plates, jugs, cutlery, a camping stove, a kettle and two pigeons on a perch. Two other women, with massive headphones, were looking important on the other side of a glass wall. Beyond them, a man was mouthing the news. A little box on the wall had lit up with the message '60 seconds to On Air'.

There it was again: easier to hear now, 'Don't want to worry you but we have company.'

'Forty-five seconds,' said Mr Featherplum, wiping his nose.

Zack backed out of the door pulling the cart. He caught a glimpse of the man who was playing the Maharajah, looking extremely pink, dropping his script, just as Mr Featherplum, his voice suddenly transformed into something full of soothing confidence, leant towards a microphone and said, 'And now we join . . .'

The girl called Miss Frankie caught the door just as it was closing and followed him out into the corridor.

'Your ice wagon was talking,' she whispered as they both progressed to the lift.

'No it wasn't, that's not possible,' said Zack briskly.

Thanks to Clovis, the cart contained a small two-way radio. The springy metal pole with the cheerful little flag on top was the aerial. The microphone and speaker were down on the side. Small brass grills.

'Do you read me?' enquired the little voice. This was followed immediately by a yelp.

'Yes, it is,' said Frankie, giggling again. 'It's barking too.'

Zack was now marching the cart to the lift. Tiny had phoned ahead of them and the welcome from the commissionaire at the front desk had been extremely cordial. He had remembered Balthazar. In fact, he remembered Balthazar's grandfather. He had agreed to wait for Zack in the lobby to let him out again.

'Goodnight,' said Zack, at the lift doors.

'I'm coming in too,' she said, grinning back at him. The doors slid open.

Zack pushed the cart inside. 'I don't think there's room for you,' he said firmly.

It was not a big lift; nevertheless Frankie joined him. They were suddenly very brightly lit and surrounded by mirrors. As they sailed upwards to the ground floor, she peered at her reflection. Met his eye in the mirror and laughed.

'I've got a brilliant idea,' she said. 'I'm going to the Scarsprings' place now with my mum. She's waiting right outside in the car. There's a big party. We're always invited. She'd love one of your ices. You can bring your ice wagon to the party. The Chief of Police will be there. He's a great friend of Steward Golightly. You'll make lots of money. I'll ask Mum now.'

Mr Featherplum would have been proud of Zack. He had become the mood and the mood was panic.

'Scarspring blokes checking drain,' hissed the cart. 'Don't come out yet.'

Too late, Zack had the idea of clapping his hand over the speaker. The lift doors opened on to the dim-lit, deeply carpeted and elegant lobby.

Sirens were wailing outside. Two police vans rumbled past with their purple light flashing.

The commissionaire nodded significantly from behind the desk. Zack came out of the lift first, doubled over, trying to keep his hand over the speaker and hissing 'shut up, shut up shut up,' into the microphone. Already he was imagining this Frankie person running to her mother's car, full of the news about the lovely ice cream cart that would be such fun to take to the Scarsprings' party. They were going to be arrested.

Frankie came bouncing after him, having paused a moment to finish checking her make-up in the mirrored wall of the lift.

'Busy night,' said the commissionaire. Silvery hair, immaculate suit. 'Your mother's car has been moved a little further down the avenue, Miss Frankie. Some gentlemen are examining a blocked drain and her chauffeur had parked directly above the manhole.'

He unlocked the doors. Frankie looked at Zack, exploded with giggles, waved and tripped off down the steps. Zack, at last, stood up straight: he patted at the side of the cart as if he had been checking something.

'Miss Frankie is of a very playful disposition,' said the commissionaire.

Zack looked after her just in time to see a scooter go past, travelling in the opposite direction to the police vans. It ploughed through a puddle right outside and a fan of water glittered upwards, as graceful as the spreading wing of a bird. Without doubt there was a very large, white dog sitting on the back of this scooter. In fact, Zack was sure it was a wolf.

'I understand that those police vehicles were on their way to a scene of some interest to us all,' said the commissionaire. 'Scarspring employees have been trying to remove a large wilderness cedar tree in Shadowcliff in order to bore for water underneath it. They attempted to cut it down last night but discovered that their axes had been mysteriously blunted. Tonight they went back with a mechanical digger. The doorman of the Shadowcliff Hotel has just telephoned me to say that the brakes failed on the digger when it was parked and unattended.' The commissionaire paused and allowed himself a discreet smile. 'In the absence of a driver it has nevertheless succeeded in negotiating several corners and has managed to end up in the harbour. A distance of six miles away.'

'All clear to come out now,' whispered the cart, sounding rather disgruntled. 'A wolf just went past on the back of a scooter. Moe got a teeny bit emotional.'

Chapter 22

'Where are you going?' demanded Clovis.

'Forwards,' snapped Zack.

'We should have turned right, I said turn right and you've just kept on straight.'

'I want to see this place where the Scarsprings are trying to dig up a tree.'

Clovis groaned. 'Brilliant idea. If you really want to meet them that much why don't we go to their party. Anshelm himself is there. I'm sure he'd like to meet us.'

'It won't take long.'

'Good, because the next thing that's going to happen will be morning at this rate. AAAH!'

The van lurched round a tight corner and nearly ran into a muddle of roadworks; temporary wooden fencing, partly collapsed; a sign saying 'SLOW'; a big hole and a number of orange lanterns.

Zack stopped the van, causing all passengers, and himself, to lurch forwards uncomfortably in their harnesses.

'Glad you stopped,' said Clovis, through clenched teeth. 'Don't get out until we're sure it's safe,' he added, as Zack opened the door and jumped down on to the pavement.

There was no one around. They were in Shadowcliff, a place of expensive houses in steep terraces, jammed between massive wedges of rock. Zack could see where the digging machine must have been. The pavement had been dug up and the mud churned by the enormous wheels of a heavy vehicle. Kerbstones were shattered further down the hill, several iron lampposts lay broken and twisted. A sign leant at a sharp angle right next to where he was standing: 'Tree scheduled for removal. Water Exploration. The Scarspring Water Company apologize for the inconvenience caused.'

A cool wind blew through Shadowcliff and the looming, stricken tree. The deep hole at its base revealed roots, scraped white, like a savage injury that exposed the bone. It was an ancient wilderness cedar, a giant of shelved horizontal branches, only a little smaller than the one which served the Jump family as a lookout back on the mountain. There were several like it in Rockscar City, standing at street corners, all of them protected by law. Until now.

Moe pressed his grizzled face to the stupid little wooden fence. He looked down into the gaping earth. His whole body seemed to vibrate with rage. He began barking. A formidable sound, worthy of a dog five or six times his size.

Clovis and Zack immediately tried to haul him back into the van, staggering and cursing, as lights in upstairs windows began to twinkle into life. Moe had somehow become extremely heavy. He remained on the ravaged pavement as if bolted. Then he wriggled free and jumped over the fence as light as a cricket and into the hole. The barking stopped.

Rattle of glass and wood: a nearby window opening.

'What's going on down there?' boomed a wealthy, powerful-sounding voice.

'Oh great,' groaned Clovis.

At this moment a coal lorry lumbered round the corner. The driver wound down his window.

'In trouble, mate? Broken down?' he shouted above the loud noise of his engine. 'Need a tow?'

'Er, no, no thanks . . .' shouted Zack. 'Just, er, just . . .' He patted the bonnet of the Ice Angel.

'Going to call the police,' boomed the person with the booming voice.

'I wouldn't put myself so near that big hole if I was you,' shouted the driver, who had now turned off his engine, the better to chat, but was competing with a tremendous scrabbling and crunching coming from the bottom of the hole.

'One of our lorries fell into a hole like that. The edge gave way. They're digging a lot of holes at the moment, all over.' He trailed off, his expression changing. 'Is that noise coming from down there?'

'Get that dog back. Do something,' hissed Clovis.

More windows lighting up.

'Moe!' called Zack. 'Here, boy!'

Zack had never addressed Moe as 'boy'. Also, Moe had never, ever come when called. Zack was not surprised, therefore, when the earth-moving sounds continued unabated. The lorry driver now got out of his cab.

'Beautiful angel,' he said.

Zack and Clovis both swung round as if attacked. The driver walked right up to the angel and touched her.

A police siren, distant but unmistakable, now rang out like a fanfare.

'MOE!' yelled Zack. 'We have to go NOW!'

The police siren, though far away, was getting louder.

Someone in a dressing gown and carrying a massive studded cudgel had opened their smart front door and was standing on the step. Presumably Mr Big Booming Voice. Zack pushed the fence over, took two steps forward, stumbled on the crumbling ground, waved his arms and began falling into the hole in the road.

'Moe!' he yelled.

However, Moe was much nearer than he had expected and there was really hardly anywhere left to fall. The white roots had disappeared. The hole had almost disappeared. In a very short time, with his small paws, Moe had almost completely filled it in.

He climbed out of it now, wagging his tail and panting slightly.

Despite the danger they were in Zack found the energy

to whisper a command. Not that Moe had ever obeyed any command, ever.

'Stop wagging your tail,' whispered Zack. 'And stop pretending to be a normal dog.'

He climbed back over the remains of the fence, accidentally kicking a lantern, which went out. The concerned resident with the cudgel was watching him. Presumably waiting for the police who would be here, of course, any minute, like eagerly-expected party guests. It was therefore very, very important that they should get back in the van and leave at great speed. However, at this minute, for some reason, Clovis and the lorry driver were hunched in conversation.

'The original chocolate recipe? You sure?' murmured the lorry driver.

Clovis, nodding, 'Even better. More ingredients.'

'The bloke that used to come round the hospitals and poor houses and—'

'Yes, yes,' Clovis whispered.

The lorry driver was pulling change and notes out of his pockets.

'CLOVIS!' hissed Zack. 'We need to GO!'

At the same moment he realized that the sirens seemed to be above them now, higher up among the tangled streets. Were they going past? On some other mission?

Clovis opened the passenger door of the cab and the smell of chocolate sauce murmured out into the night. He climbed in, unbolted the hatch above the back of the long seat and wriggled through. He returned almost immediately with a tub of Demon's Brew Chocolate Chilli Ice with Dark Berry Sauce.

The lorry driver seized it fervently.

And then, as the sirens faded somewhere further up the mountain and it did seem as if the police weren't coming this way after all, THEN, they heard the soft insistent hum of a highly-tuned, enhanced, Hillstart 10 scooter engine. Hillstarts were the machines used by the feared elite police scooter patrols.

Clovis closed the door of the Ice Angel cab.

The lorry driver shoved the tub of ice cream down the front of his jacket.

The patrolman glided to a halt. Like all scooter patrolmen he was dressed in shimmering grey uniform with a silver helmet. They were known as the shiners. This shiner was wearing a scarf tied across the lower half of his face.

Zack felt in his pocket for his identification papers. Fear had filled his mind with a frenzy of images, ending with the stinking waters of the Cat's Tail.

'Is this your vehicle, sir?' asked the shiner. 'And if you would be good enough to stay where you are,' he added to the lorry driver, who had shifted sideways, slightly.

'Yes,' said Zack, swallowing. Moe sat down on the cobbles next to him, as if they were all going to have a pleasant chat.

'This fence has been completely demolished,' said the shiner. 'I came past here less than one hour ago and it was still standing. I must warn you that any interference with roadworks, especially those relating to our water supply, is a serious matter. What is your business here?'

He was standing to the side of the van. The angel herself was still hidden from him. He only had to walk around to the front, perhaps to look at the hole, or, at least, the place where the hole had been, and he would see her.

'Perhaps you can tell me something about how it happened. Did you see anything strange?'

Zack looked sideways at Clovis. Oh no. Clovis' face was set in an expression of intense concentration.

'The troll went that way,' said Clovis suddenly, in a shaky voice. He was pointing down the street. 'We tried to stop it, with the van.'

'You saw the troll,' said the shiner. His voice had completely changed into something hungry and reverent.

'Yes,' said Zack.

'It went that way,' said the lorry driver, pointing the same way as Clovis had done.

'Yes,' said Zack again. 'We think it was filling in this, er, this . . .'

'Hole,' said Clovis.

'Describe the troll,' said the shiner, urgently.

No one spoke for a moment.

'Big,' said the lorry driver.

'Very big,' said Zack.

'Is that all?' The shiner's voice was mocking.

'No,' said Zack. 'No. It was just that it was hard to see. It was more like a sort of darkness, that sort of pressed against me. Us. And stopped us moving.'

The lorry driver and Clovis both stared at Zack. They were surprised. But it was the shiner who staggered as if the ground had shaken under his feet.

'This happened to you here, now?' he whispered, coming closer.

Zack hesitated. He looked into the shiner's eyes, fierce and bright. For a moment he felt as if the others weren't there. Even the van wasn't there. It was just him and this patrolman and, in some weird way, they understood each other.

He didn't want to lie.

'Near here,' he said. 'Tonight.'

'Near here, tonight,' said the shiner softly. Another pause.

'It had antlers,' said the lorry driver. 'It caught me on the chest, just a scrape, I'm bleeding.' He pushed his hand down his shirt and pulled it out with dark fruit sauce smeared on his fingers. It looked very much like blood.

'Antlers!' The shiner almost spat the word. 'I wouldn't be in the least surprised if you saw nothing at all, my friend. But you . . .' He looked at Zack for a long moment. 'You are not such a liar as you look, I think.'

He held his searching gaze on Zack. Zack

couldn't look away.

Neither of them noticed the police van coming down the hill. Zack only heard it and turned to see when it stopped next to the coal lorry, sweeping them all with the purple beam of light from its roof, and several policemen jumped out on to the road.

'Anything wrong?' asked the one who reached them first. 'Have either of your vehicles broken down?'

Both Zack and the lorry driver started to speak. But then someone else interrupted them. It was the man with the cudgel and the dressing gown: he had finally descended the steps from his front door.

'I'm afraid it's my fault, officer,' he said in a slightly lower version of the booming shout he had used before. 'These young gentlemen have been delivering a fridge to my house. It was difficult to park without blocking the road. These roadworks, you see.'

Clovis had started nodding already. The lorry driver licked his fingers and nodded too. Zack hadn't quite caught up yet. He seemed to be the only one who had noticed the shiner steer his Hillstart 10 quietly back to the corner, mount it and ride away.

'This gentleman had just stopped to enquire if all was well,' added Dressing Gown. 'Everyone is a little tense. The vandalism you know.' He waved a hand, encompassing many lighted windows and several open front doors, complete with staring householders, most of them armed.

'If you could all move along now,' said the policeman. 'There's a couple of big wagons full of kerbstones coming through here to go up to Storm Hill. Different route from normal because a road is closed further up. Another incident similar to the business with the digger here, vandals messing around with the search for more water.'

Everyone was nodding.

The policeman got back into the van, waved cheerily and drove off. Clovis and Zack both looked at the man with the dressing gown. He had grey hair and a neat grey beard. He smiled.

'You're having quite a dramatic evening,' he said.

'But—' began Clovis.

'I couldn't help noticing the transaction between yourself and this gentleman here,' the man indicated the lorry driver. 'I decided not to call the police after all. I was coming down to see if you had any of those Toffee Cinnamon Chunks. I remember them well. The most delicious thing I've ever eaten. The rich, melting toffee, the subtle hint of cinnamon. And no horrible Rockscar water aftertaste. Superb.'

There was a pause.

'I'm sorry, I don't think we've got any of that one,' said Clovis.

'I did try to make some, but it went wrong,' said Zack. 'I set fire to the top of the stove.'

'He'll make some more. We'll come back again soon,' said Clovis.

146

The man smiled. 'Excellent. And I must congratulate *you*, sir, on your quick thinking and imagination. Antlers and blood. Very good.'

He and the lorry driver shook hands.

'It would have fooled anyone else,' added Dressing Gown. 'But our benefactor and mayor, Anshelm Scarspring, is a different matter.'

'What do you mean?' said Zack.

Dressing Gown didn't hear him, he was accepting a little taste of the lorry driver's Demon's Brew Chocolate Chilli Ice with Dark Berry Sauce.

'Delicious,' he said, nodding, his eyes half closed. 'The sweet, sharp taste of the berries combined with the *defiance* of the chilli . . .'

'Balanced by the *rich*, comforting background of the excellent chocolate . . .' added the lorry driver. 'If this ice cream was a woman, I'd propose marriage.'

'But if you didn't call the police,' said Clovis, 'who did?'

'Probably no one. They were coming through here anyway, it seems, to make sure the road was clear. Wagons going up to Storm Hill. Usual way blocked by closed road. Traffic gets re-routed all the time at the moment. Scarsprings digging things up trying to find new water sources. Vandals interfering. Messy business.'

'But the patrolman, the shiner, I thought he came because you phoned the police . . .' began Zack.

Dressing Gown laughed heartily. 'Point One, which you should take note of for future reference, is that shiners always travel in pairs. They feel safer that way. Point Two, why did our particular shiner find it necessary to wear a scarf across his face? Not part of the uniform. Point Three, didn't you notice how interested he was when you all started talking about the troll? A masterstroke,' he nodded to Clovis.

'So?' said Zack.

'So, that wasn't a real shiner. That wasn't a policeman at all. That was Mr Anshelm Scarspring himself.'

'What?'

'In disguise. It's well known that he's desperate for any information about trolls. He really believes in them, you see. He's always looking for witnesses, for proof. Just a little bit crazy, so they say. That was him all right, visiting the sites of the vandalism, looking for clues. Incognito.'

'Maybe he likes dressing up,' said the coal man, over his shoulder, getting back into his cab.

'Our mayor really believes in trolls,' repeated Dressing Gown.

Moe, now sitting on Zack's feet, gave a mighty yawn. The lorry driver started his engine and gave a farewell salute from the cab.

'Let's go,' whispered Clovis and added, more loudly, 'We'll be back this way again next week, about the same time.'

'Excellent,' said Dressing Gown. 'I'll let a few chosen neighbours know. We'll be looking forward to it.'

Chapter 23

The same night: later now. A single peal of bells had rung out across the city and fallen silent. The midnight warning that the freight train was due to leave. Many miles of wilderness lay before it. It would not reach the nearest city inland for several hours.

Zachary and Clovis Jump and their dog Moe were already driving back up the Wolf Road. Zack and Clovis were too tired to talk: even though there was much to talk about.

Someone else who had been out in the dark was also going home. Ernesto Scarspring, heir to the Scarspring family and fortune, was creeping in through one of the several doors reserved for servants in the Scarsprings' house. He made his way along the passageway, past the kitchens where the expensive chef, especially hired for the evening, was shouting at the waiters, also especially hired.

He opened a small door on to a twisting back staircase. Some parts of his home, downstairs for example, were grand and elegant. Upstairs there was a warren of narrow wood-panelled corridors with creaking floors. No space was wasted in the city of Rockscar. Even here in Merchant's Hill the houses were built in terraces. Every house had been added to and extended, sometimes over the roof of the one next door, and all were crammed together like overcrowded teeth.

Ernesto had great-aunts and second cousins and grandparents and there was room for them all in this huge maze of a house. His own room was high up, on the fourth floor, overlooking the narrow street and the rooftops and, in the distance below, MockBeggar, SugarTown and the docks. Beyond that, the sea and the soft pulse of the lighthouse.

He went inside and closed the door quietly behind him. Then he took off his hooded coat and the tattered shoes he had been wearing. Now, safe for a while, he moved slowly, like a person in pain. He did not seem to see his cluttered room, the desk and the shelves of many books, the framed photograph of his parents, the microscope and the telescope and the gilded moving model of the planets and the sun. He was thinking only of his beloved cat, lost now for five long days.

He went to the one small window. It was wedged open, as always, for her return. Then he sat for a while staring into the salty, rainy night, tracing her favourite paths from one roof to the next, along the ledges and parapets that adorned the Scarsprings' house and those of their neighbours. Back up to this windowsill and home.

Ernesto had grown up used to loneliness. He had found

comfort in books and facts and ideas. He had kept mice and a tank of tiny red and silver flying fish. One spring he had even sent off to the mainland for a box of crickets that were sold as snake food. He had released them. He had sat watching them as they hopped and sang their way to freedom over the roofs beyond this very window.

His parents were long gone. His true comfort and companion had been his tabby cat Fisher, given to him as a kitten by the cook who had cared for him when he was small.

Now he was exhausted after the nights and days of searching for her.

He left the window, opened his dark wooden wardrobe and brought out a black suit and a starched white shirt. There was a party going on downstairs and he had no choice. He had to go down and meet the guests.

Chapter 24

There was a familiar knock at the door, discreet but insistent.

'Master Ernesto?'

Ernesto glanced at his ghostly reflection in the mirror. He straightened his collar. Then he opened the door.

Steward Golightly was also dressed in his evening clothes. He wore a white carnation pinned to his jacket.

'Your uncle is wondering when you will be joining us,' he said, softly.

Ernesto smiled a polite smile. He knew that the steward despised and resented him.

'I am coming down,' he said.

'After all this party is partly in your honour, it is only just over a month since your birthday,' continued Golightly, as they set off together towards the front stairs. His voice was heavy with pretended respect. 'All your friends are here. We all want to give you our good wishes. You are almost a man now.'

'Thank you,' said Ernesto. Both he and Golightly knew

that the only friends he had ever had were in the servants' hall. All the guests at the large and expensive party downstairs were, as always, business associates of his uncle and other powerful people from the city. The Chief of Police, bankers, casino owners, racehorse owners, the head of the planning department, newspaper editors, the Chairman of the Excelsior Broadcasting Company. There were also people who amused or interested Anshelm Scarspring in some way. Singers from the cabaret theatres. Boxers. Actors and greyhound trainers. A seemingly endless number of beautiful and exquisitely-dressed women. And so on.

They came to the gallery that overlooked the grand marble foyer. Musicians were just arriving, surely rather late, and hurriedly setting up their instruments. The great, curved sweep of the stairs was decorated with fresh flowers in the Scarspring colours, wine red and gold. White-clothed tables were piled with empty platters and crumpled linen napkins. Waiters glided from room to room with ice buckets containing bottles of the best champagne.

Here Golightly, mindful, no doubt, of Ernesto's extreme shyness, stopped beside the gilded balustrade and announced loudly, 'Ladies and gentleman, Master Ernesto Scarspring, the birthday boy himself!'

Ernesto shivered with embarrassment.

The jazz band lurched into a swelling performance of 'Happy Birthday'. The guests who happened to be in the foyer at the time started singing and raising their glasses.

Others streamed through the doors on either side, from the conference room and the ballroom. Several waiters put down their trays to join in.

'They will expect you to say something,' whispered Steward Golightly, his tone reverent, his eyes bright with malice.

Never had the song 'Happy Birthday' seemed to last for so long or to increase so steadily in volume.

Ernesto tried to continue down the stairs but the steward somehow managed to block him. As the final notes rang out, accompanied by at least fifty voices, he found himself still displayed on the gallery, blushing and starting to sweat as Golightly stepped a little away from him, made a sweeping bow, and announced him again to the crowd.

'Master Ernesto,' he boomed. His voice, when necessary, was surprisingly loud.

Ernesto grabbed hold of the balustrade. He looked directly ahead at the enormous chandelier, a great sparkling mass of glass and candle flames. Then a woman in a black dress and a feather boa raised her glass –

'To the birthday boy!'

'To the birthday boy,' yelled everyone in unison: the drummer in the jazz band struck the cymbals with a searing, silvery crash.

'Speech!' cried the woman.

'Speech!' shouted a man beside her.

'I really think you ought to say something,' whispered

Steward Golightly, smiling like a friend.

Ernesto cleared his throat. He had just noticed his uncle, Mayor Anshelm Scarspring himself, coming through from the ballroom with a slender young woman on his arm. Anshelm raised his glass to Ernesto and then stood still, waiting, with the look of someone who is thinking of other things.

'I . . . I . . . I would like to . . . to thank . . . to thank you all . . .' muttered Ernesto. He paused. Clearly it wasn't enough just to thank them: something more was needed. With the Mayor's arrival the foyer had become completely silent.

Ernesto felt sick. He looked down into the many, many faces, some openly smirking now, and he licked his lips in terror. He met the gaze of a girl who was dressed like a smaller version of all the women around her, her lips painted a dark red, a white flower pinned in her short curly hair.

She was smiling too; but it wasn't a mocking smile, it was altogether different. She raised her eyebrows as if they knew each other well and this was some secret signal between them. Then she pitched sideways with a little cry, dropping her glass, which shattered loudly, scattering the people around her, and lay motionless on the floor.

For a moment everyone turned towards her. Steward Golightly forgot his pleasant task of torturing Ernesto. Ernesto was able to push quickly past him and on down the stairs. People stepped out of his way as he crossed the floor.

He joined the guests already crouching around the girl.

Everyone was suggesting things. Air, whisky and a glass of water were all popular. A woman was loudly explaining that her dress had been splashed with wine because the girl had fallen into someone who had fallen into her.

The girl looked even younger now that Ernesto was right beside her. She was half sitting up, supported by the saxophone player from the band: a big man in a green hat.

'I'm so sorry about your dress,' she said in a dazed voice. 'I'm sure my mother will pay for it to be cleaned.'

'Don't you take any notice of that lady, Frankie,' whispered the saxophone player. 'She's got two different dresses for every day of the year and she looks like a llama in every single one of them.'

The girl made a spluttering noise.

'Can I help you?' asked Ernesto. 'Did she pass out?'

He was in a thicket of people's legs. All the members of the band seemed to be there. One of the waiters pushed past him carrying a blanket, a tray with a decanter of whisky and a jug of hot water. Ernesto toppled backwards.

'Easy does it,' said a silky voice behind him. 'If you're going to be a knight in shining armour, Ernestino, you have to be able to stay upright.'

It was Anshelm, of course, witness to every humiliation Ernesto could remember.

Ernesto struggled to his feet. The girl who had collapsed was on her feet too now, being supported by at least two members of the band. He couldn't see her face. He turned to follow them. Then he felt a hand on his shoulder.

'This is Cordelia Defoe,' said Anshelm. 'Cordelia, this is my nephew Ernesto.'

'Happy birthday,' said Cordelia.

Ernesto recognized her. She was a star from the Rockstar City Film Studios. In fact he had seen her in a film recently, what had she played, a nurse? Or was it some sort of vampire?

'Thank . . . thank you,' he said.

'Oh, come on,' said Anshelm, 'I'm sure you can do better than that. We're trying to encourage Ernesto to be a bit more talkative, Cordelia, but it's hard work.'

There was a pause. On the edge of his vision Ernesto saw the girl and the band disappearing into the crowd.

'I saw you in a film,' he said, carefully. 'Were . . . were you the demon dental nurse from hell?'

'Why, yes,' breathed Cordelia. 'However did you recognize me without the horrible wig and the warts and the false nose?'

'I didn't think you looked that much different,' said Ernesto, truthfully. Her eyes were large, slanting and the colour of new grass. They had been just the same in the film: Ernesto mainly noticed people's eyes.

'That's quite enough,' whispered Anshelm, rolling his eyes at Ernesto. He patted Cordelia's arm. 'Don't take any notice, darling, my nephew is not an expert on the movies.'

'But how could you think I looked the same with the false nose?' cried Cordelia.

'I'm sorry,' began Ernesto, hopelessly, and then he added, because it was all he could really think about properly, 'I've lost my cat. Cook gave her to me when she was a kitten. The cat I mean. I was three. She's been here all her life. The cat, I mean . . .' He swallowed painfully.

'Oh, your cat,' said Cordelia, her amazing eyes growing even larger, 'you poor boy . . . oh, you poor thing . . . but I'm sure the mayor will help you find her, he's such a good man and he knows so many people. Why don't you go on the radio, Anshelm, and make an appeal? I'm sure—'

'Would you leave us, Cordelia, dear?' interrupted Anshelm. 'I really must have a chat with Ernesto. I had sent my steward to fetch him just before that unfortunate child passed out.'

A waiter came up to them and held out a tray of glasses.

'Have some champagne,' whispered Anshelm, kissing Cordelia on the cheek. 'And I'll be back before you know it.' He took a glass and pushed it into her hand.

Then he steered Ernesto by the elbow, through the guests and around the tables and, finally, through the door at the back of the foyer which led to the private rooms.

Chapter 25

Ernesto heard the band starting to tune up again. Then the heavy mahogany door closed behind them, everything at once seemed unpleasantly quiet, and Anshelm hurried him along the carpeted corridor to the study.

This was the heart of the Scarspring empire. A room which no visitor ever saw. There was a light and sunny office for them upstairs, lined with cabinets of information concerning the charitable work of the kind-hearted Scarspring Foundation.

There were files in this office too, shelves and shelves of them. But no window. There were two desks, one for Anshelm and one for Steward Golightly, and at least six large black telephones. Anshelm's desk was covered in charts and diagrams of the water system that supplied the city: pipes, underground reservoirs, sluices and channels and sewers. Detailed street maps of Rockscar hung on the walls, studded with brass-headed pins indicating places of current interest to the mighty Scarspring Water Company. A bronze model of Anshelm's racehorse 'Beggars would Fly' stood next to a carafe of water engraved with the Scarspring crest and their motto, 'we possess'.

'Sit down, Ernesto,' said Anshelm.

Ernesto sat down.

The party, the jazz band and the girl who had fainted seemed to belong to another world. Only this dark panelled room existed. And Anshelm in his immaculate evening clothes, cufflinks gleaming, leaning back on his carved swivel chair and putting his hands behind his head.

Ernesto waited: then he couldn't help himself.

'I still haven't found Fisher,' he said. ' I haven't slept for four nights. I've put signs in the street and everything. Reward for the safe return of mature tabby cat, grey and silver. Last seen in Scarspring Street.'

'I'm sorry. We are not here to discuss your attempts to find your cat,' said Anshelm.

The gold travelling clock on the shelves behind him chimed a series of high, tiny notes. Then it struck two. Anshelm opened a box of cigars.

'Would you like one?'

Ernesto shook his head. 'No. I didn't think so.'

He blinked as Anshelm lit his cigar. A cloud of blue smoke drifted into the air.

'Why won't you have a cigar, by the way? You're old enough, you know. Or at least, you're supposed to be. Twelve, isn't it?'

'I don't want to fill my lungs with smoke,' said Ernesto, quietly.

Anshelm burst out laughing. 'Never mind, listen, this is the deal, you are the heir to this whole thing,' he waved his hand around the room,' as we both know. Well, the Scarsprings didn't get where they are today by being shy and having an interest in pet cats and butterflies and poor people, or whatever it is you are always reading about. We are, of course, admired for our good works and our acts of charity. But I'm afraid there is a little bit more to it than that. Do you want to know what has happened to your beloved flea-ridden companion?'

'Do you know where she is?' whispered Ernesto.

Anshelm sighed. He leant back in his chair again, blowing a smoke ring towards the ceiling, his eyes half closed.

'I might,' he said. 'But I don't want to worry you by saying too much.'

Ernesto jumped to his feet so fast he knocked over his chair. 'Tell me where she is!'

'Hush, now,' drawled Anshelm. 'Always so clumsy, aren't you?'

'Tell me!' cried Ernesto.

Anshelm put the cigar down on the edge of a pewter ashtray. The smoke curled upwards in a slow spiral.

'I've had a busy day,' he said. 'Being Mayor is quite demanding, you know. Being polite to people, signing things, going to meetings. And all the time looking after the interests of the Scarspring Water Company. Tedious, but it all has to be done."

Ernesto had become as still as stone.

'But then you don't like hearing about things like that, do you, Ernestino, because you like books and scientific experiments and pet animals . . . dear me, there is not as much of this excellent brandy left as I thought . . .'

He was lifting a decanter and two heavy crystal glasses on to the desk. Now he was pouring some blood-red cherry brandy into each glass and pushing one across the desk towards Ernesto. It made a sound like a whisper on the polished wood.

'If you haven't got the courage to smoke, perhaps you can at least try and drink like a man,' he said.

'Do you know where she is?' asked Ernesto, fighting to keep his voice steady.

'For goodness sake, Ernesto, you must learn to hide your emotions. You look quite deranged.'

Ernesto turned and carefully righted his chair. He heard Anshelm refilling his glass. Then, slowly, he sat down again.

'You are twelve now,' continued Anshelm. 'Steward Golightly and I have decided that it is time for us all to find out if you are ever going to be strong enough to lead the family. You are the next in line and the laws of our city require that you inherit. No one else. So you need to toughen up. Do you understand? You need to prove yourself. Just as, many years ago, I had to prove myself to my father.'

Ernesto waited, enduring.

'When I was only a little older than you I was attacked by a robber in an alley near Pedder's Square,' said Anshelm. 'Attacked by a grown man who didn't expect any trouble from someone hardly more than a boy. It was dark. I was alone. I broke his arm, Ernesto, and I threw him in the Cat's Tail.

'After that, my father understood that I was a true Scarspring. He allowed me to run certain aspects of the business. The men under my command knew what I was capable of doing. They respected me.'

'What happened to the man?' whispered Ernesto, despite himself.

'There you go! Weakness! What does it matter what happened to him? He tried to rob me. Since you ask, however, I can tell you that he couldn't swim, at least not in freezing water, with a broken arm. He was fished out like a lost shoe a few days later.'

Ernesto's eyes were wide with horror. 'He, he *drowned*? Like Mr Pimm, last winter?'

'What do you know about Mr Pimm?'

'He was found in the Cat's Tail, too. Some people said that Steward Golightly had been lending him money, and he couldn't pay it back.'

'Where did you hear such a story?'

Ernesto hesitated. Then whispered, 'Barnacle Radio.'

He was ready to jump for the door. However Anselm just stared at him. His face grey.

When he spoke again he, too, was whispering. 'Don't repeat lies, Ernesto. Show some loyalty to the house that has fed and clothed you all your life.'

He took a long draught of brandy. Ernesto felt as if the room were closing in around them.

'And do have a drink, it would make you feel so much more light-hearted.'

Ernesto reached for the second glass. He took a sip and felt as if a viper had scorched its way down his throat.

'Before we come to the matter of the tiresome feline, which I do appreciate is close to your heart, I must tell you something else. You are old enough, now.'

Anselm opened a drawer in the desk, took out a number of rolls of parchment, selected one and spread it out on the desk.

'A map, Ernesto. Rockscar is a big city, and like all big cities it likes to believe in its own might. But we both know that compared with the wilderness that lies behind it, and reaches all around it to the sea, our city is small. It really is like a barnacle, clinging on to the side of the mountain. It is the wilderness that is vast. Mountains, forest, uncultivated and feared. Stretching inland and to either side for over two hundred miles. And the wilderness begins as soon as the city ends.'

The brandy had found its way to Ernesto's brain. He felt a wave of nausea, then of courage.

'My father was killed in the wilderness.'

'Yes,' said Anshelm. 'On the Wolf Road. Here.' There was a catch in his voice. He put his fingertip on the map, high up above Storm Hill Ridge.

Ernesto shrank into his chair. Anshelm relit his cigar.

'You know the story of that night. My brother, your father, was a hero. A fighter and a leader. He and I and Golightly had been hunting for mountain lion where the forest meets the rock. No one ever dared to go there. They still don't. We followed a road that has been abandoned for years, the Wolf Road.

'It was very late. There was a waning moon but there was much cloud to cover it. We were on our way home in the deepest darkness.

'A mountain lion leapt upon us. Maybe he had followed us and then lain in wait for our return. Maybe it was a lioness, protecting cubs nearby. That lion felled your father with a single blow. I saw it happen. It knocked him off the side of the road and into a deep ravine.

'Golightly was a little way ahead of us. He turned back when he heard my cries. Together, we overcame the brute but it broke free and fled. Too late for your father. We could not even find his body.'

Silence. Except for the ticking of the little, insistent clock. Ernesto waited: he knew the story of his father's death. The cigar smouldered between Anshelm's long fingers.

'You and Steward Golightly are two of the very few living people to have survived a fight with a mountain lion,' ventured Ernesto eventually.

Anshelm laughed dryly. 'You've heard that story many times, haven't you . . . and have you never wondered how three young, strong and well-armed men could be so easily ambushed? If we had gone into the mountains for the very purpose of hunting a lion, why did we walk so casually in the pitch dark, with Golightly ahead alone? Where were our guns? The lion killed my brother, your father, the heir to our fortune and power. Why did we not shoot it dead? Why could we find no trace, absolutely no trace of your father? Have you ever wondered about these matters, little Ernesto?'

Ernesto shook his head.

'Let me tell you the answers to some of those . . . mysteries,' said Anshelm. He was speaking slowly and deliberately now; Ernesto could smell the brandy, warm on his breath.

'We did not bring back the body of the lion because there was no lion.' He paused. 'Your father was a scholar who disliked all violence, including hunting. Our presence on the Wolf Road that night had nothing to do with hunting. It was not a mountain lion that killed him. On the mountains civilization is left behind, Ernesto, and different powers hold sway, ancient powers . . . the powers of the wilderness.'

Ernesto could feel his heart thumping in his chest.

'What are you saying?' he whispered.

Sudden as a gunshot, Anshelm slapped his hand down on the parchment.

'Now!' he barked. 'You know that a wretched troll is vandalizing our property and humiliating us. The trolls don't like us looking for water beyond the edge of the city. They are possessive about the wilderness cedars, wherever they are growing. They don't like explosions. They don't like holes being made in their precious mountain. They think that the wilderness belongs to them. We have been searching for new springs here, and here and here,' he stabbed at the city map with his finger. 'And a troll is trying to stop us. But it will not stop us, Ernesto.'

'Steward Golightly says they're just a silly superstition—'

'I don't care what anyone says,' snarled Anshelm. 'Trolls exist! All sorts of things exist! This particular troll exists and you are going to catch it!'

'What?'

'You heard me. And when you have brought me the troll, then you can have your cat back. And it's no good asking me anything. Only Golightly knows where she is.'

'WHAT?'

'Just go and do it, Ernesto! Get out of your room and your butterfly books and join us in the real, stinking world!'

Ernesto couldn't speak. He stared at his uncle.

'You may go now,' said Anshelm. Reaching for his glass again, his eyes rimmed with red, already looking at something far away.

Chapter 26

Ernesto closed the door very quietly behind him.

Then he walked back down the passageway and into the foyer where he was met by the sound of the jazz band, many voices raised in conversation and an overwhelming smell of mingled and expensive perfumes. The foyer was crowded with guests waiting for their drivers to come and take them home. The party was nearly over.

He intended to make straight for the stairs and get up to his room. However, at that moment, he noticed a girl with a white flower in her hair. At first, he couldn't remember anything about why he recognized her, or what had happened. The terrible conversation with Anshelm had driven everything else out of his mind.

She was standing by the door to the ballroom. A tall woman stood next to her, already wrapped up in a massive fur-trimmed coat.

Of course, she had fainted, or pretended to faint: she had helped him. He set off towards her.

The girl was almost ready to leave. She now wore a short

grey coat of some silky material with a velvet collar and large velvet-covered buttons. As Ernesto approached she was taking the flower out of her hair and pinning it to the outside of a grey felt cloche hat. Everything about her was trim and smart and sophisticated.

She saw him and smiled a quick, secret smile.

He was almost right in front of her, having apologized and excused himself to get past person after person, when he realized that he had no idea what he was going to say. Someone brushed against him sending him stumbling forwards and his face was momentarily buried in the ample front of the tall woman's coat.

'Be careful, Master Ernesto,' she said, in a husky voice, 'I am expecting a baby.' She helped him to right himself, holding his arm. He knew he should apologize but he couldn't speak.

'Please don't worry,' said the woman easily. He swayed a little where he stood, and wondered vaguely if he, too, was going to faint. She caught his arm again and steadied him. Her voice was warm and familiar: where had he heard it before?

'My name is Ernesto,' he said.

'We know,' giggled the girl. 'I'm Frankie Brown. And this is my mum. She's a scriptwriter for Excelsior Broadcasting. We're going home in a minute.'

'Do thank your uncle for inviting us,' said the woman, still looking closely at Ernesto.

'Yes,' said Ernesto.

'Happy birthday, Mr Ernesto,' called the saxophone player from the band, tipping his green trilby hat at Ernesto. 'See you later, Rose. Don't go fainting again, little Frankie.'

'Are you all right now?' asked Ernesto.

Frankie grinned. 'What do you think?'

'I tried to speak to you, but my uncle . . . my uncle . . .' Ernesto realized with horror that his eyes were filling with tears.

'Your car is here, Miss Brown,' said a man in a wine-red uniform.

'Don't worry,' whispered Frankie. 'I pretended. I thought you knew that. I just don't like to see a person in trouble, that's all. Mum says I'm like her detective, only she's older than me. Dinah Dibbs, have you heard of her?'

Ernesto nodded. His throat had tightened. Everything around them seemed to be blurring.

He heard Rose Brown say urgently. 'He's not well, Frankie. He's had some sort of shock. Get him to a chair.'

And almost at the same time someone called, 'Miss Brown, would you join us for a word before you go, please?'

'Have to go for a minute,' whispered Rose. 'That's Mr Featherplum, he buys my scripts, you look after Ernesto for a moment, Frankie . . .'

Chapter 27

Someone was steering him through the crowd towards the door. He was crossing the pavement. He was getting into the back of a large dark-windowed car.

'Would you give us a minute, please?' said Frankie to the driver.

Ernesto found himself sitting on the plush seat with Frankie beside him. They were in semi-darkness. The air was dense with the smell of perfume and powder. He groped at the unfamiliar door, looking for the handle.

'Don't worry,' said Frankie. 'We are not going anywhere. You're a bit poorly. Mum said you should sit down so I thought this might be a good place. Away from all your not very nice guests.'

She was opening a cupboard set in the sturdy partition that separated the passengers from the driver. The sliding window above it was closed. The driver himself was standing on the pavement chatting to other uniformed men.

'I don't want a drink,' gasped Ernesto. 'Thank you.'

'It's not a drink,' said Frankie, firmly. 'It is hot sweet tea.'

She poured the tea out of an insulated flask. 'Mum never goes anywhere without a little flask of tea,' she added. 'You never know what's going to happen, do you?'

Ernesto took the enamel cup: he held it without drinking any.

'I've lost my cat,' he said. 'She's been kidnapped.'

'Goodness!' exclaimed Frankie. 'For a ransom?'

Ernesto's mind was clearing. Perhaps it was the steam from the tea, if it was tea. He breathed in deeply.

'She's a tabby, a silver tabby, and she's quite old. About nine. If you look under her paw, her front paw, two of her toes are pink underneath. All the others are black. And there's a little tiny bit missing from one of her ears. Her name's Fisher.'

'Is there a ransom note?' asked Frankie. 'Dinah Dibbs once helped to find someone who was kidnapped by identifying the typewriter which had been used to write the ransom note.'

Ernesto looked miserably into her eager face, very young under all the make-up.

'There isn't a ransom,' he said at last. 'But I know she's been kidnapped.'

He paused.

'But surely your uncle is such a powerful man,' said Frankie, softly.

'My uncle can't help,' said Ernesto. 'It is up to me. There's something I have to do. But I'm not sure I can do it—'

Someone knocked on the window and he jumped, spilling tea on his hand.

'Excuse me, Miss,' said the driver. 'They're asking me to move the car.'

'I'll go,' said Ernesto. He held out the cup to Frankie, who took it from him. Then he fumbled for the door handle and found it.

'I'll help you find her,' said Frankie suddenly.

'Thanks, but I don't see—'

'There must be something. I talk to lots of people. I could be like Dinah Dibbs, looking for clues.'

'It's not a game,' said Ernesto abruptly, shocking himself with the tone of his voice.

She tilted her chin. Her eyes looked very bright.

'For example, why can't your uncle help? Dinah would ask that right away. He's the mayor. He usually gets what he wants, doesn't he? If he wanted to get your cat back he'd have it back in half a day with a written apology from the person who took it. Probably signed in their own blood.'

Ernesto let go of the door handle. He stared at Frankie. He had never spoken about Anshelm like that, not even to Cook. He had never heard anyone else speak about Anshelm like that. He opened his mouth to argue. To say that Anshelm was a much-loved citizen, famous for his charitable work and for everything he had done for the city. But no sound came out. Instead, he felt himself starting to smile. Frankie smiled back.

The driver tapped on the window again. Then they saw Rose coming out of the doors of the Scarsprings' house and down the steps, being talked at by a busy-looking man wearing a top hat.

'I'll leave you a message,' said Frankie. 'I'm sure I can find something out.'

'Don't leave any messages for me here,' said Ernesto quickly. 'It's not very private.'

'Can I telephone you?'

'Absolutely not. Golightly would listen for sure. All the lines are tapped. And don't come here either, it could put you in danger.'

The driver opened the car door. Rose almost climbed in.

'Frankie, what's going on? I said find Master Ernesto a chair, not spirit him away to our car. People are looking for him.'

Ernesto got out on to the pavement.

'Where do you live?' he asked Frankie.

She named a place far off on the other side of the city.

'If you're feeling better, Master Ernesto, I must ask you to go back inside,' said Rose urgently. 'Frankie means well but I don't want to be accused of trying to steal you.'

He gave one last frantic look at Frankie. Her face had suddenly lit up with an idea.

'I sometimes help Mum with the stories,' she said. 'I want to be a scriptwriter. I sometimes help write the dialogue. I could put a message in the script.'

'Master Ernesto needs to go,' said Rose, very firmly.

Ernesto shook hands quickly with them both. Then, an inspiration: he pulled Fisher's collar out of his pocket and gave it to Frankie. 'I found this on the corner of Excelsior Avenue,' he whispered. 'It's hers.'

Then he walked away from the car, trying and failing to work out where he had heard Rose's husky voice before. And, all the way to his empty room, that was how he distracted himself from the fact that he was completely alone.

Chapter 28

Anshelm and Steward Golightly were in the billiard room. They were sitting in large leather-covered armchairs. All the party guests had gone home, the servants were in bed and the house above them was quiet. The glow of one muted lamp bathed the two men in soft, orange light.

Anshelm gazed at the embers in the fireplace. He was holding a charm in the palm of his hand, running the chain between his fingers. Steward Golightly seemed less content.

'You're saying that he is going after the troll?'

'He didn't say, but my guess is he will. As you predicted, he's almost out of his mind worrying about his mangy cat.'

Golightly scowled. He pulled back his sleeve and examined three deep scratches on his forearm.

'And it doesn't concern you, Anshelm, that he will be the laughing stock of every educated person in the city?'

'It doesn't concern me, no. I myself am quite sure that there is a troll. Finding it will not be a matter of physical strength, it will be a matter of intelligence. If anyone can do it, he can. He is a very intelligent young man. Also, he's not well known to the public. He can make enquiries without attracting attention.'

Golightly raised his eyebrows. 'I suggested that we took the cat just to encourage him to be a little bit more adventurous. I thought the task we would set him would be something physical, like climbing up the outside of the tide tower, or going out on one of the fishing boats and catching a shark.'

'You thought wrong,' said Anshelm. 'His task is to find this troublesome troll.'

'And if there is no such thing? If trolls are just a myth, as many people believe nowadays?'

'You surprise me. But then, you are not a Scarspring, of course, you are an inlander. You can never fully understand the deep mysteries of our city and our wilderness. Tell me, what exactly do you think it was that we encountered up there on the Wolf Road that night?'

Golightly flinched.

'The night my brother died on that road,' prompted Anshelm. 'And not just my brother, the night—'

'I know the night you mean,' snarled Golightly. 'Must we go over this again and again? The headlamps of that accursed Ice Angel van were very bright. I was dazzled. I could hardly see. None of us could. The gun went off. Everything happened so quickly.'

He smoothed his sleeve back over his injured arm. 'We were very young. I had been taken in by your family as a child. I risked my life for you. I showed you absolute loyalty, on that night. And ever since . . .'

Anselm laughed. 'You don't have a very good memory, do you?'

'I remember that I have nothing to reproach myself for . . .'

'Blessed are the self-righteous,' said Anselm, still laughing. 'For they have forgotten their sins.'

Golightly's face flared with rage. 'I've forgotten nothing, Anselm! It is you who seeks to rewrite the story to suit your own conscience. That is why you persist in speaking of trolls. You prefer to believe in monsters than to face the truth.'

He leant forward and spat into the fire.

Anselm said nothing.

Then Golightly spoke again, in a less strident, gentler voice. 'You two were talking for a long time. Did you speak about anything apart from his cat and your troll?'

'I told him that I myself was attacked by a grown man in Pedder's Hill when I was about his age. I threw the man into the Cat's Tail and he drowned. I hoped it would shock him into action.'

Golightly snorted with laughter. 'He believed you?'

'Absolutely. I've never lied to him before. Except about one thing, of course. He knows that now.'

'About the night on the Wolf Road? You told him about that?'

'I told him that his father was not killed by a mountain lion.'

Steward Golightly's freckled face grew pale.

'Relax, Stefan,' said Anshelm, smiling his dangerous smile. 'I didn't tell him anything about you.'

Golightly had gripped the arms of his chair. Gradually, he let go.

'You are so sure that you have nothing to reproach yourself for, Stefan. And yet the thought of me telling Ernesto what may have happened on the Wolf Road terrifies you.'

'I thought we agreed a long time ago that there was no need for him, or anyone to know.'

'I think we are both troubled, Stefan, in our very different ways. It has driven us both a little mad. Don't you think?'

Anshelm extinguished the oil lamp.

Pale, new light filtered through the stained-glass window: another day coming.

Chapter 29

It was the first night that Ernesto had not gone looking for Fisher. He knew now that she was not wandering the streets. His uncle and Golightly had arranged for her to disappear and Ernesto was very sure that even the very clever girl detective, Dinah Dibbs, would never find her.

It was Fisher who normally slept beside Ernesto. Fisher who had woken him each morning for the last nine years by rubbing the side of her warm face against his neck. Fisher who had followed him down the long corridors, sat with him in the sun on the roof garden, watched him as he studied, kept him company when Golightly or some irritated relative had banished him to his room.

Ernesto's mother had been ill after he was born. Then she had disappeared. His father, of course, had died on the mountain a few days later. In the lonely, sorrowful house of the Scarsprings, Fisher was loyal and told no lies.

Anshelm and Golightly had been right to believe that Ernesto would be tipped out of his private world of thoughts and books without her, and that he would find resolve and courage he didn't know he possessed in order to get her back.

He lost no time. As dawn flooded the sky he was already in the Scarsprings ancestral library. He and Fisher had spent many hours in this large, airy room together. He knew the book he wanted first. Shortly afterwards he crept back upstairs carrying one large, ancient and dusty volume bound in leather and decorated with bone.

'My JOURNAL of the MYSTERIES in the CITY
and WILDERNESS of ROCKSCAR'

By Archibald Scarspring

Ernesto sat on the bed and held the book tightly in his arms. It was written in code and, somehow, he would have to find the means to decipher it. But now it was morning and time to go down to the kitchen and fetch Fisher her favourite breakfast of sardines.

He lay back, still holding the book, still wearing his clothes and shoes. And fell asleep.

Chapter 30

The Ice Angel had been out every Tuesday and Thursday night for nearly four weeks. News had spread fast: sales were excellent.

Now it was early on the third Thursday evening and Clovis was upstairs in the map maker's shop, hoping that Mr Meakin would soon tell him it was time for him to go home.

Closing time was erratic. Customers visited Mr Meakin into the late hours and unpredictable things could happen. People arrived with their coat collars turned up and their hats tilted low over their eyes. The making and selling of maps was a sensitive business.

Not that Clovis had seen any exciting negotiations so far. He had been busy with the same task ever since he arrived to start the apprenticeship, sorting the store of old maps in the attics. The warm, dusty attic rooms had become his private workplace.

The showroom full of costly globes, known, unsurprisingly, as the Globe Room, was directly below on the first floor. Mr Meakin's Private Office was next, on the landing. However, he was usually down in the shop itself or working with the senior apprentice Mr Simou in the Drawing Room.

Clovis longed to sit there with them and start the business of learning to make maps himself. To him, the Drawing Room was a paradise. They sat at special tilted tables with special lamps: they were equipped with rolls of the best quality parchment, mysterious geometrical instruments, pots of pencils and pens and rows of bottles of coloured inks.

However, here he was, still in the attic, tidying and sorting and yawning and looking at the clock.

Mr Meakin appeared in the doorway, carrying a tray with a cup of tea for them both. He perched on the edge of a packing case, sipping and nodding, his glasses becoming mysterious with steam.

'You have sorted them very well. Very logically,' he said, in his gentle manner. 'You obviously have an excellent mind for organization.'

Clovis, faced with piles of maps, had sorted them first according to size, so that the exceptionally large ones could all be accommodated together in the only drawer that would take them.

Then, left with many smaller parchments to unroll and examine he had decided to divide them into street maps, island maps, ocean depth and pilot maps and maps of foreign places.

This left a number that could not be classified. Most of these looked even older than the rest, some were obviously damaged and all were rolled up, tied with thick black ribbon and bore the remains of wax seals, long ago broken.

They each had a small symbol enclosed in a circle drawn in the top left-hand corner. Clovis had seen this symbol before. It was a figure of a man and a dog, perhaps a wolf, drawn in various styles from one map to the next. The man was always holding the branch of a tree. The same symbol was on the map they had found in the chest hidden in the attic at home.

The parchments bearing this symbol were perplexing. Some appeared to be completely blank. Others depicted a recognizable subject – the city perhaps, or a stretch of coast – but bore no name and very little detail. Some had a name, but almost nothing else. There were blank spaces. Elegant arrows pointing nowhere.

In the end, concerned that he was not working fast enough, Clovis had put all these puzzles together in a drawer and labelled it 'Miscellaneous'.

'Have you lived here all your life?' asked Mr Meakin, examining the Miscellaneous drawer now.

'Yes,' said Clovis. Mariette had taught her sons to say as little as possible about themselves and to discourage questions.

'I see,' said Mr Meakin. 'And you attended Storm Hill School?'

'Yes.'

Mr Meakin sighed, rather as if Clovis had confirmed that he had served time in prison for a crime he had not committed.

'Do you know how many young persons sought to have an apprenticeship with this establishment this year, Mr Greenwood?' he asked, suddenly.

Clovis had no idea. He had walked in one day, secretly fascinated by the shop and the antique globes which stood in the bay window. He had asked Mr Meakin if he needed an apprentice.

'Do you recall that when you came into the shop that day, making, I suspect, an unplanned enquiry – a good map maker is drawn to the maps – do you remember that I asked you to hold something for me?'

Clovis nodded. He did, but he couldn't remember what it had been: he tried to look intelligent.

'I handed you a scrap of parchment. This scrap of parchment, in fact.'

Mr Meakin drew an envelope out of an inside pocket in his corduroy jacket. He opened it, tipped a yellowed piece of parchment into the palm of his hand and held it up.

Clovis peered at the parchment. He did remember it now. Or at least . . .

'The parchment you asked me to hold was part of a map,' he said, aware of Mr Meakin's thoughtful gaze from

187

behind the misted spectacles. 'You asked me what was on it and I said I thought it was Pedder's Town. It was very faint and worn-looking.'

Mr Meakin turned the parchment over so that he could see both sides.

'But that is just blank,' said Clovis. 'Except for that little symbol in the corner. So it can't be the same piece. There's nothing on it.'

Mr Meakin nodded, still watching Clovis closely. Then he finally looked away and took a sip of tea.

'We crowd ourselves into our city,' he said, as if talking to himself. 'We almost fall into the sea. We are so afraid of the wilderness that we have never even built roads inland.'

Clovis nodded: he tried to hide a yawn behind his hand.

'Only the freight train ventures across the wilderness,' added Mr Meakin. 'With one driver and one guard high up on an engine as tall as the second storey of this shop. Two very highly paid jobs and still very few are willing to undertake them. Driving the freight train from the docks, across the wilderness to the faraway cities inland. A few passengers in a locked coach with barred, blacked out windows.'

Clovis yawned again. It was all right for Zack, he could always have a quick nap in the day. Although he probably didn't. He was so buzzing with energy these days he was like some sort of mad wind-up toy . . . mixing, chopping, measuring out . . .

'Perhaps we are right to be afraid,' continued Mr Meakin, who clearly was in no hurry to finish this conversation, 'there are mountain lions, there are bears and there are wolves. And that is not all, of course. The wilderness is older than we know, Mr Greenwood. It holds secrets that we do not understand. Some say, dark and dangerous forces. Forces that resent our very presence.'

There was a knock on the attic door and Mr Simou came part of the way into the room, still wearing his green shade over his eyes, a pencil behind his ear.

'Mr Greenwood's brother has come to collect him,' he said. 'Will I lock up at the front now, Mr Meakin?'

'Certainly, Mr Simou,' said Mr Meakin. 'Perhaps you could offer Mr Greenwood's brother some refreshment. We will not be long.'

The door closed again.

Mr Simou's footsteps rattled away down the stairs. His pleasant and cheerful singing also faded, leaving Clovis and Mr Meakin in the honey-coloured light and the lazy, swirling particles of dust.

'One hundred and fifty young persons have asked me this year if they could enter into an apprenticeship here,' said Mr Meakin, in an altogether more business-like voice. 'One hundred and fifty.'

Clovis gasped.

'You are surprised? Last year we were approached by one hundred and thirty-four young persons. In the year before, I believe, it was nearer two hundred. I handed each of them this piece of parchment and I observed what happened next. Out of all of them, I chose only you.

'In order to acquaint oneself with some matters concerning maps it is necessary to untie the tight knots of knowledge, Mr Greenwood. To loosen the net of certainty. Take it, please. Now.'

Clovis was suddenly feeling horribly wide-awake. He took the piece of parchment from Mr Meakin's outstretched hand and held it away from him, as if it were dangerous.

'Good,' said Mr Meakin. 'Well done. Now tell me what you see.'

Clovis squinted at the parchment. The symbol of the man and the dog was hidden by his thumb. The rest of the page, which a moment ago had been blank, was once more decorated with a faded but ornate map of Pedder's Town. There were 'Secrette caves and cavernes' there, apparently, under the park. The Cat's Tail wound past the northern gates. It was labelled 'Foule and Loathsome'.

'Well?' whispered Mr Meakin.

'I don't understand,' said Clovis.

Mr Meakin removed his glasses. He took a handkerchief out of his pocket and polished away the steam. Clovis had the impression that he was trying to conceal some emotion.

'I believe you, Mr Greenwood,' he said, replacing

his glasses on his nose and looking straight at Clovis, his eyes sharp and bright. 'I believe that you do not understand at all.'

Clovis glanced at the door. 'If you don't mind, I'd like to—'.

'Stay!' Mr Meakin pulled maps out of the Miscellaneous drawer. 'I would like you to look at this, please.'

He unrolled a medium-sized parchment, swift and sure, catching the corners with his hands, weighing it down with his teacup. It was almost completely blank.

'Put your finger on the little symbol, Mr Greenwood. Your fingertip. Or, if you prefer, the ball of your thumb.'

His heart thumping, Clovis pressed the tip of his index finger on to the little man and his dog. He gave a cry. A map was appearing while he watched. It writhed on the page like something living. It uncurled and stretched and lay still.

'It's a map of the coast,' he said, fighting panic. 'And the city. But out into the water it shows the depths and reefs and rocks.'

Mr Meakin was nodding,

'And . . . and *wrecks* . . . out to sea . . . and quite close to the shore . . .'

Clovis stopped speaking. He could see a galleon now, lying close to the lighthouse point. Other ships lay stricken among the rocks further out to sea. A liner, its funnels still visible, lay terrible and broken close to the deep-water channel that would have taken it to the safety of Rockscar harbour.

Like coast dwellers everywhere Clovis had a grim respect for the sea. 'It's a map of wrecks,' he said, quietly.

'Our city exists because we have the only natural harbour along the entire coast,' said Mr Meakin. 'And even our harbour can be tragically difficult to reach.'

Clovis looked up and saw that Mr Meakin was transformed. He wasn't thinking about harbours. He didn't care about shipwrecks. He was smiling an immensely satisfied smile.

'Excellent, Mr Greenwood,' he said. 'You are the first one we at Meakin's have identified in over two hundred and fifty years.'

'Identified as what, exactly?' said Clovis.

Mr Meakin seized the map and rolled it up. 'As a map reader. A reader of a certain type of map. You have the ability to act as a bridge between worlds, Mr Greenwood. Our reality and the unseen reality which exists beside us. Overlapping in the same space. Just out of reach.'

Clovis heard Mr Simou singing on the stairs lower down the building. Then a murmur of voices. Of course, Zack was there, waiting for him. Good. In fact, very good.

'These maps are found only in Rockscar,' said Mr Meakin. 'And, likewise, those rare individuals who can read them. They date from a time when people were closer to the wilderness. I suspect that they understood it better and were less afraid.'

'I'm sorry,' said Clovis, standing up. 'I really do need to go home now, if that's all right.'

'Let me tell you what has just happened,' said Mr Meakin. 'You pressed your finger to the symbol in the circle. Then you saw the map. It appeared on the page. It did not appear for me, Mr Greenwood. I did not see anything. And when I press my finger to the stubborn little man, and believe me I have tried many times . . . still, nothing happens.'

'There will be a scientific explanation,' said Clovis. He took a couple of steps backwards towards the door.

'I've no doubt there will be. One day,' said Mr Meakin. 'But until science catches up with us, and everyone can read these troublesome maps as easily as you do, you will be a great asset to this firm, Mr Greenwood. Mr Anshelm Scarspring himself has a number of them. He will be delighted to know that I have found someone who can be of assistance.'

Clovis swayed where he stood.

'Are you unwell?' asked Mr Meakin, turning away to lock something, then turning back, eyes bright and quick, the keys gleaming in his hand.

'No,' said Clovis, feeling sick. 'No, sir. But I've really got to go.'

'Of course you have,' said Mr Meakin, smoothly. 'Your brother is down there waiting for you, is he not? I believe I met him when you arrived on your first day, didn't I? Excellent. I will come down with you. I would be most interested to meet him again.'

Clovis led the way down the twisting stairs. Towards the voices of Mr Simou and Zack. He nearly fell on a loose floorboard. It was difficult to think properly.

Chapter 31

M_r Simou poured the steaming chocolate out of the enamel chocolate pot into the large, waiting mugs.

'Of course the water is so especially foul now the summer's come, you can still taste it through the chocolate.'

'Don't worry,' said Zack. 'We're all used to it.'

Mr Simou put the pot back on the stove. 'You can actually smell the water now when you run the tap,' he added. 'Last night ours was *brown*. And the summer's hardly begun. Rain, that's what we need. No wonder the Scarsprings are so desperate, charging about everywhere looking for new sources.'

Zack nodded, raising his mug tentatively to his lips.

Mr Simou walked across the ancient linoleum and closed the door. He lowered his voice, turned to Zack like a conspirator. 'This ice van that's going round is pretty excellent. Late at night, Tuesdays and Thursdays. Just here and there. Delicious ices and decent water. I remember it from when I was a kiddie. The Ice Angel they call it. Brilliant. Only we don't talk about it too much, unless we're among friends – oh dear . . .'

Zack had started coughing.

'You *can* taste it, can't you?' said Mr Simou, fetching him a tea towel, all apologies and sympathy. 'Like bad eggs.'

The door opened.

Clovis came in, looking strange, followed by his boss. Zack put the mug of chocolate down on the table as Mr Meakin came swiftly towards him.

'Mr Greenwood, the *elder* Mr Greenwood. You'll be pleased to know that your brother is an excellent appprentice. He is *extremely* talented.'

Zack saw Clovis pulling a face at him from behind Mr Meakin's back.

'Would you like a cup of chocolate, sir?' asked Mr Simou. He was spooning yet more cocoa powder into the chocolate pot. 'We're having trouble disguising the taste tonight, I'm afraid.'

'For me, no,' said Mr Meakin. 'But I'm sure young Mr Greenwood needs one after his busy day among the maps.'

'No thank you,' said Clovis.

'Do you have a long journey home?'

'Yes. No. No,' said Clovis. 'But we need to go to um, to the Flower Market, don't we, Zack? We've got to um, um . . .'

'Get some flowers . . . for our mother,' said Zack, slowly, watching his brother's face. 'It's her birthday.'

'Have a biscuit to take with you,' said Mr Simou, opening

a battered tin with a picture of the lighthouse on the side.

'I'm OK, thanks, we're OK, we've really got to go,' said Zack, quickly.

'We've got to go,' said Clovis.

Mr Meakin reached for the biscuit tin, seemed to take it and then somehow dropped it on to the floor. Golden biscuits shot across the tiles in all directions: everyone tried to help.

'How clumsy of me, how clumsy of me,' he exclaimed, waving his arms. 'Please hold this precious parchment for me, Mr Greenwood, I can't let you young people do all the work.'

Zack was happy to be polite. He took the parchment, catching a glimpse of a little round picture of some sort just before his fingers covered it up. He stood still, anxious not to damage it. It looked very old, a torn-off piece of something bigger.

The tumult concerning the biscuits subsided. He realized that Clovis was staring at him. Raised his eyebrows in return.

'So clumsy, so clumsy,' repeated Mr Meakin. 'I don't think we should eat them now, not when they've been on the floor. Would you take them out to the dustbin, Mr Simou? No, no, Mr Greenwood, don't give it back yet. Just tell me what you think of it.'

Zack peered at the torn parchment.

'We've got to go now,' said Clovis. He looked

terrible. Was he ill? Was that why he was so desperate for them to go?

'It's a torn piece of parchment,' said Zack. Mr Meakin seemed to be waiting for him to say more. 'I don't know what else to say, really,' he added. 'I don't know much about things like this. It looks old.'

'Just blank is it?' said Mr Meakin. Zack was shocked to see him wink at Clovis, now staring at the floor.

He turned the parchment over and looked at the other side.

'Just blank,' he said. He moved his fingers. 'Except for this little circle with a drawing in it.'

'Just blank, dear me, dear me, I *am* surprised,' said Mr Meakin. He took the parchment from Zack's hand and immediately pressed it into Mr Simou's, who looked at it, and at him, in consternation.

'It's blank, isn't it?' cried Mr Meakin, glancing at Clovis again.

Mr Simou nodded. A hint of irritation, barely visible, in his thoughtful eyes.

'Well, there we are. There we are.' Mr Meakin took the parchment again, clapping Clovis on the back. 'An excellent day's work, Mr Greenwood. 'Don't let me delay you. The Flower Market closes early on a Thursday evening, you know. Make sure you get a good night's rest. You need to nurture talent like yours. Eat well, get plenty of sleep, that's the way.'

And he strutted out of the kitchen like a well-fed pigeon, looking straight ahead, as if Zack and Mr Simou no longer existed.

Chapter 32

A dry wind was funnelling up Parchment Street. Zack and Clovis stood putting their helmets on in a gust of blowing litter and crushed flower heads.

'What the heck's the matter with you?' asked Zack. 'Why were you so keen to make a getaway?'

'It's just been a very long day, that's all.' Clovis was messing about with his chinstrap. His voice was indistinct. His mind was full of maps that drew themselves: maps that he could see and Zack, it seemed, couldn't.

'Are you ill, or something? Or have you gone all white-looking because you're so talented?'

'NO, SHUT UP. I wanted to go home. OK? It's very, very . . . *intense* in there sometimes.'

'Intense? In a map shop?' Zack couldn't help grinning. A mistake.

'It's not just a shop. OK? They make maps there. And, and they read them. All sorts of maps.'

Zack frowned. 'And why was Meakin making such a fuss over a bit of torn parchment? What was all that about?'

Clovis hesitated. He jammed his helmet on his head. 'Nothing,' he said, savagely.

Zack climbed on to the scooter. 'Well, I had quite an interesting chat with Simou. He's thinking of asking you if you can do some modifications to his Bellisima Series 6. He'd like a bigger rear-view mirror, some sort of fog lamp, preferably like yours—'

'Do you know anything about invisible ink?' shouted Clovis from behind him.

Zack gave up.

'Not really,' he shouted back. 'I never did listen at school.'

They were not, of course, going to the Flower Market. They went up Parchment Street, then right, then left, on higher and higher through the narrow streets. The city was crowned with circles of wheeling sea birds. The evening was golden.

Meakin's was not the only place that was discreetly open after closing time. Most shops and businesses stayed open late in Rockscar, some all night, especially when it was known that a steamer would be coming into the harbour on a late tide. Rich travellers liked to explore before they sailed on to distant, warmer places.

Zack and Clovis passed many such well-dressed persons now, wandering in the jewellers' district, riding the scooter rickshaws with the coloured parasols.

'I bet they'd like a decent ice cream,' yelled

Zack over his shoulder.

But Clovis, worried and very miserable, only grunted in reply.

Chapter 33

The same night, much later, just before dawn. Despite being exhausted, Zack couldn't sleep.

He'd spent the afternoon doing mortal combat with a recipe for blackcurrant water ice and pistachio melts that had rapidly become pistachio cinders.

And then . . . well, anyway – he peered blearily at his alarm clock in the half-light – *anyway*, he'd been hectic all that day, burning ingredients by mistake and *then* he'd fetched Clovis from Meakin's, because Clovis' scooter needed a new tyre, not that *he'd* seemed very grateful, and *then* he'd driven the Ice Angel round the city like a maniac and here he was, finally in bed and *still* awake and any minute now it was going to be morning . . .

Moe was in his usual place next to Zack's feet: he sat up suddenly, ears swivelling.

Zack sat up too: there it was again.

A grinding and a creaking: somewhere above them.

He got out of bed, pulled back the curtains and let grey light into the room.

Moe was revealed already standing by the hatch.

'I'm coming,' mumbled Zack.

Perhaps he hadn't been as awake as he thought. Where were his slippers? Did he need slippers? He stubbed his toe on the bedstead and cursed. There it was again. A crunching of gears muffled by stone.

Zack opened the hatch, pushed his hair out of his eyes and nearly fell down the steep spiral stairs, his hands skidding on the sides, his bare feet bouncing painfully from one step to the next.

Shortly after this he arrived in Clovis' room.

The bed was empty, neat and undisturbed: it looked as if Clovis had been up all night. Zack hesitated, puzzling. Then he thought he heard someone moving about in the attic. He went up the ladder and stopped to rub his eyes.

Clovis was sitting on the floor in the middle of the room still fully dressed in the clothes he'd been wearing during the day. He had two lanterns and all sorts of other things around him; a magnifying glass, the heavy brass microscope from his bedroom, bottles of ink, sheets of paper. The chest they had discovered sticking out of the wall that night was exposed again. The lid open: the contents neatly piled on the floor beside it.

Except the map. The map was spread out on the floor. Clovis looked at Zack as if he were committing a crime and Zack had walked in on the middle of it.

'What's going on?' asked Zack. And then added, being

finally very much and fully awake, 'How did you get the chest to come out of the wall again?'

'I'm looking at this map,' said Clovis. His eyes were red. Had he been crying?

Zack lurched forward against the edge of the hatch as Moe, who was behind him on the ladder, suddenly climbed up him and over his shoulder and into the room.

'I wish he wouldn't do that,' said Zack.

'I was going to come and get you,' said Clovis. 'Depending on what happened. I got the chest to come out of the wall by working out the most likely place for the control lever. It's actually next to where the wireless aerial lead comes out of the wall in the living room. I think Dad must have installed this chest at the same time as the aerial.'

'What about the map?' asked Zack. He was used to Clovis working things out but he didn't want to hear an example in detail just this minute.

'Something happened at Meakin's,' said Clovis. 'He cornered me when I was working in the attic and showed me this old parchment with the little symbol of the man and the dog in the corner. He got me to put my thumb on the symbol. It felt really weird, sort of warm. Then I could see the map. It was on the parchment. It was a map of wrecks out to sea.'

Zack sat down heavily on a packing case labelled 'Spare Parts for Knitting Machine'.

'It felt warm? You saw things that weren't there?

Are you ill? You look awful.'

Moe was sniffing the map, the map chest and the little bag containing the watch.

'I'm not ill,' said Clovis, looking awful.

'So were the things that weren't there there or not?'

Clovis breathed in slowly, 'Well, Meakin said, well, he said that I, well—'

'He said that you should see a doctor?'

'No. Listen—'

'Because lack of sleep can make you see things. If it goes on too long.'

'NO, Zack, listen. He said that I was sort of linking realities together.'

'You were what?'

'I know it sounds ridiculous. He's probably a bit mad. I've been trying to work out what really happened. I thought I'd try it again on a different map. They've got loads with the symbol on at Meakin's. He's had me tidying them all up.'

'Perhaps he put something in your tea to make you work harder and it jumbled your brain.'

'SHUT UP, Zack. You don't understand. I'm the first one in two hundred and fifty years.'

Clovis paused.

'And you can see extra bits on maps, that other people can't see?'

'Yes. On certain maps. With the symbol on. And it's the little man with the dog, except now I'm thinking perhaps it's a wolf, and I thought I remembered seeing it on this map. This one. From the chest.'

Zack left the packing case and peered at the map.

'Look. You're right! It has got the little man in the corner! I thought I remembered it just now when you said . . . If you can do it, I'm your brother, then I should be able to do it too, other realities, here we come . . .' He leant forward, smoothing out the parchment, and thumped his hand down hard. His index finger, stained black and purple with berry juice, covered the symbol of the little man.

He stared at the map. The troll curled against the mountain, almost filling the wilderness, the little angel over his heart and the dragon in the shape of the city of Rockscar . . . the monster in the sea.

Nothing changed.

'It's not a special map,' he said, after a moment. 'I can't see anything different at all.'

He glanced at Clovis: Clovis didn't seem to want to meet his eye.

'Go on then. Put your finger on the little symbol,' said Zack. 'Do whatever you did at Meakin's.'

Slowly Clovis reached out and put his fingertip on the drawing of the little man. Immediately he shuddered and rocked backwards.

'It's all right, ' he gasped, as Zack half stood, ready to catch him. 'It's a bit like, sort of, electricity. I'm getting used to it.'

'Well,' whispered Zack.

'Pass me the pen and paper,' said Clovis. 'I'm going to copy it down.'

Zack pushed a sheet of paper towards him from the shade and into the lantern light. He handed him a pen. Wordless. The only sound now was the scrape of the nib. And Moe snuffling as he breathed, his chin on his paws.

Several minutes passed. Zack watched as, upside down, he saw Clovis draw the outline of another map, following, but not quite, the shapes within the first. He made small crosses here and there. Most in the city. Two in the empty ravine next to the Wolf Road where they had stopped the van and Moe had howled. One high up, not far from the snow line.

That done, he started writing, biting his lip, copying a line of script. Copying from the map on which Zack could see not one single cross, not one single word.

At last he was finished and he took his finger away.

Zack seized the map and swivelled it round. He pressed his fingertip as hard as he could on the little symbol. He jabbed at it. He slapped his palm down on it with all his force, hurting his hand.

But the hidden map did not appear for Zack.

'Show me what you drew,' he snapped at Clovis.

Clovis handed him the paper: Zack snatched it from him.

'Rockscar City and surrounding wilderness. Being a chart

of all water sources,' he read out loud. 'This is dynamite.'

Clovis seemed to have retreated into himself.

'That's our spring there,' added Zack. 'The one on its own near the top. This map shows our spring. It shows our caves. It shows the tunnels and the place where we keep the scooters above Storm Hill.'

'I know,' said Clovis.

'Do you think there are other copies of this?'

'I don't know.'

'Scarspring would kill to get his hands on this,' said Zack. 'Look, there's two more springs down near the Wolf Road. And I don't even think he's found all the ones in the city.'

They both stared at the pencil drawing.

'No wonder the water tastes so bad,' added Zack. 'Look how low down most of the springs are, they've practically come through the whole mountain.'

'Meakin said I had the ability to be a bridge between different worlds,' said Clovis. 'I've been thinking about what he meant.'

'And?'

'I've no idea.'

Normally Zack would have been bothered by the misery he could see on his brother's face. But he was far too miserable himself to care. He pulled Balthazar's ring off his finger. Ever since they found it he had worn it when they were out in the Ice Angel and, secretly, at night while he slept.

He threw it down on the map.

'This map is something to do with him. You can read it. Maybe he could read it too. I can't. You should be wearing this. Not me.'

Clovis picked up the ring and stared at it. The worn metal. The little row of four blue pearls and the space where the fifth one was missing.

'So?' spat Zack. ' Are you getting a message off that now as well?'

Always, all their lives, Clovis had been better at keeping his temper.

'Look, we think the person on the map, the one who is where the wilderness is, is a troll, right?'

'And?'

'And the little symbol in the corner of the map, it's a man with a very big dog. I think it's a wolf. They're wilderness creatures, right? He hasn't got the beard and everything, but he's got the wolf, next to him. I mean none of this is drawn that well. But what if he's meant to be a troll, too? Then the maps like this, with the little symbol on, would all have something to do with trolls.'

Moe yawned enormously. It was hard to believe that such an average-sized dog could have so many teeth.

'Maybe the trolls *drew* these maps,' said Clovis. 'Maybe they once belonged to them. Maybe that's the other world Meakin was going on about. Their world.'

Until very recently Zack would have made a scornful

joke at this point. Maybe about big hairy monsters with big hairy monster hands. He almost tried to now. But the truth was that he remembered the darkness that had pressed against him on Excelsior Avenue, pinning him against a tree. He had felt hot breath on his face as something turned away and let him go. He was sure of it. He had spoken about it beside Balthazar's spring in the water cave. But he hadn't told anyone else. Not even Clovis.

'You're saying they are really out there?' He jerked his head towards the shuttered window. 'And they can do things like drawing maps?'

Clovis was about to make some sort of reply. There were noises from downstairs. Moe jumped to his feet. A dull roar and a rattle from the water pipes. Mariette was awake, up and in the bathroom four floors below.

The brothers began to quickly and quietly put things away. Clovis pushed the ring into Zack's hand, closed the chest and eased it back into its hiding place in the wall. They climbed down the ladder, closing the hatch behind them.

Back in his room Zack stood, irresolute: turning the ring over in his fingers.

Chapter 34

Zack could still hear the noises from the water pipes. He looked at his alarm clock. It was six in the morning.

Leaving Moe curling up on the bed he set off again down to the floor devoted to the spectacular bathrooms: built by his great-grandfather, Izekiel Jump, a man who had loved hot baths.

Zack waited by the bathroom door. Eventually Mariette came out in her dressing gown, bringing with her a gust of steamy air and the rosy scent of soap.

'Oh, hello, Zack,' she said. She was wearing a pink plastic shower hat with a bow on the side: with her hair out of sight she looked different and older.

'Some people we were selling ice cream to said that I don't look much like Dad and that Clovis does,' said Zack. 'In fact, I don't think they thought that I looked like Dad at all.'

Mariette frowned.

'You're still wearing your bath hat thing,' he added.

She pulled the hat off and her hair unravelled on to

her shoulders and on down her back. Clovis had red hair too. And he wasn't very tall. And his eyes were like hers, brown, under straight, dark eyebrows. In these ways he resembled her. But Tiny and Mittens Muldorn had immediately realized that he was Balthazar's son. So, he must look like Balthazar, too.

Zack was pale with a bony face. He was skinny and taller and his hair that was almost black. It wasn't thick and wavy like Clovis and Mariette's. It flopped into his eyes. He had assumed, and so had Clovis, that all these features had come from Balthazar; but perhaps Tiny and Mittens were right and he didn't look like Balthazar at all.

He loomed over his mother now in the dark passageway. The lantern raised, catching them both in a net of light and shadows: sometimes at Storm Hill School he had been called BirdMan.

Mariette's hands were busy, plaiting her hair, winding the plait round her head. Her dressing gown pocket, it seemed, was full of hairgrips. She took them one at a time to fix her hair in place.

'I mean, you know.' Zack felt almost too tired to speak. 'Clovis looks like you.'

Mariette nodded. She took another grip, then another: then the last one.

'You know he loved you very, very much, Zack, don't you?' she said. 'Very much. He was very proud of you.'

'I just wondered if I'm like him at all. Clovis looks like

him, and he's good at loads of stuff, like Dad was, like doing things to engines and maps and stuff. And I don't look like him. And I'm not clever either, except I suppose, you know, making the ices and so on . . .'

'You look like yourself, Zack.' She stared at him intently. 'And you are yourself. That's what matters. I think you're clever. There's just different sorts of cleverness, that's all.'

'But, I mean, for example, was he tall? Did he have dark hair?'

She seemed to look past him for a moment. 'He was taller than me,' she said, and smiled. 'And his hair was dark.'

'Everybody's taller than you,' said Zack.

Mariette laughed. 'There was a girl at school with me, like a little doll, she was still modelling children's clothes when she was twenty, so I heard. Beautiful.'

Zack put the lantern on the floor. He felt as if he could go to sleep where he stood. A lost ship, becalmed in impenetrable fog.

Chapter 35

Two months had gone by. The Jump kitchen had become the Ice Angel factory: the family were living on sandwiches.

It was the hottest, driest summer for years. For the first time in living memory, the Scarspring Water Company had been forced to start rationing the water. Zack and Clovis were selling more ices every time they went out. People who had spent their day behind desks and counters in banks and offices now gathered in small nervous groups on certain street corners at certain times. They appointed lookouts who were more nervous still and who walked self-consciously backwards and forwards, checking their watches and occasionally knocking into bins: their smart suits visible under their especially chosen oldest coats.

In the Child of Flowers Charity Hospital nurses gave the children cups of delicious iced water flavoured with the juice of fruit Zack had bought only the day before down in the fruit markets. Fruit from the warmer countries far away in the south. Pomegranate, mango and golden blissberry.

These drinks were free, like the ones the Ice Angel delivered to the Paupers' Hospital. Dehydration was making some people ill.

All this, of course, was paid for from the profits made selling the fancy ices to the wealthier customers. Customers like the employees of Excelsior Broadcasting and the cast of *Dinah Dibbs*.

It was a Thursday. The Ice Angel drew up outside the side entrance of Excelsior Broadcasting House and the occupants stayed in the cab for a few moments longer listening to Barnacle Radio, turned down very low.

'We regret that our regular reporter, Momma Truth, is unable to bring you the news tonight,' said a man, shuffling papers about much too near the microphone. 'Water rationing continues. It still hasn't rained. Mysterious vandals continue to interfere with the Scarsprings' operations. Anshelm the slightly mad is blaming trolls. His little attack dog, Golightly, hasn't said anything. A policeman we know has suggested it's down to someone with a grudge against the Scarsprings. Plenty of possible candidates, then. Easier to blame trolls than to admit that you might have a little bit of real human opposition, eh, folks?

'And for those of you who don't have time to get to all the fashionable parties, did you know that Ernesto, the heir to our lovely Scarspring empire, was twelve years old this spring. Bit of a mystery man, isn't he? Why doesn't he come out in the daylight? Are they ashamed of him? Nice conclusion is he's just a shy individual. What did happen to his father by the way? Something of a scholar too, so they say. Killed by a mountain lion. No body ever found. Hmmm. Convenient . . .'

There was more shuffling of papers and someone coughed. Clearly this presenter was not as experienced as the formidable Momma Truth.

'Sorry about that. Right, let's have a few water statistics. Black market permits to install new bath or toilet in your home now cost twice as much as a completely new Bellisima 7 or five times as much as a completely new Tugalug 45 . . .'

'Who wants a Tugalug 45 anyway,' muttered Zack.

'However,' the presenter lowered his voice, 'it's not all Doomsville here in the Big Barnacle. Some folk have been visited by an angel. She's a bit of an Ice Queen. But she's got a warm heart. Let's hope she's going to minister to us here for many nights to come. If you're out there, pretty lady, take it easy, take care and keep watching your back. Good night and safe sailing from the voice of the outlaw truth here at Barnacle Radio.' There was a drum roll and a clash of cymbals.

Clovis looked across at his brother.

'Kings of the Mountain,' he whispered. Zack nodded, grinning in the dark.

Chapter 36

'People, people, PEOPLE,' implored Mr Featherplum, waving a bundle of scripts. 'Your attention, *please*.'

The cast of *Dinah Dibbs, Girl Detective* was gathered around Zack and the ice cart.

'As you know, our excellent writer, Ms Brown, has been in hospital for the last two weeks. I'm delighted to tell you that she has now been blessed with a healthy baby boy, but the doctors have advised her to rest for at least another three weeks. However, she has loyally continued to write our scripts for *Dinah* and her daughter Frankie has delivered these this evening. We are most *grateful* . . .'

He glared at the backs of the cast. At least they weren't actually talking among themselves, but that was probably because their mouths were full.

'*Most grateful*,' he repeated. 'But it does, of course, mean, it does mean, it, it, does . . .'

'He's going to sneeze again,' Frankie whispered to Zack.

Zack smiled, scoop in hand, busy dispensing the latest craze of the rich and successful: Pecan Nut Cream with

Exploding Alphabet Cinnamon.

'ATCHOO!' bellowed Mr Featherplum. 'Allergy,' he added. 'Do excuse me.'

Everyone was excusing him. The small freckled man who played the Maharajah asked quietly for an extra Lemon and Lime Icicle to take home for his daughter.

'So we have had no chance to *read through* this script before going live,' insisted Mr Featherplum. 'A most unusual situation for us. But I have great faith in Ms Brown, she has proved herself an excellent scriptwriter over many years. And, of course, ATCHOO! I have great faith in all of YOU.'

He wiped his forehead with his handkerchief. The air conditioning down here in the studios was old and inefficient and had to be turned off during broadcasting because it hummed.

'Three minutes,' he said, peering at his watch.

Zack had served everyone. He closed the sliding doors on the side of the cart.

'We are expecting record audiences tonight,' continued Mr Featherplum, his voice now slightly hoarse. 'As you know, a number of storylines . . .' he coughed, 'STORYLINES should be *concluding*: the mystery of the famous film star and her secret twin, the underground tunnel leading from the bank vaults to the head master's office at the school, the priceless jewels hidden in the lighthouse guarded by the luminous assassin who has been following the charming Maharajah. What a cliffhanger.' He paused to sneeze.

'Literally. We left Dinah hanging by her fingertips on to the ledge under the lighthouse window, inches from death in the savage sea.

'We believe one third of the population of our great city will be tuning in to hear what happens next. We may even be mentioned on the *news*. I, for one, cannot wait to hear what is written on these pages.'

Zack glanced at Frankie. Then looked back at her again. She had a strange expression on her face: she caught his eye and grinned and then started biting her lip.

'My mum's in hospital. She had her baby but then she had to stay in a bit longer and rest.' Now she was actually wringing her hands together.

Zack nodded.

'Don't come up yet,' said a tiny crackling voice from the cart. Clovis, back in the Ice Angel. 'Gentlemen fencing off a drain. I've got to move. Don't come out.'

Frankie had never asked Zack any questions. She didn't now. Instead she pointed at the room through the glass wall to the right.

'I'm going in there to listen to the beginning,' she whispered. 'Do you want to wait with me until your cart says it's safe?'

'Thirty seconds,' said Mr Featherplum, gliding between microphones. 'ATCHOO! The mood is *danger*, the mood is *fear*. Fingertips on that windowsill, people. FEEL the mood. Breathe it in.'

Frankie led the way and Zack pushed the cart after her. They entered the corridor and almost immediately left it again. Now they were in the adjoining room. They could see the cast gathering round the microphones, some still holding ices, finally looking at the first pages of their scripts.

He made Frankie a Raspberry Swirl. No point in panicking. Clovis could drive the van: just about.

He tried to concentrate on the actors on the other side of the glass. They were raising their eyebrows and pulling faces at each other and pointing at their lines.

Music played. The illuminated sign on the wall changed from 'Standby' to 'On the Air'.

'Oh, Dinah,' said Mrs Dibbs. 'How lovely to see you. I thought you were hanging from the edge of the windowsill under the lighthouse window by your fingertips.'

'Yes, I was,' said Dinah. 'But I was rescued by a giant albatross. It picked me up and put me down in Pedder's Town.'

'Oh good,' said Mrs Dibbs.

'It was really cute,' said Dinah.

Zack could see some of the cast who weren't in this scene turning the page to look ahead.

'The luminous assassin and the Maharajah made friends,' said Dinah. 'They both like hamsters. The Maharajah has a pet hamster that lives in a little golden hamster house. It's wonderful how pets can bring people together in better understanding and harmonics.'

'Oh yes,' said Mrs Dibbs.

'You know the film star who discovered that she has a secret twin?' said Dinah.

'Yes,' said Mrs Dibbs.

'She likes pets too. She's got a boomerang.' The woman who played Dinah looked up from her script and pulled a face at the woman playing Mrs Dibbs. 'She keeps it in the bath,' she added.

'Ah, here's your father now,' said Mrs Dibbs. 'Just in from counting his pigeons.'

'Hello, Dinah,' said Captain Dibbs in his booming sea captain voice. 'How charming you look in that grey dress. I gather lace is most terribly fashionable this summer. And what a stylish flower in your hair.'

Even Zack knew that Captain Dibbs had never shown any interest in fashion before.

'Yes, it's really important to express yourself, Dad,' said Dinah. 'Anyway, I'm opening a new detective agency. I'm going to find lost and stolen pets.'

'Oh good,' said Mrs Dibbs. 'Let's have a cup of tea.'

'The conductor of the Rockscar Sympathy Orchestra wants me to find his lost chinychinchilla. He is an egotestical git but I will do it because I love animals.'

Zack could see Mr Featherplum jumping, waving and pointing. He made frantic gestures at the cast. He drew his finger across his throat. However they were all concentrating on the script and didn't see him.

'It's pets for me from now on,' said Dinah.

For once, the cast seemed to be really enjoying the performance.

'I'm just going to count my pigeons again,' said Captain Dibbs. 'I'm a bit of a pigeon maniac, you know.'

The sound lady had boiled the kettle. Now she was pouring water in and out of cups.

'I have a healthy lifestyle with low salt and no suffocating fats,' said the Captain.

'I have taken on a very important case,' said Dinah. 'The case of the kidnapped cat. My client must remain private for his own good. But I want him to know that the collar has helped me to find a lead. I am closing in on the criminals. Take heart. You will see your cat again. Dinah Dibbs is on the case.'

There was a burst of music.

The commercial break had begun. The cast were smiling and slapping each other on the back and showing each other things on the following pages.

'All clear,' whispered Clovis' tiny voice. 'But hurry.'

Chapter 37

'Can I have a lift with you?' said Frankie. Zack pulled the cart backwards into the corridor again. He and Clovis had agreed that they must never let anyone else inside the van.

'I'm sorry, it's not really convenient,' he said, uncomfortably.

She followed him into the lift. 'Only I'm not really supposed to be here,' she added, speaking fast. 'There isn't a car to take me home. I'm in the middle of trying to solve an important case. It's my first one. I had to send my client a message over the radio. In the script of *Dinah Dibbs*. I had to take the real scripts, they're in my bag.' She patted her shoulder bag: it did look rather full. 'The scripts were supposed to go by courier but I intercepted them and brought mine instead. I came on the tram but it's very late now.'

The lift doors opened, revealing the foyer and the commissionaire, waiting, as usual, to let Zack out of a side door near the boiler rooms.

'I was just listening to *Dinah Dibbs*, Miss Frankie,' said

the commissionaire. 'Most entertaining. Your mother seems to be taking the plot in quite a new direction.'

Frankie smiled, and looked at the carpet.

'Will your car be meeting you at the front?'

She shook her head, avoiding Zack's eye. 'The car couldn't come to collect me tonight. So Mr Greenwood is giving me a lift,' she said. 'Aren't you, Mr Greenwood? Because my mum's in hospital, you know, and it's a terrible long way to walk in the dark by myself at my age on my own.'

Zack was sure Clovis would have been able to think of something to say; but he wasn't Clovis and he couldn't. A few moments later he was pushing the cart towards the Ice Angel, parked in the side road, a bit further away than where he had left it, on account of the work that had been done on the drains.

Frankie kept trotting ahead and then turning to wait for him. All the time she was looking up and down the avenue, her eyes rather wide, her hands busy with the flower in her hair, or the strap on her shoulder bag, or her long necklace of beads.

Nearly there. Zack had just had the idea of offering to pay for her to go home in a taxi. Clovis and Moe were both staring at him through the windscreen: Clovis frowned.

'Look, I didn't actually say you could have a lift—' he began.

'This is the Ice Angel van, isn't it?' She ran the last few steps and stopped in front of the angel. 'It's just like my mum described it. She remembers it from when Mr Jump, I mean Greenwood, used to come round selling ices before. She was a junior scriptwriter then. She wrote the little trailers for the next day's programmes. We know you're outlaws and everything. Everyone knows your ices are nothing to do with the Scarsprings. My mum knew Mr Jump, I mean Mr Greenwood, in the olden days, at the Midnight Café.'

Zack stared at her.

'She used to go there a lot. She knew your mum too, when your mum used to work there. Really wild times—'

'Your mum knew—'

'She reckons she introduced your mum to Mr Greenwood. Isn't that sweet? And she was there when you were born. Aren't you called Zacharias or something?'

'Zack, Zachary. My name's Zachary,' said Zack.

'But I think they lost touch after that,' added Frankie.

With a metallic clunk and a creak of hinges, Clovis opened the driver's door and jumped down on to the pavement.

'This is Frankie Brown,' said Zack. 'Her mum knew our mum and our dad, I think. At the Midnight Café. Mum used to work there, apparently. Frankie, this is my brainy little brother Clovis.'

Clovis nodded.

'She needs a lift.'

Zack pushed the ice cart round to the back of the van,

226

leaving Clovis and Frankie together.

'Oh, look at the angel,' whispered Frankie. 'She is so beautiful. Is that how your van got its name?'

Clovis nodded. 'We think so.' He had spent the day staring at shipping charts, learning to read mysterious symbols. Decoding. Now he stared at Frankie Brown: little girl face under grown-up lipstick and paint.

'Are you in some sort of trouble?' he asked.

'I just need to get home.' She managed a grin.

A tremendous bang from the back of the van: Zack lowering the ramp.

'My mum's talked to me about the Ice Angel. She reckons she introduced your mum and Mr Greenwood, at the Midnight Café. I mean, we know that's not his real name, but my mum says never to use real names if someone has a pretend one because they must have a good reason, which obviously you do, because of the ice cream and everything.'

Clovis opened the passenger door of the van. Moe jumped down and started sniffing Frankie's feet.

'They were friends for years. My mum helped your mum out and stuff. When she was pregnant. She's called Mariette, isn't she? I think it's a really pretty name. My mum nearly called me Mariette, after your mum—'

'How do you know her name? When who was pregnant? What are you talking about?'

'Your mum. You know, before she met Mr Greenwood.

227

My mum helped her out with being pregnant and everything. Helped her keep it all hush-hush. In fact, your mum actually stayed at my mum's house when she had Zacharias, I mean, Zachary. My mum was there when he was born. Because your mum didn't have anyone else to be with her. The midwife let my mum cut the diabolical cord. So that sort of makes us like family, doesn't it? A bit? This dog is really cute, isn't he? He's got such big feet.'

Clovis stepped backwards and banged his elbow on the edge of the van door. A taxi sped past and turned on to Excelsior Avenue, brakes squealing.

'What do you mean? What do you mean, my mum was pregnant before she met my dad?'

Frankie looked up at him. Her expression slowly changed.

'Oh dear,' she whispered. 'Nothing. I don't mean anything.'

She bent down again to Moe and began stroking the top of his head. 'My mum would be furious, she's always saying that I never know when to shut up.'

Creaks and thuds from inside the van: any minute now Zack would start locking up.

'Don't say "nothing",' whispered Clovis rapidly, clutching his aching elbow. 'You said that my mum was pregnant *before* she met my dad. You said your mum helped her and that Zack,' he paused, concentrating, 'and that Zack was born at your mum's house and it all had to be hush-hush . . .

you're saying that my mum had Zack before she met our dad? That's what you're saying?'

Oh great, now it looked as if she was starting to cry.

He leant towards her. He forced his voice to stay calm. 'Please would you explain what all this is about.'

'But I thought you must know. I mean, didn't you wonder why Mittens went for your brother at the Midnight Café the first night you went there?'

'*You* know about *that*?'

'I know the band. I know them really well. They were all talking about it. Everyone in the band said it was completely unrespectable and ridiculous of Mittens. People can't help how they look. They said your brother acted like a gentleman. It's not who you are, it's not who your father happened to be, it's how you conduct yourself. And your brother acted with great dignity. That's what they said.'

Clovis stared at her.

'I think he's really nice,' added Frankie.

'Hang on,' whispered Clovis, finding his voice. 'What do you mean people can't help how they look? What do you mean, *it's not who your father happened to be*?'

'They can't help who they look like.'

Clovis felt as if he were trying to dance. Something he had never been able to do. He took a deep breath. 'You're saying that Mittens Muldorn attacked my brother, when he first saw him, and didn't know who he was, because my brother looks like someone else, someone Mittens doesn't like?'

'Of course. Mittens is like that. I mean, lots of people don't like him, but—'

'Don't like *who*? Mittens?'

'No,' Frankie frowned, which made her look younger than ever. 'I don't mean Mittens, I mean—'

'Get in, get in,' said Zack, stomping round from the back of the van and taking off his white hat. 'We don't hang around on the pavement. Might attract attention.'

Now everyone was climbing into the cab. Moe was licking Frankie's hand. Clovis was fretting over the safety harnesses.

'Tell us anything you know about our dad,' said Zack, a moment later.

'The hand brake's still on,' said Clovis quietly. He was feeling as if someone had poured cold water over him. 'And we don't know where we're going.'

'JacksonTown,' said Frankie. 'I live in Jackson Avenue.'

JacksonTown was in the southeast of the city, a district well-known for its artists' studios and bars.

Zack raised his eyebrows at Clovis: he had expected somewhere a little more respectable.

'Fine,' he said. 'We can get there in about half an hour. Can you remember your mum ever saying anything about what happened to our dad? Because we don't know . . .'

Just then, Moe started to whine. It was an extraordinary

sound and not one that he made often.

'Is he all right?' asked Frankie, who was sitting next to him. 'I think he's looking in that weird mirror. Is that a periscope?'

Chapter 38

'Someone's behind us,' said Zack, who also had the advantage of the periscope. 'Looks, like, looks like . . .troll's breath! It's a police van. They're sticking really close.'

'Turn off. Next corner,' said Clovis.

Frankie was craning forward, trying to look round Moe at the wing mirror.

'Sit *back*,' hissed Clovis. 'Don't let your harness go across your *neck*. In the event of an accident—'

'They've come too,' said Zack. 'They're getting closer. Perhaps they want to buy an ice cream.'

'Are we going to have a car chase?' asked Frankie, clasping her hands. 'Let's put our feet down and make them eat our dusters.'

The brothers and the dog ignored her. The wail of the police siren burst into life. A powerful engine roared and the police van suddenly shot past, the lamp flashing on its roof, filling the cab with savage red light.

Zack braked. The harnesses locked. The police van had swung diagonally in front of them, almost blocking the road.

'Should I talk to them?' whispered Frankie. 'I can tell them my mum knows Anshelm Scarspring.'

'I don't think that would help,' said Clovis.

Zack turned off the lights of the van, hiding the angel on the front with a little bit of dark. A policeman was getting out of the car. He walked over to the driver's door and Zack wound down the window.

'Good evening, gentlemen,' said the policeman. 'And lady,' he added, smiling like a shark. He wasn't big like Mittens the bouncer, he didn't need to be, he was armed with a Rockscar Night Patrol Stun Gun: the sort that often led to accidental death.

'Can I see your papers please?'

Zack had the papers ready, as always, in the pocket on the inside of the driver's door. He pulled them out now. The policeman shone his torch on the fake identity documents for Clovis and Zack and the even more fake registration documents for the Ice Angel.

'Fridge repairs,' said the policeman. His teeth were very white, with a diamond twinkling somewhere on the top deck.

Zack nodded. Sweat pricking his skin like needles.

The policeman kept hold of the papers.

'We're stopping all vehicles,' he said. 'Looking for anything suspicious. Plus, there's been a lot of vandalism. Scarspring property.'

'We don't look like trolls, do we?' said Frankie.

Zack felt every muscle in his body tighten a notch higher. Why, oh why had he allowed this girl to get into the van?

The policeman shone the beam of his torch into the cab.

'Please excuse my sister, Officer,' said Zack. 'We had to bring her with us. Our mum isn't well.'

The torch beam progressed slowly along from one face to another. The pale, black-haired, bony-faced boy at the wheel; the round and freckled face of the solid-looking, red-haired boy in the middle; the amber-skinned, dark-eyed girl . . .

'You're a bit dolled up for your age, aren't you, darling? And who's this whiskery little gent? Oh, a *doggie* . . . Well, I don't think I'd trust you lot to mend *my* fridge . . .'

'Our dad's in hospital too,' said Clovis.

'Strangest thing,' added the night policeman. 'I can hear a humming noise coming from inside this van. Sounds very like a freezer. Plus there is a very distinctive smell. Raspberry, is it? Blackcurrant? Officer Gusto! Can you join us please? And bring that list of wanted vehicles would you, my good man?' He grinned.

A second policeman got out of the car. He came slowly towards the van, sweeping the light of his torch over the front, dazzling the occupants.

'Don't need the list, Sergeant,' he said. 'This vehicle fits the description of that one that's been going about selling ices and such. Steward Golightly was down at the station yesterday, giving us the description.'

'Our mum and dad are dehydrogenated,' said Frankie. 'It affects your electrics and makes you dizzy.'

Clovis was leaning forward, a little bit at a time: both his hands were now very near the dashboard and its long and interesting array of lights and buttons and levers.

'We really shouldn't have brought our sister,' he said. 'She's ill too. She's got a problem with her mouth.'

'Look at this, Sarge,' said Officer Gusto. He had found the angel.

'That was in the description. Angel on the front. Golightly's pretty wound up about it. Doesn't want his boss to know. Wants it found and trashed soon as possible.'

Out of the corner of his eye, Zack could see Clovis turning the switch they had never used before. They had agreed that if they were ever stopped and it looked as if they were going to be arrested, or worse, then they would use what Clovis called the turbic escape blaster. He had assured him that it could not fail. Zack had not shared his optimism at the time. He didn't now.

Yet again the policeman scanned the false papers. Mariette had always obtained the best possible documents for her sons, the Greenwood brothers. Zack knew that the policeman was having trouble finding flaws.

He glanced to his left and saw that Clovis was helping Frankie put on the spare scooter helmet. Clovis had already managed to get his own on, although it was crooked. He had jammed Moe's on too. Too far forward. Only Moe's nose was showing.

'Better search it, Sarge,' said Officer Gusto, still shining his torch on the angel.

The mention of Steward Golightly had taken a little of the swagger out of the sergeant's manner. He was quieter, but more dangerous. 'Proper procedure,' he said softly, looking up into Zack's face and smiling his unpleasant smile. 'No hurry. Don't want to push the wrong van over a cliff. These people aren't going anywhere, Officer Gusto. Not now not ever again, I reckon.'

Zack's hands on the steering wheel were slippery with sweat. His heart was pounding. He looked at Clovis. Clovis nodded.

'Just unlocking the doors,' Zack said, trying to keep his voice steady, trying to keep some pretence of calm. He leant forward as a car driver might do to reach under the dashboard and release the lock on the bonnet. Found the lever which was the second of the three controls which would engage the turbic escape blaster. Closed his hand around it. Clovis had wanted to do a practice escape up on the Wolf Road. But they never had and now this was the real thing and Zack had no idea what to expect. He pulled the lever.

Then, smiling at the policeman, he pressed the black button with the picture of the lightning bolt on it, and felt the van shudder. Something came to life at the back near the rear axle. There was a muffled roar from the engine. Louder and louder. Now it was like sitting on a volcano.

'Hold on!' yelled Clovis. 'GO!'

Chapter 39

Zack flung back the hand brake, slammed into first gear and put his foot down as hard as he could on the accelerator.

With a boom and a flash of orange flames from some pipe at the back, the Ice Angel shot forwards. Everyone inside was screaming, including Moe. Zack hauled on the wheel, they careered round the police van, mounted the pavement, frightened a lamppost and regained the road.

In another world Clovis might have become the inventor of the jet engine. It was quite possible that nothing had ever travelled so fast in history of the city of Rockscar.

As they took the first corner on two wheels Zack caught a glimpse of the scene behind them in the periscope.

The police van, the driver's door swinging open, lights flashing, front wheels already skidding on the shimmering road, made treacherous by Clovis' emergency ice dispenser.

Another corner. Tyres screeching. And then down a hill.

'Westerly direction!' yelled Clovis. 'Harbour!'

Zack leant all his weight on the wheel. All the controls felt different. Some heavier. Some alarmingly lighter. Another corner hurtled up to meet them. This was SugarTown. Now they were on the Dock Road. The van bounced and leapt over sets and cobbles. The orange glow of the hotpot curry houses and the dance halls flickered past Zack's side of the cab. On the other side, next to Moe and Frankie, the harbour itself – docked ships looming up like cathedrals, glittering with lights.

'Suggest next possible right,' shouted Clovis.

'No!' cried Frankie, eyes enormous under her helmet. 'That just goes over the railway and back round—'

But it was too late.

Zack had thought he had seen the police van in the periscope and he hadn't heard her. They lurched away from the water, up a narrow alleyway, past large buildings – actually bonded warehouses if anyone had been interested – and then they were suddenly shaken and jarred so badly Zack thought they must be losing a wheel . . .

He was throwing all his strength into trying to steer, it seemed for a terrifying second that they were about to turn over completely, they lunged through forty-five degrees and then leapt forward again.

He pulled on the wheel, it suddenly wouldn't yield – they were stuck on something and they were rocketing straight ahead –

'You're on the railway line,' gasped Clovis, his voice

239

juddering as the Ice Angel herself juddered, thumping over railway sleepers and gravel on one side, her other wheels, under Zack, trapped over the rim of the rail.

In the periscope Zack saw the lights of the level crossing swiftly shrinking into the dark. The railway cut its own path above SugarTown, following the curve of the mountain. The black backs of warehouses towered over both sides of the track.

'We've lost them,' said Zack, beaming. 'Kings of the Mountain. Was that brilliant driving or what? Did you see that corner? I thought we'd had it for sure. And that turboid charger thing. Brilliant. Absolutely brilliant.'

'It's turbic,' said Clovis, quietly. 'And we are *stuck* on the railway.'

And in the distance, as if it were joining in with their conversation, they heard the long low whistle of the freight train. Behind them.

Chapter 40

Suddenly they plunged into a tunnel.

'Full beam,' yelled Clovis.

'They are *on* full beam.'

The brick walls were blackened with soot and grime, they curved up into the darkness and the unseen roof high above. The roof of the tunnel had to be high. The Rockscar freight trains were huge.

And again, behind them, they heard the low whistle of the engine.

'It's getting nearer,' whispered Frankie. 'It sounds like something hunting.'

There was a clamour of activity in the cab.

'No!' shouted Clovis.

Moe had bitten through his safety harness. He was on his hind legs on the seat, one paw pressed against the passenger window, all growl and scrabble and snarl.

'Get down! Get him down!' cried Zack. He was clenching his teeth, clinging on to the steering wheel, fighting to avoid the sickening, metallic, sparking grind when he felt the pressure of the rail and the wheels jarring against it. He must not let it happen. Damage to the Ice Angel now would leave them stranded. Helpless in the path of the freight.

Clovis was leaning over Frankie and had hold of Moe by the scruff of the neck, having no effect on him at all. Frankie was twisted round, clutching Moe around his middle, her harness horribly and dangerously tight against her neck.

The end of the tunnel rushed towards them, they were going faster now, they shot out into moonlight, the track bending away to the right ahead, the Ice Angel doomed to follow it.

Now there was a sudden blast of cool air. Clovis yelled something. Zack was trying to ride out the corner, biting the side of his mouth and tasting blood.

'What's happened? Why have you opened the window?'

'We haven't opened it,' Clovis, sounding strange.

'It's your dog,' shouted Frankie. 'He's cut a hole in the glass with his claw.'

Zack dared a reckless glance sideways and saw Moe silhouetted, still on his hind legs, motionless at the window of the passenger door – a large and perfect circle cut out of the window, the glass presumably fallen on the track somewhere behind them, the night air streaming in . . .

'He can't have . . .'

Suddenly the cab was full of another layer of sound. A girl's voice.

'Turn it off!' yelled Clovis.

'It's not on. Look at the dial. It's off. I didn't turn it on.'

On or not, the girl went on singing. In her own strange language. Just as she had done that afternoon in the winter, when Mariette had gone berserk.

Moe threw back his head and howled. A mighty howl.

'Oh great,' gasped Zack, his head resounding like a bell in a tower. 'This is so helpful.'

'There must be another level crossing soon,' shouted Clovis, as the howl rose and fell again and the singing swelled like the sea. 'We can try and get her off there. The track will be sunk into the road, you know, to make it flat. That's why they call them level crossings, probably . . .'

Zack nodded, staring straight ahead. He had had the same idea himself. They just had to get there before the freight train caught up with them.

'If there isn't another level crossing,' continued Clovis, in the wake of another deafening howl, 'if there isn't another one we'll just go on into the wilderness. We can't outrun the freight forever. We'll have to stop and get out and leave her on the track.'

Zack had thought of this too. There were, of course, no roads between Rockscar and the cities inland. Once they were clear of Rockscar there would be no more level crossings. Only the wilderness: for two hundred miles.

He shuddered. He could feel the throb and hum of the loyal engine, the rattle and thud of the railway sleepers under the wheels. The Ice Angel. Balthazar's angel.

He whispered secretly, 'Don't worry, Dad. We'll get her home.'

'I saw a wolf,' said Frankie, suddenly. 'I saw a wolf running alongside us.'

'Probably a big dog,' said Clovis.

'I think I can tell the difference between a dog and a wolf,' said Frankie. 'And I saw a wolf. It's a case for Dinah Dibbs.'

'Listen!' Clovis, suddenly more scared.

It was the deep pulse of the freight train, vibrating the tracks. Deeper than the cacophony all around them. A feeling rather than a sound. Getting closer.

'The average speed of the freight is probably about forty miles an hour,' said Clovis. 'We can do twice that, if necessary.'

'Well, we're now doing about twenty-five and if we go any faster than this the whole van will come to pieces,' said Zack, grimly. 'She's struggling as it is, can't you tell?'

'She'll certainly come to pieces if the freight train hits her—'

'There's the wolf again, look—'

'SSH! We're trying to think here.'

Frankie pulled a face. She stared out into the night. Lower buildings now, timber yards, workshops, empty lots. She pointed towards the side of the track next to the passenger door.

'There! Look!'

'This is *not* a story,' snapped Clovis. 'Please let us think.'

At that moment the van seemed to hesitate. There was a choking sound deep inside her. She began to go slower. And slower.

'Put your foot down,' yelled Clovis. 'What are you doing? Just put your foot down!'

'Can't do anything,' Zack yelled back. 'We have run out of diesel.'

Clovis had opened his mouth to shout something else. He closed it slowly instead. The dim lights from the dials on the dashboard revealed that he had gone white.

For a moment there was something very like silence in the cab of the Ice Angel. Moe had stopped howling. Then the woman stopped singing. Only the low down roar of the freight. Like a geyser getting ready to blow.

'Switch off the headlamps,' whispered Clovis, finally.

Zack switched them off. Clouds drifted indifferently across the moon. The darkness was complete.

'How can we have run out of diesel?' said Clovis, speaking very slowly and deliberately. 'Did you forget to go to the garage at the weekend?'

'No,' said Zack. 'But we used the turbic charger, didn't we, for at least fifteen miles, before we hit the railway.'

They stared at each other dangerously.

'I can hear the train,' whispered Frankie. And then they

all heard the whistle of the freight engine one last time. Very close now. Mournful and terrible and unstoppable.

Wthout warning, Moe jumped through the hole he had made in the window.

'Oh, great,' said Zack, his voice breaking, 'the rat and the sinking ship.'

'We've got to get out.' Clvois grabbed the buckle of Zack's safety harness and started undoing it. 'I'll push you through the bloody window if I have to – and you, Frankie, get your harness off. Get the door open—'

'STOP!' screamed Zack. Although there was clearly no other way and he would have to get out, soon, now—

Then the whole front of the van tilted upwards.

For a terrifying second Zack thought that the freight engine had somehow smashed into them without them hearing or knowing; but then the van sailed forwards; not jarring or thudding or thumping, just gliding, faster and faster; he heard Clovis shouting 'Hold on!' and they went sideways, up and sideways, and landed again; and then were raised again and the back of the van swung round to straighten them up. Thud.

And they were on the ground.

With his ears full of screams, including his own, Zack pressed his face to the window of the driver's door. There was the gleam of a railway line, mysteriously high up, higher than the van and a good two metres away. Faint moonlight grew brighter.

The railway ran along an embankment here, it seemed. And the Ice Angel van was parked neatly at the foot of this embankment. Parallel to the track. Safe on solid, paved ground.

'We're off the line! We're off the line!' He heard himself shout this. Or perhaps he whispered.

At that moment the dreadful shudder and shock in the lines grew loud as an earthquake. The golden beam of the great lamp on the front of the engine cut through the dark, swamping the moonlight, gilding the tracks, sweeping across the backs of the ramshackle buildings, the van and her wild-eyed occupants. And the Rockscar freight train came thundering out of the night.

A powerful wave of displaced air buffeted the Ice Angel, even down there at the bottom of the embankment, and she rocked from side to side. The freight engine, as Mr Meakin had remarked to Clovis, was indeed the same height as a two-storey building. Smoke and sparks flared and billowed from its towering chimney. The heat from its savage furnace scorched the air.

And behind it, truck after truck after truck, each as big as a double-decker bus, loaded with goods from the merchant ships in Rockscar harbour. Timber, bales of cotton, marble blocks hacked out of faraway mountains, barrels of wine, sacks of sugar, chests of tea.

No one spoke.

Zack was still holding tightly on to the steering wheel;

despite the fact that the engine was off. Clovis and Frankie were staring straight ahead and clasping each other by the hand.

The freight train that night was not especially long by Rockscar standards: there were only about forty wagons. And, of course, the one, sealed, passenger coach. After ten minutes or so, they had all gone past. Then the occupants of the Ice Angel saw the guard's van, and the guard himself, silhouetted in the side door against the light of a brazier stove. It swung along the track ahead, the square of light from the window at the back growing smaller; the noise, the smoke, the sparks in the air and jumping off the wheels; all receding, away into the night.

Quiet.

Silence, almost.

Then, 'What happened?' whispered Clovis. 'How did you get her off the tracks?'

'I didn't,' said Zack. He started to try and let go of the steering wheel, uncurling his fingers, one by one.

'I saw something out there,' whispered Frankie.

Zack turned to look at her. He saw, and ignored, the fact that she and Clovis were still holding hands.

'What did you see, Frankie?'

He had a picture in his head suddenly. The solitary patrolman, the shiner, that night in Shadowcliff, leaning towards him, asking him the same question.

'Just something,' said Frankie. 'Just now. Something in

the dark. But darker.'

She must have let go of Clovis' hand. She raised both her own in a strange gesture, as if she were trying to hold on to the air in front of her face.

'Something that didn't look solid?' prompted Zack, softly. 'With no proper shape?'

She nodded.

'We'd better get out,' said Clovis. 'We'd better see what happened to Moe.' He and Zack stared at each other.

Then there was a knock on the passenger window.

'Girl with lantern,' said Clovis.

Zack could see the top of someone's head, and the lantern on a pole, swinging slightly. Then he saw a hand reach up to the window and knock again on the glass.

'Are you in need of help?' asked a girl's voice. The window was still closed, but there was a hole in it, of course, so it was easy to hear her.

'We've run out of diesel,' said Frankie, at once.

Both brothers glared at her.

'I've got some,' said the girl, easy and matter-of-fact. 'I've got plenty.'

Chapter 41

They sat in a semicircle in the deep, warm soul of the night.

Frankie had a blanket around her shoulders. They were all holding china mugs of tea. The girl who had knocked on the window, and made the tea, was stroking Moe gently on the back of his neck. He was lying next to her on the ragged carpet, looking extremely relaxed. He had come trotting round the side of the van, wagging his tail, as soon as they got out.

'Rat,' Zack had whispered. 'Sinking ship.'

It wasn't a house: it was a workshop.

The air smelt of engine oil.

There was a workbench behind them. A Bellisima in pieces. Other scooters in different stages of repair stood or leant in the shadows. Charts labelling each and every part of Bellisimas and Favolosas and Hillstarts and Wind Shadows and Tugalugs were just visible, pinned to the walls.

'My name is Magdalena,' the girl had said, as they climbed shakily down from the cab of the Ice Angel. 'They call me Magdalena of the Rock.'

No one had asked her anything. Even Frankie, when her feet touched the ground, had finally seemed unable to think of anything to say.

'I mend scooters by trade,' said Magdalena now, passing round a tin of raisin biscuits. 'I am mechanical.'

Zack grinned into his tea. She didn't look like a machine; she didn't look much like the girls at Storm Hill School either; she was all solid muscle and bone. Short and strong. Even her forehead was broad.

He stared around him, feeling light and strange and unreal. The shock of everything. The incomprehensible events he had just lived through. He looked at Clovis and Frankie and Moe. Perhaps we died, he thought. Perhaps we have fallen together, sideways into another world.

Magdalena was dressed in green overalls stained with oil and paint. She had flecks of red paint in her hair and on her face and hands. Her hair was all shades of yellow and very long and thick. Her skin seemed to be the same shade as goldberries.

She looked up now and their eyes met and he couldn't tell where her pupil ended and the iris began: the darkest eyes he had ever seen.

'You feel better?' she asked. 'You would like more tea?'

'I'd like another biscuit, please,' said Frankie.

'Frankie's feeling better,' said Zack, grinning again.

The engine had been turned off. He was sure. Anyway,

there had been no fuel left. And somehow the van had . . . well, travelled, travelled several metres, maybe twenty, thirty, and then lifted itself off the rails. Just in time. Somehow.

He tried to catch Clovis' eye. 'Can you come and check something with me?'

Clovis peered at him over the top of his mug.

'Won't take a minute,' added Zack.

'I'll come,' said Frankie, her mouth full of biscuit.

'No, no, you stay here,' said Zack, quickly.

'But I want to come.'

'No. Stay here.'

'I'm not scared . . .'

'Please stay here, Frankie,' said Clovis.

Frankie wiped her face, leaving a smear of lipstick along the back of her hand.

'Would you like another biscuit?' asked Magdalena. 'I will have one too, I think.'

Zack and Clovis took the lantern from beside the doors and walked out into the dark.

The workshop seemed to be on the end of a larger building. All in darkness. They were in a broad yard paved unevenly with flagstones: the far side was bordered by the railway embankment. No fence.

There was the Ice Angel, standing where they had left her. The back door must have flown open during whatever had happened. The black and silver escape scooter was lying on its side nearby.

'Where's Moe?' whispered Zack.

Moe usually followed him, even when not invited.

'Having a little rest with our new friend,' said Clovis, softly.

The lantern light caught the side of the Ice Angel.

'Do you think she's damaged?' said Clovis. They had stopped a little distance away. 'Should we check?'

Zack nodded.

Neither of them moved.

'I just wanted to have a look at the angel,' added Zack. He raised the lantern a little higher, moving the pool of light along the sleek silver flank, gliding over the sweep of the wheel arch, the long bonnet.

They crept forward. Round to the front. There was the angel herself: impassive, her gentle eyes gazing ahead, her hands clasped. Zack and Clovis stared at her.

'What do you think happened?'

'I don't know.'

'Not some other special feature of yours that you hadn't told me about?'

'No.'

A bell tolled in the distance.

'High tide,' said Clovis.

'Do you think we're still here?' said Zack, suddenly.

'What do you mean?'

'Well, it's not really . . . I don't see how it can have

happened. So if it can't have happened, how can we still be here? Maybe we didn't make it. Maybe the freight train hit us. Maybe we've all sort of fallen into another sort of reality . . .' He trailed off.

Clovis snorted. Then he clapped his hand on Zack's shoulder, causing the lantern to swing crazily from side to side.

'We're still here,' he said. 'Look.'

The swinging lantern had revealed an extra glint of metal up on the railway track nearest to the edge of the embankment. Clovis began to scramble up towards it, showering bits of loose earth and small stones back down to where Zack was standing. Now he had reached the rail.

'Get off there,' hissed Zack, very scared, despite the fact that he knew very well that there would not be another train for twenty-four hours.

Clovis arrived back beside him. Skidding and sitting down and probably travelling more quickly than he had intended. He was holding a round silver hubcap with a dent along the side of the rim.

They walked around the van. It had come from the front wheel on the driver's side.

'All right?' said Clovis. 'This must have fallen off when we . . . when the van was sort of lifted up. It landed on the track. And then there's the escape scooter.'

'That doesn't prove anything—' began Zack.

'There's an explanation,' interrupted Clovis. 'There is

always an explanation. We just don't know what it is yet. Oh, no, what the . . .'

A white shape had appeared up on the railway line. It detached itself from the darkness and cleared the embankment in one graceful leap, landing very close to where they were standing. Then, without pausing, it continued across the yard towards the lighted doorway of the workshop.

A white wolf.

Zack and Clovis crept after it. Keeping close together.

Zack could hear his own breath, very sharp and quick with fear. Wolves only ever came into the city for one reason. Hunger. And they rarely travelled alone.

Now it had gone inside. They followed. Silently. Side by side.

They were in the doorway.

Magdalena was standing trimming the wick on the paraffin lamp. Frankie, still wrapped in the blanket, was nibbling her raisin biscuit. The wolf was lying on the carpet next to Moe.

Zack and Clovis stood amazed.

'There's a black patch behind its ear,' said Clovis, eventually.

'Oh, I did not see that you had come back,' said Magdalena. 'You must not worry about the wolf, he has come to visit for his supper. His name is Cruncher. It was written on a little label on his collar. This is a terrible name, don't you think? No dignity.'

'It's *Cruncher*,' said Zack.

'You know him?' She smiled, as if it was common for people to be on first-name terms with wolves. 'I rescued him. He was tied up outside the Rockscar Ocean-Going Mariners' Bank. He didn't like to be on a little piece of rope.'

Both Clovis and Zack were unable to stop staring, as Cruncher rolled lazily on his side and crossed his enormous front paws.

'I have two cans of diesel fuel here,' said Magdalena. 'You know, it is not wise to try and drive on the railway line.'

'We didn't *try* and drive on it,' said Zack, fervently.

'Did you see us on the railway line?' demanded Clovis, one thought ahead as usual. 'Did you see what happened? Did you see how we got off there?'

She narrowed her eyes.

'I do not drive vans,' she said. 'I am expert only in affairs of the scooter.'

'But you just said we shouldn't drive on the rails,' said Clovis. 'So you must have seen *how we came off.*'

'It's nothing to boast about,' she said, her voice severe. 'You were nearly all killed – BAM!'

And she smacked her fist into the palm of her hand, causing everyone, including Moe and Cruncher, to flinch.

'There is a perfectly good road outside,' she added. 'I will show you. I suggest you always use roads from now on and for evermore. And now we will put in the fuel.'

She picked up a large can with 'Rock Scooter Repairs' painted on the side and walked out of the workshop.

No one spoke for a moment.

'She's beautiful when she's angry,' said Zack: grinning again.

Chapter 42

Another dry dawn was breaking over Rockscar. The Ice Angel, going rather slowly, had become lost trying to find the way between two unfamiliar places – a scooter repair shop in the western district known as the Rock and JacksonTown, the home address of Frankie Brown.

At last, after stopping many times to look at the map, they were approaching their destination. They pulled round the corner into Jackson Avenue and Zack allowed the van to glide to a halt outside one of the many tall terraced houses, long ago converted into flats. The sky, the building and the pavement all seemed the same colour in the grey light. It was five-thirty in the morning.

Someone in stained white clothes was dragging a dustbin up the cellar steps. He hauled it to the kerb. A sign on the railings said 'Sleepy Dog Diner'. As they had come through JacksonTown they had passed many restaurants and bars and jazz clubs. It seemed a strange place for Frankie to be living; but then, she was pretty strange herself.

'Yes, this is the one,' whispered Clovis, peering up at the

front of the stone-faced building. 'Number 27.' He was whispering because Frankie was asleep.

A smell of some sort of cooking was coming in through the perfectly round hole in the window of the passenger door.

'What should we do?' Zack whispered back. 'We've got to get home. Mum will be fidgeting like a ferret.'

'Someone's coming out,' said Clovis.

The door of number 27 had opened and a man was coming down the steps. He was big. He was wearing a black suit and a green trilby hat. Zack recognized him. The saxophone player he had seen playing at the Midnight Café.

He came striding down the steps and straight over to the Ice Angel, where he stopped at what was left of the window in the passenger door.

'Have you got Miss Frankie Brown in there?' he asked, in a quiet and dangerous voice.

'We've given her a lift from Excelsior Broadcasting,' said Clovis, rapidly. 'She was delivering some scripts.'

'She had no business delivering anything. Get her out this minute. And don't think you're going anywhere. You're going to tell us exactly who you are and what you have all been doing since 11.30 pm, when she was seen leaving Excelsior House with a teenage ice cream salesman.'

Zack recognized other members of the band coming down the steps now. They were all much bigger than he remembered. Didn't anyone ever go to sleep anymore? Why were these men here, at this horrible time in the morning, looking so alert and healthy and terrifying?

The saxophone player had put his arm through the round hole in the glass and opened the passenger door of the van. Moe tried to lick his hand.

'We were chased by a police van and we got lost,' said Clovis, sounding reasonable and calm and also slightly muffled because Moe had jumped on to his lap. The man was trying to undo Frankie's safety harness. She had still not woken up.

'You got very lost,' said the saxophone player. 'It is now nearly a quarter to six. You got lost for . . .' He had undone the buckle and was pulling Frankie towards him. 'You got lost for six, for six hours . . .'

But Clovis took hold of Frankie, too. And he didn't let go. At least not until he fell out of the cab, his fall broken because he landed on Moe who had taken the precaution of leaping down first.

'How do we know who you are?' he demanded. 'We're looking for her family. You haven't said—'

At that moment, Frankie woke up. 'Oh, hello, Uncle Hat,' she said, sleepily. 'Zack and Clovis brought me home. You'll never guess what happened. We got *stuck* . . . it was amazing, we . . .' She yawned. Her eyes were brighter now. She glanced down at Clovis. 'Well, anyway, we got stuck,' she concluded.

'And lost,' said Clovis.

'Thanks ever so much for the lift, Clovis,' said Frankie. 'I don't know how I would have got home without you. You are both perfect gentlemen, helping me out like that.'

'Not at all,' said Clovis, going slightly pink among his freckles.

The band were towering around him. Weren't musicians supposed to be kind, relaxed sort of people? Then there was a thump from the back of the van and he heard Zack's voice, full of good cheer.

'We've got Sharp Lemon Shocker with Fizzing Sorbet Sticks, that's a nice one if you're feeling a bit tired. And some really good Slow Burn Chocolate Velvet, a welcome taste of sophistication for the cultured palette, secret recipe, of course, but I can tell you there's best stem ginger involved, and a hint of smoking fire seeds.'

'It's the new generation Ice Angel, Hat,' said a sad-faced man who Clovis thought was possibly the drummer. 'Remember? Balthazar's kid and the other one. Showed up at the Midnight and got Mittens all of a dither.'

Clovis had managed to stand up now. Moe was sticking close to him, growling very softly. He reached out to put his hand on the rough fur on the back of the dog's neck and gasped out loud in surprise. Moe seemed much taller than normal. His back was as high as Clovis' waist.

'Remember, Hat?' said the drummer. 'Give the kids a

break. Looks like they got her out of trouble, not into it.'

'And they've got the real ices,' said someone else. 'No Rockscar water taste. The real thing.'

Gradually the band were moving away from Clovis and gathering around Zack.

Only Hat stayed. He put Frankie down and she smiled: he didn't smile back.

'Go and get yourself an ice cream,' he said. Frankie went.

'We're her family,' said Hat to Clovis. 'Her mum's in hospital right now. Anything happens to Frankie, anything at all, and we'll come looking for whoever's responsible and it's . . .' He drew his finger across his throat. 'You understand me?'

Clovis nodded. 'With all due respect, sir, if it wasn't for us, she'd probably still be wandering about somewhere now, trying to get home,' he said. 'She's not as grown up as she thinks.'

Hat took off his hat and wiped his forehead. Then he wiped his eyes.

'Tell me about it,' he whispered, in an altogether more pleasant voice. 'It's like trying to look after some sort of wild animal that won't go on a lead and keeps running into the road.'

'But she's very funny and clever,' added Clovis, going pink again.

'Hey, Hat,' called the sad-faced drummer. 'Isn't it time

you were *on the air*.'

Hat frowned at him.

'Relax, Hat,' said someone who Clovis now recognized as the bass player, 'We're all outlaws here.'

The rest of the band laughed. Quietly, because their mouths were full.

Moe jumped back up on to the passenger seat: just another smallish, scruffy-looking dog.

Chapter 43

Anselm Scarspring walked along the cool tiled passageway and out across the courtyard into the blazing sun. He climbed a flight of stone steps. Then, shielding his eyes from the glare with his hand, he turned through an archway into the green and sparkling water garden: built by his ancestors on the roof of their house.

Here he walked beside a long channel lined with turquoise and jade mosaic. Little flying fish rose shimmering, scattering droplets, and then dived under the surface again. He stopped and sat down on a bench shaded in an alcove of woven branches, a stone child knelt on the rim of a dish of water lilies.

This was Anselm's personal refuge. Even Golightly did not dare disturb him here. And it was now the only place in the city of Rockscar where fountains still played. Everywhere else, including the hospitals, water was rationed.

Anselm leant back and half closed his eyes. He had summoned Ernesto to meet him here at noon. After a welcome moment of peace he heard his nephew's footsteps approaching. Walking with the same uneven and irritating stride as his dead father.

Anshelm gritted his teeth. Touched the charm he carried in his pocket. Murderer's guilt.

'Good afternoon, Uncle,' said Ernesto.

'I expect you know what I'm going to say,' said Anshelm. 'It's been six weeks without rain. We have been stopped in every attempt to find new springs on the edge of the wilderness. You will be aware that we are now rationing water to every citizen—'

'Except ourselves,' said Ernesto.

'Two reservoirs are now dry. Something which has never happened before. The pump in Candlemas stopped working earlier this week.'

'They say it had become polluted,' said Ernesto, quietly.

'DON'T SPEAK! I have entrusted you with the task of finding and capturing this troll. YOU HAVE DONE NOTHING.'

Ernesto had taken a step backwards, out of reach. He knew that Anshelm, should he get angry, was as fast as a hawk.

'You are very like your father, Ernesto, you don't know that, do you? Contrary to the lies we have allowed the public to believe, Zoran was not a fearless lion-hunting warrior. He never went hunting in his life. He liked books and history. He had come to believe that trolls exist, but his stupid and dangerous solution was to try and befriend them. In fact, I

265

think he believed that he *had* befriended one of them. *That* is what killed him that night on the Wolf Road.' Anshelm paused. 'His own foolishness.'

Ernesto was still standing in the full sun. His dark, formal clothes did not help him in the heat.

'You have one more week,' said Anshelm. 'After which, who knows, maybe Steward Golightly will drop your precious Fisher into the Cat's Tail, all cosy in a little sack of stones.'

Ernesto shuddered. His voice, however, was steady.

'I have finished my preparations,' he said. 'I have identified the living descendant of the ancient family of troll hunters.'

'*Troll hunters!*' Anshelm almost leapt off the bench. 'But I have never heard of such people.'

'Our ancestors employed them as members of their households. Troll hunters could track trolls days after they had been sighted. They knew how to keep them at bay. They knew where it was safe to go and where to avoid. There are examples of them bargaining with trolls and persuading them not to damage property. They advised on the proper use of guardians and charms.'

Anshelm kept his eyes on Ernesto's face. 'You have found out about these, these hunters from books . . .'

'Books and records,' said Ernesto. 'And family journals. Here in our library. There were a number of journals kept in code and I deciphered them.'

'Journals?' Anshelm was growing paler.

'Yes, Uncle Anshelm,' said Ernesto, very calm. 'Journals. Archibald Scarspring kept one for several years. And there were others.'

'Anyone I might have heard of? More recent?'

'A few pages which I think were written by my father, in which he describes how my mother became ill after I was born. In his last entry he says that she is being cared for by a new friend and that he is going to visit her.'

'Are you saying that he knew where she was? Someone was caring for her? Who?'

'It doesn't say. But something else is worrying him too. He doubts the loyalty of someone in our household.'

'Who? Why?'

'I don't know. But he was concerned for you too, Uncle Anshelm. And for me. He uses the word traitor. He is going to find out more. Until then he doesn't want to tell you because you will not believe him. But that's the last entry.'

'Traitor? Probably some servant with a grudge, long gone now.' Anshelm shrugged. 'We looked for your mother for years,' he added. 'I hope you know that. We offered rewards.'

'I will find her,' said Ernesto, simply.

'Don't you think that if she were alive she would have come back to you? Especially when the papers and the radio were full of Zoran's death,' said Anshelm, more softly. 'She had nothing to fear from me. And she loved you more than life itself.'

Ernesto couldn't speak.

'She was a shy person, Ernesto, very private. Good-hearted. And fine-looking. Dark in her skin and her hair. The photograph you have doesn't do her justice.'

Abruptly, Anshelm put his face in his hands.

Ernesto took a step towards him and then stopped.

The silence continued, broken only by the soft splashing of the water in the small fountains and pools.

Anshelm spoke without looking up. 'And are there any descriptions of trolls, in these journals you have so cleverly deciphered?'

'There are several descriptions,' said Ernesto, carefully. 'But they are never first-hand. Trolls are usually described as male, two or three times the height of a human, bearded, possessing great physical strength. Sometimes they have horns, sometimes antlers, sometimes claws.

'The only person who claimed to have seen one himself was Archibald. He would never describe what he had seen. He was said to have suffered from something called the Curse of the Scarsprings.' Ernesto paused. 'People thought he was mad.'

'Leave me now,' interrupted Anshelm suddenly. 'Go.'

He was whispering, but his voice could have cut through stone.

Chapter 44

For some time after Ernesto had gone away down the stone steps and into the house, Anshelm stayed alone in the quiet and sunny water garden.

As so often happened, even here, he felt the sharp cold of that night on the mountain. He saw the steep bend in the Wolf Road, barely visible in the light of a waning winter moon. His brother Zoran had come here to meet someone, he and Golightly had followed him, to this rendezvous, spying on him, no other word for it. Zoran had been desperate with worry when his wife became ill. When she disappeared without trace a few days later he had seemed to lose his mind, refusing to speak to Anshelm, insisting on walking alone into the wilderness. Who knew what rogue or trickster might be leading him into harm, fooling him with lies and promises?

But if that unknown person was there at all they must have been in the shadow of the trees. Anshelm had not been able to see him. Or her.

It was Golightly, of course, who started the argument.

Clever, clever Golightly whose motives for everything had always been just around the corner of Anshelm's understanding. Whispering to Anshelm as they crept behind him that Zoran must be keeping dangerous secrets: that he did not show Anshelm the trust and respect due to a brother.

Now, twelve years later in the water garden, Anshelm shivered and clasped his charm in his fist. The Wolf Road. Nothing understood or as it seemed.

Hot-tempered. He had always been hot-tempered. Anger. Fear. Act first, think later. And that night Zoran had seemed a stranger. Full of rage in return. Shouting at him to take Golightly and go. Commanding him. Swinging punches in the dark.

Golightly at a distance. Watching.

Then the Ice Angel van had come grinding up the hill. The wretched Jump family, the outlaw ice cream sellers that the Scarsprings had never been able to catch. The headlamps had lit up the shameful sight. He and Zoran, right on the edge of the road, hands on each other's throats; rolling and kicking like two stupid, bar room brawlers.

Anshelm had glimpsed Golightly, his rifle raised. Had gasped to breathe, to shout 'No!'

The door of the van had swung open, the driver had leapt out.

In that instant Anshelm had been knocked off his feet by something he couldn't see. Crashing down, still clutching

Zoran, his fingers digging into his Zoran's neck, Zoran falling with him . . . Something dark in the darkness. Enormous strength. Pinning him to the icy ground.

A gunshot echoing off the mountain. Figures silhouetted. Screams. Anshelm felt the ground shifting, giving way. Tried to keep hold of Zoran, feeling him slipping, the sounds of rocks falling . . .

The air itself suddenly alive, in turmoil.

Anshelm, fighting the unseen force that held him, suddenly free.

Struggling to his feet.

Only Golightly was there. Zoran and the ice cream seller were gone. The edge of the road had crumbled. They were gone into the merciless ravine, many metres deep.

Anshelm had swayed and staggered. His head was bleeding. He had walked forward and leant against a great wilderness cedar tree, right on the broken rim of the ravine. Everything here lit by the headlamps of the silver van. He had looked down and seen the little metal charm on the ground. An angel. Greenish metal. Very old. He had picked it up.

They had come back in the daylight. The van had gone. Anshelm, himself, had climbed down into the ravine. He had always been a good climber. Not that it was any use. There was no trace of anyone, alive or dead.

And Steward Golightly and Anshelm had become murderers. A secret that slammed them together and held them like a vice.

Anselm opened his eyes. Or perhaps they had been open all along. He saw the stone child and the water lilies. He took the charm of the little angel out of his pocket and kissed it. Then he stood up and walked slowly down the stone steps and back into the house.

Chapter 45

'Anshelm!'

It was Golightly. Face flushed: sweat sticking his hair to his forehead. They almost collided in the corridor leading to the offices.

Anshelm side-stepped neatly: always quick on his feet.

'Another little crisis, Stefan? Can't you manage anything on your own?'

'You've received a telegram, Anshelm, I've been looking for you, no one seemed to know where you—'

Anshelm held out his hand.

'I opened it,' added Golightly. 'I thought it might be urgent.'

'Of course it's urgent,' said Anshelm. 'It's a telegram. A telegram addressed to me, which I now see you have read.'

'It is from Meakin. Meakin the map maker.'

'So it is, let's see, "have taken on an apprentice who has great skill art of map reading stop he has been working here some weeks much time practising stop today he managed to read our oldest and most worn map without difficulty stop

273

suggest you bring material to shop six pm stop fee . . ."'

Anshelm laughed out loud. The fee for Clovis' skills would have bought a small house in Merchant's Hill.

'Meakin is a cunning operator,' he said. 'The sense of drama created by a telegram, a masterly stroke.'

'Do you know what he refers to?' asked Golightly. 'Can map reading be so difficult? And what is this material he believes you to have?'

Anshelm folded the telegram until it was small and put it in the pocket of his waistcoat. He turned towards the door of the office. He was no longer laughing: his expression, as he looked away from Golightly, was one of secret triumph and excitement.

Golightly followed him.

Without speaking, Anshelm unlocked a cupboard, moved boxes and papers and then opened some hidden compartment at the back. He drew out a roll of parchment, yellowed and frayed with age.

'I don't remember seeing that before. Did it belong to Zoran?' Golightly lowered his voice, mentioning the dead man's name.

'Yes,' said Anshelm, closing the cupboard. 'And to our father, and his father and his father before him. But now it is mine.'

He pushed things out of the way and unrolled the square of parchment on the desk.

'I don't understand,' said Golightly. 'It's just a primitive drawing. There is no skill here. Here, some sort of crude symbol. I suppose that is the signature of the artist. The whole thing is poorly executed. It would not surprise me if it is the work of a child.' He suddenly snatched at the map, but Anshelm was too quick for him.

'Yes, yes,' said Anshelm, smiling. 'It is clumsily done and no doubt of little consequence but you must indulge me, nevertheless, Stefan. I would like to show it to Meakin's talented apprentice.'

'And pay the rascal all that money? For what? What if this gets in the papers? They are already saying you are mad with your endless hunting for trolls.'

'Are you saying you don't want to accompany me?'

'No, of course not. Of course I want to be there.'

'I thought you might,' said Anshelm.

Chapter 46

Zack had already become lost twice. He was on his blue and silver Bellisima, with Moe on the back, trying to find the scooter repair shop belonging to the girl called Magdalena of the Rock.

What with one thing and another, the night before, he hadn't noticed the name of the street.

When he stopped for the third time and started yet again to unfold the cumbersome map, Moe jumped off the back of the Bellisima and started to walk off down the pavement. He came to a corner and looked back over his shoulder.

'Oi!' shouted Zack.

'Oi yourself, Beaky!' shouted a girl on the pavement. 'You shaving yet?'

Zack wobbled the scooter into the kerb and nearly fell off. One of those really nice girls from Storm Hill School. She screamed with laughter: especially loud, no doubt to be sure that he could hear it above the noise of the street.

Moe, meanwhile, stuck his chin in the air, turned the corner and disappeared from sight.

The street was busy. Lots of offices to do with the shipping lines and import and export businesses: smartly-dressed men and women, all with briefcases.

'Oi!' shouted Zack again. 'Come back!'

Several people looked at him. He revved the engine: the only choice was to follow Moe.

He spotted him waiting under a lamppost. As the scooter approached, Moe set off again. He crossed the road, entered a side street and Zack followed him, cursing and sweating. However, after a few more corners and junctions his language improved. They had reached an area of warehouses which seemed familiar. Then he realized that they were parallel to the railway.

This was the district known as the Rock.

Finally, with a triumphant wave of his tail, Moe halted in a cobbled street.

There was the long wooden building. Not the back and the yard where the Ice Angel had so mysteriously arrived the night before. The front. 'Rock Scooter Repairs'. White painted letters: faded with time.

Moe led the way along the side, through the gate and into the yard. Everything looked a little smaller and more ramshackle in the bright daylight than it had in the dark. The large doors of the workshop were propped open. A man was standing just inside, talking to a young woman dressed in overalls. Moe trotted up and licked her hand.

Diesel and petrol were not cheap in Rockscar and Zack

had an envelope containing money ready to offer to Magdalena. He waited now, unsure, holding his helmet in one hand and the envelope in the other.

The customer was collecting his scooter, a beautiful vintage Favolosa Mark A with the original fog lamp. Clovis would have gone wild just to see it.

'Excellent work,' said the man. 'It's always worth the trip to bring it to you. The way you modified the suspension, last time. It's as if I'm gliding along the road.'

'Thank you,' said Magdalena, in her unusual, musical accent.

Money exchanged hands. Then the customer opened his briefcase and took out a bottle wrapped in tissue paper. Expensive wine?

No.

'I'd like to give you this,' he said, lowering his voice. 'It's Ice Angel water.'

Zack recognized the blue-green bottle: he was amazed.

'Please,' said Magdalena. 'This is not necessary.'

'Have it,' said the customer, whispering now and speaking quickly. 'The rumour is it comes from high up, somewhere near the glacier. It's delicious. Everybody's thirsty with this rationing. Terrible drought. The Mayor doesn't seem to be able to find any new water sources. Too distracted, wasting his time looking for trolls. All this vandalism, terrible.'

'He should not be looking on the edge of the wilderness. And he should not be disturbing ancient trees,' said

Magdalena in the same stern voice she had used when advising Zack and Clovis not to drive their van on railway lines.

'The water arrangements he has should be quite enough,' she added.

'Please accept it,' said the customer. 'None of that disgusting aftertaste.'

'Thank you,' said Magdalena. 'You are most kind.'

Zack stepped back as the man steered the beautiful scooter past him and into the sunlight. He nodded politely to Zack, put on a Wind Shadow helmet, the most expensive and safest in Rockscar, started the sweet engine and drove away.

Zack stayed out there in the heat a moment longer, Moe panting discreetly beside him.

'Why don't you come in?' called Magdalena.

Zack sauntered into the workshop. He swung his helmet. Casually.

'Aah!'

Magdalena leapt forward: they collided. He had knocked into a Hillstart, propped up and with a wheel missing, but she somehow managed to catch it before it hit the floor. Some of her hair had caught on a button on Zack's cuff. She jerked her head to free it and he winced as if the pain were his own.

He picked up the envelope, which he had dropped, and held it out.

'For the fuel,' he said, breathlessly. 'The diesel you gave us last night.'

'No, it is not necessary.'

She left him standing and went over to the workbench. Moe followed her.

'Excuse me. I am very busy.'

Zack and the envelope were left next to the scooter he had so recently knocked sideways. He raised his head to scratch his forehead where his helmet always left a red line and saw a long, long strand of hair trailing from his cuff.

She started hammering something.

'We don't know how our van came off the railway line last night,' said Zack.

She continued hammering. He stared at her back, like a door, locking him out. He had ridden for ninety minutes in the hot afternoon, knowing that this would happen. She half turned, without looking at him, and took a box of nuts and bolts or something from a shelf. In the van going back up the Wolf Road last night Clovis had cheerfully suggested that she was actually a boy.

Wrong.

Zack shifted his weight from one foot to the other. Ignored by his dog. Unnecessary to the scene. Unable to leave.

Then he heard footsteps. The creak of a scooter as it was pushed into the yard from the street. Magdalena swung round. He saw her eyes black and wide and scared and a spasm of shock contracted under his ribs. He turned too.

There was a lanky boy standing there. Out of breath, hot, too many clothes, parking a chunky, workaday Tugalug, the most unfashionable scooter in the city.

Zack recognized him as he began to speak: it was the person who sat in the middle of roads near to blind corners in the rain and the dark, looking for his kidnapped cat.

'Good afternoon,' said the boy, removing his unstylish helmet. 'My name is Ernesto Scarspring, I am looking for someone known as Magdalena of the Rock.'

He stayed a few steps away from the doorway, raising his hand to shield his eyes from the sun. Long fingers. Very clean nails.

So this was the mysterious heir to the Scarsprings. Cat Boy. And what would such a foolhardy and downright peculiar person want with Magdalena? Zack tried to signal to Moe, who was under the workbench eating something.

Magdalena wiped her hand on the leg of her overalls and came out into the sunshine. 'I am Magdalena.'

Not too busy to talk to him, then.

'I need your assistance,' said Ernesto.

'And this is the scooter?'

'Tugalug, the farmer's friend,' said Zack, helpfully.

They both ignored him.

'My request does not concern my scooter.'

'Our affair is only with the scooters,' Magdalena frowned.

At that moment Cruncher came over the railway line and across the yard towards them. He walked on into the workshop and Moe gave the yelp of greeting that he usually reserved for Zack.

Ernesto did not seem surprised or alarmed by the sight of a wolf wandering about. In fact he nodded, as if it was what he expected.

'Are you aware of your ancestors, Miss Magdalena?'

'We are scooter specialists.'

'But are you aware that you are the direct descendant of the great troll hunters, who served the Scarsprings and other powerful families for many generations?'

She straightened her back, although it was perfectly straight already. She folded her arms across her chest.

'Yes,' she said.

'Then I must ask you, on behalf of all the Scarspring family, to assist me in capturing the troll whom my uncle believes is vandalizing our attempts to find fresh water.'

'Perhaps your uncle is looking in the wrong places. Perhaps he should not be disturbing the wilderness. Or harming the roots of ancient trees.'

Moe pottered out of the workshop and came up to Zack as if he vaguely remembered him from somewhere.

'I agree with you. But I have no control over my uncle's activities,' said Ernesto.

Zack picked Moe up. Not something he usually attempted but he wanted to be able to leave quickly if necessary. Moe was much heavier than he looked and quite possibly heavier than normal. He stretched out all his limbs in lazy protest, causing Zack to stagger where he stood.

'And this must be your dog!' exclaimed Ernesto. 'He has webbed feet. I was reading about such a dog only last night. This is amazing. A troll hound. And there, the long retractable claws for climbing trees.'

Ernesto was now actually touching the naked soles of Moe's paws, something no one in the Jump family would ever have dared to do.

'And the unusually long whiskers. Larger pupils for improved night vision—'

'This is my dog,' said Zack.

'*Your* dog—'

'Yes, and I've got to go now.'

'But this is a coincidence of the most extraordinary proportions! Stop, please. This animal could be of immeasurable help to us. All the troll hunters were accompanied by troll hounds. He is a prince among dogs.'

How did this Ernesto person manage to speak like this all the time? The prince breathed right into Zack's face. Horrendous.

'Do you know what a troll looks like?' asked Magdalena, abruptly.

Ernesto shook his head. 'Only traditional descriptions

exist, never first-hand. Usually they mention that the troll was a male, similar to a human, but larger, with horns. A cunning and dangerous monster. Uncivilized and with no sense of right and wrong. Some records suggest that they eat human children. In the past they were accused of poisoning wells, stealing cattle, and summoning storms. They also possess extraordinary strength.'

He was still holding Moe's paw. It was true, there were triangles of almost transparent skin between his toes. Like a frog.

'And when you catch this troll, what will you do?' asked Magdalena.

'My uncle is anxious to imprison it, I suppose,' said Ernesto. 'There is a dungeon under our house. Very old. It is never used. Perhaps he will put the troll down there. I, myself, do not agree. But there is a reason why I must comply with his wishes.'

'And if I do not agree to help?'

'Then, of course, I will attempt to get other assistance. There are no other descendants of troll hunters that I have been able to trace, but I have heard of a detective who has recently retired, a good friend of my uncle. I will ask him.'

Magdalena frowned. Zack had the impression that she was thinking very hard.

'I think it is best if I help you, Mr Ernesto,' she said, finally. 'There is no need to ask any very good detective.' She glanced at Zack. 'And this boy and his special dog will help too. He owes me a favour.'

Chapter 47

It was later on the same day. The blazing afternoon had turned into a sullen, sultry evening. Mr Meakin had asked Clovis to stay at work a little longer than usual. Then he had disappeared into his Private Office. There was a client, he was not to be disturbed.

At six o'clock, when he should have gone home, Clovis was sitting at the crooked kitchen table, nursing a half-empty cup of lemonade. The water tasted so bad, even the lemons and sugar could not disguise it.

He had spent the last two weeks reading the hidden maps. Mr Meakin had buzzed around him, nodding and smiling, urging him on, not allowing him to do anything else.

It had become easier to read them. He could see more now. And he understood more: he understood that Silas Meakin wanted him for some very specific purpose.

Clovis sipped his foul lemonade. He was exhausted. He rested his head on his arm. Immediately the nightmare plunge along the railway line roared up in front of him. He sat up with a jolt and stared round the kitchen. Took another mouthful of lemonade.

Then, without meaning to, he put his head down again and a different horror engulfed him. The mystery he didn't want to solve, or even name: about Zack, the careless remarks of a certain Frankie Brown, and the photograph of Steward Golightly and Mariette on the wall of the Midnight Café.

Gradually, miserably, he dozed into sleep.

He was woken by the creak of a cupboard. Mr Simou, the senior apprentice, was now filling the coffee pot with the stealth of a coffee-making burglar.

Clovis blinked his bleary eyes.

'Are you all right?' whispered Mr Simou.

'Tired,' Clovis whispered back.

'Why haven't you gone home?'

'Mr Meakin wants me to do something for him. Some client he wants me to meet.'

Mr Simou's kindly face became anxious. 'Well, I hope it's not the one he's talking to in the office at the moment.'

'Who's that?' Clovis still didn't feel completely awake.

'Mayor Scarspring, himself,' said Mr Simou, still in a low voice. 'And his dangerous little friend, Steward Golightly.'

Clovis' eyes and mouth all opened wide. Mr Simou, the kitchen and the steaming coffee pot all snapped into focus.

'Have this,' said Mr Simou, pouring and stirring. 'Best to

have all your wits about you.'

Clovis took the enamel mug. It was Mr Simou's own, with his initials, S.S., scratched on the handle. He sipped carefully. The coffee was very hot and very strong.

'I don't want to meet them,' he said.

'Just keep your nerve,' said Mr Simou. 'I might stay late myself, then you can tell me what happened afterwards.'

Clovis managed a smile. Mr Simou was a hard-working, law-abiding and gentle person. If he had any idea about Clovis' real life he would probably run a mile.

'Thanks,' he whispered, trying to smile. Mr Simou smiled back.

The door of the kitchen burst open.

'Ah, there you are, Mr Greenwood,' said a familiar voice. 'Would you join us upstairs? I have some clients who are most anxious to meet you.'

Mr Meakin had descended the stairs silently, it seemed.

'Mr Greenwood was feeling unwell, sir,' said Mr Simou, stooping over the sink. 'He's just finishing a cup of coffee.'

'Really?' Mr Meakin barely looked at either of them. 'Well, come along, Mr Greenwood. You go home now, Mr Simou. I'm sure your wife and your little son and the new baby will be wondering where you are.'

'Yes, sir, thank you, sir,' said Mr Simou.

Clovis' heart sank. He stood up, feeling very alone, and observed that Mr Meakin was dressed even more smartly than normal. Dark velvet jacket, despite the heat, embroidered waistcoat, pearl earring: an air of suppressed excitement. He clapped his hand on Clovis' shoulder.

Steward Golightly appeared in the kitchen doorway, quick eyes, taking everything in. He was carrying a hunting rifle. Clovis had never seen him up so close before.

'Steward Golightly, sir,' said Mr Meakin, fulsomely. 'This is my apprentice Mr Greenwood.'

Golightly nodded at Clovis. Stared pointedly at Mr Simou.

'Good night, Mr Simou,' added Mr Meakin, raising his voice very slightly. 'We mustn't keep you. Mr Simou has recently become a father for the second time, Steward Golightly, a beautiful little girl, only two months old.'

Steward Golightly smiled and turned back towards the stairs. 'Such a vulnerable age,' he said, over his shoulder, raising the rifle to lift it over the banister. He was short and broad shouldered. Very different, in that way, from Zack. But his eyes were light-coloured, like Zack's. And his hair, like Zack's, was dark. Clovis thought of this frightening man singing side by side with Mariette at the Midnight Café all those years ago. He felt sick.

'Excellent, excellent,' murmured Mr Meakin, hustling him out of the kitchen. Clovis glanced back at Mr Simou but he was busy at the sink again, and didn't meet his eye. No choice but to follow Steward Golightly upstairs, step by step, towards the half-open door of Mr Meakin's Private

Office. His mouth was dry. Sweat was spidering across his scalp.

Up ahead in the office, a chair creaked.

Chapter 48

The Private Office was lined with book-laden shelves. Portraits of Mr Meakin's father and grandfather watched genially from above the fireplace.

Anshelm Scarspring sat with his back to the window, his face hard to see. A map was spread on the table in front of him.

'Allow me to introduce you,' said Mr Meakin, from behind Clovis. 'This is Mr Clovis Greenwood, our junior apprentice. Mr Greenwood, I've no doubt you recognize our esteemed Mayor, Mr Anshelm Scarspring.'

Everyone was now in the room, making it even smaller and stuffier than normal. The brass fan on the ceiling turned elegantly, but to no effect.

'Mayor Scarspring has a map he would like you to read for him,' said Mr Meakin, bustling with anticipation. 'Sit down, Mr Greenwood, and make yourself comfortable.'

Clovis sat down opposite Anshelm. Steward Golightly and Mr Meakin remained standing.

Anshelm unrolled a parchment and spread it out. Clovis

kept his eyes down, postponing the moment when he would have to look him in the face. Anshelm was securing the corners of the map with the glass paperweights that Mr Meakin kept on the table for this purpose. He held the last one for a moment in his long fingers. It contained a swirling blue sea and a white-sailed ship. He put it in place: the room held its breath.

'Now, Mr Greenwood,' said Anshelm. 'If you would be good enough to share your knowledge with us.'

Clovis stared at the parchment. No colour, just faded black lines drawn without the help of a ruler. There was nothing like this in Mr Meakin's collection. It was the floor plan of a house, six storeys high, including the cellars. To one side, in very faint, simple lettering, he could make out the word, 'Scarspringe'. Opposite, equally faded, there was the symbol of the man and the wolf, awkwardly drawn.

'If you would put your finger on the symbol, Mr Greenwood,' prompted Mr Meakin. Clovis could see him out of the corner of his eye. He was leaning forward slightly, his eyes at their brightest. Golightly, of course, was out of sight. He was standing directly behind Clovis. Very close.

Clovis put his fingertip on the symbol.

He knew more about map reading now. He felt a jolt of heat. This map had been left undisturbed for a long time.

'What do you see?' Golightly. Making him lurch forward with fright.

'Hush, Stefan,' said Anshelm. 'Don't distract him.'

For a moment Clovis thought that something was wrong. The map held no secrets. Or his own strange skill had inexplicably left him.

Then, faint, so faint, words started to form.

First, the rooms were labelled. Wine cellars. Storerooms. Kitchens, an armoury, a great hall. Retiring chambers. Servants' quarters. Outside there were stables and something called the water garden which was actually on the roof. All identified in unsteady, child-like lettering and eccentric spelling.

He licked his lips, making ready to speak.

He could hear Golightly breathing.

More words appeared. Coaxed back from long ago, slowly, slowly. Clovis looked up to find Anshelm staring, not at the map, but straight at him.

'Well, Mr Greenwood?' he whispered.

'This is a map of a house,' said Clovis.

'Surely you mean "floor plan",' said Mr Meakin. 'I have taught you the correct language, have I not—'

'Ssh!' hissed Golightly. He put his hand on Clovis' shoulder and Clovis could feel each individual finger.

'It shows all the rooms,' said Clovis, still looking at Anshelm.

'And?'

'I think it's very old.'

'And?'

'The full title of the map is "Melisande Her Secret Place". There is a cross here, in the water garden and, next to it, some writing, very small, which says "secret place under the roses behind the pond with the little stoney boy keep out private."' Clovis swallowed. 'I think that this map was made by a child,' he added. 'And here, it says, "For Melisande on her seventh birthday from her special secret friend from the wilderness."'

'That can't be all it is,' spat Golightly. 'The Mayor has not paid all this money just to find out where some kid played in a garden!' The grip on Clovis' shoulder tightened even more. 'And how could your respected ancestor Melisande have a friend from the wilderness? No one lives there. I suggest this boy is lying. This jiggery-pokery is all a trick, Anshelm.'

Anshelm, however, seemed unperturbed.

'It is well-known in the family that Melisande insisted all her life that when she was a child she had met a little girl, of similar age to herself, and that this little girl was, in fact, a troll. Perhaps it was true. Perhaps that little troll child drew this plan of the house and garden.'

'That is absolutely ridiculous, Anshelm.' Golightly's voice shook. 'You are joking, of course.'

'Of course,' said Anshelm. He stared directly at Clovis, he was almost smiling. 'Thank you, Mr Greenwood.'

Then he looked up at Mr Meakin and Steward Golightly. 'If you would leave us, gentlemen. I would like to speak with Mr Greenwood alone.'

Golightly's sharp intake of breath. Cutting the air just behind Clovis' head.

'Of course, sir,' said Mr Meakin.

'Right away from the door,' said Anshelm, his eyes on his steward. 'If you don't mind.'

Clovis didn't look around. He heard the door opening and felt Golightly's rage as he backed out of the room. Then there was the sound of footsteps receding on the stairs.

'Good,' said Anshelm. 'We have disposed of the greedy shopkeeper and the dangerous monkey.'

He moved the glass paperweights off the map and allowed the parchment to curl back and roll itself up. Then he pushed it to one side.

Clovis barely moved at all. His mind was sparking with fears and possibilities. He watched Anshelm as he drew a long ivory cylinder from inside his coat. It was decorated with the Scarspring crest, the mountain lion.

There was a quick grace about Anshelm's movements. He had a pale, bony face and a hooked nose. His dark hair fell across his eyes and he pushed it away. Now he was teasing a cloth out of the end of the cylinder. It came free and he tipped another roll of parchment on to the table.

'You will tell no one that you have seen this,' he said, busy with the paperweights again.

Clovis looked down at the map and just managed not to cry out. He put one hand on the edge closest to him and pressed downwards: in that way, he stopped his hand from shaking.

'Let us begin,' said Anshelm, softly.

Clovis stared down at the landscape. The troll, hunched and powerful, covering the wilderness; the dragon that was the city of Rockscar; the blue monster that was the sea. The map was exactly the same as the one they had found in the secret chest at home.

'Wait!' whispered Anshelm.

Clovis was more than willing to wait. Anshelm moved silently from behind the table, past Clovis, to the door.

Clovis looked over his shoulder, saw him turn the handle with great care and then fling the door back.

There was no one listening on the landing. Golightly's harsh, brief laugh echoed up from the kitchen, where Mr Meakin was no doubt making a celebratory pot of chocolate.

Anshelm closed the door again; but not before he had taken the key out of the lock on the other side. Mr Meakin must have left it there, in all his excitement. Clovis watched, his stomach clenching with fear, as Anshelm locked the door and put the key in his pocket.

'Golightly can't bear to be left out of anything,' said Anshelm, smiling. 'And your boss, Meakin, is obsessed with money. The amount he is charging for this little favour would buy a house. I wouldn't put it beyond him to spy on us, in case he can milk a bit more cash from me.'

Clovis tried to smile back.

'My family have waited for generations to read this map,' continued Anshelm, sitting down again. 'The other one...' he pointed to the first roll of parchment, 'that was just to put Golightly and Meakin off the scent. This one also belonged to my ancestor Melisande, but it is far more valuable.'

He rested his fingers on the edge of the parchment spread before them.

'Let's not delay, map reader,' he said. 'This map is of great interest to me.'

Clovis tried to swallow.

'Is there a problem, Mr Greenwood?'

'I can't do it. I can't read this one.'

Anshelm didn't seem surprised. He sat back in his chair and loosened his collar. 'What would it take? Money, I presume. You have realized that my interest in this map is very great and you have decided that you want your share of the benefit. Name your price. I can be very generous to people who help me.'

Clovis stared down at the map, imagining the pattern of crosses which would take shape when he put his finger to the symbol in the corner. The hidden springs in the wilderness and the city – and the Jump family caves in the mountain.

'This is dynamite,' Zack had said. 'This could kill us.'

'It's not about money,' said Clovis. 'It's nothing to do with that. I don't want anything.'

'Put your finger on the symbol, Mr Greenwood, tell me what you see.'

Clovis knew that he must lie. He must quickly invent something. He put the tip of his middle finger on the little symbol of the man and the wolf. Familiar curling writing uncoiled itself, deepened and darkened. 'A Chart of Water Sources in the City of Rockscar and the Surrounding Wilderness'. The Wolf Road snaked from the edge of the city up the mountainside. The cave system took its familiar shape. The tiny crosses blossomed in the body of the dragon, three more in the wilderness, two springs in the lifeless ravine, and, finally, the one high up near the snow line. Home.

He could feel Anshelm's eyes on him. Looked up to see that he was smiling. 'It's a map of the wilderness,' began Clovis.

'We know that,' said Anshelm. 'That observation requires no special skill.'

Clovis had seen many secret maps here at Meakin's. Buried treasure. The location of the dens where bears hibernated. Places where certain medicinal plants might be found . . .

'It shows the wilderness cedars,' he said. He paused to clear his throat. 'The ones that are planted in the city. And wild ones, in the wilderness.'

'Very good,' said Anshelm. 'Thank you.'

Clovis felt as if the room were moving and dissolving

around him. He took a deep breath: relief.

'As I said,' continued Anshelm in the same easy, friendly voice he had been using all along, 'this map also belonged to Melisande, the little girl who liked to hide in the water garden. My goodness knows how many times great-grandmother. She seems to have been an exceptionally secretive woman. And when she died, her secrets died with her.'

Clovis nodded.

'So tell me what you really see, Mr Greenwood. It is a map of water sources. We know that, you see. We have always known.'

Clovis sat as if turned to stone.

'Is there a problem, Mr Greenwood?'

Clovis searched his brain desperately for an answer. Any answer. He remembered Mariette saying: 'Balthazar always believed that no one should touch the wilderness. He could have looked for other springs and made himself rich. But he thought it would be wrong . . .'

'I can't help you look for water sources,' he said. 'I think it is wrong to disturb the wilderness.'

'Whatever your views, I think you can allow me one piece of information,' said Anshelm. 'I feel certain that you can.'

Silence.

'I have reason to suspect that there is a source of exceptionally pure water high up on the mountain, somewhere close to the glacier,' he continued, watching Clovis as he spoke. 'Long ago, when Melisande was an old lady, our family somehow divided itself. The Scarsprings stayed in the city. One of the daughters married a man named Jump. We believe that they laid claim to a spring in the mountains. At one time I had reason to believe that a descendant of theirs still lived up there, in fact that he was selling ices and water from an extraordinary van which people called the Ice Angel. But that stopped twelve years ago.'

'I can't help you,' said Clovis, his voice almost cracking with fear. He clung on to his first excuse like a man near drowning, clinging on to a sinking piece of driftwood. 'I think it is wrong to disturb the wilderness. I feel very strongly about it.'

He thought he heard a creak of footsteps on the stairs. But everything beyond the locked door seemed to be part of another world. His own world had shrunk to the size of this room, this table. And this map that could destroy everything.

'You realize that you are defying the most powerful man in Rockscar,' said Anshelm.

Clovis nodded.

'And that I only have to click my fingers and Steward Golightly will come in here to help me persuade you, and he is not a gentleman.'

They stared at each other.

'You have gone white,' said Anshelm, after a long moment. 'Perhaps I should tell you that I will not be summoning Golightly. There has been enough violence already. And this map is not for his eyes.' He sighed very heavily. It seemed that he was weighing up some decision. Then he drew something out of his pocket, a charm, and brought it to his lips.

'Let me ask you a question, Mr Greenwood,' he said. 'Do you think I am mad?'

'I don't have any logical reason to think you are mad, sir.'

Anshelm reached up and turned on the lamp directly above the table. The rest of the room faded back into shadow, leaving them together in a stark pool of light.

'People in our city are saying that I am. They are saying that I am too concerned with trolls and not paying enough attention to my work as Mayor and the urgent matter of water shortages. Do you think trolls exist, Mr Greenwood?'

'I don't have enough information to make a decision,' said Clovis.

Anshelm laughed.

'I am going to tell you something no one else knows,' he said. 'It is a confidence which I ask you to respect. There is no water shortage.'

Clovis' mouth fell open. 'But—'

'You look amazed. But it's true. There is no water shortage. We have pumping stations, we have sluice gates, we have underground reservoirs which we can draw upon, or not, as we wish. We have hundreds of miles of emergency pipes, we have emergency tanks, we have the most elaborate, superbly engineered water system imaginable. My ancestors were brilliant engineers, Mr Greenwood. And because of them this mighty city has grown to the size it is today. The water does not taste very sweet, it comes down to us through the mountain, through many layers of rock; but we do not need sweetness to survive.'

'But the reservoirs and the pumps and the drought, there's been no rain—'

'Yes, yes, a couple of the reservoirs are dry, there's been no rain. Do you think this is the first summer that we've had no rain for a few weeks? We have other reservoirs, plenty of other supplies, filtered, clean and stored away.'

Clovis, for the first time, wondered if perhaps Anshelm were crazy after all.

But there wasn't much time for contemplation.

'There appears to be a water shortage,' said Anshelm, staring at him intently, 'because I have given orders for various sluices to be closed. For taps deep in the caves under Shadowcliff to be turned off. Only I know the whole system, and only I know that I have created this crisis by myself.'

'But why?'

'Because then the Council at the Town Hall give permission for the Scarspring Water Company to dig and disrupt in each and every place I want. My employees are supposedly looking for springs and underground lakes and so forth. But I know there are no springs and underground lakes in the places where they go and dig their holes. So, can you guess what I am about, Mr Greenwood?'

Clovis frowned with concentration. He was almost too interested to be scared. But not quite.

'You do the damage,' he whispered out loud. 'You disturb the ancient trees. Then the vandalism happens. Some people say a troll is doing it . . .'

'Exactly,' said Anshelm, his eyes widening. 'I am trying to trap the troll. I am luring it to the edge of the wilderness and into the city. Everything I am doing is bait. The troll hates damage in the wilderness. It hates explosives and digging and the uprooting of trees. It has been creeping into the city to try and stop the work my men are doing. Just as I hoped it would. Every night, I visit all the places where the so-called vandalism is occurring. All I care about in life, Mr Greenwood, is finding the troll. Meeting it face-to-face. I have my reasons, and they are more serious than you can possibly imagine.'

'But the map,' began Clovis, and checked himself just in time. 'The map that *you say* shows water sources . . .'

'The Jump family, the ones who were related to the Scarsprings many generations ago and went into the wilderness, they professed to have befriended trolls, to live near their home.' Anshelm's ghostly face was flushed. His eyes were bright. 'I believe their spring to be in a cave, high up the mountain. It is the only spring that interests me and it should be on this map. If I find that spring then I am much closer to finding the troll.'

He paused and looked away from Clovis. 'If it is mad to devote all your thoughts, every waking minute, to trying to find something that others say does not exist, then, I am mad. I am mad, indeed. But we will sit here until you help me, I can wait all night.'

Clovis felt as if his mind was emptying of any ideas, or hope of ideas.

He watched Anshelm settle himself in his chair. Close to, in the harsh light of Mr Meakin's expensive lamp, it was evident that his eyes were an almost colourless beige, the iris rimmed with black. He had unusually smooth skin for a man. Nose like the beak of a bird of prey.

Yet again he raised his hand in a quick, fluid gesture and brushed his dark hair away from his eyes. Not thick hair. Straight. The sort that slides. And his hairline formed two arches, meeting in the middle of his forehead. That's why his hair kept falling forwards, of course. What did Mariette call it when someone's hair grew like that? A widow's peak.

In this wretched moment, when he thought all might be lost, Clovis suddenly realized something. The shock was so great that he shuddered. Perhaps Anshelm interpreted this as an acknowledgement of defeat.

'I'm waiting, Mr Greenwood,' he said.

Clovis liked precision. He liked facts. He had never gambled.

But he chose to gamble now.

Anything rather than betray his family.

He took a deep breath. 'I know that you have a son,' he said softly. 'A son born fourteen years ago. You probably met his mother at the Midnight Café. She knew Steward Golightly. She was not from a wealthy family. You did not stand by her. She was left to bring up your son without you.' He felt as if he might be going to pass out, he breathed again.

'I don't think the voters of Rockscar would like to think that their respectable, honourable Mayor, who gives so much to charity, had abandoned his own child. I have friends in Barnacle Radio. They could have the story tonight.'

Anshelm's eyes flared with amazement. He seemed unable to speak. He brought the charm to his lips.

'You're saying that I have a son?'

Clovis had not expected this. He had assumed that Anshelm already knew. That he would want the matter kept secret.

'Perhaps you have heard the gossip that I would have liked to have *had* a son,' said Anshelm, rapidly. 'That I despair of my nephew Ernesto's ability to lead the family. That Golightly has ambitions to take over in his place . . .'

'I can tell you the name of the woman,' said Clovis. 'Just

her first name. So you know it is not a lie.'

Anshelm fell silent. The silence grew longer. He kept his eyes fixed on Clovis. And then, yet again, something happened which Clovis did not expect.

'You do not have to tell me her name, Mr Greenwood,' whispered Anshelm, at last. 'I have never forgotten her. And now I see her in the colour of your eyes. The shape of your brows. Your dark red hair. She is your mother, is she not? And this boy, my son, is her son too.'

Chapter 49

Clovis listened to Anshelm's footsteps going slowly down the stairs. Then he, too, stood up. He didn't want to meet Mr Meakin, who must still be somewhere in the building. With the map still unread, perhaps he would not be getting the fat envelope of banknotes Anshelm had brought him.

He didn't want to meet anyone.

He closed the door of Mr Meakin's Private Office very quietly, leaving the key in the lock. The landing and the stairs were in darkness.

He stood still, listening.

Then he heard a murmur of voices. Anshelm, Golightly and Mr Meakin came down the corridor and past the foot of the stairs: the visitors were being escorted to the front door of the shop.

'Excellent,' Mr Meakin was saying. 'I'm so glad we were able to give satisfaction.'

Anshelm, it seemed, had chosen not to tell Mr Meakin anything. He spoke softly in reply: Clovis couldn't make out what he said.

'Do come back to us with any other documents,' said Mr Meakin. 'My apprentice will be most happy to oblige.'

At that moment Anshelm glanced over his shoulder, up into the darkness at the top of the stairs. Clovis froze like a rabbit.

'I look forward to meeting him again soon,' said Anshelm, speaking a little more loudly. 'He is clearly a very resourceful young gentleman. I hope to learn a great deal more from him. There is someone he can help me find.'

Steward Golightly followed his gaze and looked up. Pinned Clovis with a stare like a spear.

Mr Meakin opened the door into the shop and the three men stepped into a triangle of grey-blue light and disappeared from view, their voices receding with them.

'Psst!'

Clovis looked round, wide-eyed, heart racing.

'Up here!'

Someone was leaning over the banister of the stairs up to the attics. It was Mr Simou.

'Quick!'

'What is it?'

'Just come up here, quick!'

Mr Simou sounded so earnest, and so different from his usual cheerful self, that Clovis obeyed: treading swiftly across the creaking landing and on up the first flight of worn, uncarpeted stairs.

'In here,' hissed Mr Simou, hustling him through

the door to the storeroom, directly above Mr Meakin's Private Office.

This room was rarely used. The small window was without curtains and the glass was dirty. There was a trestle table on end, leaning against the wall.

Mr Simou closed the door behind them, his finger to his lips.

Clovis held his breath.

Silence.

More silence.

Then the sound of the door of Mr Meakin's Private Office opening and closing beneath them. Now there was a rustling noise. Clovis was surprised by how much he could hear: Mr Meakin was humming to himself, straightening chairs, putting things away. There was a rattle of keys and a metallic clunk. Must be a safe, probably behind one of the ancestors: now home to the fat envelope.

At last, Mr Meakin, still humming, left his office and locked it behind him.

Clovis looked at Mr Simou.

'Why are we—'

'I think you should see this.' Mr Simou crouched on the floor and rolled back the tattered piece of carpet.

Bare boards. And a neat round hole in the wood. Big enough to look through, if you didn't mind lying on your face. Or to listen through, if you didn't mind lying on your ear.

'You can hear everything that's said in his office from here,' whispered Mr Simou rapidly. 'This sort of thing isn't uncommon in this part of town. Jewellers', map makers', moneylenders'. Precaution. He'll send me up here to make notes of everything that's said. Prices agreed. Delivery dates. Usually when he doesn't know the customer. Sometimes he thinks they might be planning to try and rob him. Calls out to me as he's offering them a chair, "You busy up there, Mr Simou?" And I shout "Yes, Mr Meakin." And they know someone's listening.'

He replaced the carpet. 'I'm afraid your private dealings with Mayor Scarspring were not very private at all.'

Clovis managed to speak. 'You mean you were listening?'

'Me? No, certainly not.' Mr Simou paused. There was the distant thud of a heavy door closing. Mr Meakin leaving the shop and locking it behind him.

'Golightly and Meakin came down to the kitchen. I had taken the precaution of staying on, to make sure that you were OK.'

'You stayed because of me?'

'I thought Meakin seemed restless. I think he wanted to come and use the spyhole himself, but he didn't dare leave Golightly. Then a late night customer rang the bell. Meakin had to deal with them. Golightly suddenly claimed that he needed a breath of air. He left the kitchen. I followed him—'

'What? You did what?'

'I followed him, after a moment, to see where he'd gone. He wasn't at the back door. He'd come upstairs. Perhaps he'd thought of listening at the door to the office but then thought one of us might see him. Maybe he knew the spyhole is here. Maybe he had a lucky guess. I looked everywhere. There was nowhere else he could be. He stayed in here until a few minutes before Mayor Scarspring came out of the office. Then he came back down to the kitchen and waited with us, cool as you like.'

Mr Simou paused. He looked extremely serious and stern. 'Steward Golightly is outside on Parchment Street now. He has an accomplice. His chauffeur. An unpleasant person. I think that they are waiting for you and they mean you harm, Mr Greenwood. Or should I say, Mr Jump.'

Clovis gasped at the mention of his true name. He stumbled backwards against the wall and stayed there, leaning, eyes like marbles, staring at Mr Simou.

Mr Simou, however, seemed too preoccupied to notice. He took the three steps necessary to get to the window and looked down into the yard. Then he beckoned the stricken Clovis to join him.

Down below, in the dull light, the Favolosa gleamed with extra mirrors and extra lamps. Next to it, Mr Simou's wholesome green-and-black bicycle with the basket on the front.

'You will have to borrow my bike,' whispered Mr Simou.

'You can lift it over the wall. I'll take your coat and helmet, they might think I'm you. Anyway, I'll create a diversion.'

'I don't understand,' said Clovis, in a hoarse voice.

'Your mother contacted me when you got your apprenticeship. Asked me to keep an eye out in case things got rough. Which they have.'

'My *mother* contacted *you*—'

'Yes. Let's go and look out of the front.'

Clovis followed Mr Simou up another floor and into the attic overlooking the street.

'My mother . . .'

'Yes, yes. Your mother, Mariette. She used to work at the Midnight Café, Tiny is my cousin. Ah. They're there, all right . . .'

Mr Simou stepped back a little from the gabled window.

'Be careful. Stand a bit to one side.'

Clovis peered down at the pavement opposite. A rickshaw toiled past.

'In the doorway of the estate agent's,' whispered Mr Simou.

Two men were visible in the shadows. One of them appeared to be holding something, partially hidden by his coat. He stepped out of the doorway into what was left of the daylight and consulted his watch. Then he turned up his collar. It was Golightly. Holding his hunting rifle.

'You're sure they're waiting for me?'

Mr Simou nodded. 'It's not my business to know the

312

details, but I understand that Mayor Scarspring brought a map for you to read, using your particular skills.'

'You know about that? I mean, about my map reading?'

'I guessed. I knew your father, Balthazar. He had the ability too.'

'YOU knew my father?'

'There's no time for all that now. All that matters is that whatever happened in the Private Office between yourself and the Mayor – Steward Golightly heard most of it. He is absolutely ruthless, of course, and he means to control the Scarspring empire, one way or another. Young Ernesto has probably only survived this long because Golightly thinks he's a weakling. So. Do you think he might have some questions he would like to ask you? Questions prompted by whatever he heard you tell Mayor Scarspring?'

Here, Mr Simou turned away from the window and looked directly at Clovis. He spoke slowly and deliberately. 'Questions that he and his chauffeur friend might make you answer *whether you wanted to answer or not?*'

Clovis couldn't speak.

'You understand, don't you?'

Clovis managed to nod.

'Then you will also appreciate that, when you've told him everything he wants to know, you will be found in the Cat's Tail, or simply never found at all. Ever?'

'Look, wait a minute,' said Clovis, his voice shaking. 'Can't we call the police?'

Mr Simou laughed briefly. 'Golightly owns a fair number of the police. That's a police truncheon the chauffeur is carrying. And there's no point in trying to contact Mayor Scarspring either. Most of the staff at the Town Hall and Scarsprings' house answer to Golightly. He is a skilled blackmailer. You wouldn't stand a chance of speaking to the Mayor.'

He set off down the stairs.

'The only reason those two out there haven't come knocking on the door already is undoubtedly because they are waiting for what is known as "back up". Get a couple of uniformed officers and you can kidnap someone in broad daylight. It's been done plenty of times.'

A few moments later they were in the hall behind the stairs, next to the back door and the coat hooks. Mr Simou was now wearing Clovis' jacket and helmet. The jacket was too small. While Clovis watched him, in terror, he unlocked the door into the yard. A moment later, Clovis handed him the ignition key to the Favolosa. Mr Simou began to wheel the scooter down the stone passageway which led to the door on to the street. The only way out of the map maker's, apart from through the shop itself.

'I'm coming with you,' said Clovis, suddenly.

'No,' said Mr Simou, straightening the helmet. 'That would just make it even more dangerous for both of us. I can look after myself. And I telephoned someone. They are coming to my assistance. When my friend and I have got their full attention, you get the bike. You get the bike over the wall, you'll be in the yard belonging to the ironmonger's on Bloom Street. Get home as quickly as you can. Put my coat on. And helmet, it's in the basket. Different sort of helmet, still important.'

'But, I don't want you to get, to get—'

'Knocked about?'

'I don't want you to get hurt on account of me.'

Mr Simou's face broke into his familiar grin. A shade wider than normal. 'It's not me that's going to get hurt, Mr Greenwood.'

He opened the door and wheeled the Favolosa on to the pavement. 'I'll lock this,' he hissed. 'And you get out of here. As soon as you can.'

Clovis tried to grab his arm, but he was too quick. The door slammed. Clovis heard the key turn in the lock on the other side. Now both doors on to the street were locked – and he didn't have a key for either of them.

He did not rush straight to the yard and seize the bicycle as he had been advised. Instead, he flung himself back down the passage, in through the back door and up the stairs to the Globe Room on the first floor. He stopped a moment in the doorway, remembered not to turn the light on and crept towards the window.

Mr Simou, dressed as him, had positioned the Favolosa on the cobbles and was leaning over, as if adjusting the angle of one of the mirrors.

'Just *go*,' groaned Clovis.

But the Clovis down below did not seem to be in a hurry. Now he was fiddling with the headlamp.

Golightly and his chauffeur moved out of the shadows. The fake Clovis chose this moment to start messing about with the chinstrap of his helmet.

'No! No!' mouthed the real Clovis, in anguish at the window. 'Just go!'

But the fake Clovis straightened the helmet as if he had all the time in the world. Then he turned towards his two assailants just as they reached him. Golightly with the gun raised, the chauffeur beside him with the truncheon.

Clovis at the window reeled in horror. He picked up an enormous, gem-encrusted globe and heaved it on to the windowsill. He had in mind to drop it on Golightly's head somehow. He rattled frantically at the window. It was locked. He couldn't open it.

He didn't need to –

Astonishing things started happening very quickly down on Parchment Street.

Mr Simou had leapt up into the air and landed, standing, on the seat of the scooter. He gave a wild yell, kicked the rifle clean out of Golightly's hand and it smashed through the estate agent's window.

Passers-by stopped to scream.

Golightly jumped backwards, his face contorted with shock; the chauffeur swung the truncheon savagely at Mr

Simou's legs. Mr Simou jumped as if he had springs. The chauffeur missed him completely, staggered off balance, and Mr Simou landed neatly back on the seat of the scooter like an acrobat in a skipping game.

He made a gesture at the chauffeur which was well-known throughout the city and which told him exactly what to do with his truncheon.

Up at the window, Clovis was wringing his hands in terror and amazement.

Golightly said something to the chauffeur. They stood together in the middle of the street, facing Mr Simou and the scooter. Confident and dangerous again. Waiting . . .

A siren wailed, getting closer.

Clovis hopped from foot to foot. 'Go *now!*' He shouted, unheard. 'Before they get there! Go!'

He was supposed to be going himself, of course. But he couldn't even look away from the window.

The siren grew louder and louder. The chauffeur and Golightly grinned at Mr Simou. Mr Simou made a gesture concerning the appearance and lifestyle choices of their mothers and the police car came roaring up the hill and skidded to a stop.

The doors flew open. Two uniformed men scrambled out.

'. . . he owns a fair number of the police,' Mr Simou had said to Clovis.

'Arrest this man!' yelled Golightly.

317

This was it, for sure. It was going to be four against one.

The street was full of people now. They were climbing on things to get a better view.

Clovis, who had the best view of all, screamed, 'Go! Go!' at the top of his lungs. He had improved his Favolosa so many times. He knew it could easily outrun a police car. He knew Mr Simou could still save himself. He kept shouting and banging his fists on the window. But the noise of the crowd was louder than he was and there was no time to do anything else.

Golightly, the chauffeur and the two policemen advanced towards the scooter. Spreading out, like a pack of dogs closing in on the kill.

Closer and closer.

Then, in one whirling leap, Mr Simou kicked Golightly in the chest; the steward fell violently backwards; Mr Simou wrenched the truncheon off the chauffeur; reached quickly down and started the engine of the scooter, and then jumped back, standing, on the seat.

The engine snarled. A mean and moody rumble – very different from the sound of a normal scooter.

The Favolosa moved forward. The chauffeur and the two policemen flung themselves out of the way.

Mr Simou had neatly angled the front wheel. The scooter was going in a circle, as wide as the narrow road: faster now, and Mr Simou was steering with his foot; slapping the truncheon into his palm. Smiling.

Golightly lunged at his legs. The chauffeur rushed at him from the other side.

Mr Simou jumped out of Golightly's reach, landed facing the other way and sent the chauffeur sprawling with a kick.

One brave policeman got too close and was sent flying into the crowd. Golightly tried to grab the scooter by the handlebars. It ran over his foot. He staggered forwards and threw his weight against it. The Favolosa veered off course and fell over.

Clovis was scrabbling at the window catch as if he could break the metal lock with his bare hands.

Mr Simou landed on his feet, picked up the chauffeur and threw him into the window of the perfume shop. Sounds of breaking glass.

The second policeman leapt at him.

Mr Simou twisted his truncheon out of his grasp and hit him with it.

Golightly was on his feet, swaying, keeping back. He shouted with rage.

Mr Simou began to juggle with the two truncheons. There was a circle of space all around him and the fallen scooter. No one, not even Golightly, was getting any closer.

The crowd fell silent. They all just kept watching. It was obvious to eveyone that Mr Simou could go if he wanted to, now. He could pick up the scooter, jump on and drive off and no one would have cared to try and stop him.

But Mr Simou was in no hurry. He kept juggling,

throwing the truncheons higher and higher.

Suddenly the onlookers parted. A huge man came bellowing through, swinging his arms, a little round hat jammed on the back of his head. His long grey coat surging around him.

Clovis gasped. It was Mittens from the Midnight Café.

Mr Simou waved a cheery truncheon in greeting.

Mittens picked up the scooter, and Steward Golightly, and put one tidily by the kerb and the other upside down in the front of an open-topped car. He noticed the chauffeur, who, realizing himself noticed, pushed rudely through the crowd and ran away. The two policemen, who had no personal involvement and had only been obeying orders, also seemed to be losing enthusiasm. Mittens sat them side by side on top of a bakery van and they stayed there.

Mr Simou steered the scooter round to face up the hill, Mittens jumped on behind him, nearly knocking it over again, and the Favolosa accelerated up Parchment Street, aided by Clovis' modifications and therefore much faster than the driver, the passenger or the dazed onlookers expected. People screamed, the crowd scattered, Mitten's hat flew off and they were gone; the engine roaring and the whole thing only bouncing very slightly on the cobbles, protected by Clovis' suspension system, involving extra buffers and springs.

Chapter 50

Clovis couldn't think, his mind was chaotic with relief. He stayed a moment longer at the window of the Globe Room. Steward Golightly was being helped out of the open-topped car. His shoulders seemed to have become wedged in the footwell on the passenger side. Now he was on the pavement, dusting off his clothes, pushing away the people who had helped him. He looked up and down the street. Then at the map maker's, where Clovis stepped back from the window just in time.

The steward's face was grey and venomous. Clovis was suddenly terrified again. He was by himself in the dark in the ancient shop. Soon it would be night outside. And all the violence he had just witnessed had been because of him; the police and the gun and the truncheons had been meant for him. Mr Simou and Mittens had saved him from the Cat's Tail.

His legs almost buckled. He leant against the wall and put his hands to his face. His skin was cold and clammy. He took a deep breath. Then he risked another look out of the window.

Golightly was shouting, pointing the way Mr Simou and Mittens had gone. The policemen jumped into the car and started the engine. The chauffeur got in the back. The siren started to scream – they sped off.

Only Golightly was left. He had retrieved his rifle.

He stood among the broken glass in the doorway of the estate agent's across the street. Took a cigarette from his pocket and lit it. Stared at the map maker's. Terrier at a rabbit hole. Waiting.

He must have decided that the real Clovis could only be still in the shop. Alone. He would have to come out eventually. And then one man and one gun would be enough.

Clovis stepped back from the window. Forced himself to the top of the stairs. The darkness at the bottom terrified him. Clinging on to the banister. Down slowly. Heart thumping. Every board creaking under his feet.

He was in the yard. He tried to straighten Mr Simou's cycling helmet on his head. It kept slipping sideways and forwards over his eyes.

There was Mr Simou's bicycle, leaning against the wall. Dim in the failing light.

He scrambled on to the pile of logs left over from the previous winter. From there, it wasn't too difficult to get on to the top of the wall. He paused, looked around the small yard. More frightening to stay still than it was to keep moving.

Logically, if he straddled the wall, and leant down and grabbed the bike by the handlebars and *braced* himself, he should be able to lift, well, to drag, to *heave*, to . . . heave—

Clovis fell off the wall, on to a pile of sacks in the ironmonger's yard with Mr Simou's bicycle on top of him. Fortunately for him the pile of sacks was high, and the sacks were full of wood shavings.

A few anxious moments later and he was through a gate which opened on to a narrow alleyway. His nose was bleeding and the handlebars on the green-and-black bicycle were bent. He pushed the bike in as straight a line as he could manage and, grazing a row of dustbins, he emerged on Bloom Street. If he turned left he would come to the junction with Parchment Street. He turned right.

And so it was that, sometimes riding and sometimes pushing Mr Simou's bicycle, Clovis toiled back up to Storm Hill and on to the secret entrance to the caves. It took him four hours and he arrived there just after one o'clock in the morning. When he reached the bushes by the road, almost too tired to walk, and had manhandled the bicycle on to the hidden path, he saw three people waiting by the gate with a hooded lantern. His mother, her fists clenched in the pockets of her apron; and, leaning on the wall of rock, his saviour Mr Simou and Mittens from the Midnight Café.

Mariette ran forwards. 'Mr Simou told me what happened. And they've brought the Favolosa back. Zack doesn't know anything yet, he's still out in the van looking for you . . .' She stopped. Her jaw was set. Her eyes swollen from crying.

Clovis stared from one face to another.

'And I believe you've met my brother, Mittens,' added Mariette. 'Your uncle. I'm afraid we had a bit of a falling out a long time ago . . .'

Mittens shuffled from one foot to another like a bear in shoes. Mr Simou looked solemn and polite.

'Let's go back to the house,' said Mariette, brightly. 'We all need a cup of tea.'

Clovis pushed the bicycle the last few steps to the gate. He stumbled and Mr Simou caught his arm. Mr Simou who, it now turned out, was some sort of deadly fighting expert.

'All right?' whispered the deadly fighting expert.

'Just want to thank you,' mumbled Clovis. 'Saved my life.'

'Think nothing of it,' said Mr Simou. 'We enjoyed ourselves.'

Until now Clovis had believed that no one except his own family knew about this gate: so very skilfully hidden on the edge of the wilderness. But then, of course, if Mittens was Mariette's brother that made him family. Amazing thought. And hadn't Mr Simou said something about Tiny being his cousin. He looked at them all and for a moment he thought he was going to laugh. Heard Mr Simou's voice.

'I think he's feeling faint.'

Clovis breathed in, allowed himself to be steered through the gate and on down the passage to the caves. The lantern bobbed ahead of him. Mariette's face turned towards him, pale, very hard to see, nodding like a puppet.

'I've got to talk to you,' said Clovis. 'In private. It's very important.'

Chapter 51

It was the next morning. Zack was by himself.

The night before had been horrible. He and Moe had gone looking for Clovis in the van; found Parchment Street and the map maker's deserted with broken glass everywhere and then cruised around, imagining every awful thing possible. He had arrived home when it was almost light to discover that Clovis was safe and Mr Simou from Meakin's and Mittens from the Midnight Café, of all people, had just left.

Apparently, Mittens was Mariette's brother and they'd had some sort of row a long time ago. Then last night, when Clovis was so late, Mittens had gone looking for him, or something, with Mr Simou from Meakin's. Maybe they'd brought him home. Maybe the Favolosa had broken down. It certainly looked a bit dented.

The atmosphere had been very awkward and strange. Neither Mariette or Clovis wanted to talk to him. In the end, exhausted and miserable, he had gone to bed.

When he woke up again he discovered that Clovis

was in the bath. Mariette was mysteriously busy somewhere else upstairs. He decided to go down to the spring.

It was a wild, windy morning full of sunshine. Big, white clouds were sailing inland from the sea, each one perfect and separate, like a child's drawing. Zack took a lantern and leapt neatly down the path, calling to Moe, ready to tell Balthazar about Magdalena and Ernesto and the troll hunt.

'Come on, troll hound,' he called to Moe. Trying to fight off the worry that he couldn't put into words.

When he reached the spring he thought that perhaps he should fetch some more ice. He was planning to try out a new recipe. He decided to go back up to the house and get one of the metal buckets: it wouldn't take a moment. He put the lantern down by the pool, went back outside and delayed a few minutes longer, checking the tyres on the van, running his hand along the curve of the angel's wing. Her wooden feathers were already warm in the sun.

Then he went back to the front door, which was slightly open, and stopped to get a twig from between his toes. And stayed there, leaning against the wall, standing on one leg, because he heard Clovis' voice coming from inside, almost shouting, hardly sounding like Clovis at all, 'So, I'm right, then?'

'Don't ask me that.' Mariette at her coldest. 'I don't know how you dare ask me that. And now that you have bothered to come downstairs I would be very grateful if you would explain what on earth happened at Meakin's and why you were "running for your life" as Mr Simou so charmingly put it.'

'I *am* right, aren't I?'

Silence.

The creak of the kitchen door. Floorboards.

Zack straightened up and took two steps, maybe three, in through the front door and then stopped again. The room was empty. Now they were in the kitchen. Moe stood beside him. Ears up.

Clovis again, 'Well, he's going to find out himself, isn't he? Wouldn't it be better if you were the one to tell him?'

Another silence.

'He needs to know now for his own safety, Mum.'

Zack knew that he must make himself known immediately. He tried to cross the living room to the half-open door into the kitchen. He couldn't.

'I know running the van is dangerous, Clovis, but I couldn't stop him.'

'Too right it's dangerous, I should know,' Clovis even closer to shouting now. 'But this isn't to do with that. This is to do with who he really is. You're the one who should tell him. How's he going to feel if he finds out from someone else?'

'That's not possible,' said Mariette. 'Balthazar took him in when we married, and he gave him his name. That's all that matters. Only a very few people knew who his real father was and they are far too considerate and sensitive to start

328

making announcements about something which is not their business.'

'Well I *worked it out*.'

'And I trust you aren't going to start making any announcements either, Clovis.'

Zack had crouched down beside Moe. He had his arm round Moe's chest. They were both staring at the kitchen door.

'Look, a lot happened at Meakin's. The Mayor came to the shop for me to read a map of his. I'm good at reading very old maps. I gather Dad was too, so I expect you know what I mean, although it's yet another thing you never told us about. Anyway, the point is that it was all supposed to be very confidential, but your very good friend Golightly was there—'

'He is NOT my friend!'

'Well, he was once, wasn't he? We've seen the photograph of the two of you at the Midnight Café. You looked pretty friendly to me. And that's his gun you've got hidden inside the sofa. The one with the initial G on it. A little present, was it? We're not stupid.'

Zack lurched to his feet. He didn't wait to hear any more. He didn't run into the kitchen and confront them. He reeled around as if someone had punched him in the face and he stumbled and skidded down the path, his arms flailing, his hair in his eyes.

He ran on, falling, running again, down to the caves.

Chapter 52

Zack stood by the spring, gasping in the cool air, everything beyond the lantern light very dark after the bright blue day outside.

Moe sat down on the floor of the cave beside him, whining quietly.

The spring rippled.

Slowly, like a wounded man, Zack sank to his knees. His eyes were tight shut. A thousand secret words had been whispered here. Childhood news, festivals and presents; stories about Clovis and his maps and engines; the misery at Storm Hill School; and then, at last, the triumph of the Ice Angel.

He was starting to shake.

'I don't think you're my real dad,' he whispered. 'I think you must have sort of adopted me. Mum had me already. Clovis is your son. But I'm not. So I'm not really a Jump at all. I didn't know. Clovis has found out somehow. And I think my real dad,' he paused, 'I think my real dad is Stefan Golightly.'

He had one hand to his face. The other was pressed hard down on the dusty ground, as if he could root himself there, and never leave again.

'I'm so sorry. I'm so sorry, Dad, I didn't know. Maybe I shouldn't have come and talked to you all these times . . . I expect you would have liked Clovis to tell you stuff. He looks like you, I think. And he's good at all the things you were good at. Are good at . . .'

Silence.

'I'm so sorry,' added Zack again. 'I feel like it's all my fault.' Although what it was that was his fault, or why, he didn't know. Everything.

'I'm sorry,' he dropped his voice to the faintest whisper. 'I love you.'

Then he took his hand from his face and opened his eyes. There was the cave. The spring in its rocky pool. It was just that he felt hopelessly different and alone.

He shifted his weight and looked down and saw his palm print in the dust, lit by the lantern.

Moe gave a soft yelp.

Zack stared, transfixed.

The print was spreading. It was changing. The edges were shifting in the dust. Slowly, the familiar shape of his own palm was disappearing. It became wider, the fingers and thumb shortened and strengthened until they were broader and blunter than before.

Then it stopped. Finished and perfect.

As if someone else had pressed his hand exactly where his had been. And kept it there, as he had done.

Chapter 53

The workshop door stood open, but there was no sign of Magdalena. Zack parked the Bellisima just inside. His heart was racing, he almost dropped his helmet. He could smell the engine oil and the diesel and, riding above them, a layer of some other, very different scent.

Something moved in the corner of his vision. He swung round thinking of the wolf; but it was only Moe, walking away across the flagstones towards the giant wilderness cedar tree.

'Moe!' called Zack. Feeling worse than ever. 'Keep away from the track.'

Moe turned and looked back over his shoulder, wagging his tail.

Then Zack realized that something was different. There was a ladder against the trunk of the ancient tree. More than a ladder: a flight of very well-worn and very steep wooden steps.

Displaying his unexpected skill with the vertical, Moe launched himself upward and began climbing. Zack ran across and looked up into the dense architecture of the branches and saw platforms and banisters high above. A bigger and much more elegant version of the lookout tree back home.

'Moe! Get down here!'

No reply. He pulled himself up. As he climbed, the smell of engine oil and diesel receded. A light and mysterious scent grew stronger, mingled now with the odour of the cedar itself, dark and green and full of shadows.

He progressed from one landing to another, passing a businesslike, short-handled axe leaning against the tree trunk. The rooftops of the warehouses and the other buildings of the Rock spread below him. The sea shone like steel in the distance. He kept climbing.

Then, at last, he reached a platform with a railing all around it and one last short ladder, leading up to an open door. He was looking at the most elaborate and beautiful tree house he could have imagined.

'Hello,' called a voice. Magdalena's voice. 'Come in.'

Zack climbed into a curved wooden room, with round windows, bookshelves, a stove and a thick carpet on the floor. Moe, predictably, was already stretched out, getting his neck stroked. Another ladder led away, higher: other rooms, above this one, further up the tree. A low door stood half open, revealing a glimpse of something that might be a kitchen.

'You look hot,' said Magdalena. 'Would you like

a cold drink? We have the plumbings. Or perhaps the cup of tea?'

She was dressed almost entirely in black, with some sparkling bits here and there. A short black dress with a mysterious spiky skirt that stood out like the sort ballet dancers wore, with silver net underneath. Black boots with thick silvery soles. Elbow and knee protectors, also black.

'Perhaps the coffee?'

Her lips were painted the colour of dark plums. Or maybe they were always like that.

'Thanks,' said Zack. 'Chocolate would be nice.'

'I didn't say I had chocolate. I don't have chocolate. I have tea or coffee.'

'Yes. That's what I meant.'

She was wearing a necklace made out of pointed teeth.

'Which?'

Now she was smiling. Something warmer. Gone though. Almost immediately.

'I will make you tea. I believe it fortifies the brain.'

She went through the door at the other end of the room. He heard water running.

Then he looked up and noticed a row of skulls on the wall above the bookshelves. At first he thought they were deer; but they were too broad. The eye sockets looked forwards, small black caves. He took a couple of steps closer. They couldn't be deer. They looked far too much like human skulls. Very much like human skulls except they had antlers, one on each side of the head, sweeping out gracefully and then branching into three curved points like those of young stags.

Zack stared at them. They had teeth. Human type teeth.

'You would like sugar?'

She came back into the room carrying a tray with a china teapot, a cup, a sugar bowl covered with a beaded cloth and a jug of milk. All matching and daintily decorated with flowers.

'Oh, you have seen the skulls,' she said. 'These are the trolls my grandfather killed, of course.'

She looked away from him as she said this, pouring the tea.

'These are the actual skulls of actual trolls? And you've got them here in your living room?'

'Obviously.'

'They really exist, then—'

'Oh! Goodness me. Here is the boy Ernesto.'

She and Moe had both crossed to one of the neat round windows.

Zack joined them, holding his teacup as delicately as if his grip might break it.

Down below in the yard, Ernesto Scarspring was peering into the workshop. A tall man was with him, lightly built. A black Wind Shadow 5 was parked near the side gate: only one lamp on the front, only two, perfectly-angled mirrors. The most elegant, most powerful and most expensive scooter in Rockscar. The man removed his helmet. He turned his head from side to side, freeing his long dark hair.

Magdalena breathed in sharply.

'Anshelm,' she whispered, 'The Water King himself.'

Zack stepped back from the window as if he'd seen a sniper.

'You are afraid of him?' said Magdalena. 'I am not afraid of anyone.'

Now Ernesto had seen the wooden staircase. He looked up. His agitation echoed around him. He dropped some papers that he was carrying. He bent to retrieve them.

'I'm not scared of Mayor Scarspring,' said Zack. 'I just don't want him to see me, that's all.'

Magdalena had picked up a battered-looking bag from beside the stove. She slung it on to her shoulder.

'My equipment,' she said.

Zack nodded. What would that be, exactly?

'You will have to meet eventually, you know,' she said, heading towards the ladder.

'What do you mean?'

Perhaps she hadn't heard him. She paused, straightening an elbow protector, and then climbed down out of sight. Moe trotted towards the ladder to follow her.

'Hey!' hissed Zack. 'Just whose dog are you anyway?'

Moe sat down with a thump and stared back at him with his large, thoughtful eyes. Then he tilted his head on one side and folded an ear.

'Oh for goodness sake,' said Zack. 'There's no need to look like a birthday card. It's just that, well, it's just that you seem so at home here. It's just a bit weird, that's all.' He sighed.

Moe gave a low, questioning bark.

'All right,' said Zack. He took a sizeable gulp of tea and put down the cup. She must have used some of that Ice Angel water he had seen the customer giving her. There was no Scarspring aftertaste at all.

Zack stepped off the last step at the bottom of the tree. Moe followed him, coming down headfirst.

Ernesto was already greeting Magdalena and introducing her to his uncle. Anshelm Scarspring held up his long hand to shield his eyes from the sun.

'You must excuse my nephew,' he said, as Ernesto tangled his words. 'He is happier reading than he is talking.'

'He is a very clever person,' said Magdalena. 'This is evident.'

'That's what I'm hoping.'

Zack stayed back in the shadow of the tree.

'So you are truly a descendant of these people who were called troll hunters?' said Anshelm.

She nodded.

'And there is only you?'

She nodded again. 'I lost both my parents. It is over twelve years now.'

Zack frowned. How old was she, anyway? Had she brought herself up?

'And your friend over there?'

Anshelm was standing almost with his back to Zack, who had stayed quite still. Not still enough to go unnoticed, it seemed.

'That is the person who has the troll hound and has been kind enough to agree to join us,' said Ernesto.

Zack stepped forward into the sunshine. For the first time in his life he was knowingly walking right up to Anshelm Scarspring. One of the two men who might have killed his father. And, in that same moment, crossing the dusty yard, everyone's eyes upon him, he remembered yet again that Balthazar was not his father, after all. All morning he had been ambushed by that knowledge. Over and over and over, each time as fresh and harsh as a slap in the face.

Balthazar was not his father. Unbelievably, unbearably, his father was Stefan Golightly.

Zack looked from one person to another. Glanced down for the reassuring sight of Moe. Moe wasn't there.

'May I enquire as to your name?' said Anshelm.

'I'm sorry,' said Ernesto, quickly. 'I didn't introduce you.' His light brown skin flushed with an undertone of pink: clearly, correct introductions were important in the Scarspring household.

'This is, this is Mr, er, Mr . . .' He looked at Zack, frowning with anxiety.

'Greenwood,' said Zack. 'Zachary Greenwood.'

It had been dark the first time they met and Anshelm had worn his silver shiner helmet and the scarf across his face: only his eyes had been visible. Now they stood together in a blaze of sunlight. Each could see the other clearly. Anshelm's eyes swept over Zack. Then he took a step towards him, and stumbled slightly on the uneven paving stones.

'Yes,' he said, softly. 'Greenwood. Of course . . .' He paused, nodding, his gaze taking in every detail of Zack's face. 'I believe I've met your brother.'

Zack flinched with surprise. A moment later, he was more surprised still.

'But I wonder,' continued Anshelm, with the same strange intensity, 'do you know who I am?'

Zack darted a glance at Magdalena. It looked as if the rumours that Mayor Scarspring was a little crazy were not far wrong. Or perhaps he thought that Zack looked stupid. That was probably it.

'You're the Mayor, sir. You're Mayor Anshelm Scarspring,' he said, carefully. 'Head of the Scarspring Water Company.'

Anshelm nodded again and then looked away.

'You are right,' he said. 'And these are fancy titles that mean nothing.'

There was an awkward pause. The sun felt very hot on Zack's face.

'So,' continued Anshelm, turning to Magdalena. 'If I had known your family existed I would have sought you out long ago myself. I am most interested to meet anyone who has first-hand experience of trolls. In fact, because of an experience which I have had, an event in my life which remains unexplained and which haunts me more tenaciously than I can say, I would very much like to describe something to you and for you to tell me if that description fits with your knowledge, your understanding, that is, of trolls . . .'

The elegant, composed Mayor of Rockscar City had gone. At that moment Anshelm had become as humble as a pilgrim.

'Have you got a radio?' said Ernesto, suddenly.

Three pairs of eyes turned to him in surprise.

'It's very important,' said Ernesto.

'Of course,' said Magdalena. 'In the workshop.'

'I need to listen to a short programme in five minutes and thirty seconds' time,' said Ernesto, looking at his watch.

'I will show you how to tune it in. It is moody.'

'If you will excuse me,' said Ernesto, with a courteous nod towards his uncle.

Anshelm raised his eyebrows but he said nothing; and Magdalena and Ernesto crossed into the shadows of the workshop, where Zack remembered seeing a large, many-dialled wireless on a shelf above the workbench.

Their voices receded, leaving Zack and Anshelm alone.

Despite having seen photographs in the newspapers for as long as he could remember, Zack had imagined that Anshelm was broad and burly. A brawler in expensive clothes. However, the real Anshelm was almost thin. He had large eyes in a pale, bony face. He looked exhausted.

Then Zack suddenly ducked and yelled. The yard was reverberating with a high-pitched droning, loud and piercing and savage. He caught a glimpse of something out of the corner of his eye, a scarlet flash in the air, something too fast to see, weaving around him, closer, further, diving closer again, choosing how it would attack, the face, the eyes, the throat—

'Stay still!' Anshelm shouted. 'Lightning flies! Don't move!'

Zack was cowering on the ground with his hands over his face. Everyone knew that you must cover your face. One bite and he'd be unconscious in minutes. He had been going to run for the workshop. Something in Anshelm's voice stopped him. He could see between his fingers, Anshelm a dark shape, a sudden blur of violent, decisive movement—

'It's safe now,' said Anshelm.

Zack shifted and looked around. He stood up slowly. Then he saw them. Two lightning flies. Dead on the ground.

'What happened?'

'I knocked them out of the air,' said Anshelm,

grinning. 'With my hand. Party trick. All to do with speed and reflexes.'

'You knocked . . . but how could you even see them? They're so fast . . .'

Zack looked down at the two flies. He had only seen pictures of them.

'They're so fast and so little. At school the Health Person from the Town Hall said that it was pointless trying to swat them, you'd always miss.'

Anshelm stood on the dead flies and crushed them with his foot. Now they were just two smears of red and black on the paved yard.

'I didn't miss,' he said, quietly.

'Thanks.' Zack paused. He felt as if his heart was going to beat out of his chest. 'You probably saved my life.'

'My pleasure. The least I could do.'

They both looked down at the paving stones.

'We'll ask the young woman if she would be kind enough to pour a little petrol over them,' added Anshelm. 'To neutralize the poison.'

Zack nodded. He raised his hand to brush away the hair that was always falling across his eyes.

He saw Anshelm's expression flicker into shock. Staring at his fingers. They were stained purple with berry juice. He made so many ices these days, he rarely got rid of the stain completely. He looked up again to see that Anshelm had gone white.

'I make fruit pies,' said Zack, rapidly. 'I help my mother. It looks like blood but it's only berry juice.'

'The ring,' whispered Anshelm. 'That is a very distinctive ring. I believe I have seen it before.'

Zack was only wearing one ring, of course. The one he and Clovis had found hidden in the chest in the wall at home. Balthazar's ring.

The radio chatted busily in the workshop. Magdalena was saying something to Ernesto. Zack tried to seize on to what was happening. Anshelm had recognized the ring. Had he seen it on Balthazar's finger? When? Where? What had been happening?

'Mayor Scarspring,' he said, lowering his own voice in turn, speaking in a rush, 'Have you ever travelled the Wolf Road?'

Anshelm seemed to sway where he stood. He drew a charm out of his pocket and held it to his lips. Zack saw that it was an angel, made of some greenish metal. A tiny version of their own angel on the front of the van.

'Have you ever travelled the Wolf Road?' whispered Zack, again. Terrified.

'Where did you get that ring?' said Anshelm. 'Five blue pearls set in twenty-five carat gold. If you turn it slightly we will see the place where a pearl is missing. It was always missing. That ring has been in my family for over four generations. It first belonged to my ancestor, Melisande.'

'But we thought, we thought . . .'

'That ring was mine,' said Anshelm. 'I lost it on a terrible night, in the dark, during a, during a,' he sighed, 'during a struggle. After everything had happened, and I was home again, I discovered that it had come off my finger . . . it was always a little loose . . . 'I ask *you*, Zachary Greenwood, have you ever travelled the Wolf Road?'

Suddenly there was the sound of a car screaming to a halt outside. The metallic thud of the door slamming, brisk footsteps, someone rattling the side gate and a voice calling, 'Anshelm, are you here?'

'Damn him,' whispered Anshelm. He looked quickly around and then pointed at the steps leading up into the tree house.

'Go up there,' he said, urgently. 'Now. I don't want him to see us side by side.' Zack goggled at him.

'It's Golightly,' said Anshelm. 'If he realizes who you are he will mean you harm. Get out of sight. NOW.' He seized Zack's shoulders, spun him round and shoved him towards the tree.

More noise from the gate. Someone kicking it.

'Is Mayor Scarspring there? I need to see him. Open this gate immediately.'

Zack hesitated for a moment. Glimpsed the crushed lightning flies near his feet. Ran to the wooden steps.

Anshelm was walking over to the gate. Unbolting it. Zack reached the second platform, stopped, breathless, and stood there, in the shelter of the branches. Watching.

It was Stefan Golightly.

Zack froze. Every particle of his being focussed on this man. Fourteen years after the photograph had been taken in the Midnight Café, Golightly's handsome face didn't look so different. However, in the spotlight next to the young and sparkling Mariette Muldorn he had been smiling. Now he looked dishevelled and limping and dangerous.

'If he realizes who you are he will mean you harm,' Anshelm had said, whatever that meant.

Zack steadied himself against the carved handrail of the platform.

'I've been looking for you all night, Anshelm, where have you been?' Golightly's words tumbling.

'I had a lot on my mind after our visit to the map maker's, Stefan. You know how I like to roam the city alone. I returned for breakfast and found young Ernesto setting out to come here. I decided to join him.'

'They said back at the house that you and Ernesto are visiting some charlatan who pretends to be a troll hunter.'

'That's right. It is a public holiday. I am allowed a little sight-seeing.'

'And do you realize that a journalist is trying to find this place as we speak? This will be a delightful scoop for him. You and your troll obsession will make the front page yet again.'

Golightly stared around the yard, took in the doorway of the workshop: looked Anshelm up and down. 'If they photograph you now you will look as if you have slept in your clothes. Where is this so-called troll hunter anyway, too scared to show himself now I'm here?'

'If anyone should be scared to show his face it is you, Stefan,' said Anshelm, evenly.

Zack could see Golightly's face. The steward certainly didn't look scared. He breathed in now, looking back at Anshelm, nodding, seeming to try and calm himself.

'I understand that you told someone something extraordinary last night. I am praying that it was a lie.'

'You're the one who's told lies, aren't you, Stefan? I've had all night to think about it. You sent away the woman I loved because you discovered she was carrying my child. You told me she had vanished. Takes the night train inland. What lies did you tell *her*? That I knew she was with child? That I wanted nothing to do with her and her baby? Or did you just threaten her so badly that she ran away? And then, I believe, you concocted a story for her monstrously large brother, all about me ill-treating her. He threw me out of the Midnight Café. Literally. '

Up on the platform Zack's hands were clenched around the wooden handrail. He was recognizing things. People. Mittens Muldorn. It had to be. Which meant that the woman Golightly had sent away was Mariette. Which meant . . .

'I had a son, apparently,' said Anshelm, his voice as dry as bones. 'You made sure that I didn't know. But I know

now, Stefan. Were you spying on my meeting at the map maker's?'

For a moment Zack didn't hear anything clearly. The scene below and the platform around him swam and blurred and the loudest sound he could hear was his own heartbeat.

Then Golightly, shouting, 'I did it to protect *you*, Anshelm! *Everything* has been for you. I have made you the richest, most successful man in this city. She was nobody. Unworthy of the house of Scarspring. A peasant—'

'Do you think I cared? I would have married her!' Anshelm's face, white with rage.

'I'm a servant of your family, Anshelm, I protected you. That woman and her brat are in the past. You need my protection again right now. Do you realize that there are water protests going on all over the city? That a march is planned tonight and that some mean for it to end *outside our house*? Tell me. Is it true that you have brought about this water crisis yourself? Tell me it is not true, Anshelm. I beg you.'

But Anshelm leapt forwards, swinging his fist, as fast and as sure as when he had knocked the lightning flies out of the air and saved Zack's life. He punched Golightly on the mouth and Golightly staggered backwards and fell.

'Go!' he shouted. 'And that is for my son, and the years that separate me from him. Fourteen long years!'

Zack stood transfixed.

Golightly struggled to his feet. His hand to his mouth. His face was very pale and there was blood between his fingers. When he finally spoke it was obvious that he was using all his energy to keep his self-control.

'Come with me now, Anshelm,' he said. 'Come away from this place and this so-called troll hunter. Come home now.'

'Don't you want to know what happened?' cried Anshelm. 'Do you want to go on believing that we are murderers until we lie in our graves ourselves? There was something else on the Wolf Road that night. You know there was. Something invisible, powerful. I was arguing with Zoran, I don't deny that. We had followed him. I told him that trolls don't exist. I said that anyone who claimed that he could meet one was lying. Tricking him . . .'

'Sound familiar?' spat Golightly.

'He told me to go home. He was always sending me away. He was the clever one. He said he didn't need my advice. His wife was still alive. She was there, in the wilderness. He was going to see her. I thought he must truly be losing his reason. How could she be there, on the mountain, in that freezing night? I seized him, I had him by the shoulders. I don't deny that. Then that extraordinary van came out of the dark. The ice seller, Jump. Zoran tried to knock me away . . .'

Up in the wilderness cedar Zack leant forward as far as he dared, his scalp pricking with fear.

'The ice seller flung himself out of the van. Who knows what he made of what he saw? You were there, waving your stupid rifle.'

'*You* had your hands round Zoran's throat,' snarled Golightly. 'You have never been able to control your temper. If it wasn't for me—'

'Something happened . . .'

'Yes, something happened. You struck him and he fell off the side of the road.'

'I did *not* strike him.'

'Just as you struck me now.'

'There was a singing, a young woman's voice suddenly singing in a strange language, what was that, Stefan? Can you explain that? Something struck me. Something darker than the darkness. I felt its heat. I was knocked down. It held me there on the ground. I heard you fire your gun. And the ice seller went spinning sideways. There was screaming. The air seemed to be ripped open like a curtain. Then the weight was off me. And there was just the two of us. And scattered, broken things on the ground. And that van. And the angel on the front . . .'

Golightly was shaking his head. Slowly. His split lip ugly and swollen.

'There was *something there* on the Wolf Road,' Anshelm's voice was full of pain. 'Did it drag Zoran out of my grasp? Did it throw him into the ravine? The ice seller fell with your bullet, over the edge. I saw him. I can see him now. I see him every night when I close my eyes. Silhouetted in that blaze of light. His hand clutching his face . . . You always have been a good shot, Stefan, let's hope he died quickly and the wolves didn't pull him to pieces while he still breathed.'

Zack screamed.

Both men looked up at the tree.

Zack ran towards the top of the ladder. He turned, half leaping, half falling, down from rung to rung. He reached the next and final platform. Not a ladder from here. The curved wooden steps.

He ran forwards. The top of the steps. The yard below.

Heard Golightly's voice again. Golightly who was not his father after all. Golightly who had murdered Balthazar.

Zack's breath like fire in his throat. Every muscle, every fibre of his body electric with hate and pain.

Then he stopped. As if he had run into a wall. He stopped at the top of the staircase, pushing against a darkness that made no sense. That held him. And then, unbelieving, uncomprehending, he felt himself slowly lifted backwards. And something steadied him. And he sank down on to the platform, his arms by his sides.

He tried to throw himself forwards, to use his whole body against the unseen force. But he was trapped.

Something breathed on his face.

Golightly's voice, down in the yard, shaking with rage . . .

'I know what I did. I did it for you. I don't indulge myself in ridiculous excuses and explanations. The outlaw ice seller had obviously tricked Zoran into meeting him in that forsaken place. He intended some crime. Maybe even murder. Maybe he planned to sell Zoran more lies about his lost wife. Zoran would have given him anything he asked. Good riddance to the ice seller, he was bad for business anyway . . .'

Zack clawed at the thing that held him. He tried to cry out and felt something cover his mouth. Something very like a human hand.

'You need to believe that trolls are real, Anshelm,' shouted Golightly. 'I don't.'

'*There was something there, Stefan.*'

'You saw something that wasn't there, Anshelm. That's the Curse of the Scarsprings. In your head. And now it's consuming you. You're throwing everything away. All our years of hard work. Everything.' Golightly's voice rang out, ricocheting in the yard like gunfire. 'The people will rise up against you. You're blind to what is happening.'

A creak and the slam of the side gate shutting.

The thing which held Zack was gone. He almost fell down the steps and saved himself, clinging on to the banisters, gasping for breath, although no breath had been denied him. Then he stayed there, looking down, staring at Anshelm, who stood in the middle of the yard, holding the angel charm against his cheek.

352

Slowly, because he was aching all over, Zack went down the wooden steps that led to the foot of the tree. He reached the bottom and stopped again.

Anshelm looked up. Managed a crooked smile.

Then Magdalena came out of the workshop, packed with health and energy, with Moe beside her carrying a biscuit in his mouth. Surely she had heard the shouting. She must have decided to stay out of sight.

'Forgive me,' she said. 'It takes some time to tune in my wireless, there is a problem with my amplifications and then the programme Mr Ernesto wished to hear was a little bit postponed because the news was extended by talking about the water protests . . . Oh, you two, you look like . . . two ghosts . . .'

Her words faded. Her face was changing. Some shock had engulfed her. She was staring at Anshelm and the charm he was holding. Her mysterious eyes grew dark, and darker still.

'I must ask you something,' said Anshelm. 'I must ask you, it is about the nature of trolls. Is it possible, are they ever responsible for . . .'

Now, again, there was shouting outside at the gate.

'. . . responsible for a sort of energy, something which doesn't seem to have a shape, but which is dark, and can impose itself, push people, perhaps even larger things, like trees or machines . . .'

The gate rattled. More shouting.

'Excuse me,' said Magdalena. She marched over to the gate. 'Who are you?' she called, sternly. 'What do you want?'

'Do you mean something that seems to be alive?' whispered Zack.

'Yes,' Anshelm nodded. 'Definitely alive. Why?'

Magdalena was running back towards them. Her thick yellow and gold hair swung round her like a cape.

'Mayor Scarspring, there is newspaper person at the gate. He says am I a troll hunter and where are the evidence and do you also believe in fairies? He has a camera and he proposes climbing over the gate very soon.'

'Is there another way out of here?' Anshelm, very quick and crisp.

'Yes. If you will bring your scooter, I will escort you. There is a little path on the other side of the railway line. It will take you all the way back into SugarTown.'

The gate rattled. Scrabbling. Someone was trying to climb over.

Magdalena ran over to the Wind Shadow and started to wheel it towards them.

Anshelm turned to Zack, lowering his voice. 'Tell me how you obtained the ring.'

'We found it,' said Zack, blushing like a thief.

'Where?'

'With some papers and things . . . at home . . .'

Much cursing from the gate. The top of a head appeared

briefly, only to vanish again, followed by the thud of someone falling heavily back to the ground.

Anshelm grabbed Zack's arm.

'How could it be in your home?'

'I don't know. Maybe she, someone found it. You said it must have come off, you said it was loose—'

'You did not know it had belonged to me?'

'No, of course not. I thought it had belonged to my father.' Zack felt the word catch in his throat. His eyes stung with tears.

'Your father?'

Zack nodded. He couldn't speak.

'Your father is dead?'

'I thought he was my father,' Zack whispered.

'Mayor Scarspring, you must be quick,' called Magdalena. Already pushing the scooter at a diagonal up the side of the embankment.

Zack began pulling the ring off his finger.

Anshelm stopped him. Clasped his hands over Zack's. Just for a moment.

'Keep it,' he said, softly. 'From me. Wear it. Until we meet again.'

Then he turned and ran up the steep slope and he and Magdalena hauled the Wind Shadow up on to the railway line and they disappeared over the other side.

Just as a small-faced man with a camera fell heavily off the top of the gate on to the paved yard.

Chapter 54

'So who exactly are you?' repeated the newspaperman again, sitting up, brushing dust off his clothes.

'I make pies,' said Zack, who had said all this already. 'Fruit pies. Meat pies, then I deliver them round the workshops and places at lunchtime.'

'I can't see any pies,' said the man, tetchily.

His camera was broken, his knuckles were bleeding and his glasses were bent.

'No. That's because today I'm just collecting orders. We've got some new recipes in. We only come round twice a week, you see.' Zack was trying to sound calm. A huge effort.

'Only I heard there was someone here who pretends to hunt trolls. And that our excellent Mayor, Mr "I Believe in Fairies" Scarspring, is visiting them. Meanwhile, our citizens are suffering. People are getting sick. The hospitals are full. Protests and demonstrations all over the place. My sources in the police say it is only a matter of time before there is a dangerous riot. People are very, very angry. All because there is not enough water. And our esteemed Mayor and Head of the Scarspring Water Company is sneaking around talking about trolls.'

The man was now holding a folded banknote. Quite a large one. He unfolded it and smoothed it out. Then he flicked it with an inky finger: it made a crisp, inviting sound.

'You wouldn't happen to have seen him, would you?'

Any minute now Ernesto would come ambling out of the workshop. Innocent, polite and happy to talk to anyone about anything: banknotes not required.

'I can't help you,' said Zack. 'I don't know what you're on about at all.'

Something caught the sun, something on the edge of his vision: a flicker of gold up on the railway line. Magdalena? He turned but there was no one there.

The newpaperman was still holding out the money; he was also glancing around, towards the entrance of the workshop and the faint chatter of the radio.

The painful chaos in Zack's head cleared. He saw Anshelm Scarspring knock the lightning flies out of the air: Anshelm who turned out, face to face, to be as lightly made and skinny as Zack himself.

'I don't know what you're on about and I think you should go now,' said Zack. He clenched his fists and took a step forwards, and was amazed to see the newspaperman get quickly on his feet, grab the remains of his camera and cram his broken glasses into his pocket.

'Now,' continued Zack, not recognizing anything about himself. 'Get out. My friend will be back in a minute and I don't want her upset.'

'OK, squire,' muttered the newspaperman, retreating towards the gate, still looking around. They arrived there together and Zack let him out and locked it behind him.

Then, feeling as if nothing were real, he walked over to the door of the workshop and went inside.

Chapter 55

Ernesto was crouched on a stool next to the workbench. The wireless was beside him. Moe was stretched out at his feet.

'Fat lot of use you were,' hissed Zack. Moe was unimpressed. He thumped his tail gently on the floor.

'Ssh!' hissed Ernesto, one finger to his lips, the other gripping a stubby pencil, poised over a notepad. 'I'm listening for clues.'

It was the *Dinah Dibbs* show, of course. And Dinah was speaking now.

'The hamster Tippy Toes the Third had been *trained* to gnaw through wires on burglar alarms,' she said, fervently. 'That's how the burglars burgled the bank. The judge said it was not his fault and he walked free with no stains on his characteristics. He's going to live with my dad's pigeons.'

'That's nice, dear,' said Mrs Malone.

'And I have a message for my friend whose pet was kidnapped,' said Dinah. 'I have great news. I know where his pet is hidden. The one who likes fish. He must meet me exactly where we met before. I will tell him the location. I will be there at six o'clock tonight.'

'Goodness,' said Mrs Malone. 'How exciting.'

'One of my pigeons has laid an egg,' said Captain Malone. 'Some say we are fiction. But you can't argue with an egg.'

There was a little burst of music and then there was the announcer, smooth as ever, 'Here is an extra news bulletin. It is the hottest day of the year so far. The water protests are continuing in the city this afternoon and a large demonstration is planned for this evening. There are rumours that some of the protestors plan to march from the City Hall to Merchant's Hill. Illegally distilled liquor had been widely distributed. Police are advising citizens to stay at home. The crowd outside the City Hall is already over one thousand strong. Any disorderly behaviour will lead to immediate arrest.

'And after the weather forecast we will be having a special interview with Mr Edgar Featherplum, the director of *Dinah Dibbs, Girl Detective*, to discuss the runaway success of the recent change of direction which has resulted in the highest listening figures in the history of radio serial dramas.'

Ernesto leapt into the air, surprisingly high, and started bouncing around the workshop as if he were on springs.

He paused to turn off the wireless; then he started bouncing again.

'That message is for me, that message about the cat, it's for me, my cat's called Fisher, you see, the one who likes fish, and I've got to meet Dinah outside our house at six o'clock tonight. Well, not actually Dinah, she must have found Fisher.'

There was a sound from the doorway and they both turned. Magdalena stood silhouetted, framed by her glittering hair.

'But Dinah says that she will tell me the location,' added Ernesto, stationary at last.

'Mr Ernesto,' said Magdalena. 'I have a proposition. Your uncle Mr Anshelm has a little green charm in the shape of an angel on a chain. Do you know the one I mean?'

Ernesto nodded. 'It is very precious to him,' he said. 'It belonged to my father.'

'Get me that charm and I will get you your cat. Wherever she is. Whatever it is necessary to do.'

'You can do that?'

She nodded. 'Of course.'

'But I would be stealing. If you are sure that you can get my cat then perhaps you would accept money instead.'

'You will not be stealing,' said Magdalena. 'I have seen the charm today. It once belonged to my family.'

'Then it wasn't my father's? My uncle has always said that it was. That is why he values it so much. He found it on the

361

ground where my father disappeared.'

Magdalena seemed to consider how to reply.

'I believe that your uncle found it. But it was not your father who dropped it. It was someone else.'

She came out of the doorway and into the workshop and, as she did so, her face became visible again. Zack was startled to see the intensity of her expression.

'There are many shops in the jewellers' quarter selling beautiful charms,' persisted Ernesto. 'Many people carry them, it is like having a guardian on your automobile. I would be most happy to buy you one. I have saved up a lot of money. I never spend it.'

Magdalena had clasped her hands together. Her eyes had become huge and fathomless.

'The thing is, Ernesto,' said Zack, surprising himself yet again, 'I think it must be a very particular charm of great sentimental value. It can't be replaced with another one.'

He realized that Magdalena was looking at him. 'Isn't it, Magdalena?'

She nodded.

'I think it might still be stealing,' said Ernesto, very sadly. 'But he took my cat. I should harden my heart.'

'*He* took your cat?' exclaimed Zack.

'Well, Golightly did. He is powerful, you know, behind the scenes. It's to make me use my initiative and face danger. In order to get her back, I must catch the troll that is carrying out the vandalism. I think that part must have been my uncle's idea. Golightly doesn't believe in trolls. I think he would like me to have been set a task like climbing up the outside of the tide-bell tower or the lighthouse. Then maybe he could have tried to arrange for me to be pushed off.'

'*Push you off?*' gasped Zack.

'It is possible.'

'You're saying he would kill you?'

'If it could seem like an accident, yes, I think he would. Now that I am almost grown up.'

'But, surely your uncle—'

'Golightly has some sort of hold over my uncle. With me out of the way and this power he has over my uncle, he would be running the family, and the Water Company and the City Hall for the rest of his life. I have known this for as long as I can remember.'

Zack shuddered: in comparison to this, Storm Hill School seemed almost cosy.

'Please get the angel charm for me, Mr Ernesto,' said Magdalena. 'Go home now and get it, I'm sure you can. And we will meet you outside the Scarspring house at six o'clock tonight and the person from the wireless will tell us how to rescue your cat.'

'When you say we—' began Zack.

'Yes,' said Ernesto, his eyes shining. 'I will do it. We will meet on the stroke of six pm.'

He held out his hand to Magdalena and she shook it solemnly.

Then he climbed on to his Tugalug and put on his helmet. Zack unlocked the gate. The Tugalug puttered away down the street: overtaken, as it went, by several faster-moving pedestrians.

Chapter 56

Zack and Magdalena walked back into the yard where Moe was rolling on his back, waving his unexpectedly large feet.

'I must ask you,' said Zack immediately. 'I must ask you. What the Mayor said, about a sort of darkness that presses on you, stops you moving . . .' He was watching her face closely. She had no expression. Her slanting eyes were almost closed against the sun.

'Do you know about it? I mean, has it happened to you? Here? It happened to me just now, in the tree. You were in the workshop with Ernesto. Golightly came in the yard. They argued. But I was up there,' he pointed at the wilderness cedar, ' and it stopped me coming down. And it happened to me once before in the street. Golightly was there that time too . . .'

He trailed off, frowning. He had only just realized that Golightly was the common factor. And, each time, Zack had been prevented from reaching him. What had he planned to do outside Excelsior Broadcasting? Just get closer, see the car, see who was in it; then Golightly had come out of the building . . . And today, when Anshelm had accused Golightly of shooting Balthazar; today he had been out of control, desperate – rushing like a storm to confront the steward – full of hate and rage.

He looked into Magdalena's unreadable face.

'Do you think maybe trolls can make themselves sort of dark and invisible and they work for Golightly, and they protect him, or something?'

She burst into laughter. But Zack was used to girls mocking him back at Storm Hill School.

'I've got an idea,' he said, 'I know what I'll do. I met someone who works on Barnacle Radio. I'll tell them about it and they can do an item, you know, on their news and they can say, has anyone else had this happen to them, has anyone else been sort of stopped by something they couldn't see, please get in touch, and then . . .' He looked at his watch. 'I can go up there now. I know where they live.'

'No. Don't. Don't talk to the radio.'

'But it's a brilliant idea. Maybe lots of people have had it happen to them and they're all scared that they're mad so they don't tell anyone.'

'Please. Not the radio. No.'

'But you want to catch one, don't you? I thought that was the whole point.'

Magdalena put her hand on his arm and looked into his face. It stopped him speaking as neatly as flicking a switch.

'I will tell you some things,' she said. 'But they must be a secret between us.'

He waited. She leant towards him and there was that scent he had noticed in the tree house. She spoke softly, as if they might be overheard. 'There are no such things as trolls, Mr Zachary.'

'What!'

She nodded, smiling.

'But . . . but . . . the troll hunting . . . the skulls . . .'

'My ancestors made the skulls. Real people skulls from the graveyard with antlers attached. To impress the wealthy clients. They made a living pretending to know everything about something that never existed in the first place.'

He was speechless.

At that moment Moe stood up and yawned. He pottered towards them. Ears larger than ever.

'No,' said Zack. 'No. You can't mean it. What about Moe being a troll hound? Ernesto's read about them. Webbed feet, climbing trees . . .'

She held out her hand to Moe and he came up to her and sniffed her fingers.

'There are probably many dogs in Rockscar with webbed feet,' she said, still looking down at Moe. 'Perhaps to do with fishing in old times.'

'Are you sure? What did they do? Jump off the side of the boat and *herd* the fish into the net?'

'I don't know. Maybe. Who cares?'

Zack felt like a soldier who had to keep stumbling on across the battlefield: explosions, gunfire, shock after shock after shock.

'Are you telling me,' he said, his voice rising, 'that you aren't anything you said you were? And it's all been lies?'

She didn't reply. Still stroking Moe.

'I have just found out who my real father is,' said Zack. 'Just now.'

Moe rolled on to his back again. Magdalena knelt down beside him and tickled him under his chin.

Zack looked around the yard. The wilderness cedar that contained an extraordinary tree house; the embankment and the railway line where the Ice Angel van had somehow saved itself from being smashed to pieces by the freight train; this girl or woman or whatever she was, with her unlikely accent and her bold, mysterious face.

'Something was up there in the tree with me,' he said, slowly. 'And something stopped me from getting near Golightly on Excelsior Avenue. Something just like the ... the Mayor said, something dark and—'

'You are imagining,' said Magdalena. 'You have so much drama in your life rushing about in your van, driving on railway lines, it has affected your brain with stress. This explains the whole experience. There really is no such thing as trolls.'

'So, you are tricking Ernesto Scarspring, a strange but decent human being. You are going to hunt for a troll that you know isn't there. How much will you charge him for all this?'

Magdalena patted Moe and stood up.

'I make no charge. The boy Ernesto will get his cat. I will make sure of that. Wherever it is. And, if he still needs proof of trolls, I will provide skulls and footprints and all those things, just like troll hunters have always done. And everyone will be happy.'

But Zack was chasing something, just ahead of him, a thought, an important one. 'And the vandalism? How do you explain that?'

He jammed his hands in his pockets and rocked from foot to foot.

'The damage to the Scarsprings' equipment? How do you explain that?'

Her expression changed. He took a step backwards.

'The vandalism will stop when the Scarsprings stop digging their stupid holes in the wilderness, and hurting the sacred trees, leaving them bleeding and dying, with the wind burning their roots.'

He stared at her in yet more amazement. She was bristling with energy.

'What I mean is that there are people in the city who do not like to see the trees damaged and the wilderness disturbed,' she said, in a slightly calmer voice.

Zack felt like someone who has pushed against a locked door only for it to fly open. He had fallen into the truth.

369

'It's you, isn't it?' he whispered. 'You are the vandals. You.'

She didn't move or speak. On the warm stones at her feet, Moe became watchful and dangerous.

'You live in a wilderness tree,' said Zack, his heart racing. 'You love trees. You do the vandalism and you pretend that trolls are doing it. You pretend to find the evidence. You pretend to bargain with the trolls. You advise the Scarsprings not to dig in certain places. To leave the trees alone. You say that then the trolls will go away. But there aren't any trolls. It's you. Your family have been protecting the wilderness all this time. You're the fake trolls and the fake troll hunters. Both.'

Magdalena still didn't speak straight away. Then she took a step towards him and put her hands on his shoulders.

'Do you think you will tell your friends at the Radio Barnacle?' she said, softly.

He shook his head. At this moment any thinking seemed ambitious. Could he think?

She brought her face close to his. She smelt of flowers. Was she going to kiss him? Did she want him to kiss her? She brushed her cheek against his. Then she stood back, still with her hands on his shoulders: looking at him.

'You must come tonight, with your van with the angel and the ice cream,' she said. 'Bring your brother, yes? Because when I have the charm, my charm, it will be the

370

best night of our lives. Or the worst. We shall scream with joy or grief. All of us.'

And suddenly she hugged him very tightly, and he realized that she was crying.

Chapter 57

'And she wouldn't say why?'

'No. Just cried for a bit. And then said she had to mend a scooter, or something, and I should go and you and me should meet her at six o'clock et cetera.'

Clovis broke off a very small piece of bread and dipped it in honey. They were sitting on the highest but one platform of the lookout tree.

'It's a lot to take in,' said Clovis, replacing the lid on the honey jar.

Zack didn't reply.

It was late afternoon. The forest stretched below them, dark and dusty and dreaming in the heat.

'She's not a real troll hunter. There's no real trolls. There's no water shortage . . .'

Clovis let his list stop there: they both knew the rest. Anshelm Scarspring was Zack's real father. Golightly had killed Balthazar on the Wolf Road, probably with the hunting rifle which Mariette kept hidden in the sofa. She had found it, no doubt. Afterwards.

They hadn't told Mariette about Golightly and Balthazar yet. Or about the truth about the water shortage. Or about trolls.

She really wants to talk to you,' said Clovis, after a while. 'She's been in a terrible state all day.'

'Probably because you don't dare go back to Meakin's and your precious apprenticeship is in danger.'

No, Zack. She's upset about you. You know that. How you feel. Whether you're angry that she didn't tell you . . .'

'Too right, I am.'

'Yes, but, you know, Golightly told her that Scarspring didn't want anything to do with it. I mean you. Her. And he threatened to kill the baby. You.'

'She should still have told me. I even look like him.'

Zack hadn't eaten. He gave Moe a piece of bread and Moe ate it for him.

'He saved me from those lightning flies, you know.'

'I do know, yes, you told me.'

'But it doesn't mean I don't, you know, care about Dad. I mean, Balthazar. That won't change.'

'Of course it won't,' said Clovis. 'It wouldn't be logical to stop caring about him. Either of us. Even though he's dead and we're never going to see him. Ever. It wouldn't be logical to stop caring. We'll always care.'

Another silence. A mountain hawk swerved over the tops of the trees.

Clovis coughed.

'Sky looks weird, sinister clouds over the sea,' he said. 'Have you noticed?'

They both stood up and gazed out towards the bright sea and the band of dark grey sky just above it. Two wise old weathermen, making predictions. Wiping their eyes with the backs of their hands.

'Looks like a thunderstorm might be coming,' said Clovis. 'Finally.'

'None of it makes sense,' said Zack.

Chapter 58

It was late afternoon. Ernesto Scarspring crept along the passageway that linked the many bedrooms on the fifth floor of the Scarspring house. Past Golightly's south-facing chamber, always locked. Then, the larger room kept ready for his grandparents who visited during the winter but lived for the rest of the time on the mainland. Past other guest rooms, so many minor Scarspring relatives to consider.

And now, stealthy as a hunter, past his parents' room, untouched, the furniture draped in sheets to protect it from the dust. Sheets which were now grey and grimy with dust themselves. A room he chose never to enter.

He had reached the end of the corridor. There was only one door left. It stood slightly ajar. He peered in, his heart pounding.

Anshelm was lying on his back, asleep on the bed. He lay fully clothed on top of the covers, his eyes restless behind bluish lids. Dreaming uneasy dreams.

But where was the charm? Ernesto thought he knew.

There was a little table beside Anshelm's bed. A lamp decorated with coloured glass. A clock. A fountain pen. His expensive watch made here in the jewellers' quarter of Rockscar City.

Ernesto crept very slowly forward. With each step the floor creaked and he stopped and watched Anshelm's face. Another step. Anshelm continued to dream.

The little green metal angel on the chain was nowhere to be seen. It was, Ernesto was sure, in his uncle's waistcoat pocket. And Anshelm was wearing his waistcoat.

Years of trying to be inconspicuous had made Ernesto skilled in the art of moving quietly. He reached the bed. Now he was so scared he was starting to sweat. He kept his eyes on Anshelm. His uncle's jacket was open, and Ernesto could see the slim silk pocket in the lining of his waistcoat, on the side furthest away from where he was standing.

He bit his lower lip. A seabird flew past the window and gave a harsh cry. He almost toppled on to Anshelm in fright.

Then, slowly, slowly he leant across and reached his hand down between the warmth of Anshelm's body and the cool lining of the waistcoat, instinctively matching his breath with Anshelm's own, to hide the sound.

Ernesto pushed his finger and thumb into the waistcoat pocket and felt the chain between them. He began, slowly, to draw it out.

Anshelm's eyes flew open and he seized Ernesto's wrist in a grip of iron. Ernesto screamed. He tried to break free, still pinching the chain between his finger and thumb. He flailed with his free hand. Trying to fight.

But Anshelm was older and stronger.

'What are you doing, Ernestino?' he whispered. 'For a moment, I thought you were Golightly come to kill me.'

Ernesto didn't speak.

Anshelm sat up, still holding Ernesto's wrist, and they faced each other in a horrible intimacy.

'Or were *you* trying to kill me? I have had such surprises in the last twenty-four hours, nothing would shock me now.'

'No, no.' Ernesto made one last attempt to pull himself free. And failed.

'What's that you've got, Ernestino?'

Ernesto shook his head: so near to saving Fisher.

'Show me.'

He shook his head again; he had managed to draw the charm into his palm; he closed his fist around it. And then they both turned their heads sharply towards the door.

Chapter 59

It was Steward Golightly.

He had pushed the door open and stood on the threshold. Full-length coat, despite the heat. His hat tilted back.

'What a touching scene,' he said. 'I am so sorry to interrupt.'

'Touching or not, Stefan,' said Anshelm. 'It is no concern of yours.'

Golightly smiled. 'Everything you do is a concern of mine, *Mayor* Scarspring.'

Ernesto struggled; but Anshelm had not forgotten him.

'I thought I might find you here,' said Golightly.

'I must ask you to leave us,' said Anshelm. 'Since I have learnt that you cheated me in the matter of my own son I have no wish to accommodate you, or employ you, or speak to you again.'

Ernesto, still a prisoner, looked from Anshelm to Golightly. There was no time to wonder about this matter of a son. He understood that something terrrible was happening. He had known these men all his life; but he

378

didn't feel he knew them now.

'People are calling for you to resign as Mayor, Anshelm,' said Golightly. 'There is a great crowd of them this very afternoon outside the City Hall. The Scarspring Water Company has never been so despised. Am I to tell them that *you, yourself* have engineered this dangerous water shortage?'

He smiled horribly at Ernesto. His damaged lip was encrusted with dried blood.

'Don't look so stricken, boy. Madness is all part of being a Scarspring.'

'Get out,' said Anshelm, his voice rising. He stood up. 'I should have thrown you out long ago.'

'But you couldn't, could you, Anshelm . . .'

Golightly took a few steps into the room. Ernesto saw his chauffeur just behind him in the passageway. Holding a rifle.

'Because I know too much.'

Ernesto felt Anshelm's grip on his wrist tighten even further. Then, suddenly, it relaxed. He had let him go. In fact, he was pushing him away. The chauffeur had come right into the room. He and Golightly were side by side, blocking the doorway. The chauffeur pointed the gun at Anshelm. Golightly turned and locked the door.

'Anshelm murdered your dear father, Ernesto. No mountain lions, no trolls, just Anshelm. I saw it all. They were arguing. Anshelm pushed Zoran into a ravine.'

'That's a lie,' shouted Anshelm.

Golightly clapped his hand on to the chauffeur's shoulder.

'And now this gentleman is prepared to swear that he just happened to be out hunting that night, on the Wolf Road. And he saw exactly what I saw. He was too afraid to speak. Until now.'

'It's not true, Ernestino!'

A terrifying silence.

'Who cares?' whispered Golightly. 'He will be well paid. Money talks. It can say anything.'

Anshelm lunged at Golightly; but the chauffeur was quick on his feet. He jammed the gun into Anshelm's face. Slammed him back against the wall.

'The guilt has gradually driven you into madness. You are desperately searching for an imaginary troll to take the blame for your crime,' continued Golightly, softly. 'You see things that aren't there. Hallucinations. The Curse of the Scarsprings is well-known. You have lost your mind, just like your great-grandfather Archibald. I have tried to reason with you. But you will not listen. Now, in your despair, you are going to take your own life.'

Anshelm had seized the barrel of the rifle. 'Get out, Ernestino, run!'

He tried to force the barrel upwards: the rifle went off, shattering a mirror behind him, the chauffeur wrestled it out of his grip and swung it violently; hitting him on the side of his head; sending him stumbling back into the wall again . . .

Ernesto tried to duck past Golightly and Golightly

caught him by the hair.

'Leave him alone!' shouted Anshelm, gasping for breath.

'If only we could.' Golightly twisted his hand deep into Ernesto's hair, making him scream. 'But you see, he is all that stands between me and my future. So, in your madness, afraid that he too will suffer from the family curse, you have decided to throw him to his death out of this very window. I've made you a new will. If anything happens to Ernesto, I get everything you own. I forged your signature. I've been forging it for years.'

He began to drag Ernesto across the room. The window wasn't wide. But it was wide enough.

'No! No!' Anshelm sounded as if he were choking. The chauffeur shouted some curse. Ernesto couldn't see them – Golightly's face was filling his vision, contorted with effort . . .

'And I will find your son,' snarled Golightly, 'And I will . . . kill . . . him . . . too.'

Ernesto knew exactly what lay beneath the window.

This room was on the fifth floor, directly above his own.

He bit Golightly's hand. Was hit across the mouth. Golightly lifted him and pushed him through the narrow opening, backwards; Ernesto's jacket caught, material rending and tearing; he clung to the stone edge of the window, feet scrabbling on the sill; he managed to turn his head and saw the drop over his shoulder . . .

Then Golightly, leering, prised Ernesto's fingers off the

window frame, slammed a damp hand over his face and gave him a blow in the stomach that doubled him up like a rag doll.

Ernesto fell backwards, writhing in the air.

The steward stayed at the window long enough to see him hit the flat roof of a bay window two floors down and roll off it out of sight. Then he turned away, to attend to his next task in the room behind him.

He did not know how well Ernesto knew the rooftops and the ledges. The places beloved by Fisher: places where Ernesto himself had secretly climbed in the moonlight, accompanying his cat.

Ernesto hit the little flat roof, rolled dangerously off, clung on to the gutter and then, kicking his legs, he inched along to a ledge which ran along the side of the building. Slippery with ancient bird dirt.

The drop below swerved on the edge of his sight. His fingernails were broken and bleeding; the pain from the punch in his stomach made him retch; he braced his leg against a drainpipe . . .

Shouting from the room above. Crashes.

Ernesto's mouth was full of something burning. For an instant he thought he saw Fisher, her calm green eyes watching him. Then, exactly where he had seen her, he saw a deep crack in the weathered stone. With a desperate, agonizing effort, he gripped it and pulled himself up – struggling for footholds – until, at last, he was back on top of the bay.

He looked up at the open window.

He looked down and to the side; there was a way there, if you dared, along ledges and balconies, round the side of the building to lower roofs and the water garden. Escape.

Ernesto put his bleeding hand in his pocket and felt the angel charm.

Then he heard Golightly shouting and Anshelm's voice, shouting back that Golightly was a coward.

He began climbing. Not downwards to safety. Higher up. Back to Anshelm.

Two long, terrifying minutes later and he was lying along the ledge on his front immediately above Anshelm's window. He leant over, upside down, and looked inside.

The chauffeur was sprawled motionless on the floor. Golightly had the rifle now. Rammed against Anshelm's chest. Every piece of furniture had been overturned or broken. Was Anshelm injured? His hands were behind him, out of sight.

Golightly had his back to the window. Only Anshelm saw Ernesto. His eyes widened. He made a tiny movement with his head that Ernesto knew was a command to him to get away.

'You will be found with the rifle in your mouth,' Golightly was saying, surprisingly softly. 'And your brains decorating the wall. It will be suicide. Don't worry, I'll help you pull the trigger. Just like I've helped you all your stinking life.'

He moved the barrel of the gun closer to Anshelm's face.

Then Ernesto slipped, and saved himself, and gasped in pain, and Golightly looked over his shoulder and saw him.

With a roar of rage Golightly charged. He thrust his head and shoulders through the window. He twisted around violently and immediately found Ernesto, on the narrow ledge, only inches above him. He forced one arm through the little remaining space and swung it, clawing, trying to get a grip on Ernesto's torn clothes and drag him off the ledge. Ernesto managed to haul himself on to his feet.

Golightly had climbed right out of the window now. He was standing on the sill.

Ernesto shuffled a little further along the ledge, just out of reach. He pressed his body back against the wall.

Golightly lunged again, snatching to get Ernesto by the leg and pull him off balance. But it was not Ernesto who lost his footing.

Ernesto looked down, screaming, and saw Golightly fall backwards on to the roof of the bay window, and roll off, just as he had done himself.

But Golightly had not spent his childhood creeping about on rooftops. He was bigger and heavier than Ernesto and he could not save himself with his fingertips on gutter and stone.

Instead he fell further, striking a carved lion that stood out like a gargoyle, and then he fell further still, and went on falling.

Chapter 60

Ernesto was hurting in every muscle and bone. He crawled in through Anshelm's window. Tried to stand. Crawled again. It seemed dark in there after the sickening sweep of rooftops and sea and sky. He peered into the debris of the fight and saw Anshelm trying to stand, leaning against the tilting remains of the four-poster bed.

'Ernestino?'

'I'm here.'

'Are you hurt?'

'A bit.'

Ernesto managed to get to his feet. He stepped over the chauffeur, who groaned and shifted in the tangle of carpet and broken glass.

'Where's Stefan?'

Ernesto had reached Anshelm now. He discovered that his hands had been tied behind his back. He looked round for something to cut the rope and picked up a piece of glass.

Anshelm's face was grey with pain. When the rope was finally severed, he still did not move.

'Where's Stefan?'

Ernesto put down the piece of glass. He was starting to shake: his teeth were chattering so hard, he couldn't speak.

Groaning and gasping for breath, Anshelm walked unsteadily to the window; he looked out, and down; he stayed absolutely still; then he turned back to face Ernesto.

Ernesto was holding out the blood-stained angel charm, lying on the palm of his hand.

'What did you want it for?' asked Anshelm. Not taking it. Just staring. As if he was asking about something that had happened in another lifetime.

Ernesto shook his head. He was still shaking.

'I feel very cold,' said Anshelm. 'We need to go downstairs.'

They held on to each other and made their way slowly across the ruined room to the door. The chauffeur stirred again and started to sit up. Anshelm locked the door behind them.

It seemed to take a very long time to get downstairs. The house was deserted. When they finally reached the office, Anshelm wrapped a rug round Ernesto's shoulders and poured them both some brandy.

Ernesto held the glass to his lips and his teeth chimed against the rim. Anshelm steadied his hand.

'You were very brave, Ernestino,' he said. 'I thought, for a little while, in there, that I had lost you.'

Chapter 61

Zack was standing by the spring in the cave. It was late afternoon. In a few minutes, he and Clovis and Moe were going to set off in the van to go the meeting place outside the Scarsprings' house.

He put the lantern on the ground and knelt down.

The spring whispered to itself.

'I've met my real, I mean, my other father,' he said.

Even this near the entrance, the cave felt almost cold.

'But I still love you,' he was rushing the words. 'So, it's up to you, because I'll always love you. If that's all right. If you don't mind.'

He leant over and put the tips of his fingers in the water.

'He seems sort of OK. He saved me from some lightning flies. Very quick – Zap! Zap!'

Zack sliced the air with his hands, flicking his face with drops of water as he did so.

'But that doesn't mean I don't love you.'

He wiped his eyes.

'And I think I've got something called the Curse of the Scarsprings, I see things that aren't there. I haven't told Clovis.'

He didn't dare put his palm down on the floor of the cave again, in case nothing happened. In case there was no answering print in the dust, and that had all been in his imagination too.

Chapter 62

They were driving in silence. All the windows wound down: the air hot and heavy. The sprawling streets of Storm Hill were deserted. In the distance the sea and the sky looked like two sheets of metal, reflecting each other.

They drove down into Pedder's Hill and the stink of the Cat's Tail filled the cab. Then on into a district of offices and imposing buildings: towards City Hall.

'Everyone's gone to the water protest,' said Zack. 'Public holiday. Heatwave.'

'Let's hope so,' said Clovis. 'Because I really don't want anyone to see us. What with Golightly wanting to kill me. And you. And the police already looking out for a silver van with an angel on the front. Stop!'

The Ice Angel almost skidded to a halt. Moe was leaning as far as he could out of the passenger window. He was swivelling his ears, slowly, from side to side.

'Can you hear that?'

It was the distorted voice of a person shouting through a megaphone. And then, the answering roar of a substantial crowd.

'That must be the protest,' said Clovis. 'Outside the City Hall. We'll have to go another way.'

More shouting. A wave of applause, echoing off the buildings. Yells and chanting. Zack shuddered. The crowd sounded like a big, dangerous animal.

'People are very upset,' said Clovis. 'It's only logical that something like this would happen. Rationing. Sickness . . .'

'I know,' said Zack, softly.

A pause.

'So, do you really think he was speaking the truth when he told you that he'd made it all happen himself?'

'Oh yes,' said Clovis. 'I believed everything he said. He's too extreme to lie. He's a man possessed.'

Zack didn't reply. He started the engine and then turned uphill at the next corner. They went to the street where the Scarsprings lived by a long route, leaving the sound of the demonstration behind.

Merchant's Hill was in a very old part of the city. Much older than the broad and tree-lined Excelsior Avenue, or the scattered buildings of Storm Hill. The Scarsprings' house stood on a steep, cobbled street that wound down towards MockBeggar. They parked the Ice Angel a little higher up, facing downhill, the fastest escape route, towards the harbour.

It was six o'clock in the evening.

'I still don't see why we're doing this,' said Clovis, leaning over to peer into the periscope for about the tenth time. 'Golightly could come round the corner at any moment. This is, by far, the most dangerous place for us in the whole blessed Barnacle.'

'Magdalena seemed to think it was very important.'

'So what exactly did happen between you and our scooter mechanic friend? Apart from what you've already told me?'

Zack looked straight ahead through the windscreen.

'Why are you looking like that? You didn't kiss her, did you? Did you kiss her?'

Moe burped.

'Good grief. I don't believe it. You kissed her, didn't you?'

'There was no kissing,' muttered Zack. ' And anyway, I don't think she really meant it.'

He stared down the narrow street, dustbins and litter along the pavement: a pile of rags by the kerb. Then he turned on the radio. Permanently tuned to the Barnacles these days. Six o'clock news.

Momma Truth was back. 'Too hot, much too hot,' she whispered, warm and mellow as ever. 'Three more lightning flies have been seen, well, almost seen, in SugarTown. No casualties as yet but the City Hall have warned us all to watch out for the next few days. It's the time of year, folks, and the very unusual heat and the lack of wind, apparently.

'The water demonstration which began as a peaceful march and a rally outside City Hall has become just a little bit ugly. Momma Truth says don't go down there, my children. The word is that smuggling gangs from SugarTown have got involved. Looking to settle a few scores with the police. Handing out Dragon Breath Rum to anyone stupid enough to drink it. Some excitable folks have set out for Merchant's Hill. They're heading for the Scarsprings' House.

'And where is our esteemed Mayor and troll scientist Mr Anshelm Scarspring? Nobody knows. No comment from City Hall. No sign of Golightly either. Perhaps they've both gone to the park. Have a nice cool drink for me, gentlemen. In fact, have one for all of us.'

There was the sound of a baby crying in the background.

'Got to go,' said Momma Truth. 'Stay out of trouble.'

Zack turned the radio off again. Moe growled.

'Can you hear that?' hissed Clovis.

There was a noise in the distance. Like something boiling. Different sounds coming to the surface. Voices. Hooters. Screams. Gunshots.

'Sounds a bit unpleasant,' said Clovis.

'Just a bit.'

'And it's coming this way, according to Momma Truth.'

'Certainly sounds like it.'

'One way and another, this really isn't an ideal spot for us to park.'

At that moment an automobile swerved into view from a side street. Big headlamps, rusted chrome radiator, iron bear guardian tied on with rope. It ground to a halt a little way beyond the dustbins and the litter, making a mighty rattling noise.

'Definitely not a Scarspring vehicle,' said Clovis. 'Loose exhaust pipe. Datchet Sedan. Must be nearly twenty years old. It's little Frankie. Look. She's coming to see us.'

Frankie came clattering up to the passenger window of the van. She was wearing high-heeled shoes. Clovis opened the door and jumped down.

'Hello,' she said, breathlessly. 'What are you doing here? Are you selling ice cream?'

'No,' said Clovis. 'This would not be our vending site of choice.'

'I've come to meet someone. Only he's not here. And Hat won't let me out of his sight. That's him in the car. My mum's come home with the baby.' She pulled a face. 'I'm under a sort of curfew thing.'

'We know who you're meeting,' said Clovis. 'Ernesto Scarspring. About his cat. He told Zack all about it. We're meeting him too.'

Zack was watching the Datchet Sedan. He could see Hat inside. Then, suddenly, Hat was getting out. And, despite his size and his suit, he was almost running up the hill.

Hat didn't stop until he reached the dustbins and the pile of rags. He was staring at something. No, not some*thing*. Someone.

'I'm going down there,' said Zack, rapidly. 'See, where

Hat is? There. There's someone lying there. I thought it was just a pile of old clothes and stuff. I'm going to look.'

He was snatching at the buckle of his harness. Something was wrong. Horribly wrong.

He jumped out of the cab and ran down the pavement, closely followed by Clovis, Frankie and Moe. The wall of the Scarsprings' house looming alongside them. Locked, wooden gates, banded and studded with iron.

Hat was absolutely still, looking down at the pile of rags. Something dark gleamed wet on the dusty cobbles around it. Something that had collected here and there, making tiny rivers and pools.

Moe got there first. Hackles up. Silent.

Then, Zack and Clovis. Frankie screamed and grabbed hold of Clovis' hand. Zack was bending down, trying not to scream himself.

'He's dead,' he whispered.

'I can see that,' said Clovis.

Golightly lay on his back. His eyes open.

'He's dead,' repeated Zack.

Hat crouched down and took Golightly's wrist. He held it. No one spoke.

'There's blood everywhere,' said Clovis. 'It's Steward Golightly, isn't it . . .'

'OK,' said Hat, standing up. 'He's dead for sure. Not so long ago. I suggest we all get out of here, right now.' He looked over his shoulder down the hill, the noise was getting much louder. 'Whatever's happened here, we certainly don't want a part of it. Come on, Frankie.'

'But my message,' said Frankie, who was hanging on to Clovis as if her legs were giving way. 'My message for my secret client. From Dinah Dibbs.'

'No time,' said Hat, scanning the street again, looking back at Stefan Golightly's drained face. 'I should never have agreed to bring you. If Rose finds out . . .'

'But it's important,' cried Frankie.

Hat stepped round Golightly, seized hold of her and lifted her clean into the air.

'Stop! Put me down!'

'Frankie,' said Clovis, white-faced, 'Frankie. Listen. It's Ernesto Scarspring, isn't it? Give us the message. We'll see him. We'll wait for him.'

'Scarspring!' Hat hissed. 'We're waiting here, risking our lives for some Scarspring! No way! We are all getting out of here *now*. There is a very important dead man on the road and it doesn't look too much like natural causes to me. Plus it sounds like a war is marching up this hill, in case none of you have noticed.'

Frankie looked down at Golightly and began screaming.

Hat turned, swung her on to his shoulder, and started striding to the Datchet.

Clovis gave chase.

'Tell us the message,' he gasped.

She was writhing and kicking her legs. Trying to get

something out of the pocket of her dress. An envelope. She threw it and Clovis picked it up. Then everyone was running. Zack, Clovis and Moe headed for the cab of the Ice Angel. More gunshots from down the hill. Sounds of breaking glass –

'But what about Magdalena,' said Zack, stabbing at the ignition, missing, dropping the key . . . 'We can't just leave her.'

The Datchet Sedan thundered past them, bouncing and rocking up the hill, the exhaust blasting a cloud of black smoke. Now the shouts and chants and crashes were echoing off the buildings. These buildings.

'That's not a demonstration,' shouted Clovis. 'That's a riot. Start the engine.'

'But Magdalena—'

'We're not *leaving* her. She isn't here. She's quite tough enough to look after herself *plus* she's probably heard all this and turned back. Plus, in case you haven't noticed, the lunatic Ernesto isn't here either.'

'But what if—'

'*Start the engine, Zack.*'

Zack stared down the hill. Past the incomprehensible, huddled body of Golightly. Towards the approaching sound of the riot.

'She won't turn back,' he said, almost quietly. 'It was too important to her.'

Clovis scrabbled on the floor and found the key. Moe

was whining like a creature in pain, pawing at the dashboard. The horn sounded. Then the lights came on.

'You're in love with her, aren't you? We're about to get blamed for a murder. Or attacked by a mob of drunken maniacs. And *you* are in love.'

A police van came hurtling from behind them, siren blaring, and shot on past down the hill.

'She wants that charm very, very much,' said Zack. 'But I don't know why.'

'She"s out of your league, she's a totally grown woman. Start off with someone your own age.' Clovis was almost crying with frustration. He leant over and tried to get the key into the ignition himself.

'Oh yeah, like someone who dresses seventeen and is actually quite possibly nine?'

'Do you want to die here, you unbelievably stubborn, hopelessly unrealistic person?' screamed Clovis.

'Here she comes now,' said Zack, looking in the periscope. 'On a Wind Shadow,' he added. Despite the cobbles the Wind Shadow was gliding, absolutely smoothly.

'That's it!' exclaimed Zack. 'It was her!'

'What was?'

'That night. The night Moe arrived. It was her, on her scooter. Do you remember? I saw a red light on the Wolf Road. Going along so smoothly, remember? That's the scooter. The Wind Shadow. I heard a customer telling her how brilliant she is at fixing the suspension. I bet it was her.'

'And you think we need to discuss this now?'

The Wind Shadow came to a soundless halt just under the window of the driver's door. Magdalena was wearing goggles. Her black and silver dress, her golden skin and the scooter itself were all covered with a layer of sandy dust.

Clovis had his head in his hands.

'There's a lot of trouble down there,' she said, pushing the goggles on to her forehead. 'I had to come a different way. Where is the boy Ernesto, does he have the charm?'

'Let's just *get out of here*,' groaned Clovis.

'But my charm—'

'Look,' said Zack. 'The gates.'

The fortified gates of the Scarsprings' house were opening. Or, at least, one of them was, although not by very much.

Two figures came out on to the pavement. They hesitated. They stood, holding on to each other. Then they moved forwards, slowly, towards the body of Stefan Golightly.

The noise of the riot was exploding. Another police van scorched past the Ice Angel, making it shake. Zack could see figures pouring out of an alleyway in the distance. Spreading out. Throwing things. The air smelt of smoke.

'It's Ernesto . . . and the Mayor,' said Clovis. 'They look like they've been in an accident.'

Ernesto and Anshelm were standing beside Golightly's body.

'Perhaps we should all be going now,' said Magdalena.

Voices were ringing up the street, full of violence. 'SCAR-SPRING. SCAR-SPRING.'

Zack watched Anselm turn round and look down the hill. His movements seemed slower than normal. Not good in the present situation.

'Get them into the van,' yelled Zack. 'Now. Get them *in*—'

Clovis hit the pavement, fell over, stood up and flung himself towards Anselm and Ernesto.

'Quick! Get in our van! They're coming!'

Only a hundred metres away the steep street was filling with people: they wore masks and scarves over their faces, they were lurching and crashing, throwing things at windows, waving sticks and pieces of metal. A whole wall of police suddenly surged round a corner. Gunshots. Screams.

Clovis was hauling Ernesto towards the Ice Angel.

Anselm, however, stayed still. He was staring down at Golightly again. A brick hit the wall behind him. He ignored it.

Zack scrambled out of the cab. The crowd was shouting for someone's blood. And that person was standing right here on the pavement, in plain sight, like a dazed and flightless bird.

'You've got to get out of here,' shouted Zack. Anselm didn't hear him. His face was bruised down one side. There was blood at the corner of his mouth. His jacket was hanging off his shoulders, torn and jagged. He was staring and staring at Golightly.

Zack grabbed his arm and began to pull him towards the van.

'I take him. On the scooter,' said a calm voice behind him.

He looked round into Magdalena's black eyes. She had brought the Wind Shadow right up to the kerb. There was a terrible crash of breaking glass. Someone had thrown something through a first-floor window of the Scarsprings' house.

'That's him! That's the Mayor!'

People running towards them now. Shouting.

Anshelm suddenly seemed to wake up.

'Get out of here, Zachary,' he yelled, gesturing at the scooter. 'Save yourself.'

'*You* get on the scooter.' Zack grabbed him and started pushing him towards it. 'I'm going in that van.'

Anshelm saw the Ice Angel. He saw the angel herself, facing him.

'Get on the scooter,' screamed Zack.

Magdalena was already revving the engine. Anshelm struggled up on to the back. The Wind Shadow cut through the crowd, sending people reeling backwards.

Zack ran to the van. Clovis had started the engine and Zack skidded on to the seat and flung the gears into reverse. Ernesto and Clovis fought with their harnesses. Moe leant out of the window snapping and snarling, grown suddenly as big and dangerous as a lion.

The Ice Angel shot backwards, arced into a side street on two wheels and then roared forwards again, up the hill. Magdalena and Anshelm on the Wind Shadow, steady and sailing behind them in the eye of the periscope.

Chapter 63

Storm Hill Ridge. High on the ragged edge of everything. Baked all that long hot day. Now striped with tapering shadows. The Ice Angel pulled up on the verge: as good a place as any.

'Smoke,' said Clovis, pointing between trees and buildings where the city plunged steeply below. Zack frowned.

'Looks like it's coming from Merchant's Hill,' said Clovis.

'Not necessarily,' said Zack.

'There is no need to protect my feelings,' said Ernesto. 'It is very likely to be our house. I'm not stupid.'

The Wind Shadow came to a neat stop behind them. Zack's wing mirror was filled by Magdalena and Anshelm, dismounting. He saw Anshelm shake Magdalena's hand.

'What happened to your face?' asked Clovis, abruptly.

'Steward Golightly pushed me out of a very high window,' said Ernesto. 'But I was fortunate enough to be able to climb back in again.'

Zack and Clovis looked at each other, wide-eyed.

'He tried to kill Uncle Anshelm, too. He tried to put a rifle in his mouth and make it look like he killed himself. He intended that my uncle's brains should decorate the wall. He planned to tell everyone that my uncle had killed my father and that the guilt had finally driven him to madness and suicide.'

Moe growled, softly.

'Your dog got bigger when we were all escaping from outside our house,' added Ernesto. 'Is that something troll hounds can do?'

There was a pause. Uncomfortable because of the shocking account of the events in the Scarsprings' house that afternoon, told in Ernesto's strange matter-of-fact way; also because he still thought Moe was a troll hound, and now they knew that troll hounds were an invention.

'We like to think it's an optical illusion, just because he's trying to make himself look scary. Making his fur stand on end.'

'Oh no, I don't think so,' said Ernesto. 'He definitely got bigger. About three times his normal size.'

And there was another uncomfortable pause, because what Ernesto said was true and could not be explained.

'We've got a letter for you,' said Clovis, raising his eyebrows at Zack. 'From your friend. She did come to meet you, she just couldn't stay.'

He handed Ernesto the envelope and Ernesto began to open it slowly. His fingers and palms were scoured red and

403

raw. He realized that they were both staring at him.

'I hurt my hands,' he said, finally pulling the folded letter free. 'And it really hurts here,' he touched his side and traced a line under his ribs. 'And here,' gently pressing on his chest. 'When I breathe. I think he broke one of my ribs. Or maybe two.'

'Good grief,' whispered Zack.

Ernesto examined his letter. They could see a hand-drawn crest at the top. A picture of a magnifying glass and the words 'Dinah Dibbs: Detective. Cats a Speciality'.

Zack looked in the wing mirror and saw Magdalena still framed there, crouched down in her savage ballerina dress, adjusting something on the Wind Shadow. Anshelm had sat down on a rock. He was using a piece of his shirt to dab blood away from his mouth.

'It is a simple matter,' said Ernesto. 'Listen. "Dear Friend and Client. I have excellent news. It was not really a very clever thing to find your cat. I was lucky. I was at Excelsior Broadcasting House on business and Mr Featherplum, the director, was sneezing and sneezing and someone asked him why and I think it was the Maharajah and he said it was an allergenic reaction to a cat he was looking after for a friend. The Maharajah said that if the allergenic reaction was so bad he would look after the cat for Mr Featherplum. But Mr Featherplum looked worried and said Oh no it is Steward Golightly's cat and he had better not let the Steward down, despite nasal discomfort.

'"Well, the next time I went to the Broadcasting Studios I took the collar you gave me. I showed it to him and he was ecstatic with relief and said that is her collar wherever did you find it I lost it when I was taking her from my studio to my car to drive her to my house. So, dear friend, your cat is at Mr Featherplum's house" . . .' Ernesto's voice faltered. 'And she gives the address here, in code.'

He looked at Zack and Clovis, his sharp face engulfed by a huge smile, despite the blood and bruises. They both smiled back.

'I don't have to catch the troll,' he said, looking at Zack. 'I don't have to do anything. I will just go to this Mr Featherplum's house and explain that Fisher is my cat.'

'Well, done, Dinah Dibbs,' said Clovis. Still smiling.

'Pretty good for someone who's only eight years old,' said Zack.

'She is *not* only eight, Zack.'

'Why are you going pink, Clovis?'

'Maybe it won't be that easy,' said Ernesto, suddenly, his smile gone. 'Maybe the police are looking for me and Uncle Anshelm. Right now. For the murder of Steward Golightly.'

Two pairs of eyes fixed on him, getting rounder by the second.

'We didn't murder him,' added Ernesto. 'He murdered himself, by mistake. This can happen when you try to push other people out of windows.'

At this rather chilling moment, Anshelm appeared round the side of the van. He stopped in front of the angel, then he came round to Zack's door.

'You're a good driver,' he said, quietly.

'Thanks.'

'We had to teach him from a book,' said Clovis.

'Hello, map reader,' Anshelm grinned. One of his teeth was broken. 'And this is *your* van?'

Zack and Clovis both climbed out of the cab, leaving Ernesto re-reading his letter. The angel was covered all over with a layer of Rockscar City dust, as if she had been frosted wih gold.

'This was Balthazar Jump's van,' said Anshelm.

'That's our real name,' said Zack. 'That's who we are.'

'Balthazar Jump,' repeated Anshelm. 'So, we are all connected.'

He turned at a distant sound from the city. Gunfire again. A haze of smoke, very definitely over Merchant's Hill.

'And now, I think, we are drawn together more tightly still. Something is happening, I've no idea what; but we are past the point of no return. At last.'

Magdalena walked towards them, brushing the dust from her clothes. Moe jumped out of the open window of the cab and greeted her as if they had been parted for days.

'He's your dog, isn't he?' said Zack. 'He's been your dog all the time.'

She shrugged her shoulders.

'You were in the forest on the night of that storm. The night he came to our house.'

'Fisher is at the home of Mr Edgar Featherplum, Director of Radio, in West Street, Shadowcliff,' shouted Ernesto, still in the cab, fumbling with his harness. 'I thought she'd written the address in code. But it's just her writing. I think she must have written that bit when she was in the car, bouncing about.'

'We'll go there soon, Ernesto,' said Anshelm.

'I want to go now.'

Ernesto climbed out of the door and then leant against the Ice Angel and held his side.

'We'll take you,' said Clovis. 'We promise. Just let me ask Magdalena something.' He breathed in as if he had been running. 'Magdalena, are you saying that you *brought* Moe to us. To our house?'

She narrowed her eyes. 'When you say Moe, you mean this dog?'

'Of course he means this dog,' said Zack. '*Our* dog.'

'He is not your dog,' said Magdalena. 'He has never been your dog.' Her voice was scornful.

Zack looked at Moe, who was now standing beside her. He was the size of a wolf. In fact, he looked exactly like a very large wolf. With gold eyes.

'Some people recognized him from before,' he said. 'Tiny at the Midnight Café thought he was Dad's, I mean, Balthazar's dog. We thought maybe he had come back.'

407

'He is not Balthazar's dog or your dog. He is nobody's dog. He belongs only to himself,' said Magdalena. 'And his name is not Moe. This is a ridiculous name. You are very foolish.'

'This is the troll hound?' said Anshelm. 'He certainly looks like no other dog I've seen.'

'Don't get your hopes up about troll hounds,' said Zack.

'Wait a minute,' said Clovis. 'You found our house. It was *you* that set off the alarms. *You* brought Moe to us. Why?'

'She called us,' Magdalena pointed at the angel on the front of the van.

'The angel? She *called*. To you?'

'Of course. And then Moe stayed to protect you because you were planning to start taking the Ice Angel out again.'

'Protect us,' said Clovis, slowly.

'We have always offered the Jumps our protection.' She turned to Anshelm. 'But now I must have the charm. It belonged to my father. He is the one who has dropped it. I must have it. It is not a charm. It is a key.'

Anshelm folded the bloodstained piece from his shirt and stood up slowly. He walked up to Magdalena.

Moe drew back his lips and snarled.

'I have the charm,' said Anshelm. 'I have it here. Tell me something that proves it is yours.'

'Give it to me,' said Magdalena. 'And follow me. You will see that it is mine. We will find out the truth. All of us.'

'Hang on a minute,' said Clovis. 'When you said that the angel on the van called to you. And that Moe protected us. Does this have anything to do with that night on the railway? Because that voice started singing then.'

'Yes, she called me. Because your idiot driving nearly got you all killed.'

Zack gasped.

But Clovis, ever methodical, persisted. 'And how did we come to be lifted off the railway line?'

'I told you, the creature you call Moe, the troll hound. He has protected you. When the Jumps came to live on the mountain my family promised to protect them. The troll hound was doing as I asked. To honour our promise.'

'Who are your family?' Anshelm spoke each word with effort, like throwing heavy stones. '*Tell me who you are.*'

'Give me the little angel. The key,' said Magdalena. 'Give me the key that my father dropped.'

'Can Moe make himself into something hard to see? And dark. Something that can hold you and stop you, something very strong. Strong enough to lift something very heavy, like a van?' Zack was speaking fast, looking at Moe.

Magdalena snapped her fingers in exasperation.

'This is obvious. How do you think he saved you from the freight train and stopped you from walking straight into Golightly that night outside Excelsior Broadcasting, and later, in the tree . . .' she tilted her head, contempt in her voice, 'when you were wild and crazy and flinging yourself

409

down the steps . . .'

Everyone looked at Moe. He put his head on one side and folded one ear and became small. One cute little birthday card dog.

'Is this creature a troll?' cried Anshelm. 'Is that what trolls are?'

Magdalena turned from one shocked face to another. She was glittering with rage. A beautiful, dangerous woman.

Silence. No one breathed.

'Is this what they call the Curse of the Scarsprings?' whispered Zack. 'Seeing the darkness he makes?'

Still she said nothing. The she pulled her goggles down over her eyes.

'I suggest that you travel in the angel van, Mayor Scarspring, because you look unwell. The hound can come on my scooter. And then, if you will all follow us in the angel van . . .' She hesitated. Her eyes were filling with tears. 'All your questions will be answered. And mine. My questions will be answered too.'

Chapter 64

It turned out that Ernesto was able to wear Moe's safety harness, when it was extended as far as it would go. He sat by the window, clutching his letter from Dinah Dibbs.

Anshelm was beside him, then Clovis. Zack at the wheel.

Something had spilt in the back of the van. There was a strong smell of chocolate and cinnamon.

For a while no one spoke. They followed the Wind Shadow and the golden blur of Magdalena's hair. Zack could see Moe on the back of the scooter. Ears in the wind. Medium-sized.

She led them along the arc of Storm Hill Ridge.

'Where do you think she's going?' said Clovis.

It was Anshelm who answered. 'I think perhaps we are going back to the beginning.'

A few moments later the Wind Shadow turned off the ridge. Not down towards the city. Up on to a rocky track, crowded on both sides with gorse and low-growing trees.

Taller trees looming ahead. The Wolf Road.

'Yes,' whispered Anshelm.

Zack, as always, slowed the Ice Angel to Tugalug speed. He steered around the potholes and ridges. He knew them all. Even with all his care, however, and Clovis' excellent work on the suspension, the van bounced and jarred and Ernesto and Anshelm reached out and tried to hold on to the dashboard. Meanwhile the Wind Shadow sailed evenly ahead, barely slowing down.

'It was her, all right,' said Zack. 'That night in the storm.'

'I know,' said Clovis. 'You don't think that we're going, you know . . .' he glanced sideways at Anshelm and Ernesto, dropped his voice to a whisper, '*to our house?*'

'We're going to the ravine,' said Anshelm. 'We're going to the place where it all happened. You can be sure of that.'

The Wolf Road began its steep, sickening climb. Now they were surrounded by pine trees. Now suddenly the city lay deep and distant beside them in the evening haze. Now, trees again.

Anshelm and Ernesto were both still leaning forward. Zack was hunched over the steering wheel. Clovis caught the resemblance in their profiles. Saw himself, solid, round-faced, a wise owl perched with bright-eyed crows. And now something else was about to happen; whatever it was, it would probably change everything.

'We're still brothers, aren't we?' he whispered to Zack.

'Always. Kings of the Mountain. Always.' A quick grin, too busy to look away from the road ahead. But enough. More than.

Chapter 65

Magdalena had parked the scooter, removed her helmet and was sitting under the wilderness cedar, all by the time they arrived.

Zack stopped the Ice Angel on the side of the narrow track away from the edge of the ravine. Everyone climbed down from the cab. The barren place which Balthazar Jump had called the garden of the trolls lay in shadow below them.

'Where's Moe?' said Zack to Magdalena.

'He has gone to fetch the person who is not here,' said Magdalena.

'Who?'

'Your mother.' Magdalena's face was set like a warrior. No emotion. 'When she is here, we are all here.'

Everyone, except Magdalena, was standing close together.

'By the way, map reader,' said Anshelm, 'I thought you showed great courage at Meakin's, when we had our little conversation. Great courage. And great intelligence.'

'Thanks,' said Clovis. He shivered, although he was far from cold.

'Please, don't any of you stand near the edge . . .' Anshelm grabbed hold of Ernesto's arm. ' Do you think we are to believe that the creature who can be a wolf and a dog and a darkness is also a maker of maps?'

'I don't know what to think,' said Clovis.

Anshelm nodded. 'We do not yet have the truth,' he said, quietly. 'Only a part of it.'

'Here they are,' said Zack.

Mariette was running towards them, stumbling on the uneven ground, with Moe springing along at her side. She stopped when she saw them all. Her sons. Ernesto. Anshelm Scarspring. Then she walked forwards as she had done on that freezing night, her hand over her mouth.

Anshelm gave a cry. He shook his head. He called, 'Golightly is dead, Mariette. He has lied to us all.'

'Are you all right?' shouted Clovis.

She nodded, her eyes on Anshelm, gradually coming closer.

'Please hurry.' It was Magdalena. 'And Mayor Scarspring, please give me the key.' Moe ran to her.

With all eyes fixed on him, Anshelm brought the angel charm out of his pocket. Magdalena took it and held it up.

'This is the only key to the garden of the trolls,' she said. 'The key my father dropped in the dark. Zoran Scarspring came to meet him here. My family had been caring for Zoran's wife. Here, in our garden. Zoran had come to visit her.'

Anshelm began to speak. She held up her hand.

'But Steward Golightly and Anshelm Scarspring had secretly followed Zoran that night. He had not told them about my father, and his friendship with him, or the other world, which is so close to this one. Our world, where the garden lies. We are wilderness dwellers. We are the people whom you would call trolls.

'They started quarrelling.' She paused. 'I know, because I was there. A little girl. Over there, standing under the tree. I saw Anshelm and Zoran. And I saw Golightly. He had his rifle.'

Magdalena looked from one face to another.

'Perhaps you do not remember, Mayor Scarspring, how Stefan Golightly came to be a member of your family?'

'He was found wandering the streets in Merchant's Hill, I believe,' said Anshelm. 'My father took him in. He was very young, so was I. We grew up together.'

'He was not wandering near your house by chance,' said Magdalena. 'And he was not so young as he seemed. He crept into the Scarspring family like a rat creeping into a grain store.'

'Are you saying that a child, a child of three years old –'

Magdalena's black eyes flashed. 'He was not three years

416

old, Mayor Scarspring. That was how he chose to seem. To put everyone at their ease.'

'That's not possible,' whispered Mariette.

Magdalena drew back her shoulders. Her mantle of hair seemed to rise and float behind her, even though the air was still. As they watched, huddled together, they saw her face soften and lose its boldness. Briefly, for a few seconds, she became a little girl.

Then she was herself again.

No one spoke.

'Golightly was a member of my family; but he was cruel and scheming,' said Magdalena. 'He left us. He turned his back on the wilderness, which it is our duty and purpose to protect. He went down into the city and he set out to seize the House of Scarspring and take it all for himself. Slowly and cleverly. Time is different for us, you see.

'That night, as he and Anshelm followed Zoran to this place, here on the Wolf Road, Golightly must have realized that Zoran had found a way to meet and speak with my father and his people, the wilderness dwellers. He must have been very afraid that Zoran might speak of this "Golightly" and that my father would recognize his own missing kinsman – and that he might warn him that Golightly was dangerous and could not be trusted. Perhaps he thought that my father might tell Zoran then, that very night.

'Golightly knew that he had to kill Zoran. At once. Before

the friendship deepened. Before Zoran learnt any more. Before he told Anshelm whatever he knew. Before the doorway into the garden was opened.'

Magdalena looked from one shocked and staring face to another. She breathed in deeply, as if the air would give her strength.

'I have had many years to understand what I witnessed,' she continued. 'Golightly knew that he must kill Zoran. Then the Ice Angel van came up the road from the city, on its way home. Balthazar Jump was my father's friend. The angel on the front knew that there was great danger and she began to sing. In the light of the headlamps Balthazar Jump saw Zoran and Anshelm Scarspring wrestling like stupid children right on the edge of the ravine. Shouting into each other's faces . . .' Magdalena's voice faltered. 'He saw Golightly raise his rifle, pointing it at Zoran. Trying to find the best, most deadly shot. The troll hound, the one you call Moe, was with him travelling in the van. They both leapt out. Balthazar Jump was very brave. He ran at Golightly. Golightly fired. He missed Zoran. He shot Balthazar.

'The hound jumped on to Zoran and Anshelm and knocked them to the ground. His darkness hid them. Golightly, my kinsman . . . Golightly could not see them to shoot anymore. But the ground was giving way.'

Magdalena was starting to sob. All her listeners moved towards her. Zack put his arm around her shoulders. She pointed to the rim of the road where it crumbled steeply into the ravine.

'It was all in the same instant. My father let go of my hand. He unlocked the door. It flew open. I think he hoped to get us all away from Golightly and his gun and into the garden. But they fell. My father and Zoran Scarspring and Balthazar Jump fell. They fell off the road and into our world.'

She took a deep breath.

'And the doorway slammed shut. And they were inside. And I was outside. And the only key was lost. The door cannot be opened without it.'

Silence.

'Golightly knew exactly what had happened,' she said, looking at Anshelm. 'When you found the little angel he knew that it belonged to my father, not Zoran, and that it was not a charm, it was a key. Every time he saw you hold it to your face, he knew that you had the means to find and free your lost brother, Zoran, right there in your hand.'

'But if what you are saying is true,' cried Anshelm. 'If these extraordinary, unbelievable things are true, then why didn't you come to me and tell me?'

'You trusted Golightly. He would have recognized me. That would have been my death sentence,' said Magdalena. 'I had no way of opening the garden and I was very young. We do not age as you do. I went down into the city and sought the protection of the nurses at the Child of Flowers Hospital. I worked there, cleaning the floors, in exchange for shelter and food. Later I went down to the Rock and reopened my father's workshop. That has been my living. I have lived there alone ever since.'

'You poor girl,' gasped Mariette.

'It has not been easy for you either, I think,' said Magdalena.

'And do their bodies lie here? In this other world you speak of?' Anshelm ran to the wilderness cedar and pushed against the huge trunk.

'Wait,' cried Zack. 'Just tell me something. Does this, this garden, this other world, does it reach high up the mountain. Does it go as far as the ice caves and the spring, the one near our house?'

'It may.'

'Because, then, I think Dad, Balthazar, is alive—'

'Please, I am begging you, everybody,' cried Anshelm. 'Please open this door.'

'Time is different in our world,' said Magdalena. 'Maybe only a few days have passed. And my father and mother are skilled healers. So it is possible that they are all alive, and your mother, too, Mr Ernesto . . .' she paused and gently pushed Zack away. Her warrior face was returning. 'Or they may all have died long ago. And I may only find their bones.'

'I'll come with you—'

'No, Zack, I will go alone. You must all wait here. The doorway is fragile. If they are there, they will come to you. I promise.'

Zack seized her arm. What was happening? She was changing again. She was not a grown woman anymore. She whispered, 'If I can return, then I will, Zachary.'

And now she was his own age. She looked up into his face, her eyes huge with fear. And he bent to kiss her. And her hair floated and billowed around them.

Then Magdalena walked to the tree and Anshelm stepped aside to let her pass. She ran her fingers down the trunk. Finding some place that she recognized, she pressed the angel charm against the bark.

For a moment, nothing happened.

Suddenly it seemed as if the air split open. The warm evening on the Wolf Road was flooded with sunlight. Everyone saw the ravine transformed, they were looking down on the tops of leafy trees. Another landscape, stretching away as far as they could see.

Mariette Jump, holding on to both her sons, was once more engulfed by the scent of sweet, lowland flowers.

Chapter 66

Edgar Featherplum braced himself and blinked into the early light. It was five in the morning. A visitor at this time was either a stranger who was drunk or some other species of bad news. He opened his front door.

A sharp-faced, brown-skinned boy was standing on the step. Beside him, a dark woman and a pale, black-haired man. Mr Featherplum had a good memory for faces. His job at Excelsior Broadcasting involved attending many parties and public functions. The boy was Ernesto Scarspring, he looked as if he'd been in an accident.

But the other two, standing with their arms around him as if they never wanted to let go . . . surely not, it couldn't be . . . was he still asleep?

It was the cat who let him know that it was all real. She was sitting on his shoulder, her claws pricking him through his dressing gown; she suddenly made the most extraordinary noise in his ear, leapt clear, sailed through the air, landed on Ernesto Scarspring and began rubbing her face against his in a great explosion of purring.

Mr Featherplum sneezed.

Lose the beard and this man looked exactly like Zoran Scarspring, And wasn't this his beautiful wife? Mr Featherplum had been to the wedding.

'Would you like an ice cream?' said Ernesto. 'I'm sure you deserve one, after looking after Fisher for so long.'

Mr Featherplum stepped out into the street. The fountain on the corner, which had been turned off for weeks, was splashing and busy. There was a silver van with an angel on the front parked in the middle of the road. The boy who came and sold ices at the studio was there with his ice cart. He was pouring chocolate sauce over a pot of ice cream.

'The water shortage is over,' said Ernesto. 'And you can have any ices you like. The Jump family are my friends.'

Anselm Scarspring was there, looking as if he'd been in the same accident as Ernesto. He was sitting on a black and silver scooter, eating a cornet, talking to a red-haired boy.

Several of Mr Featherplum's neighbours came out of their houses in their nightclothes, clutching purses, interested in buying ices.

Mr Featherplum advanced a little further into the street. He nearly tripped over. One of his slippers was rather worn. A small woman with long red hair and a brightly-coloured knitted cardigan caught his arm. She escorted him to the ice cart, smiling at him as if he were an honoured guest.

'Good Morning, Mr Greenwood,' said Mr Featherplum, still feeling a little dazed.

For some reason two people greeted him in return. One was the boy, Greenwood, who came round the studios with the cart every Thursday: looking a lot more relaxed than he did normally. The other was the short, heavy-set man beside him. He had a recent scar that ran down the side of his temple and into his hair. Mr Featherplum suspected a glancing bullet wound.

'This is Balthazar Jump,' said the ice cream boy. 'Mr Jump, may I introduce Mr Edgar Featherplum.'

'Delighted,' said the man with the scar, in an easy, gentle voice. Were all these people always so cheerful at this time in the morning?

Mr Featherplum chose a lemon sorbet. Nothing too rich. He thought of going over and exchanging a few words with Anshelm Scarspring. No harm in trying, good for his career. But the Mayor looked busy, sharing some joke with the red-haired, round-faced boy. And the ice was so delicious. He stayed where he was and nibbled a little bit more.

He looked at the angel on the front of the van. She had a wise, understanding face: not easily shocked. Then he looked all around him. There was a queue at the ice cart. People were milling about, talking quietly, eating ices, licking sauce off their fingers.

Some were sitting with their feet in the pool around the fountain.

Mr Featherplum took a deep breath; he stepped out of his troublesome slippers and rolled up the legs of his pyjamas, just enough to clear his ankles; then he walked towards the fountain and the inviting, sparkling water. He had stopped sneezing.

He felt the Mood. He was the Mood.

And the Mood was good.

A message from Momma Truth at Barnacle Radio:

Rockscar isn't the only place where getting clean, safe water can be a problem. If you want to know more about how you can help go to www.wateraid.org

Acknowledgments

Many thanks to the people involved in the production of this book:

At A P Watt, Literary Agency: Caradoc King, Elinor Cooper and Louise Lamont.

At Hachette UK: Beverley Birch, Naomi Pottesman, Sally Critchlow, David McDougall and Jessica Smith.

For comments on early text and presentation: J M Henderson, Joanne Wilson, Rick Adair and Ian Gundy.

And my apologies to anyone I may have missed out.

Read more from Charlotte Haptie in
Otto in the Time of the Warrior

Otto Hush

Ice-makers and fire-makers. Lamp eyes, dammerung, mat flyers, artists, whisperers, counterfeiters. Multiples. These are the Karmidee. The last truly magical people, hidden and far away in their secret City of Trees, their last refuge from our world, where they would be put in laboratories, or zoos, or worse . . .

Once there were many such people and creatures living among us. They are all there in the stories. Even mermaids. Even fire-breathing dragons, dreaming on the edge of volcanoes. But those are stories for children now.

Don't be deceived. Magical people exist and they are

called Karmidee. But they are not like the people in the fairy tales. They do not twinkle. They are real flesh and blood and bone.

Their City was discovered in the end, of course. Humans get everywhere. There was an earthquake, a crack opened in a mountain and explorers found their way through. They took over, as explorers often do.

However the Karmidee managed to seal the City again. And now three hundred years have passed. The outsiders, now known as Citizens, are very many and very powerful. They believe that the City has always been theirs. But they are wrong. And even though it is their home, the City of Trees is far greater and far more mysterious than they know.

The Karmidee have a King. He is a gentle, mild-mannered person who lives as a Citizen among the Citizens and comes to the aid of his people in times of trouble. He was chosen, like all Karmidee Kings and Queens, because he was born with a birthmark in the shape of a butterfly.

His name is Albert. Albert the Quiet.

His son is Otto Hush.

Strange Events
ON THE
Roof Garden

'. . . and one of them was carrying a bicycle in its beak,' added Otto Hush, over his shoulder.

His father, Albert, librarian and quiet King, was climbing up the creaking stairs behind him. This was the last flight, up to the roof garden on the top of Herschell Buildings. It was nearly midnight and the air hung very still. There was a mutter of thunder in the distance.

'That way,' whispered Otto, pointing.

Not that any pointing was needed. Two crate birds were making a nest in among the neglected flowerbeds and the chaotic garden furniture. Already, it loomed impressively over the smaller trees. The penny-farthing bicycle could be seen clearly, interwoven with some pieces of drainpipe and a great many mattress springs.

'Isn't it great?' whispered Otto. 'We'll be able to see her eggs, and the babies, really close.'

He and Albert both suddenly ducked and tripped over things. A crate bird, really close, had come gliding in to land. He hit the ground on splayed feet, swayed slightly, shook his massive wings and nodded peaceably to Otto and his father. Crate birds look like giant storks. They are usually about three metres tall. Fortunately they are vegetarians.

'Perhaps time to go,' said Albert, softly, as the crate picked his way over to the nest on his long legs.

'What's that?' whispered Otto.

'What's what?'

'There, coming towards us . . .'

There was something coming. Very hard to see.

Many of the roof gardens in the City of Trees are joined by narrow rope bridges. There was a bridge across Parry Street leading to the much tidier gardens on the roof of Owen Mansions. Otto knew that it was possible to go from Owen Mansions to the gardens above the street behind and, by other bridges and along other rooftops, all the way to the Boulevard. It was dangerous. Some of the bridges were in poor repair.

Someone, or something, didn't seem concerned about

the seven-storey drop on to Parry Street. The bridge swung from side to side. A shape came over the tops of the lime trees. It moved slowly and awkwardly. It was small.

Not a person. Otto realized. A dog?

The dog, if it was a dog, came over the parapet with a scrabble and a thud. Then it seemed to become entangled with the bushes. Finally it rolled across the stone floor and came to a stop right in front of Albert.

The bushes kept rustling as if they had come alive.

'Well, what have we here . . . ?' muttered Albert in his calm way. 'Ah, a bear cub,' he added. 'A very young one . . .'

He crouched down and the bear cub stayed still, looking up.

There was a crack of thunder. The bear cub made a small sound and the bushes shivered, although there was no wind.

'Hard to see in this light . . .' murmured Albert. 'I wonder where the parents are.'

He stood up slowly and looked back across the bridge. No longer swaying.

'It looks as if it's got a pattern on its back,' said Otto. Even in the night-time shades of black and silver and grey he could make out shapes behind the bear cub's ears. Repeated again, along the spine and flank. These shapes now began to shift and change.

'It's going stripy,' he whispered.

'I believe you are right,' said Albert, as if bears did this all the time.

There was a small sound, like the breaking of a small, dry twig.

'The bushes,' whispered Otto.

'That'll be them,' said Albert. 'Ssh . . .'

He picked up the bear cub and it licked his face.

'Honourable greetings,' said Albert, rather more loudly, addressing the bushes. 'I, Albert, King of the Karmidee, known as Albert the Quiet, am honoured that this bear cub has been brought to me for my protection. I undertake to shelter her in my family and care for her as I know her parents would . . .' he paused. The bushes had become completely still. 'If they could.'

Albert is known for his ability to help and care for Impossible animals. There was a moment of silence on the roof.

Then Otto heard something move and turned in time to see the rope bridge sway, very gently to and fro.

'What the skink—'

'Time for us to go home I think,' said Albert. 'Try to avoid the word skink, Otto.'

'But what the—'

Albert kept his voice to a whisper. 'You've heard

stories about chameleon animals, all completely Impossible, of course. Well, except for actual chameleons, which are a sort of lizard, I think—'

Otto was still gazing at the bridge. Without doubt something had just walked back across it.

'I saw a chameleon fish once,' he said, looking back at the little bear. 'At least I think I did. I saw the tank.'

'Well, this is a chameleon bear. Of a very small variety. There would no doubt have been much bigger ones too. Maybe there still are. They used to talk about them in the mud towns when I was a kid. Different chameleon animals. The bears were supposed to live in the forests above the mud towns . . .' Albert stroked the cub's nose. 'I thought they'd died out long ago, if they'd ever been there at all. No one can see them, obviously. They can change colour, blend in. Makes them invisible. Safe from hunters and so forth. When the Normals came they hunted everything.'

'Well it's not exactly hard to see this one, Dad.'

'Exactly. Something's wrong. She keeps changing, look now, hard to see in this light, anyway she's not only not invisible, she's very visible. Not safe for her. Not safe for the others with her. Not safe at all. It looks like her mother has kept her as long as she dared. Now they're asking us to look after her, which is quite an honour, when you think about it, poor little thing.'

There was another crack of thunder. The storm was coming closer. The bear cub made a snuffling sound and Otto patted her head, feeling large and protective.

In truth, strange dangers awaited them both, as yet unknown. Otto reached down again now, and felt the anxious beat of the little bear's heart through her fur. He did not imagine that she would one day save his life.

They all stood there on the roof garden for a moment longer, under the clouds and stars, while around them the great City of Trees mirrored the sky, with lamps and lights and mysteries of its own.

'I'll stay a bit,' whispered Otto. 'Just for a minute.'

Two massive shapes loomed ponderously out of the darkness.

'Look, Dad, they've got an old sink——'

'I'll see you down there,' said Albert, pitching his voice below the noise of the mighty wing beats.

The crates were taking off again, cooing hoarsely to one another.

'They might bring something really big next, like, you know, a bath.'

The bear cub yawned. Albert carried her to the stairs, leaving the door standing open.

Almost immediately there was a crack and a jolt of lightning and thunder and, in the same moment, a gust of cooler air rushed across the roof garden, spinning and twisting, and Otto, amazed, saw a funnel of blue light spiral into existence between where he stood and the foundations of the crate nest.

He ducked down, watching through leaves, as the light spread, paler now and very clear, revealing a tall boy, almost a man, standing looking down at something in his hand. He wore dark, sparkling clothes and a billowing cape. His feet were bare. His black hat was pushed back on his head. He looked up and then, slowly, as if searching, he looked around him. Not close by. Into the distance. He turned and Otto saw him very clearly. He had a pale, freckled face.

He stayed quite still.

Otto didn't even breathe.

The boy glanced up at the storm clouds and muttered a curse. It seemed that he had no wish to be on this shabby roof garden. He was holding what looked to be a sphere of blackglass. He tossed it in the air with one hand and caught it with the other. Smiling to himself, all grace and menace, he put it back into his pocket, jumped into the air and disappeared.

Otto didn't move. He stared at the place where the boy had stood, while the light that had surrounded him faded into darkness.

Then it started to rain. Massive, splattering drops. The crate birds returned, bringing umbrellas, and began trying to open them and build a roof. Otto stood up slowly. He had no umbrella. He decided to go back inside. He walked backwards to the doorway.

Win an Ice Lolly Maker!

We are offering three lucky *Ice Angel* readers the chance to win a *Zoku Ice Lolly Maker*. This fab device can make ice lollies in seven minutes, and will help you create ice lollies to rival Zack and Clovis' from the *Ice Angel*!

To enter the competition, all you have to do is sign up at
www.hodderchildrens.co.uk/iceangel

Only one entry per person.
Closing date: 1st April 2011
The winners will be chosen at random.

Competition only available to UK residents.

For full terms and conditions go to
www.hodderchildrens.co.uk/iceangel

If you're feeling inspired by Zack and Clovis' flavoured ices from *Ice Angel* then check out the simple recipes below. Wow your friends and family with these deliciously icy treats!

To make the ice lollies you will need some ice lolly moulds. These are super easy to find in the shops, or over the internet. Alternatively you can just use some plastic cups lying around in the kitchen, and old ice lolly sticks (that you've washed before hand!).

Frozen Bananas

The easiest ice lolly of all! All you need is a banana – unpeel it, insert a stick in one end, and pop it in the freezer for a couple of hours.

For a slightly more extravagant banana lolly, dip the end in chocolate – or yoghurt if you're feeling healthy – and then pour sprinkles or nuts over the top before putting in the freezer.

Milkshake Lollies

Another super simple, but delicious ice lolly. All you have to do is mix your favourite flavour ice-cream with milk to make a batch of milkshake (or if you're feeling lazy you can use pre-made milkshake straight out the bottle), pour it into your moulds, then freeze.

Fruit Ices

For a really refreshing and healthy lolly why not try a fruit ice. Just like the milkshake lollies, pour your favourite fruit juice into the ice lolly mould and freeze.

If you're feeling adventurous also try multi-coloured ices. Start off with one fruit juice – pour it into the mould a third of the way up and freeze as normal. Once frozen, use a different colour juice and pour it into the mould over the already frozen juice, two thirds of the way up.
Freeze again, and repeat with one last juice.

From war-torn Olympus to stormy
New York City, mythology and reality collide
in a breathtaking adventure.

OUT FEBRUARY 2011

9780340997406 £5.99 PB

Hodder
Children's
Books

www.hodderchildrens.co.uk